The cells in the cellar at Bendlerstrasse resemble cages at the zoo. Thick vertical bars separate them from the corridors, along which guards perambulate continually.

'Pigs, dirty pigs,' whispers an artillery Hauptmann in the cell next to Oberst Frick. His face is beaten up and swollen. One eye is completely closed.

'What in the world has happened to you?' asks the Oberst, quietly. His body begins to tremble.

'They beat me,' whispers the artillery officer. 'Smashed my teeth in, sent an electric current through me. They want me to confess to something I never did.'

'Where are we?' asks Oberleutnant Wisling, curiously.

'Third Army Court Martial Unit, section 4a, directly under the jurisdiction of the J.A.G.,' a Stalbszahlmesiter replies. 'Don't expect anything good! It's like living in a railway station. You get the impression that half the Army's up for court martial. There'll be nobody left soon. They say we're short of soldiers and yet we're shooting our own quicker'n the Russians can.'

D1319801

Also by Sven Hassel

THE BLOODY ROAD TO DEATH
BLITZFREEZE
REIGN OF HELL
SS GENERAL
ASSIGNMENT GESTAPO
LIQUIDATE PARIS
MARCH BATTALION
MONTE CASSINO
COMRADES OF WAR
WHEELS OF TERROR
THE LEGION OF THE DAMNED
O.G.P.U. PRISON

and published by Corgi Books

Sven Hassel

Court Martial

Translated from the Danish
by Tim Bowie

CORGI BOOKS

COURT MARTIAL
A CORGI BOOK 0 552 11168 6

First publication in Great Britain

PRINTING HISTORY
Corgi edition published 1979
Corgi edition reprinted 1980
Corgi edition reprinted 1981
Corgi edition reprinted 1983
Corgi edition reprinted 1984

This book is set in 10pt Plantin

Corgi Books are published by Transworld Publishers Ltd.,
Century House, 61–63 Uxbridge Road,
Ealing, London, W5 5SA.
Made and printed in Great Britain by
Hunt Barnard Printing Ltd., Aylesbury, Bucks.

To the memory of Ernst Ruben Laguksen,
Commander of the Finnish armoured regiment,
Nylands Dragoon Regiment.

The tragedy of the German soldier is his belief that there is a sensible reason for continuing the resistance and for losing his life. Day out and day in he goes on making inhuman sacrifices for a cause long since lost.

Oberst Graf von Stauffenberg shortly before his execution 20 July 1944

This book is dedicated to the city of Barcelona where I have met with the most exceptional hospitality and where the majority of my books have been written.

The loss of a leg or a foot is not half as bad. These new artificial limbs have joints which often work better than the real thing, and if you get arthritis you can cure it with an oil-can.

> Porta to Tiny, 125 miles north of the Arctic Circle.

Porta whinnies with pleasure and offers her a seat on the rotten bench we are occupying.

She laughs, the sound ringing deep into the woods. She is standing with the sun behind her and we can see her body in silhouette. Her grey summer uniform skirt is made of thin transparent material. We'd like her to stay there for ever. Her hair is long and golden, like a ripe cornfield. She cannot speak German and we have to make ourselves understood in a queer kind of lingua franca. Porta speaks something he says is Finnish, but the girl doesn't understand him.

Splashes jump out in the river. They are like big raindrops.

'They're shooting,' says Gregor laconically. 'Waste o' time!'

'Waste of *powder* at this distance,' says the Old Man, lighting his silver-lidded pipe.

The spurts of water seem to race one another across the river.

'You not frightened?' asks the girl soldier, smoothing her skirt.

'No,' laughs Porta carelessly. 'They're pitiful, those gun-crazy idiots!'

'I never see them shooting before,' she says, stretching her neck to see better.

'We can get a bit closer,' suggests Porta, helping the girl up. 'We're laughing at them here!'

'Can you take a picture of me?' she asks, offering a Leica to Heide. She positions herself on top of the hill.

Heide takes a photograph of her, making sure that all the bullet splashes on the river are included.

'Let's take one with you in the middle of me an' Tiny,' shouts Porta, with a big smile.

She laughs, and puts her arms around their shoulders.

Heide squats down like a real professional photographer.

The explosive bullet tears away half her face. Flesh, blood

9

and splinters of bone spray over Porta. A torn off ear dangles from Tiny's chest, like a medal.

'A sniper, a rotten bloody sniper!' shouts Tiny, dropping down alongside Porta.

They push the dead girl's body in front of them for cover.

THE BRIDGE

'No. 2 Section! Ready to move off!' orders the Old Man, and swings his *Mpi** over his shoulder. He looks tired and discouraged. A grey stubble of beard covers his face. His ancient silver-lidded pipe hangs sadly from the corner of his mouth.

A few of the section get up and begin to get their weapons and equipment together.

Porta and Tiny stay down in a warm hole they have found, and look as if none of it was any of their business.

'Didn't you hear the order?' shouts Heide officiously, inflating his chest to *Unteroffizier* size.

'There 'e goes again,' says Tiny, furiously, pointing with his Mpi at Heide. 'What'll we *do* with 'im?'

'Shoot him when we get the chance,' decides Porta, briefly.

'Say we tie 'im to the bridge just 'fore we push the bleedin' 'andle, an' liquidate 'im an' cremate 'im in one go!' suggests Tiny, delightedly.

'Swine,' snarls Heide angrily, and moves away.

'Get your fingers out, you lazy sacks,' shouts the Old Man, irritably, pushing Porta.

'You've got it all wrong. I don't move a step till I've had my breakfast coffee,' answers Porta, unconcernedly.

Tiny begins getting ready to boil up. He fills the kettle with snow, and soon has a pleasant fire going.

The Old Man's face has taken on a coppery-red tinge.

'What kind of a rotten monkey's been chewing *your* arses? On your feet in five seconds, or *I'll* make you a cup o' coffee you'll *never* forget!' He swings his *Kalashnikov* above his head like a club.

Porta just manages to duck away as the butt comes flying at his head.

'Hell's bells, old un, you might've *hit* me! You don't have to

* Mpi/Maschinenpistole = machine-pistol.

start beating people up just because they want a cup o' coffee for breakfast!'

'Coffee,' shouts the Old Man, in a rage. 'What do you think you're on? An outing to look at the Northern bloody Lights?'

'Sod what I'm on,' says Porta, stubbornly. 'I *still* want coffee! My brain doesn't start working till I've had my coffee.'

' 'E's right,' Tiny agrees. 'This bleedin' army can't do what it likes with *us*. We got a right to coffee. It says so in Supply Regs. Ivan's snot-'eaded coolies even, they get coffee 'fore they go out 'n get theirselves shot dead.'

'You! You've not got the right to a fart,' shouts the Old Man, furiously, 'and if you don't get your kit together and lift your arses off the ground double-quick, I'll blow the shit out of your stupid heads!'

'Do it! Get it over with now!' Heide prompts him eagerly.

Porta is pouring water on the coffee beans. A delicious aroma rises towards the tree-tops.

Our nostrils begin to quiver. Soon the whole section is sitting down, sharing Porta's coffee. Even the Old Man sullenly accepts the mug which Tiny graciously offers him.

'To the devil with the lot of you,' snarls the Old Man, blowing into his mug. 'The rottenest section in the whole army and I had to get it! A shower of arseholes is what you lot are!'

' 'E's no gentleman, is 'e?' remarks Tiny to Porta.

'A proletarian prick I'd say he was,' declares Porta. 'About as useful as a hole in the head!'

Tiny crows with laughter. He thinks Porta's remark is the joke of the year.

'You take that?' asks Guri, the Laplander, his face splitting in a typical Lapp grin.

'Damned if I do,' shouts the Old Man, vehemently. 'You heard me. I gave a direct order: Section, march!'

'Don't shout so loud,' warns Porta. 'The neighbours might hear all that German piss. It's dangerous to talk German in these parts!'

'That does it,' roars the Old Man, wrathfully, taking his Mpi from his shoulder.

'Shoot and you're dead,' threatens Tiny, swinging the muzzle of his *Kalashnikov* towards the Old Man.

'Let a man have his coffee in peace,' says Porta pettishly. 'There'll *be* no war till I've swilled my tonsils clean!'

12

'Up my arse,' the Old Man gives in, and slings his Russian fur-cap far away amongst the trees.

'Mind you 'air don't freeze,' says Tiny, in a kindly voice. 'They didn't issue us them 'ead-cosies for parade purposes only, y'know!'

Porta is quietly making a new pot of coffee. His breakfast ration is five cups, as a rule.

'Tell me,' says the Old Man in a dangerously quiet voice, 'just how long do you reckon this coffee party is going to go on?'

'Only idiots expect people to chase around all over the map before they've had their coffee,' says Porta, calmly, filling up the mugs again.

The Old Man accepts his with a shake of the head, but jumps when Tiny starts to make toast.

'I'm reporting you for refusing to obey orders, when we get back,' he threatens, shaking with rage.

'Tell me,' Porta turns to the Legionnaire, 'you're the oldest member of this shootin' club, did they ever send you foreign legion lot out to get your throats cut by the Muslims without a cup of coffee under your belts?'

'*Non, mon ami*, I never remember it happening,' answers the Legionnaire, well aware that it would not be diplomatically wise, and productive of incalculable problems, to do anything but agree with Porta on the subject of breakfast coffee.

The Old Man loses his patience, throws his mug from him and kicks the toast out of Tiny's hands.

'Up on your feet! Up! Now!'

'Don't treat good food like that,' Porta scolds. 'How d'you know how soon *you'll* be hungry!'

'I've said it before an' I'll say it again. 'E's no gentleman,' sighs Tiny, patiently collecting the toast from the ground.

'Watch your blood pressure, old 'un,' advises Porta. 'You'll shorten your life, going off like that!'

Shortly after this episode we are moving on our way, slipping and sliding down the steep slopes. By dinner time we have reached the road leading to the ice-free port, a long way to the north. A little to the east runs a notorious railway, built at the cost of the lives of thousands upon thousands of prisoners. Rumour has it that it is built on human bones.

We lie in the snow and watch endless transport columns roll past our position.

'Up on the road,' orders the Old Man. 'Follow me in single

file! If we're challenged nobody answers but those of you who speak fluent Russian. The rest of you are just deaf and dumb.'

'*Merde aux veux!* Let's hope Ivan doesn't smell a rat,' mutters the Legionnaire uneasily. He seems to become smaller.

'Jesus wept!' hisses the Westphalian, sourly. 'This is the last time I go on a trip behind the neighbours' lines. Soon as we're back I'm going to put a bullet through me foot.'

'Cost you your old turnip if they find out,' says Porta with a sarcastic smile.

Slightly north-east of Glenegorsk we find the first of the hidden bridges.

Four long goods trains are held up, on camouflaged tracks, waiting for the green light, and a couple of kilometres further back a fifth train is waiting.

We prepare the explosives inside the fringe of the woods. We have five sledges loaded with the new Lewis bombs, which we have just begun to be supplied with.

Porta and I get the first guard. We couldn't care less. We can't sleep anyway. We're full of pervitin pills. The Russians call them *pryshok porokh**. One pervitin can keep a man awake for a week, and they can be a lifesaver for men working behind the enemy lines.

'You're off your head, man,' I protest, when Porta lights up a cigarette. 'They can see you from here to Murmansk!'

'Don't piss your drawers, son,' mumbles Porta. 'The Red Army sparkles all night! Why shouldn't I?'

'It'll be your fault if we get knocked off!'

'You'll never feel it!' says Porta, callously, taking a long draw at his cigarette so that it glows brightly.

Early next morning we are listening to Heide, our explosives expert. He is standing up on a windfall to get a good view of us all.

'Listen to me, and listen good, you arseholes,' he shouts. 'As you can all see, what I have in my hand looks like a lump of rubber, and you can do almost anything you like with it without anything happening. Throw it in the fire and what you get is a thick, sticky mass. It looks like chewed-up gum, but it isn't. This shit consists of a quarter thermite, mixed with metallic oxide, and three-quarters plastic explosive.'

'What's plastic?' asks Tiny, blankly.

'No bloody business of yours. All *you* need to know is it's

* pryshok porokh (livening powder) = anti-sleep pills.

14

called plastic.' Heide holds up a copper tube.

'This is a copper and aluminium tube, which contains a detonator.'

'What's a detonator?' asks Tiny, lifting his hand like a schoolboy.

'No bloody business of yours, either,' Heide rebuffs him. 'All *you* need to know is it's called a detonator. And don't keep interrupting me with stupid questions! I'll tell you all you need to know an' that's enough. As you can see there are eight bends on this tube and these represent eight different time intervals, so that we can decide when she goes bang-bang. The lowest is two minutes, and I wouldn't advise using it. The highest is two hours. The tube itself' – he holds it up proudly, as if he himself had invented it – 'contains a mercury compound. You bite through this little glass chap here, the acid inside runs down and dissolves the seal holding the striker in position. The striker shoots forward and primes the bomb. The process has commenced.'

'An' then it goes bleedin' BANG!' shouts Tiny, with a big grin.

'Idiot,' snarls Heide, irritably. 'Cut those interruptions out! Don't you realise I'm an *Unteroffizier*, and your superior?'

'If you'd been in the cavalry you'd 'ave been a *Unterwachtmeister*, and if you'd been in a Alpine Regiment, you'd 'ave been a *Oberjäger*. You could also've been – if, that is to say, you'd been in the paratroops, like Gregor 'ere . . . '

'When the detonating process has commenced,' continues Heide, with a superior air, 'enormous heat is generated, and it is this which ignites the plastic explosive mass.'

'An' it goes BANG!' says Tiny, jubilantly.

Heide sends him a killing look.

'All known metals, even the heaviest steel, melt in seconds. Without this clever little device called the detonator you can play about as you like with the plastic. Nothing will happen, except you'll get your fingers sticky. You can jump into a fire with your pockets full of it. It won't go off! Put it under a steamhammer. No bother! But once the detonator's blown, watch out for it! Run for your lives. Once you've bitten through the glass, get moving! Put sixty yards, at least, between you and the explosion centre. Inside that distance your lungs'll be hanging out of your arse and throat. I'd prefer seventy yards myself. When they were demonstrating it for us at the Army

15

Ammunition Depot at Bamberg, they lost two ammunition experts. They thought they could play games with Lewis bombs.'

'Bamberg! I know that place,' shouts Tiny, happily. 'We used to blow up trains an' lorries with some bleedin' stuff they called TNT. There was a couple o' them ammo bleeders went up there too. One on 'em was in 'is bed at the time. It turned out as 'ow some wicked bleeder of a Gefreiter 'ad shoved a load under 'is bed an' sent 'im to kingdom come that road.'

'Squad leaders on me,' orders the Old Man, brusquely.

'Peace in our time,' says Tiny, laconically, fishing a huge cigar out of his gas-mask container. He always smokes cigars. He considers them high-class.

Our squad has the job of looking after the bridge to the north of Pulosero. Trees have been planted to camouflage it and the work has been so well done that we are only a few yards away when we discover it. It is an enormous railway bridge. The steel supports stretch right into Lapland. We have been detailed to blow up bridges and dams all the way down to Pitkul. A stretch of around 150 kilometres. This should put the railways and the most important road communications out of commission for a considerable time.

'Wonder if we'll get leave after this, so we can get 'ome an' 'ave a gander at the *Reeperbahn*?' dreams Tiny, his eyes swimming at the thought.

'They'll piss on us and send us on a new outing, without even giving us the chance of a sauna,' reckons Barcelona, pessimistically.

'Should've been a Finn,' says Porta, decisively. 'They get treated like people.'

'Don't look on the dark side,' shouts Gregor, optimistically. 'They're sure to pin a few medals on us for this.' He loves fruit salad, just as Heide does.

'*Par Allah*, all I want is a *Heimatschuss** and a good sleep in a clean hospital bed,' sighs the Legionnaire, tiredly.

'Be satisfied if you get home alive,' advises the Old Man, drily.

'Can it,' shouts Tiny. 'Let's get these bridges blown away, so's we can get a bit o' fun out of this bleedin' war.'

The explosives are shared between us. Our special packs are full. We say good-bye to one another before we disperse silently

* Heimatschuss = (Blighty wound).

16

into the white desert and are swallowed up by the forest on the far side of the frozen lakes.

Our squad goes round the river bed and continues along the road leading north. We are challenged several times by drivers and guards who, because of our uniforms, take us to be security troops.

Tiny brings us close to catastrophe when he shouts '*Arschloch*'* after a Russian truck, which splashes snow over us.

At the road bridge south of Lapland we say good-bye to the Legionnaire's party.

'Do it proper, now,' Tiny exhorts them, paternally. 'Make it go off in one long bang, my sons, or else nothing'll 'appen to the bleedin' bridge. If I was you I'd've asked me to do it for you!'

'*Merde*, you are not the only one who knows how to blow things up,' answers the Legionnaire, and disappears at the head of his party.

'Bridges are 'bout the 'ardest thing there is to blow up,' Tiny tells Porta. 'If the charges ain't right even a million o' them Lewis bombs won't do it.'

'Watch out you don't make a balls of it some day,' says Gregor, grumpily. He has a neurotic aversion to anything that can be called an explosive.

'It'll never 'appen,' boasts Tiny. 'When a bridge 'as a run-in with me, it's the bridge what falls on its bleedin' arse!'

A few hours later we arrive at our bridge. Tiny goes round patting its huge steel girders appreciatively.

'Lord love us, ain't she a lovely bridge?' he grins.

A goods train a kilometre long thunders across it. A fur-clad soldier waves to us from a brake-van.

'That boy doesn't know how lucky he was catching that train,' says Porta, thoughtfully, 'the next one'll get blown all to hell!'

The bridge is tougher than we'd expected. It is unbelievably difficult to clamber up on the ice-slick concrete, and there is nothing to get a grip on. Only ice, and rough concrete that rips our hands to shreds.

Tiny raves like a madman each time he slips down and slides comically along on the ice of the river.

'Who the hell's the idiot, who didn't think we'd need

* Arschloch = (German) = arsehole.

17

climbing irons?' Porta curses viciously, as he slips back down for the twentieth time.

When we finally get up there, after several hours of exertion, we run into a new obstacle which comes close to discouraging us.

We sit down silently and stare at the coils of wicked-looking barbed wire with which the immediate under-pinning of the bridge is thickly entangled to prevent access to its most vulnerable parts.

'Jesus, Jewish son of the German God,' exclaims Porta, 'all we need now is for the lot of us to be booby-trapped, and them and our Lewis bombs'll get us out of uniform quicker than Hitler got us in!'

'Piss'n porridge, there wouldn't be a button left,' mutters Tiny, peering under the barbed wire.

'Oh well, with the Blessed Virgin and good German know-how on our side we'll probably get by,' says Porta, philosophically.

'If we should 'appen unexpectedly to touch something or other off,' says Tiny, 'it'll be us as gets blown up for a change!'

'Some nerve,' sniffs Gregor.

'Hold on to your hats!' warns Porta, and begins to cut the wire.

The first rusty strands whip past our faces. Porta tires quickly, and hands the wire-cutters over to Tiny who goes at the wire like a bulldozer.

'Hell, watch out you fool,' warns Gregor, terrified. 'You cut just one wrong wire and we've all had it!'

' 'Ere's a fuckin' mine,' shouts Tiny in amazement, bending forward. Carefully he pulls the T-mine towards him. 'Wires are ''ere,' he goes on, pointing to a row of grey cables running under the mine.

'Careful, careful,' shouts Porta, nervously. 'Leave it where it is and screw off the cap! We'll climb down while you're fixing her. No need for the lot of us to get killed!'

Unworriedly Tiny starts disarming the monster, screws out the detonator and leaves the mine dangling down amongst us.

We're so frightened we hardly dare breathe.

'Be more careful for Christ's sake,' Porta shouts up to Tiny, who has found three more mines, of a type we've not met before.

'Look at these!' shouts Tiny absorbedly. 'There's a little bleeder 'ere you can *bend*!'

'Christ man, don't bend that!' howls Porta, fearfully. 'It's the sodding detonator!'

'What you want me to do with it, then?' asks Tiny, blankly. 'Kick it in the soddin' teeth?'

'Leave it be, for heaven's sake,' moans Gregor, wild with fear.

'I can't go on cuttin' wire, without it goin' up,' explains Tiny, poking cautiously at the nearest mine.

'Isn't there a red flap on the one side?' asks Porta, getting well down behind a heavy concrete column.

A goods train rattles over the bridge. All talk stops as it passes over us.

'Blimey, it's rainin',' says Tiny, wonderingly, when the train has passed.

'One of the neighbour's boys has pissed on you,' shouts Porta, convulsed with laughter.

'I'll strangle the bleeder,' roars Tiny, shaking his fist at the train roaring in the distance. 'Nobody gets away with pissin' on me! Stink like a backyard shit'ouse, I do! Commie shit all over me lousy 'ead too!'

'You can have a wash when we get back,' grins Porta. 'Better to get hit with shit than shrapnel! See if there's a red button on one side of those rotten mines!'

'There's a red flap,' states Tiny, 'an' a big 'un too. There's the 'ole 'istory of the socialist revolution written 'longside of it.'

'What's it say?' asks Porta.

'They ain't started payin' me Russian translator money yet,' says Tiny, insolently.

'Now, let's go slow on this one and see what happens,' says Porta. 'Push in the red flap and hold on to that lever at the same time. If the lever shifts, then up she goes!'

'*Very* interestin',' bawls Tiny, his voice echoing under the bridge.

'Mad as a bloody March Hare,' groans Gregor, resignedly, pushing himself deeper into the snow.

'No need to take cover,' comforts Porta. 'We're relatively safe down here. Mines always blow upwards!'

'What about Tiny?' I ask, innocently.

'He will have died for the honour of Greater Germany, and

his name will be engraved on the heroes monument outside the barracks,' intones Porta, fatalistically.

'I've pushed the flap in,' shouts Tiny, unconcernedly. 'Now what?'

'Bend it inwards, but slowly! If it begins to fizzle, jump down to us, but *move*, unless you're tired of living!'

'She's dead as a nit,' replies Tiny. 'But I reckon she's maybe just lyin' doggo!'

'Now open the lid,' explains Porta. 'Put your hand into the slot, feel round for a little square gadget and pull it downwards.'

'Got it,' says Tiny, in a satisfied tone, hurling the mine over the edge. 'I'll fix the rest quick as a randy Turk shaggin' a bunch o' bints!'

'Careful,' warns Porta, 'careful and hold on tight to that lever! If you let go of it, you've met your last mine!'

'Wait a bit 'fore you shit yourself,' boasts Tiny, self-assuredly. 'I ain't never lost one yet. It's all right to come up again now!'

'Look where you're cutting now,' says Porta. 'A cable might have got entangled in that wire, and if you cut it we'll get our arses blown off!'

We lay the disarmed detonators under the great steel cylinders. Porta feels they cannot do much damage there.

We work our way slowly through the wire in to the supporting girders, taking care not to touch off a mine.

I am sweating with fear despite the arctic cold. I am just as afraid of the mines as Gregor is. During the many hours we have been working under the bridge, countless trains have passed above us. We hold our groundsheets over our heads in order to avoid an experience like Tiny's.

When we are finally finished with the barbed wire the serious job of getting the explosives up from the sledges begins. I get the worst job, carrying the Lewis bombs from the sledges to the foot of the various piers. After a couple of hours of this I am so worn out that I drop on the snow and refuse to continue without a rest. My arms and back are aching so much that I'm ready to scream at the slightest movement.

Porta and Tiny are engaged in a bitter argument as to which of them is to place the explosive.

'If we take a pier each, it'll go quicker,' says Tiny, who is mad keen to get at the Lewis bombs.

'You do as I tell you, you walking shit-house, you,' shouts Porta, throwing a spanner at him.

'You ain't no more'n me,' rages Tiny. 'An Obergefreiter's an Obergefreiter and neither God nor the Devil can tell one of *them* what to do. Where'd we be, I'm askin', if any bleedin' Obergefreiter was to get up an' go round orderin' other Obergefreiters about?'

'I attended the Army School of Ammunition and Explosives at Bamberg,' crows Porta, 'while you were pissing about at the Army Catering School learning how to ruin sauerkraut! Even *you* ought to be able to accept that on this job, I'm the boss!'

'Strike me blind,' answers Tiny, resentfully. 'As if I 'adn't been at Bamberg. They even give me a medal for exceptional diligence, costin' the lives of two instructors!'

After a great deal more quarrelling and argument they agree to share the work between them. Tiny finds a clever way to fix the bombs to the piers so that they do not slide down. But the most important thing of all is still to get them wired up properly.

It is far into the night before we get one side of the bridge finished, and then Porta demands his dinner.

'The rot's spread from your arsehole to your brain,' cries Gregor, excitedly. 'It's suicide to sit down to dinner right here, under Ivan's own bridge!'

' 'E'll 'ave a stroke if 'e finds us 'ere, won't 'e?' grins Tiny, unconcernedly.

But Porta still stubbornly demands his dinner, which he has a right to according to HDV*.

While we sit eating, NKVD security guards cross above our heads. They are so close to us that we could touch them by merely putting our hands up between the planks of the bridge.

It's a break-neck trip over to the other side of the bridge and several times we are close to falling. When we get there, there is more of that damnable barbed-wire to cut through.

We throw the explosives from base to base of each pier. The primary charges are the most dangerous. A knock can set them off. If we dropped one the security guards would be all over us in a minute, and we have no illusions about the treatment we'd get from them.

'You're pretty good at it,' Porta praises Tiny, patting him on the shoulder.

* HDV (Heeresdienstvorschrift) = Army Service Regulations.

'Long as we keep the wolf from the door,' Tiny grins with pleasure, ringing the nearest concrete base with Lewis bombs.

He swings under the bridge, with the agility of a monkey, to make the wiring fast.

It makes me dizzy just to look at him.

'How the hell's he *do* it?' mumbles Gregor, nervously.

'For the love of the holy St Agnes, don't ask him,' warns Porta, 'it'd make him fall! He's no idea how piss-dangerous it is!'

A faint noise makes us look up. Three security police are crossing above our heads. We can hear the warning clank of the Mpi's.

'Adolf ought to 'ave a go at this,' roars Tiny suddenly, his voice ringing through the silence.

I tear my Mpi from my shoulder and aim at the security guards on the bridge.

A train comes thundering in the distance. The sound of the salvo drowns in the noise.

Three men in long fur coats topple over the low fence along the bridge and whirl down between the ice-blocks far below.

Porta peers cautiously up between two sleepers. Luckily there were only three of them.

With a steely roar the train crosses the bridge.

'What you shootin' for?' shouts Tiny, in amazement, looking round a concrete pier. 'Tryin' to shit-frighten everybody, are you?'

'Because you can't keep that bloody great Hamburg gab of yours shut,' answers Porta, viciously. 'Didn't I tell you not to talk German in these parts?'

By flashing signals to one another we manage to bite the glass capsules open at the same time, ensuring that the explosions are synchronised. This is very important with a bridge of this type. Otherwise the bridge will break at only a few points along its length, and the Russian engineers can easily repair these.

Porta is last man off the bridge. He trails a thin wire after him, and behind the bend in the river he connects it to the plunger box which Tiny is carrying on his back.

We ready ourselves at a safe distance from the bridge on the opposite side of the lake.

Tiny swings the handle like a mad thing in order to build up enough of an induction charge for the explosion, while

22

Gregor watches the meter which tells us when there is enough current available.

Tiny takes a short breather after his strenuous work and lights one of his big cigars. A solemn moment like this, he feels, is worthy of a cigar. With the expression of a padre throwing earth on the remains of a fallen field-marshal, he pulls the plunger to the ready position and gives out a belly chuckle of innocent expectation.

'Grab your 'ats, boys, she's ready to go,' he says, solemnly, patting the box.

'Don't you push that till I say so,' Porta admonishes him, nervously. 'The priming charge has got to go first or not a shit will happen to that damn bridge!'

'Jesus wept!' cries Tiny, in horror, 'that'd be like goin' to the pictures an' findin' some Yid 'ad 'ooked the bleedin' film.'

'That can happen,' says Porta, seriously. 'Happened to me once in Berlin.'

'Don't be fright,' Tiny assures us. 'I never met one I couldn't beat yet! An' this fiddlin' little bridge ain't goin' to be the first!'

'*Little* bridge, you say?' asks Gregor, in surprise. 'It's the biggest I've ever seen!'

'Enjoy it while you can, then,' laughs Tiny, raucously, 'couple o' minutes' time an' it won't be there to enjoy!'

A goods train pulled by two large steam engines rolls slowly on to the mined bridge. A red flag flutters from every other wagon.

'Holy Agnes, God's stepmother,' shouts Porta, his eyes bugging. 'An ammo train!'

'An' look at them tankers piss-full of pet,' shouts Tiny, pointing towards the road, where a long line of trucks are moving along beside the railway line.

'Get a good grip on the ground,' says Porta, worriedly, 'or you can risk flying off it together with that blasted bridge!'

'Hope they don't notice the priming charges begin to fizzle,' says Gregor, darkly, watching the kilometre-long petrol column through the glasses. 'God save us all, there's enough gas there for a whole army!'

'Balls,' Tiny quiets him, in a fatherly tone. 'They'll be flyin' around the Milky Way lookin' down at us before they've time to wonder about anythin'.'

'Bugger, we should have fused 'em shorter,' says Porta, in

annoyance. 'Shouldn't believe everything those Bamberg dopes tell you. We know more than they'll ever learn.'

'Like Christmas ain't it? When you're 'avin' a peep through the key'ole to see the Christmas tree your ol' dad's pinched, and tryin' to find out what the presents are they've bought on the never-never,' says Tiny, with a happy expression on his face.

'If it doesn't go, we're for a court martial,' says Gregor, darkly, bringing the glass up to his eye again.

'If it does go,' laughs Porta broadly, 'and Ivan gets us, then we'll have another kind of court martial!'

'Oh, stop thinkin' so much,' says Tiny, optimistically. 'Whatever you do they can 'ave you for it in the army! Court martials're always ready an' waitin'!'

With a noise like distant thunder the train rumbles across the bridge, and from the other end another train begins to roll on to it.

'Pity, only returned empties,' sighs Tiny, sourly.

A couple of flames shoot up suddenly at each end of the bridge.

'Primers gone,' cries Porta, staring expectantly towards the long bridge.

Tiny comes down on the plunger with all his weight.

A single fantastic yellow-red flame shoots towards the sky and spreads into a mushroom-shaped cloud of enormous dimensions. The bridge is lifted up, along the whole of its length, towards the grey, threatening clouds. Both goods trains go with it, without a single wagon tipping over. Then everything bursts into millions of separate parts. A set of bogies crashes down a few yards from us.

The tankers are moving so closely behind one another that they have no possibility of turning. They are whirled up into the air, and flaming streams of petrol pour out over the frozen lake.

Heavy tankers are thrown about like toys. Petrol spurts everywhere, creating new redly glowing bonfires. Then, slightly delayed, the blast hits us with terrible force.

I am thrown many yards across the ice. But everything happens so quickly that I don't even have time to be frightened.

Tiny, with box and torn-off cables trailing behind him, flies like a bullet right across the lake and disappears in the trees on the far side.

Porta is thrown up into the air in a crooked curve, spins around his own axis several times and lands in a giant snow-drift.

Gregor has disappeared completely. We find him far down the gulley, jammed in a cleft between two storm-twisted trees. We have a lot of trouble freeing him.

'Holy Barbara,' cries Porta. 'Those Lewis bombs certainly make a job of it!'

'They'll tear our balls off, if they get hold of us,' predicts Gregory, ominously, peering around nervously.

'Ivan's got other things to think of, just now, than looking for *us*,' says Porta, optimistically. 'That'll teach 'em to drive their rotten trucks with lights full on, as if we didn't exist!'

'Now they know there's a war on, at any rate,' says Tiny, with a satisfied grin.

'Let's get moving,' says Porta, decisively. 'It's only a few hours to the rendezvous point, and they're not waiting for any-body! I don't much like the idea of us four having to make it home on our own!'

They are all there when we arrive, but the action has not been carried out without serious losses. No. 1 Section were ambushed before they reached their target. They were executed on the spot, and their bodies left in the snow for the wolves. No. 2 Section, the Old Man's, has lost nine men. There are only five men left of No. 3 Section. The rest were killed when the explosives blew prematurely.

'Blown to dust,' explains a gefreiter, with expressive gestures.

'That was a hell of a noise you lot made,' says the West-phalian. 'What the devil was it you did?'

'We took along a couple of tons of their ammo, while we were at it,' answers Porta cockily.

'And you weren't even hurt?' asks Barcelona, in amazement.

'Only in our feelin's,' answers Tiny, laconically.

Leutnant Blücher has disappeared without trace, together with most of No. 4 Section. Only eight men get back to rendezvous point, and they are in such a state of shock that we can get no proper explanation from them. They babble about security people and torture and they will probably wind up in one of the Army Psychiatric Sections when we get back. The strange sickness which gets soldiers engaged in guerilla warfare behind the enemy lines has got hold of them too.

We lie dug-in in a *balka* for three days, waiting for the

Russian activity to quiet down before moving off. A couple of times we hear their skis squeaking on the snow not very far from where we lie waiting.

We can't sleep, any of us. The pervitin pills see to that.

Porta shortens the waiting for us by telling us the story of a Gefreiter he met once at the Army Ammunition and Explosives School at Bamberg.

'He was a mad type, from Dresden,' he begins. 'Mad as that Russian who came over to us at Charkow and ate cloth, as if he were some kind of a moth. This Gefreiter from Dresden was a professional glass-eater. Soon as he saw a mirror or any kind of expensive glass, he'd grab it and eat it. Very soon there's not a mirror left in the company. This glass-eating Gefreiter from Dresden has eaten the lot.

'The other companies used to come over to us every evening, with mirrors and things, and he'd eat 'em all. They had to pay to see him do it, of course. I was the treasurer. After a bit he'd got through every mirror in the regiment. Eaten every single one of 'em. The price of mirrors increased noticeably.

'We got round the mirror shortage by hooking mirrors in town, and before very long there wasn't a mirror left in the whole of Bamberg. Of course the case got to the Kripos.* At first they laughed at it, and wanted to know who'd be crazy enough to pinch mirrors, and put the chap who reported it in the clink. But when they found out all *their* mirrors were gone too they soon changed their tune.

'Soon after this the Gauleiter's mirror went. Then the Commanding General's. It was a wonderful business, and I could have gone on with it all the time I was at Bamberg if that crazy glass-eater of a Gefreiter hadn't gone and asked for a posting to KdF.† The idiot had got delusions of grandeur and persuaded himself he was an artiste and that Adolf might be interested in seeing him eat mirrors. The Director of Army Entertainment at Bamberg, a padre he was, threw him out on his ear.

'Glass-eating's not an *art*,' he screamed after him, quite worked-up. 'You'll hear more of this, you Gefreiter you!'

The watchdogs took him the same evening. The parson had seen to that. I got things moving to get him out again, of

* Kriminaldolizei (German) = Criminal Squad.
† KdF (Kraft durch Freude) = Nazi holiday and entertainment organisation.

26

course. There was money in the chap. But, unfortunately, he'd hanged himself in his cell. He'd written his last words on the wall:

'Glass-eating *is* art! Heil Hitler!'

'I once knew a bloke as used to eat razor-blades, an' shit 'em out in little steel bars,' recounts Tiny. ' 'E used to sell 'em to drunks on the Reeperbahn!'

Early on a grey morning we get back. The dead from the night's shelling are still lying around. The Russians had shelled the area for about thirty minutes. Revenge when they realised we had managed to get through again.

Trucks pick us up later in the afternoon. We are off-loaded so far behind the front that we can only hear the guns as a muttering in the distance. But for several days we are in a queer state and still go around turning our Mpis on anybody we meet and shouting:

'*Stoi!*'*

All in all we haven't much else in our heads but the rattle of Mpis and the swish of battle-knives, but after a few turns in the sauna, and a bit of fun with the girls in uniform, it slowly goes away. Only No. 4 Section fails to shake off the sickness, but they have it so badly that we have to tie them up with their own belts until they can be taken away to the psychiatric section. We never see them again.

When it is time to move back up, and the holes in the unit have been filled up with new men, we are almost completely well again and have got rid of the continual fear of being killed wherever we go.

---

* Stoi (Russian) = Halt!

When those who, acting in good faith, raise their
voices against the reign of terror, themselves are sent
to the concentration camps and stamped as slan-
derers, then something at the very core of this movement must be rotten.

Colonel-General von Fritsch
6th June, 1936.

During the trip back to the forest camp Tiny holds his head out
of the window the whole way, in order to let the wind cool the
holes he has got in his face after a bitter three hour long bout of
catch-as-catch-can wrestling with a giant Finnish woman. The
prize for beating her was 1,500 Finnmarks and twelve bottles
of vodka.

'It's as good as ours,' said Tiny, as he ducked into the ring.

First she bit off half his nose and chewed on it like a dog with
a sausage. Then he lost part of his left ear. When he still
wouldn't give in she broke three fingers on his right hand and
tore the little finger off the left. He didn't declare himself
beaten until she began crushing his balls.

As they were both taken away to the field sanatorium, we
wondered why she was walking backwards. We found out later
that Tiny had wrenched both her feet round so that they
pointed the wrong way.

In the back of the truck some very queer soldiers we have
been sent to pick up are screaming and shouting. They talk as
if they had a red-hot potato in their mouths. None of them are
wearing badges of rank. They belong to a fortification battalion
with a high number and carry no weapons. When we sound off
at them they laugh as if we had said something funny.

The Old Man is the first to discover that they are mentally
deficient. Before the big offensive opens they are chased out,
under the command of some SS Dirlewanger people, into a
minefield, to set it off. In 1940 the French Army used pigs for
that purpose. But, in accordance with the new German racial
purity laws, all useless human material is to be eliminated. And
so the staff of fortification battalion 999 had conceived this

idea, thus making some use of the weak-minded instead of just sending them to Giessen and killing them with an injection. A way of doing things which was called by the rather nice name of 'euthanasia'.

THE BATTLE GROUP

The trees creek with cold. The storm blows powdery snow into frost-bitten faces. We had never imagined it could be so cold. We are living deep-frozen meat. Our bones rattle inside us and our flesh hangs in ribbons. Human parts and bloody entrails dangle from the snow covered bushes.

An MG-42 spews out death, heavy mortars spit out their grenades with a hollow plopping sound. A reindeer falls from the sky, its legs pointing upwards. It screams shrilly as it falls. It hits the hard-frozen snow and splinters into a shower of blood and guts.

Two Russian officers in long fur capes come reeling out of the bushes. Who is supporting who it is impossible to tell. They are splitting their sides with laughter. Are they mad? Or mad with drink? One of them has lost his fur cap. His close-cropped red hair sticks out like the bristles on a pig. The frost has eaten great holes in his face.

The Legionnaire swings the barrel of the MG towards them. Tracer tracks eat their way into the two officers' stomachs. With arms still round one another's shoulders they fall into the snow, which rapidly becomes red. Their crazy laughter dies away in a long death rattle. A Stalin organ roars and howls. Rockets tear up trees by the roots, and the snow bubbles like porridge. A poisonous reddish-grey smoke rolls along close to the ground.

Some of us put on gasmasks. The smoke burns in our lungs. Why shouldn't one of the sides have begun to use gas? All of us have got gas-shells, and we haven't brought *ours* along just for fun, have we?

I search for my gasmask and then remember that I threw it away a long time ago. The bag it was in is full of all sorts of other things, but no gasmask. It's a good place to keep cigarettes dry in. I am not the only who is searching in vain for his gasmask.

The smoke rolls along concealing everything. We cannot see anything to shoot at but we keep shooting till our weapons are red-hot.

An armoured sledge rushes past us like a ghost, with long tongues of flame spitting from its forward shield. It is so close to us that we need only to reach out to be able to touch the flailing snow-chains.

Porta slings a mine up under the turret. Human parts fly out of the trap-door. A giant yellow-red flame shoots up towards the sky, and a wave of heat sweeps over us like a warm blanket.

'Hell!' mumbles Porta, in disgust, throwing a torn-off arm to one side.

Steel clashes against steel and the frozen earth creaks and groans. A sickening stench of blood and hot oil envelops us. From the forest we hear animal-like screams and a horde of fur-clad soldiers storm forward. The breath smokes from their mouths. Machine-pistols snarl until their magazines are empty. Then the fighting continues with battle-knives, bayonets and sharpened infantry-spades. The fighting is so intense in this devilish man-to-man encounter that no one has time for the fear of death.

My eyes are smarting, pain jabs at my heart like a bayonet. My hands are sticky with blood. I swing my spade in front of me like a flail. Above everything I've got to keep them at a distance from me.

A flame-thrower roars. There is a stench of burning flesh and hot oil. It's Porta. Tiny carries the full container. Again and again the horrible flame roars out across the snow.

Human bodies are burning. Trees are burning. Even the snow looks as if it is on fire. The devil himself would be stiff with fright at the sight of a flame-thrower in action. It would be a refinement even for hell.

Fire spurts at eyes. Faces are crushed like eggshells. Bodies are thrown up towards the Arctic sky and fall back into the snow. The dead are killed over and over again.

A *Rata** howls out of the clouds, and rushes like a comet straight into the ground. It explodes like a giant golden fire-cracker.

The Northern Lights flash across the heavens like a wild,

* Rata = Russian fighter-bomber, used for the first time in the Spanish civil war.

32

mad sea of flame. The earth is one huge slaughterhouse, and stinks like a bubbling latrine.

I feel a blow on my shoulder, snatch the MG* to me and rush forward, panting and coughing. Heide, who is close behind me, stumbles and goes head-over-heels down a slope.

A machine-pistol stammers a long, wicked burst, I spread the supporting legs of the MG, throw myself down behind it and press the butt to my shoulder. Heide guides the long cartridge-belt.

I glimpse them. The MG rumbles, and tracer bullets track between the trees.

A white shape throws up its hands. The *Kalashnikov* flies up above his head. A long ululating scream. A hand-grenade whirls through the air.

A dull thud and all is silence.

'Let's move,' snarls Heide. He is already on his way.

I wrap the cartridge-belt round the breech, sling the MG on to my shoulder and dash after him. I don't want to get left on my own.

'Wait for me,' I scream.

'Piss on you,' he shouts without slackening pace.

There is nothing worse than a retreat. You run for your life with death at your heels.

Porta catches up with me. Passes me in a flurry of snow. Tiny comes struggling along behind with the two heavy flame-thrower containers on his back. He holds on to his light grey bowler with one hand.

I fall, press myself down into the snow. I drop away for a moment into a dream of fear.

'Up you get,' roars Gregor, 'or I'll kick your arse from here to kingdom come!'

Rage gives me strength. I come to my feet and stagger on through the deep snow.

Back in the depths of the forest we pull ourselves together and make up a battle group. A queer mixture of all kinds of regiments! Gunners without guns, tankmen without tanks, cooks, medical orderlies, drivers, even a couple of sailors. A mixed lot.

An infantry oberst we've never seen before takes command. He has a monocle stuck fast in one eye. He knows what he wants.

* MG = Maschinengewehr = Machine-gun.

'Let's get out of this as quick as we can,' says Barcelona, pushing a fresh magazine into his Mpi.* 'This lot stinks of heroes and Valhalla!'

'Where the hell's Ivan got to?' asks Porta, wonderingly, peeping over a great wall of snow.

In the course of the night we dig in and build machine-gun posts out of blocks of snow. We make a fire and heat flat stones. These are tied round the locks of the machine-guns with woollen underclothing. Life in the Arctic has taught us a lot of things they didn't think to teach us in training.

Before we are finished building up the position we have to withdraw again. We have over three hundred wounded with us. We have nothing to help them with. All our first-aid packs are long since used up, and we use filthy rags of uniforms as bandages. A stench of rot rises from these living corpses. They stretch out skeleton arms to us and plead for help. Some ask for a weapon to end their hell of pain. Others lie quietly and look at us with eyes that beg for mercy.

'Don't leave us, comrade,' whispers a dying Feldwebel, as I pass him with the MG on my shoulder.

'Don't leave us to the Russians,' groans another.

I look straight in front of me, won't look at them. Luckily the orderlies come and lift them up on to the heaps of branches which serve them as a bed. We take them with us as the Oberst has ordered. Nobody is to be left behind.

We make sledges of thin tree trunks, and lay the wounded on them. When they die we throw them off and go on.

Four days later we reach two odd-looking hills, shaped like sugar-loaves. It has grown so cold that our noses become plugged with ice, and tears harden into icicles. Metal shatters like glass, and trees split with a loud crack.

Gregor looks at his nose. It is lying in his hand. He feels at the hole in his face. Looks at the nose in his hand, perplexedly.

'What the hell,' he cries and starts to scream. He throws the nose and his Mpi from him. Only Heide, the super-soldier, keeps his head. Like lightning he has Gregor on his back. The Legionnaire has picked up the nose.

'Hold him,' snarls Heide. 'We've got to sew it on again!'

'Is it worth it?' grins Porta. 'It wasn't a very handsome nose, anyway!'

Taking no notice of Gregor's babbling, Heide sews the nose

*Mpi (Maschinenpistole) = machine-pistol.

on again, takes a bloody bandage from a body and binds it tightly round his face.

'Wouldn't it be better to sew it double, so 'e can't pull it off again?' suggests Tiny, holding out a reel of heavy thread.

Gregor whines and moans. Despite the anaesthetic effect of the cold it is still terribly painful.

Heide is not exactly a cosmetic surgeon. The needle he uses was given him by a veterinary surgeon who used it to patch up horses.

'Slacker,' he scolds, and pulls at the nose to make sure it is firmly attached.

'Can a bloke's prick drop off from frost?' asks Tiny, worriedly.

'Can happen,' smiles Porta. 'The Army Institute of Science at Leipzig has compiled statistics on the subject, and these tell us that thirty-two per cent of all soldiers exposed to arctic conditions come home without a joy-stick!'

'Jesus Christ almighty, son of the German God,' groans Tiny. 'What'd you be able to tell the 'ores if you went back to the Reeperbahn with no prick?'

'You'd have no future as a pimp, at any rate, if the polar bears had made a meal of your old John Thomas,' smiles Barcelona.

A tall, thin Pioneer feldwebel gets up suddenly from the bed of branches, tears the blood-soaked bandages from his body and, before anybody realises what is happening, rushes out across the frozen lake.

A couple of orderlies chase after him, but he disappears in the mist. His madness is infectious, and shortly after, two more of the wounded follow him.

The Oberst is furious. He orders a guard mounted over the wounded. Things really begin to go wrong when a guard falls asleep with an Mpi across his knees.

A wounded SS-Unterscharführer creeps silently across the floor and gets hold of the Schmeisser. A rain of bullets sprays the wounded who roll about desperately on their bed of branches. His eyes burn madly and froth rims his gaping mouth. When the magazine is empty he crushes the guard's skull and attacks the wounded nearest to him with the butt of the weapon.

The Legionnaire is the first to arrive on the scene. He throws his Moorish dagger and it bores into the madman's throat.

35

With a gurgling death-rattle the SS-Unterscharführer collapses.

All hell is loose in the blood-bespattered igloo. The wounded run amok. An infantry Leutnant commits *hara-kiri* by thrusting his bayonet into his stomach and cutting upwards. His entrails pour out over his hands. An artilleryman gets Porta by the throat and tries to strangle him.

A shot cracks. The artilleryman falls backwards.

Shortly after this we have other things to worry about. The Russians start an attack under cover of heavy mortar fire. The attack lasts only a couple of hours. Then the snow envelops them again and they disappear into it like ghosts.

Death is so close to us that we feel it already has us in its grip.

Schnapps is issued. A water-bottle cap full to everyone. No. 2 Section gets half a cap more.

'You know what that means,' grins Porta, ominously. 'They don't give you a schnapps ration because they like the colour of your eyes. Famous last drink this is!' He throws the schnapps down in one go.

' 'Eroes' piss,' grins Tiny, 'couple o' pints o' giggle water an' I'll go out an' get me a Knight's Cross with vegetables an' a table knife.'*

'*Nom de Dieu*, it's more likely to be a wooden cross,' smiles the Legionnaire, handing Tiny his schnapps ration. He is a Mohammedan and does not touch spirituous liquors.

'Out of 'taters, into 'taters, then piss it up the wall!' grunts the Old Man, trying to get his silver-lidded pipe going.

'*C'est la guerre*,'† sighs the Legionnaire rolling a little machorka in a piece of Bible paper, and getting a kind of cigarette out of it.

'Give us a puff,' begs Tiny.

The Legionnaire hands him the bent-up cigarette in silence.

All through the night we battle our way on against a howling arctic storm. The snow whirls about us so thickly that we can only just see the man in front of us. Which is an advantage. It means the Russians will have a job finding us. Now and then we hear them behind us.

'They're so certain of us, those yellow monkeys, that they can't be bothered to conceal themselves,' says Porta, downheartedly.

* Slang for Knight's Cross with Oak Leaves and Sword.
† It is war.

'Anybody 'ere still believe in the Final Victory?' asks Tiny with a broad grin.

'Only Adolf and his faithful unteroffizier, Julius Heide,' Porta gives out a typical Berlin laugh.

'Why *did* we go to war, anyway?' asks Tiny wonderingly 'What they got in Russia anybody'd *want*?'

'So that Adolf can be a really great warrior,' answers Porta. 'All those shits who've crept up on top of the heap have to have a war so they won't be forgotten again.'

'Hear me now!' Heide's voice is heard from behind the snow curtain. 'They hang defeatists!'

'And twisted-up bleedin' abortions like you, they put in cages,' shouts Tiny harshly.

Late on the following day the Oberst orders a halt. The battle group is simply unable to continue. Many of the group have been left behind in the snow to freeze to death.

Our rations have run out. Only a few, like Porta, have some crumbs left. He is chewing on a frozen crust, the remnants of a Finnish army loaf.

'Are you hungry?' he asks, putting the last bite into his mouth.

'Rotten swine,' snarls the Old Man.

'Anybody got any vodka?' begs Gregor. His face is dark blue in colour and has swollen up enormously after Heide's surgery.

'Lost your bleedin' mind, 'ave you, well as your snout?' shouts Tiny, jeeringly.

'Vodka!' says Porta. 'It's so long since we've had a drop of that Russian piss I can't recall the taste of it.'

'I could eat a pensioned-off whore from Valencia,' asserts Barcelona. 'I haven't been so hungry since I was inside a Spanish prison camp.'

Porta and the Legionnaire begin to debate just how many juniper berries one should put into a venison dressing.

'Six, I feel,' says Porta, knowledgeably.

'*Impossible*,' the Legionnaire rejects the suggestion, 'but do as you wish. If you include six berries I would not even have to bother to taste the dressing. It would stink to heaven. It is also of importance that the correct kind of pot is used,' he continues. 'If you wish to achieve a true venison dressing you cannot use *any* ordinary kind of pot.'

'True, an antique pot should be used,' agrees Porta. 'And the best of these are made of copper. When I was in Naples, I got hold of one which Julius Caesar's chief cook used to make *bouillabaisse* for the spaghettis' kaiser.'

'Take a trip to Marseilles, and taste the queen of all soups: *Germiny à l'Oseille*,' suggests the Legionnaire. 'After this I would suggest *Pigeon à la Moscovite* with *Champignons Polonaise* and *Salade Béatrice*.'

'I once dined with a chap who, God save us all, forgot to put truffles in his *Perigourdin*,' says Porta. 'He lived on Gendarmenmarkt and was celebrating his release from Moabitt prison. We had actually expected to see the wreck of a man. He'd been in the cage for five years, so you could hardly expect anything else, could you? Some people are completely crushed for ever and ever after a short turn in 'the dark', but this fellow was as chipper as could be, and so healthy it seemed almost indecent. But the worst thing anybody can do, in my opinion, is to be late for a meal. It ruins a meal when you have to rush through the soup and fish to catch the other shits up.'

'Have you tried blue fish baked in the oven with *Sauce Bearnaise*?' Gregor interrupts. 'It's simply heavenly. Me and the general loved it. It was our favourite after an especially bloody battle.'

'I do hope we're in the neighbourhood of this lake, when the herring roe season starts,' says Porta, expectantly.

'When we get 'ome,' says Tiny, by home he means the German lines, 'I'm goin' to organise a goose, fill it up with prunes an' apples, an' eat the lot myself.'

'I'd rather have a turkey,' says Barcelona. 'It's bigger!'

'I can't bloody *stand* it any more,' shouts Porta, desperately, jumping to his feet. 'Come on, Tiny, get hold of your rocker and fill your pockets with grenades.'

'Where we goin'?' asks Tiny, readying his Mpi noisily.

'We're going over to read the neighbour's menu,' answers Porta, swinging the *Kalashnikov* over his shoulder.

'Want me to take a sack?' asks Tiny optimistically.

'No, Ivan's got sacks,' considers Porta.

'Anybody who won't take a risk to get grub's a bleedin' idiot,' Tiny belly-chuckles.

'You'll get shot,' the Old Man warns.

'You're nuts,' answers Tiny, unconcernedly. '*We're* the ones who do the shooting!'

'We're looking forward to some of that real Russian hospitality they're so famous for,' adds Porta as he disappears into the snow with a short laugh.

'One of these days they're not going to come back,' mumbles the Old Man pessimistically.

Several hours go by with no sound but the howling of the arctic storm. A long vicious Mpi salvo breaks the stillness.

'A Schmeisser,' says the Old Man, looking up.

Shortly after there is the sound of three handgrenade explosions, and a series of flares send a brilliantly white light out over the terrain.

'They've met the neighbours,' whispers Gregor, in terror.

'If they get through all right,' says the Old Man, worriedly, 'the devil take those two maniacs!'

'You ought to report them,' says Heide, officiously. 'It's a serious breach of discipline. The enemy will be able to use it as propaganda. I can just see the headlines in Pravda:

GERMAN ARMIES STARVING
Suicide missions sent out to
steal bread from the Red Army!'

We sense, more than anything, the muzzle-flame from a heavy gun depressed to ground level. Loud screams and a long series of explosions follow. A couple of Maxims bark angrily.

A long silence falls across the snow desert. Even the icy storm quietens. It feels as if the whole of the Arctic is taking a deep breath, and readying itself for something quite special.

A colossal explosion which seems as if it will never stop rends the stillness of the night.

'God save us all,' pants Barcelona, shocked. 'They must have mistaken the ammunition store for the kitchen!'

'Alarm, alarm,' our sentries scream hysterically, certain that an attack is on the way.

A gigantic column of flame goes up to the north-east of us, and the earth shakes to a long rolling explosion.

A group of officers with the Oberst in the lead come rushing out of an igloo.

'What in the world are the Russians doing?' asks the Oberst, nervously. 'Can they be fighting amongst themselves?' He turns to an infantry major: 'Have we anybody out there?'

'No, Herr Oberst, this battle group has no contact whatever with the enemy.'

Oberst Frick jams his monocle tighter into his eye and looks sharply at the major.

'Do you *know* this to be true or do you merely *think* it to be so?'

The major is obviously uneasy and has to admit that he really knows very little about what is happening within the group. He is a signals officer and has never before been with a battle unit.

A long series of explosions and a snarling MG salvo bring his eyes round to the north-east, where sharp tongues of flame can be seen against reddening clouds.

'There's some devilry going on,' mumbles the Oberst. 'Find out what it is.'

'Yes, Herr Oberst,' replies the major, unhappily, and with no idea of what it is he has to find out about.

A few minutes later he is passing the buck to a Hauptmann.

'I want a clear picture of what is happening! Understand me, Herr Hauptmann? There's some devilry going on. Some damned devilry!'

The Hauptmann disappears behind a clump of trees, where he runs into a Leutnant.

'There's some devilry going on. You understand me?' he roars at the Leutnant. 'I want your report here in ten minutes time. Somebody is annoying the enemy!'

The *Jäger*-Leutnant jogs off down the narrow track where he runs into No. 2 Section. He points at the Old Man with his Mpi.

'On your feet, Oberfeldwebel! What a pigsty this is! The enemy's worked up and I want to know why. Understand me? I want to *know*. Even if you have to get it from the Russian CO in person!'

'Very good, sir,' the Old Man replies, moving around as if he were preparing to go.

The Leutnant disappears between the trees and decides to find a hiding-place where the Hauptmann will never think of looking for him.

The Old Man sits down quietly, and puffs his pipe.

During the next hour we hear dispersed firing, first from one direction then from another.

'They're dead long ago,' says Barcelona, blackly, listening to the sound of a long, vicious Mpi salvo.

The depressed gun roars, and several handgrenades explode. Through all the noise we hear the sound of a great roar of happy laughter.

'That was Porta,' mumbles the Old Man, fiddling nervously with the silver lid of his pipe.

Dawn is near and the storm has slackened off almost completely. Only occasionally icy gusts whirl the snow up around us.

'I doubt if we'll see them again, now,' states Heide. 'Nobody can hang about in the middle of an enemy retirement as long as they have without getting scalped.'

'I'm afraid you're right,' says the Old Man quietly. 'If only I'd forbidden them to go.'

'*Par Allah*, you couldn't have kept them back,' the Legionnaire comforts him.

A well-known sound brings us to our feet with our weapons at the ready.

'Ski-troops,' whispers Heide, tensely, taking cover behind a tree.

I am down in a hole with the butt of the MG pressed into my shoulder. The snow squeaks and crackles. There is a strange kind of grunting noise. Again a sound like the hiss of skis sliding through frozen snow. I crook my finger on the trigger. There is a shadow moving amongst the trees.

'Don't fire,' shouts Barcelona, jumping to his feet. He has seen Porta's cylindrical yellow topper, which seems to be bobbing about strangely high up amongst the trees.

'What the hell?' cries the Westphalian, astoundedly.

Half fearfully we stare at the floating hat as it comes bobbing towards us. If Porta is wearing that hat he must have grown at least six feet. Then the riddle is answered. A reindeer comes snuffling out of the snow. It looks as if it has been rolling in cotton wool. It is pulling an *akja** behind it, fully loaded with boxes and sacks. On top of the load Porta and Tiny sit majestically.

'Was it you doing the shooting?' shouts the Old Man.

'Sometimes it was,' answers Tiny, with an air of superiority. 'But the neighbours' lads got shot of quite a pile of Uncle Joe Stalin's shit, too.'

'We ran into a crazy sod of a *politruk*,† with a face that thin he could've kissed a *kz*‡ goat between the horns with no

* akja: Finnish reindeer sledge.
† politruk: political commissar.
‡ kz: concentration camp.

41

trouble,' explains Porta, waving his arms about. 'We had to take aim twice before we could hit him. Then some bungled-up arsehole starts nattering at us out of the dark, and then he begins shooting at us. We aimed at his muzzle-flash and that soon cured *him*.'

'But we went the wrong road,' Tiny breaks in. 'It was black as the backside of a nigger's bollocks. We blunders into some staff quarters where a load o' military geniuses was discussin' 'ow to win the fuckin' war. There was some *vojemkom** pushin' out a load o' pig-latin. I pointed me old rock-a-bye 'ere at 'is fat gut, an' 'e stopped talking quite sudden-like! "*Germanski!*" 'e screams, and didn't 'ave time to say any more 'fore 'e was a goner. Porta swept the rest of 'em under the carpet!'

'You brought their charts back, I hope?' asks Heide, professionally. He thinks of nothing else but military objectives.

'What the 'ell'd we want with them?' asks Tiny, blankly. 'They wasn't what we'd gone out to get. And, any road, we knew the way back!'

Heide can only shake his head despairingly.

'What a row there was then, both south and north,' explains Porta. 'When we got outside we got tumbled head-over-heels by a whole shower of 'em, and some cunt of an officer gave us a real shellacking. He was that mixed up he never even noticed when Tiny answers him: "*Jawohl, Herr Leutnant!*" '

'Almost more'n a bloke's life was worth to be out in the open there,' Tiny goes on, lighting up a cigar.

'Well we kept walking about a bit and watching the confusion,' laughs Porta, heartily. 'A major, red in the face as a boiled lobster, gives us another bollocking and orders us to help get a PAK-gun† into position. An order's an order in any man's army, so we got on with helping the anti-tank boys to get their pea-shooter set up where Major Ivan wanted it.'

'All 'ell'd broke loose up the other end of the camp,' grins Tiny. 'Up 'ad gone an ammo stores an' there was an awful din goin' on. We thought for a bit it was you lot come to give us a 'and. Somebody blows the alarm whistle an' all the stinkin' Russians dashes over to where the bullets are flyin'.'

'Now we had some elbow-room,' says Porta, loftily. 'We pushed our nuts into the various companies just to say hello, and suddenly there we are with the catering boys.'

* vojemkom: regimental commissar.

† PAK-gun (Panzerabwehrkanone): Anti-tank gun.

'I doubt if any German soldier 'as ever seen so much perishin' grub at one time in all 'is born life,' interjects Tiny, rolling his eyes ecstatically heavenwards. 'They'd got every-thin'. Wobblin' pork, smoked reindeer, pickled gherkins, the *lot*!'

'Yes, a comparison of Russian army catering with German ditto,' remarks Porta, drily, 'makes one realise that belief in the Final Victory can only be supported by faith alone!'

'There was a fat sod of a cook-sergeant, lyin' there 'avin' a wank at a picture o' Marlene Dietrich,' Tiny gives a dirty chuckle. 'Biggest load 'e shot in 'is life was the last, when rock-a-bye-baby 'ere pushed forty-two tracers right up 'is bleedin' jacksey!'

'We had to move fast, now,' says Porta, with a short laugh. 'We grabbed everything we could get our hands on. When we found out we couldn't carry the half of it we went out to try and liberate a sledge. That's how we met this Commie reindeer, who did *not* conceal from us that he was a critic of the system, and since he also had an *akja* with him, well, we enlisted him on the spot.'

'I 'ad to promise 'im some Finnish, capitalist reindeer cunt,' grins Tiny, 'and 'e's goin' to get it too, if I 'ave to bend over an' supply German arsehole to 'im, personally!'

'Don't tell me this unit's going to be cluttered up with a reindeer, now?' shouts the Old Man, furiously.

'We can discuss that later,' answers Porta, off-handedly. 'While the neighbours were shadow-boxing and banging away at one another, we popped in on the QM. There was only one man on guard and he was asleep, so he didn't even notice it when we shot him.'

'Asleep on guard,' shouts Heide, indignantly. 'He *deserved* to lose his life!'

'Well, I'm quite happy to find that the majority of soldiers are bad soldiers,' replied Porta.

'*Beseff** that is because most soldiers are poor people,' says the Legionnaire. 'Life has taught them that however hard they work they will still continue to be poor.'

'Ah! But poor soldiers make good killers,' says Tiny, 'an' they've got sharp eyes an 'ears. That's because they've 'ad to keep 'em open for the bailiff an' the bleedin' coppers since they was nippers!'

* Beseff (Arabic): To be sure (quite certainly).

43

'When we dropped in on the butchers' store,' continued Porta, 'Tiny came near to killing us. He dropped a hand-grenade into a box of flares. They fizzed about all over the place and a couple of Ivans got hit and were rendered down in two shakes. But our visit was remunerative. There was coffee, pure coffee all the way from Brazil. I don't think Adolf, even, can get it any more. It was as easy as walking into the grocer's and asking for a pound!'

'Easier,' grins Tiny, euphorically. 'You didn't even 'ave to queue up and slip your coppers to some bint behind a cash-box.'

For the next couple of hours we eat as if we were preparing ourselves for three years of famine.

'Shouldn't we give some to the wounded,' feels Heide, the humanitarian.

Tiny almost chokes on a huge mouthful of pickled herring.

'What sick soddin' monkey's been bitin' on your arse? They're goin' to kick the bucket any bloody road.'

'They are our comrades,' Heide instructs him, angrily.

'Maybe they're yours, I don't know any of 'em,' replies Tiny, carelessly, pushing another pickled herring into his mouth.

'Tiny's right, you know,' says Porta. 'If we give the wounded anything we'll have old Monocle-Charlie, the Oberst, on our backs. He'll want it shared out to the whole of the company. It's better, in my opinion, that a few of us get enough, than that everybody shares and still gets too little to do him any good.'

Suddenly the Old Man goes red in the face. He tries to hit himself on the back. His face goes slowly purple. Gurgling, he rolls over on his side. He is choking. We roll him on to his face and hammer with our fists on his back.

'He's dying,' says Porta, with conviction. '*People!* Why can't they chew their food properly?'

'' E ain't gonna die,' says Tiny and gripping the Old Man by the ankles he bangs his head against the ground repeatedly whilst the Legionnaire hammers him on the back.

Half a block of liver paste flies out of his mouth.

'God save us,' stammers the Old Man, straining to get back his breath. 'Think, to die in action choked by enemy liver paste!'

'It's all one,' says Gregor, with a lop-sided smile, 'whether you get choked by liver paste, or get your guts blown apart by explosives!'

We take a break from eating, but after ten minutes we start in again.

We are no longer eating to still our hunger, but from mere gluttony.

'*Santa Maria del Mar*,' groans Barcelona, with a long drawn out belch. 'I'm dreaming. Pinch me, somebody, am I still here?'

'You're still here,' I answer, cutting myself a large slice from a haunch of reindeer.

'Hell's bells,' he cries, toppling a shivering goatsmilk cheese into his widely gaping mouth.

'What the devil's that?' cries Porta, in terror, throwing himself head-over-heels into covers behind a snowdrift.

We scatter like chaff before the wind. In a moment we are lying in wait for the unknown who has given us warning of his coming. The automatic weapons are at the ready. Fingers curl round triggers.

We lie like this for some time, waiting, tense.

'Gas shells,' says Porta, fearfully, fumbling for the gasmask he has long since jettisoned.

Then the Legionnaire laughs hysterically and points up into the sky.

'*Sacré nom e Dieu*, there are your gas shells!'

We gape at the heavens and cannot believe our own eyes. V after V of wild ducks flap noisily past above our heads.

'Holy Mother of Kazan!' cries Porta, getting up on one knee. 'There goes a whole supply depot and we're doing nothing about it!'

'What in the world are they doing here?' asks the Westphalian, thoughtfully. 'Ducks fly to the warm regions in wintertime.'

'Maybe then they're Eskimo ducks, on their way to cool off their arses on the damned icebergs,' says Tiny, licking his lips, hungrily. The sight has made him forget completely the fact that he is no longer hungry.

'I can't imagine what they can live off up here,' continues the Westphalian, stubbornly. 'There's nothing here for ducks to fill up on.'

'Maybe the travel agency they bought their tickets from has gone broke,' suggests Porta, staring after the ducks which have disappeared across the Lange Lake.

'Wild duck is wonderful,' says the Old Man, dreamily. 'If only we could have potted a few of 'em down!'

'I've never tried it,' says Heide. 'Is it as good as ordinary duck?'

'Better,' Porta assures him. 'Kings and dictators serve it at great banquets to which they invite the highest in the land. I have the English king's recipe for wild duck. I got it from a cook in the English Life Guards whom I met in France.'

'Was he an Englishman you had taken prisoner?' asks Heide, interestedly.

'No, he was a chap I said good-bye to on the beach at Dunkirk, when Churchill's army went off back to London to patch up their uniforms.'

'You allowed a prisoner to escape?' asks Heide, in amazement.

'Hell no. That's what I'm trying to tell you. He just went off home!'

'They're coming back,' screams Tiny, excitedly, pointing out over the lake.

'Devil take me if they're not,' shouts Porta, throwing a stone up in the air in the vain hope of hitting a duck.

The Old Man catches up a carbine and shoots into the flock. Tiny and Porta stand watching like a pair of bird-dogs.

The rest of us pick up our carbines and Mpi's. Shots hail up at the quacking flock, but not a single bird is hit. They disappear behind the hills.

'Oh *shit*!' says Porta, in disappointment, dropping down on the snow.

'It'd have been the first sensible shot fired in the whole bloody war!'

'If a bloke'd been a fighter pilot it'd've been easy to fly under 'em an' pick 'em up on the wing,' says Tiny, swallowing involuntarily.

Long after the wild ducks have flown past we are still talking about them.

'They're best with apple sauce and a special kind of gravy,' says Porta. 'And, most important thing of all, the skin must be crisp. It should crackle slightly between your teeth.'

'They don't understand that in Spain,' says Barcelona. 'They stuff them with oranges and boil them till its like chewing on a limp prick.'

'People who do that ought to be shot,' decides Porta. 'It's blasphemy to ruin a duck like that.'

We are on the march again, and pass through a narrow cleft

still talking about ducks. High walls of snow and ice enclose us on both sides. An acrid smell of death fills our nostrils.

Wonderingly we look around us for the bodies. Much later we realise it is we who are carrying that horrible, sickly-sweet stench about with us.

'We'll stink of corpses the rest of our lives,' says the Old Man, quietly.

He's right. After four years at the front the death smell has penetrated us so deeply that it will be hard for any of us ever to get rid of it.

On the march we talk of peace. Some of us have been in uniform since '36 and simply cannot realise what it will be like to wear civilian clothing again, and to be able to go to the loo without clicking our heels together and asking permission first. We don't really believe in peace any more. Porta thinks it will be a hundred years' war. He has worked out a complicated equation which he says demonstrates how it can be done. Every year some youngsters become old enough to be called up and get themselves slaughtered on the altar of the Fatherland. The subject is so interesting that we call a halt to discuss it in more detail.

Officers of the battle group, which we have joined up with again, strangers to us, begin to shout at us and chase us forward. They are scared and nervous, unused to being inside enemy territory the way we are. A special kind of man is needed to carry out this kind of task.

A good guerrilla fighter should not, first and foremost, be a sporting fool, nor a product of the usual kind of military academy. He should have a good bit of the villain in him and have the mentality of a sixteen-year-old boy, so that he has no real understanding of the fact that he himself is just as easy to kill as the other fellows he mows down with his machine-pistol.

Shadowy forms jump at us from the darkness. Bayonets flash and machine-pistols sing of death. It takes only a few minutes. A few bodies in the snow mark the episode.

The battle group marches on in a long column of route. The officers are irritable, shouting and screeching at the men to conceal their own fear.

No. 2 Section pulls away from the group a little. If the neighbours come back we'll do better on our own, and we know he *will* be back. Siberian units like to make a lightning swoop and then to disappear like ghosts into the snow.

47

'Think if it was going to be all over tomorrow,' says Gregor, his face taking on a strange expression, 'and you got your nut caved in today! Make you look, wouldn't it?'

'*C'est vrai, mon ami*, it can happen like that if your luck's out,' says the Legionnaire. 'I had a comrade in the Second Regiment of the Legion. He had been with us everywhere where we had seen hard and dirty fighting, without having received a scratch. On his chest they had hung every decoration it was possible for an NCO in the French Army to win. After eighteen years he decided to leave the service. His papers were clean and he had a job to go to in Customs and Excise. He had been up to say good-bye to the Colonel and had taken a glass with our O.C. Coming downstairs from handing in his arms to the armoury, he jumped happily from one landing to the next and came down with his foot in a bucket of soapy water. He went head first down the rest of the way, and smashed his head into a rifle-rack at the foot of the stairs. Dead on the spot. Both neck and back broken!'

'You can choke on a chunk of meat while you're sitting having a shit,' says Porta, who often lunches in the latrines.

'Think I'll keep a better eye out in the future,' says Tiny, thoughtfully. 'Think o' breakin' your neck in a bucket! Wicked to bleedin' think on ain't it?'

We are tired and pessimistic on the march back. Only Porta is happy as a lark. He is selling part of the Russian supplies. But suddenly his growing business effort comes to a stop. The sledge disappears in the course of the night. The following day the reindeer comes back, but with an empty sledge. Porta cries with rage.

For a moment he suspects Chief Mechanic Wolf, but puts that right out of his head. Wolf would never get anywhere near the front, not even when one took his psychotic greed into consideration.

'Let me just get hold of that rotten crook,' he howls, punching the snow helplessly, 'and I'll wind these well-manicured fingers round the bastard's neck and squeeze an' squeeze till there's no more life left in the son of a whore. Oh, he's *got* to be some wicked old pervert. It *can't* be Chief Mechanic Wolf. He's a thieving, money-grabbing pig like the rest of the top lot, but he's not filthy enough for this. In some ways he's like me. If some wicked sod's got to be relieved of the burden his life must be to him then we help him off with it in a pleasant, civilised manner. I know Wolf like I know myself. No sneaky crookednesses, 'less they're agreed on in advance. No, he'd never pinch what I've had to labour for in the sweat of me brow. Well, at any rate, he'd leave half of it behind, if he did. If it can't be Wolf, though, then who *can* it be? It's *got* to be somebody who doesn't know me.' He looks up at the driving clouds and folds his hands. 'Dear God, help me get hold of that dirty viper, that cursed snake, so I can whip his arse to shreds with red-hot barbed-wire!'

'The devil take this horrible weather,' groans Gregor stopping for a moment to scrape the snow from his face.

'We'll never get through,' whines the Westphalian, resignedly. 'Let's sit down and wait for them, and get it over with!'

'You're out of your mind,' shouts Porta, contemptuously. 'Don't shit yourself before it gets dark even!'

'I can't go on,' weeps the HJ* leader, heartrendingly, throwing himself down in the snow.

' 'Itler's boy's capitulatin',' grins Tiny, pleased, swinging the SMG over his shoulder as if it were a spade.

'Get him on his feet,' orders the Old Man, roughly.

'Come on up,' snarls Heide, ready for action. A born bully, recruit-chaser, this is what he really loves doing.

'Let me be,' howls the HJ leader, kicking out at Heide.

'You've got ten seconds, you yellow-gutted cur,' hisses Heide, pushing the muzzle of his Mpi into the boy's stomach.

'You wouldn't dare,' screams the HJ lad, in terror. 'It's murder!'

'Wouldn't I, though?' Heide grins like a devil, and sends the snow alongside the boy spurting up with a burst of bullets.

Shakily the boy gets to his feet, and reels after the section which is already some way ahead.

'March to attention,' rages Heide. 'Straighten your legs, stretch your feet out! Pull your rifle-sling taut, you quivering jelly-bag, or I'll blow your arse from under you!'

'You're raving mad,' protests the HJ boy.

Heide steps to one side, lifts his Mpi like a club and smashes it with brutal force into the boy's face.

'This time you get away with it,' he snarls with satanic glee, 'but next time you lie down without an order, I'm gonna pluck you! March, you sad sack! At the double, if you please!'

* HJ (Hitler Jugend) = Hitler Youth.

With blood streaming down his face the HJ boy doubles along with Heide at his heels. He has got so much speed up that he almost runs past the section.

'Ho! Where you goin', Son of 'Itler?' shouts Tiny, in amazement. 'If it's the leave train you're chasin' it went off long ago!'

'Why is he bleeding?' asks the Old Man, threateningly.

'He fell down,' grins Heide, 'and hit his face on his carbine, which he was carrying in an unregimental manner. Right?' he questions the HJ boy, with a wicked expression on his face.

'Yes, Herr Unteroffizier,' shouts the boy. 'I fell down.'

'Let's see your Mpi,' demands the Old Man, holding out his hand for Heide's weapon. He examines the barrel briefly. 'Another time I'd be very careful, Unteroffizier Heide, that people don't fall down and hit their faces, when they're standing near you! Hear me, you'll fly straight in one long arc into Torgau, if I catch you laying a finger on a subordinate. And I don't care *how* tight you hold on to the Führer's arse!'

Heide goes chalk-white in the face, and stares at the Old Man furiously for an instant.

'You could have left out the last remark. You might come to repent it bitterly some day!'

'You can leave it to me to sort out what I'll repent and won't repent,' smiles the Old Man, condescendingly, 'but I'd watch myself if I were you! You want to stay on in the Army after the war. You're no fool, so watch your mouth or it may be the Army won't have you when they're putting the pieces together again after this lot's over!'

'You think we're going to lose this war?' asks Heide, with a hint of a threat in his voice.

'Don't you?' asks the Old Man, turning on his heel and moving off.

To the north-west the reflection of a huge fire lights up the sky.

'Petsamo's burning,' confirms Oberleutnant Wisling.

We all stare towards the north. Petsamo. It seems like a hundred years since we were there.

'*Merde, alors*, how people can live in this cursed land,' remarks the Legionnaire, tired and freezing. 'I am sick with longing for the Sahara and the hot sand!'

'One thing's for sure. I'm cured of winter sports for the rest of my life,' smiles Barcelona, bitterly, clapping his hands together. His face hidden behind a mask of ice.

'What in the hell does Adolf *want* with this country?' asks Porta, in a voice which sounds as if it came from the grave.

'*Im Osten, da leuchtet eine heiliges Licht ...*' sings Gregor, jeeringly.

Far out in the neighbourhood of Motowski Bay the battle-group halts. That night fifteen men are shot in the head. We are nervous and irritable. Our nervousness shows in the fact that our sentries shoot three of our own men.

'They're getting cheekier and cheekier,' says Porta, examining with interest, the bullet-hole in one of the bodies. 'Right between the eyes!'

'*C'est la guerre!* But why don't we show them we're still here?' suggests the Legionnaire.

'Ye-e-ah! Let's go make us some Russian corpses,' grins Tiny, murderously, swinging his Mpi round in an arc.

An attack group is formed under the command of a Finnish forest-runner, one of those tough Commie-eaters who consider every live Bolshevik to be an insult to God and to Finland.

Silently we sneak through the snow and lie in ambush a kilometre on the opposite side of the bay.

They arrive a couple of hours later on squeaking skis in single-file, without the least suspicion. We pull back on our triggers until the magazines are empty.

They fall forward and sideways like corn going down before a sharp scythe.

We go over them quickly and take what is usable. A few are still alive. The forest runner looks after them. With a wicked grin of hate he places the muzzle of his weapon between their eyes and fires. Their skulls break up like eggshells. They are Siberian troops and have plenty of fine-cut machorka in their pockets. Smoke soon scents the air around us. Their water-bottles are filled with vodka.

Porta guesses they have just been issued their weekly ration. We discover it to be Thursday, Ivan's vodka day. Perhaps they were half-drunk when they got here. It could explain the absence of scouts and the way they went headlong to meet their deaths.

They have photographs of their families in their wallets. We sit on the bodies, soon frozen stiff, and discuss the photographs. The ones we don't like we flip away on the arctic wind, but the young sweethearts and wives we keep. We cut the men away; They only disturb our fantasies about the women.

51

Shortly after midnight all hell breaks loose. Automatic weapons spit death from every angle. In long snow-capes and on short skis they come rushing at us. Even their faces are covered by white snow-masks. It is like being attacked by an army of ghosts. As suddenly as it started it is over. In many places the snow is blotched red with Finnish and German blood. Wounded men babble heart-rendingly, but we are too worn out to bring them in, and it is not long before the icy cold puts an end to them. Death comes quickly north of the Arctic Circle.

The battle group is shrinking. Far more than half the number are the wounded we are dragging along with us. Our strength ebbs away hour by hour. We begin to drop the wounded and let them lie. They only hold us back. The spirit of comradeship of which we sing is not worth much to a dying battle-group in the Arctic.

Many put an end to their lives with a bullet.

The Oberst bends over his adjutant, a young Leutnant, lying in the snow. Both his eyes have been blasted by explosives. He closes the lids of the dead man's eyes and walks silently, his face impassive, along the rows of groaning soldiers.

Sanitätsgefreiter Krone, the former chaplain, kneels by the side of Leutnant Kraus. In a clear voice he prays to God for mercy.

The Oberst stops for a moment and looks at Leutnant Kraus, whose skin is already the parchment colour of death. His teeth seem to project strangely from between his purple lips, which are pulled back in a canine snarl. The hero's death is not a particularly beautiful one, thinks the Oberst, bitterly. It hardly resembles the fantasies of the war-correspondents.

Shortly after, he collects the officers of the battle-group around him. They arrive one by one. Leutnant Linz from No. 1 Company, Hauptmann Bernstein from No. 2, Leutnant Paulus from No. 3, Oberleutnant Wisling from No. 4, Major Pihl from No. 5, Leutnant Hansen from No. 6. Last to arrive is Leutnant Schultz.

'Let us sit down, gentlemen,' says the Oberst, with a gloomy expression. He throws a brief glance at their faces. He knows which of them he can count on, and which of them would prefer to spit in his face. 'Gentlemen,' he begins, tiredly, 'I have ordered you to come here to discuss the future of this group. I can, of course, order whatever I feel to be the proper action. That is why I am in command, and you must obey my

52

orders. Protests are considered as mutiny and in the situation we find ourselves that means a drumhead court martial and immediate execution. This is the case, not only in our own army, but in all others.'

He pauses, blows away some snow from the lock of his Mpi, and listens for a moment to the muffled groans coming from the igloo in which the wounded have been placed.

'In my opinion, our situation is completely hopeless. Our ammunition is about to run out. So is our strength. Over half of the group's personnel are wounded. If we continue as we have been doing, we shall all soon be dead. Under these circumstances I do not wish to give my next order until I have discussed our situation with you, but you must understand that whatever your opinions may be, the final decision is still mine. I am not attempting to cover myself.

'I know what my responsibilities are, and I am thinking, first and foremost, of the wounded, who are suffering most terrible pain. Many of them have gangrene, and we have no drugs, no bandages, nothing at all with which to help them. It is very doubtful that we will be able to get through to our own forces. The scouting party which has just returned to us has informed me that there are large bodies of Siberian infantry in front of us. We must also reckon on the presence of an armoured sledge battalion. If we split the battle group into three there is a small possibility of our being able to fight our way through.' He pauses again, and smashes the butt of his Mpi into the snow. 'But without the wounded, it must be understood!'

An angry murmur goes up from the assembled officers.

'Leave the wounded, by God?' shouts Leutnant Schultz, the youngest of them, who has been steeped in the ethic of heroism.

'I am speaking, Leutnant Schultz!' snarls the Oberst, rebuffing him angrily. 'You may have your say when I have finished. We can also stay here, extend our igloos to build up a hedgehog position, and hope that our own forces will come to get us. But that I feel to be a vain hope. My personal opinion is that HQ have long since written us off.'

'What about an SS-regiment?' asks Leutnant Schultz, childishly hopeful.

'If you are in touch with the Commanding General, Herr Leutnant, you may suggest your idea to him,' sneers the Oberst. 'Perhaps you would inform him at the same time where he can *find* an SS-regiment!'

'SS-Gebirgsdivision-Nord is in Finland,' says Leutnant Schultz, triumphantly.

'True, but *they* don't know where *we* are,' snarls the Oberst, irritably, 'and even if they did know they would not come to fetch us! We are in a catastrophic situation. The Finnish soldiers seconded to us have disappeared in the course of the night. *They* know that their only chance is to fight their way through in small groups.'

'That's desertion,' screams Leutnant Schultz, furiously.

'You are mistaken,' smiles the Oberst, condescendingly. 'The Finns are not under German command. None of them have taken the oath of loyalty to the Führer. Ten kilometres east of us there is a Siberian ski-battalion. It is a heavily over-strength battalion and it will very soon attack and destroy us.' He polishes his monocle, thoughtfully, with a snow-white handkerchief. 'I suggest to you that we leave the wounded here with a few volunteers to look after them. This may sound unfeeling, even brutal, but is the only chance for the remainder of the group. To stay here and fight would be suicide. And as soon as the fighting was over the wounded would be shot out of hand. Wounded men are always troublesome and particularly enemy wounded. If we leave the wounded here with an unteroffizier, who has orders to make contact with the Russians as soon as the battle group has departed, there is a possibility that the Russian commander will not order them to be executed in cold blood.' He sits down heavily on the snow, and points at Leutnant Schultz whose frost-bitten face is now a coppery-red. 'Now it is your turn, Herr Leutnant. I shall be pleased if you have a better plan to suggest!'

White-hot with stifled rage the young officer gets to his feet and stares at the Oberst with contempt and hate in his eyes.

'What you suggest is the filthiest thing I've heard of in my life,' he says, harshly. 'To leave our wounded comrades to the mercy of the Bolsheviks is not only treason, but deliberate murder. You talk all the time of saving the group, getting through, as if that means something. *Fighting* is what means something! Fighting as our German forefathers fought. Most of us will be dead before the Final Victory, but that is unimportant. As long as some of the best live to see it. The cost of that victory will be the greatest price ever demanded of a Fatherland, but a thousand years from now they will look up to those of us who have paid it. You call yourself a German officer. I

54

call you a cowardly wretch. Until this minute I have regarded you as an honourable German soldier who did his duty, respected his oath to the Führer and knew what that oath entailed. I see now that I have been bitterly in error. But I swear to you that as long as I can lift a weapon, your filthy suggestion will not be carried out. If it is it will be over my dead body. I promise you, too, that I shall see to it that you answer to a court martial, if we get back.'

'Are you finished?' asks the Oberst, matter-of-factly. He turns to the No. 2 Company O.C., Hauptmann Bernstein, who remains seated and throws out his arms resignedly.

'Herr Oberst, what am I to say? I await your orders. Whether or not I agree with them is of no importance. I shall carry them out.'

'Is that all?' asks the Oberst, with a resigned smile.

'It is, sir. I cannot see that there is anything to add.'

'Major Pihl, what is your opinion?'

The Major stands up. He is a line officer. That is obvious. He bobs up and down, arrogantly, from the knees, as is the habit of Prussian Guards officers.

'Herr Oberst, I do not understand you,' he trumpets. 'Have you thought your suggestion through properly? That is, nevertheless, no affair of mine. I agree with Bernstein. You give the orders, we carry them out without discussion.' Straight-backed, he sits down alongside Hauptmann Bernstein. He lights a cigarette and appears to take no further interest in the proceedings.

Leutnant Linz from No. 1 Company jumps noisily to his feet, clicks his heels loudly three times and gives the Nazi salute.

'Do you no longer use the Prussian salute, with your hand to your cap?' asks the Oberst, smiling, 'or do you think you are with the SS, Herr Leutnant?'

The tall, thin Leutnant goes red in the face, and kicks shyly at the snow. A lump of it flies into Major Pihl's lap.

'Leutnant Schultz has already said what I have to say, sir!' He clicks his heels again three times and this time salutes in the regulation manner. He takes a seat next to Leutnant Schultz as if seeking safety there.

Leutnant Paulus from No. 3 Company is next. He gets up without unnecessarily theatrical gestures, like the slow-moving Frisian he is. He neither salutes nor clicks his heels.

'Herr Oberst,' he begins, in his slow deep voice, 'I have commanded a company of your regiment for fourteen months now. I know you are not what Leutnant Schultz has accused you of being. I believe that you have not arrived at your decision without long and deep consideration. I am not able to decide whether it is right or wrong. I am under your command and await your orders.' He sits down beside Hauptmann Bernstein, who presses his hand in silence.

Little Leutnant Hansen from No. 6 doesn't much want to state his opinion. Inside he agrees with the Oberst, but he has spent seven months in Torgau for a slight offence and if there is anywhere he does not want to see again it is Torgau. He glances at Leutnant Schultz, who is watching him with ice-cold eyes.

'Well, Herr Hansen,' the Oberst presses on. 'What is your opinion?'

'Herr Oberst, I do not like your suggestion. The enemy will merely kill all the wounded with a few Mpi bursts, and I'd like to know who'll volunteer to stay behind with them. You can't *order* soldiers to give themselves up. Have you forgotten Lemberg, where they liquidated hundreds of wounded with a shot in the neck and crucified the priests on the doors. You can't leave comrades to that sort of fate. I must say no to your suggestion, Herr Oberst.' He sits down again on the snow and avoids Oberst Frick's eye. He knows his answer was a cowardly evasion, but Torgau looms, like a brutal threat, in his thoughts.

The last to reply is Oberleutnant Wisling from No. 4 Company.

'Sir, I am in complete agreement with you. You have no other choice. In your place I would give the order, and if anyone complained I would convene a drumhead court martial for him. Whether you agree or not, orders are to be obeyed. Any recruit knows that!'

'Another cowardly, traitorous swine,' shouts Schultz, indignantly.

'In your position, Herr Oberst,' continues Oberleutnant Wisling, ignoring Schultz's hate-filled shout, 'I would myself remain with the wounded. Otherwise you will have to defend yourself in front of a German court martial. The result of that can be in little doubt.'

'Thank you, Wisling, it takes guts to state your opinion as you have done, but I do not fear a German court martial, I shall know how to defend my decision, if it comes to that.'

Oberleutnant Wisling shrugs his shoulders. Oberst Frick gets to his feet and adjusts his monocle.

'It has been informative hearing your opinions, but they have not changed my decision. I will not allow soldiers under my command to be slaughtered to no purpose. As commanding officer it must be my chief duty to bring as many effective men back as possible. Dead soldiers are of no value.'

'Running away from these *untermensch*!' screams Leutnant Schultz into the arctic night, placing his hand theatrically on his pistol holster. 'Is there nobody who puts duty to Führer and Fatherland first? Every German soldier has sworn an oath to risk his life where it is required. Millions of brave soldiers have already given their lives for the Führer. To stay alive, is that your only object, Oberst Frick? God be praised there are only a few of your kind. For the sake of the army you must retract your order. Let us build a hedgehog defence position, and fight the Bolsheviks, kill as many as we can before we ourselves are killed. We owe this to the Führer and the magnificent ideal he has given to the German people.'

'The discussion is closed,' states the Oberst, decisively. 'The wounded will remain here. The group will march off in one hour's time, No. 5 Company leading. Schultz, you will take the rear with the heavy company. And I am sure I do not have to tell you that from this moment failure to obey my order means a court martial on the spot. I will have no protests. Is that understood?'

'Understood, sir,' comes half-audibly from Leutnant Schultz.

The Sanitäts-Gefreiter, the former chaplain, and two ski-troopers with frost-bitten feet volunteer to stay with the wounded.

Soon after, the group marches off. The last thing we see is the chaplain standing on a snow hillock waving to us.

About an hour later we hear the chatter of machine-guns behind us. Some say they can hear screams. We were never to know what really happened to the wounded and the three volunteers.

A rattling noise makes us dive for cover.

'*Panzer*,' shouts Porta, going like a bullet into a snow-drive.

Orange lightning flashes across the desert of snow. The report that follows is short and flat.

'Tank-gun,' groans Heide, in terror.

'*Merde, alors*, they must be mad,' says the Legionnaire. 'Tanks cannot be used here!'

'You'll soon be wiser, my old sand-flea,' laughs Porta, sarcastically, tying hand-grenades together to make an explosive charge, as he speaks.

'Ivan can do things you'd never believe. Just wait! Your tongues'll fall straight down out of your German arseholes when you find out what Ivan *really* can do!'

On the far side of the frozen river some ghostly black boxes are crawling slowly along. The noise leaves us in no doubt of what they are. The howling of the tracks and the infernal roar of the engines makes our blood freeze with fear.

Two, three, *five* T-34s rattle towards us through the snow. They slide sideways down the ice-covered slope to the river. For a moment we nourish the vain hope that they will turn over but they continue out on to the ice with a deafening din, whipping up the snow in clouds behind them. In silhouette they are almost beautiful. A T-34 attacking over an open field of snow is an impressive sight. Like some great, lithe carnivore. All its angles are rounded and smoothed down, so that it is almost a pleasure to see what human hands can create from the harshness of metal.

We grab hand-grenades and tie them in bundles. It is the only weapon we have against tanks.

I pull one leg up under me and get ready to jump. The trick is to jump at the right moment, just when you are inside the tank's blind-spot. I tense myself like a cornered animal which can only save itself by killing its attacker. Courage has nothing to do with it. Sheer terror, fear of death, is what drives us to the desperate attempt of attacking a T-34 with nothing but a bundle of grenades and an Mpi.

The leading T-34's machine-guns sputter wickedly at us.

A squad which has tried to run for it goes down under the concentrated fire. Not all are killed. A Feldwebel stops, lifts his arms to the heavens as if in a last prayer, rolls forward and then lies still on the snow.

Another squad runs zigzagging across the ice. A T-34 catches up with them and we hear bones and weapons crunch under its broad tracks.

The tank revolves on the spot crushing their remains into the hard packed snow. Blood splashes up its sides.

'Keep down,' rages the Old Man.

Two T-34s rock up over the ridge in front of us. The closest of them swings its machine-gun a little to the left.

'The swine's got you in his sights.' I think and can almost feel the gunner's eye on me. 'If he fires you've had it.' I know what it is like inside those damned 'Tea saloons', as we call the T-34s.

The front gunner is sure to be an experienced tankman, who knows it's not clever to waste too much time in thinking about what to do. Keep doing something and keep doing it quickly is the watchword.

'Shoot everything you see in front of you, never mind what it is?' That is the order imprinted on every tankman's consciousness.

'If you want to stay alive forget you're human. If you can't shoot 'em, mash 'em with your tracks!'

I jump up, slide down the ice-smooth slope and land in a soft snowdrift. Porta comes sliding down after me.

'The devil,' he pants, readying his bundle of grenades. 'This lot stinks of Valhalla and a short life!'

The leading T-34 stops with a jerk.

We hold our breaths in expectant fear. Tanks only stop when they are going to fire their gun. With tensed faces we wait for the short, wicked thud, and the roaring of the explosive shell which will tear us to pieces. They can't have missed seeing us. The observation slits in a T-34 are very good. Much better than in our own tanks.

The muzzle report is deafening. Flame shoots from the long-barrelled gun. A wind hot from the jaws of hell blows over us. There is a nasty plopping sound in the snow only a few centimetres from us.

Missed, I think, and stiffen like a frightened animal at the mercy of a rattlesnake, but no explosion follows.

'Dud,' mumbles Porta, staring in fascination at the hole the shell has made in the snow. 'Holy Agnes! A dud! Maybe the parson *is* right, and the German god *is* looking out for his own!'

'Let's get out of here,' I say, and start crawling towards the tank, which has begun to speed up its motor.

'Holy Mother of Kazan,' shouts Porta, terrified, 'we've bought it! Get down, she's coming for us!'

The T-34 roars into top revs and seems almost to go into a crouch as if ready to spring. In its oil-reeking interior Leutnant

Pospelow presses his forehead against the rubber cushioning of the observation window.

'Turret, two o'clock,' he orders.

Less than three hundred yards in front of the tank a small body of men close together show up against the snow.

Leutnant Pospelow smiles in satisfaction, and orders his four other tanks to swing into line to give them a broad field of fire. He does not remove his eye for a second from the observation glass. He is imbued with the hunting fever. This is a tankman's dream. The targets are beautifully placed, as if for an execution, which in reality it is.

A 20 mm anti-tank gun barks angrily and sends its small, useless shells to splinter on the T-34's skin. Machine-guns spit tracer.

The tank driver, Corporal Baritz, gives out a laugh.

'Those dumb Germans think they can knock us out with MGs!'

'*Job tvojemadj*,'* laughs the front gunner. 'We'll blow them a pretty tune on our golden trumpet in a minute!'

'Explosive, fragmentation,' orders Leutnant Pospelow, coldly.

The shell clatters into the chamber, and the breach snaps closed.

The Leutnant's hand hovers for a second over the red button as if in doubt, and then comes down on it. The gun roars, flame gouts from the muzzle. The T-34 curtsies. The hot casing rings on the steel floor of the turret. A second later the breach snaps to again and a new fragmentation shell is ready in the chamber.

Again and again the gun fires. The snow in front of the T-34 is blackened with soot. Three hundred yards away it is red with blood. It looks as if a madman had been throwing buckets of jam on it.

Millions of stars dance in front of Leutnant Pospelow's eyes. He is struck violently on the chest. He slides half-way down into the turret.

The driver, Corporal Baritz, is thrown backwards with terrific force. The loader strikes his head on the turret machine-gun, and gets a deep slash in his forehead. The air is blown out of the forward gunner's lungs, and he loses consciousness for a moment.

'Bleedin' lot o' sods,' rages Tiny, banging the snow with his

* Job tvojemadj (Russian) = Go home and fuck your mother.

fists. The mine he has thrown is not powerful enough to penetrate the T-34's steel skin.

The Russian tank crew has been saved by a miracle from being burnt to a crisp.

'*Bysstryj, bysstryj*,'* roars Leutnant Pospelow to Corporal Baritz, who is fumbling with his instruments and pedals. His head is still humming like a beehive. He can hardly understand how he can still manage to move and to think reasonably clearly.

The tank jumps forward, away from that suicidal German out there in the snow, who is probably already preparing to throw another mine. Unpredictable desperadoes like that are deadly dangerous to any tank. You either have to run them down or get away from them.

Leutnant Pospelow decides to run for it.

'*Karbid*,'† he roars, furiously, kicking Corporal Baritz in the back.

With a sulphurous oath the corporal treads on his accelerator without knowing that he is moving directly towards the very thing he wants to get away from.

Porta and I lie in the snow with our bundles of grenades and wait for the right moment to attack the monster approaching us, with snow spurting out to both sides.

One of the turret hatches is thrown open and a leather-helmeted head appears.

'Kill them, the cursed dogs,' the Leutnant screams across the snowy wastes. It is the scream of a frightened man.

'All right then, Ivan Stinkanovitsch,' grins Porta, demoniac-ally, running in short bursts towards the T-34, which has stopped again to fire.

It is amazing how the Leutnant can miss seeing him.

The bundle of grenades flies up under the T-34's turret. In one long jump Porta is behind a wall of snow, and pressing himself down into it to avoid the storm of steel parts the air is soon filled with.

Two other T-34s are working together. They herd the running soldiers into a group. When they are sure of their prey, they back a little then move forward side by side. Alongside the group they reverse their outer tracks so that the noses of their

* Bysstryj (Russian) = faster.
† Karbid (Russian) = top-speed (tankman slang).

61

vehicles smash together in a rain of sparks, crushing the trapped men to a bloody porridge.

'Let's give up,' says a Flak-Unteroffizier, with tears running down over the open frost-sores on his cheeks. 'They're butchering us!'

Porta stares at him for a moment, then laughs aloud.

'Don't forget there's a war on, son, and both sides seem to be taking it seriously!'

'Probably thinks we're makin' a film. Verdun's silent, deserted ruins, or something,' jeers Gregor, throwing an explosive charge like lightning up on to the rear hatch of a T-34 as it roars past. 'Regards in hell!' he screams as he dives for cover.

As if at the blow of a giant hammer the hatch-cover is blown in. Leutnant Pospelow screams like a woman, as he is pinned between the heavy cover and the sharp edge of the hatch. He screams for a long time as the red flames lick up around him.

The loader is thrown out of the other hatch opening, and rolls around screaming in a sea of flame which melts the snow around him. Slowly he crisps like bacon on a frying-pan, and turns to a glowing mummy.

'Out!' roars the tank driver, Corporal Baritz, tearing the hatch open. He is running as he hits the ground. A shower of machine-gun bullets sends him kicking.

The forward gunner is only half-way out of the hatch when the tank is thrown up into the air like a football. It goes end over end and lands with a ringing crash, before it is blown to pieces by a colossal explosion inside.

A little distance away another of them is going in circles. Faster and faster. Red flames and black oily smoke are pouring from the hatches. Only one of the crew manages to get out of the red-hot steel coffin. He runs over the snow like a living torch. His screams are terrible.

We can feel the heat right over where we are lying. The Legionnaire raises his Mpi and sends a long merciful burst at the burning Russian writhing desperately in the snow.

'Padaerscha, padaerscha!'* he roars, stretching his burning arms out towards us.

Several Mpis are turned on him. Shortly after, he collapses. The body melts down to a tiny crisp.

The commander is still trying to free himself from the turret

* Padaersche (Russian) = Help.

62

of his T-34. He does not scream, nor plead, but is exerting himself to the utmost to get free of the burning steel box. His face is burnt black, crusted. Oddly his eyes still shine clearly. His lips are charred to cinders. His nose is a strange twisted lump of meat. His hair is burnt off in patches. His hands are the worst. Blackened knobs of flesh with which he is still trying desperately to force open the hinged hatch cover.

'My God,' I groan, and hide my face in my hands. The stench of burnt meat turns my stomach and I vomit on to the snow.

'Cut it out,' snarls Porta. 'It was them or us! This is a big fight we're in, and we've promised our big neighbour one on the schnozzle!'

'It's dreadful,' I whisper.

'It's war,' replies Porta, harshly. 'I'm not that happy to have Ivan on my tail. Up with you! Get hold of a charge! The knockin' off whistle hasn't gone yet. There's the last of those "Tea saloons" fellows comin'!'

An Mpi cracks from some stunted bushes. A burst falls around us.

Like lightning I sling a grenade into the bushes.

A tankman springs into the air, blood spouting in a thick jet from his mouth.

I sweep him with a burst from my Mpi.

With a long-drawn scream he collapses, rolling in the snow.

'What a dope,' says Porta, pityingly. 'People are bloody stupid! Heroes to the end! Well, that's one fool less in the world!'

A terrific blast throws us from our feet and sweeps us through the thick brush. We are forced down the narrow gorge and crash into the rocks at the bottom so hard that we are both unconscious for a moment.

Porta's reindeer comes flying through the air with all four legs splayed out and strikes the yard-thick ice wall with a hollow thud.

My body feels as if every bone in it were broken. All around us is a sea of glowing metal parts, which shortly before had been a tank. Round about lie the tank crew frying like rissoles.

'Fuckin' "Tea saloons" ain't much when you know what you're at,' boasts Tiny, forcing his way up out of the snow.

'You ought to have your arse reamed out by a gorilla, you mad sod,' rages Porta, passing his hands gingerly over his aching body. 'You nearly killed the lot of us.'

'Can't make omelets without breakin' eggs, can you?' says Tiny, philosophically.

Slowly we fight our way onwards. A snow-storm is beginning to blow up.

The Oberst is almost done. He leans on Oberleutnant Wisling. Leutnant Schultz is almost finished too. He stumbles continuously and can only get up again with difficulty. Nobody helps him.

Tiny tries to whistle a Reeperbahn song, but fails. The Legionnaire raves of the Sahara and the hot sand. The Old Man rolls along in his own bow-legged style. He finds difficulty in keeping his silver-lidded pipe going. His hands are buried deeply in the pockets of his greatcoat. His Russian Mpi hangs at the ready on his chest.

'Gawd'struth, I wish we was home again with them Finnish spuds and pork gravy,' sighs Tiny, hungrily.

'I hope we're somewhere near Lange Lake when the herring-roe season is on,' says Porta, smiling with frost-chapped lips.

The Legionnaire lifts his hands towards the heavens and says 'Allah commend us!' in Arabic.

It is beneath the dignity of a German to ill-treat defenceless prisoners. Cases of this nature should be reported immediately and guilty persons punished most severely.

Rudolf Hess, 10th April, 1934.

'God bless you come Sunday,' says Porta, treading on the commissionaire's toe, as, together with Tiny, he swings in to Kempinski's,* where he intends to celebrate his birthday.

'This is my sister,' he tells the commissionaire, pointing to a well-developed lady in the middleweight class.

'Then my brother's been fuckin' his sister,' she screams delightedly across the overcrowded restaurant.

Tiny pushes himself up on to two bar-stools.

'One for each cheek, cock,' he says to the bartender and orders a double vodka and a bottle of red wine. He throws back his head and empties the glass with a loud, slobbering noise. 'Another little taster, if you please,' he grins, jovially.

This scene is repeated eight times. Then something happens which later nobody can explain. At any rate a lady in a long green gown suddenly finds herself with a full basket of fish on her head.

Tiny grabs a bowl of jam and throws it in the headwaiter's face, who in return hits him over the head with a bottle of beer. Tiny revenges himself by sticking a fork in the headwaiter's arm. The latter rushes, screaming like a madman, into the street, with the fork still sticking in his arm.

The middleweight lady reaches for a waiter's masculine equipment and gets a good grip.

He gives a shrill scream, and brings both his knees up to around his throat.

Another waiter comes waltzing out of the kitchen with a large dish of *Eisbein*. The whole lot shoots up towards the ceiling and is distributed over the nearest tables, whilst the waiter does a nose-dive under another table.

A party in formal dress open their eyes widely and attempt desperately to get out of the way of Tiny, who is ploughing his

* Kempinski's = an elegant Berlin restaurant.

way across the restaurant like a Stalin tank which has taken it into its head to win the war on its own.

He hears a thunderous bang and is certain he is about to die. But it is not so serious. He staggers to his feet, butts someone or other in the face and sways out to the kitchen where he finds Porta engaged in a furious argument with the cook. Together they reduce the kitchen to a heap of ruins.

When the riot squad arrives, they withdraw to 'The Bent Dog' on Gendarmenmarkt, where they hear that a battalion of English paratroops has landed at Kempinski's.

COURT MARTIAL

Leutnant Schultz loses no time after we get back. Inside an hour he is reporting to the NSFO*. In every corner there is muttering against the malicious Nazi-Leutnant. A couple of Finnish *Jägers* suggest we kick his balls in and toss him over to the neighbours.

'I'll blow his candle out,' threatens Porta, pulling his Nagan from its yellow holster.

'You stay where you are,' decides the Old Man, brusquely. 'Let's keep out of the officers' private quarrels.'

'It could've been one of us,' protests Porta, tensely. 'That Schultz is a real bastard.'

'Maybe he is,' says the Old Man, unsympathetically, 'but it's *not* one of us he's informing on! If an officer needs to be revenged then let the other officers see to it themselves!'

'Piss,' Porta gives in, 'but if that arsehole ever gets in front of my gun-muzzle, you'll see a pair of balls wither away sharply!'

'That's murder,' shouts Heide, indignantly.

'No it bloody isn't!' answers Porta, furiously. 'A bastard who runs off at the mouth don't count!'

We discuss Leutnant Schultz for a long time. One thing is certain when the discussion in the Finnish *Jägers* sauna is over. Leutnant Schultz won't need to worry about his old age.

Tiny has been filing away at three bullets while we've been talking. Dum-dum bullets make an enormous hole in a man.

The following day a Major from the Secret Security Police comes for Oberst Frick, and Oberleutnant Wisling is picked up in the middle of technical service.

They are put immediately into a JU-52 and flown to 6th Army at Munster to go in front of a court martial.

* NSFO (Nationalsozialistischer Führüngsoffizier) = Nazi political officer.

The final verdict is deferred until evidence can be taken from others belonging to the battle group. In the meantime the two arrestees are sent to the military prison Torgau where they are placed in the boot squad, together with countless others taken into custody. Prisoners who have been sentenced are given much harsher treatment.

Every man in the boot squad is issued each morning with ten pairs of new, iron-hard army boots of smelly yellow leather. The squad marches for one hour in each pair of boots. To attention and at the double. Round and round the great parade ground. When the hour is over a whistle shrills, and everyone changes like lightning to a new pair of boots. Then 'Qui-ick march!'

This goes on without a break from 05.00 hrs to 21.00 hrs. Some faint. Feet swell up and become lumps of bleeding meat. Blisters burst and new blisters form. No attention is paid to this. In Torgau pity is an unknown term. It is a military prison, notorious for its strictness, and the permanent staff are proud of their reputation.

'March, march, you lazy men,' roars the Feldwebel, standing on a box in the middle of the parade ground. 'Do you call that parade marching? Get your legs *up*, you fucking bastards! Stretch those insteps! Hands level with the belt-buckle and *down* again smartly! *Smartly*, I said!'

A Major-General collapses. He is an elderly man who comes from a soft job in an outlying garrison.

Curses and oaths rain down on him but he stays down. It takes the fire-hose to get him on his legs again.

'An hour's extra marching for you,' orders the Feldwebel, jovially. 'It'll be easier, soon as you get that lazy sweat out of you!'

And the Major-General continues making hard boots supple, so that the fighting-men in the trenches won't have the trouble.

Every evening between 21.00 and 22.00 hrs each man in the squad hands ten pairs of softened-down boots into the Quartermaster's Store and receives instead ten pairs of hard, stiff ones in replacement. These are to be marched supple by the following evening.

In front of Oberst Frick runs a Feldwebel with red shoulder straps, a political prisoner. Behind him is a Gefreiter with green shoulder straps, a criminal, and behind the Gefreiter an artilleryman with purple shoulder straps, a religious deviator.

Then comes a Rittmeister with white shoulder straps, a defence saboteur. There are many in the squad with white shoulder straps. Only two have black shoulder straps. These are men who have insulted the Führer. They are certain to receive the death penalty. Both of them are from the Navy.

After six weeks on the boot squad, Oberst Frick is done for. His feet are in ribbons, swollen pieces of bleeding meat. In the prison infirmary they amputate two of his toes. Oberleutnant Wisling lies in the bed next to him with broken ribs and concussion. He fainted once too often on the boot squad. The GvD* was in a bad mood. But the Torgau infirmary is not a place where prisoners are allowed to stay long.

Limping and with faces drawn with pain the two officers report to the armourer's workshop for temporary light duty, a duty any prisoner at Torgau would prefer to avoid.

After a couple of weeks with the armourer they are sent to the convalescent squad, which drills from early morning to late at night.

On the wall at one end of the parade ground is painted in large white letters:

GELOBT SEI, WAS HART MACHT†

The worst thing of all in the military prison was that Iron Gustav‡ was there. Torgau's feared Hauptfeldwebel, who sneaked around on rubber soles like an avenging angel in infantry uniform. The prisoners and the permanent staff feared him equally. Experienced men, who had spent a long time at Torgau, on one side of the cell doors or the other, contended that if Iron Gustav looked at a man for more than three minutes the unhappy person would just drop dead. A glance from Iron Gustav's icy blue eyes was enough to freeze the blood. Another unusual thing about this little, strongly-built, iron-hard Feldwebel was his voice, which sounded like the cracking of dry sticks. He always used as few words as possible. But every word contained as much as a whole book. Even a mentally defective deaf mute could understand the words that shot from Gustav's tight mouth. He never shouted, as did other Unteroffiziers. If you were not standing close to him you could not hear what he said. But that wasn't necessary.

* Gefreiter von Dienst (German) = Corporal-in-charge.
† Gelobt sei etc (German) = Praise be, for that which makes hard.
‡ Iron Gustav = see March Battalion.

There is a story about a totally paralysed Unteroffizier who was lying in the infirmary here. The Army Medical Commission from Berlin had declared him completely paralysed. It had, therefore, been decided to pardon him and send him home. This was so shockingly unusual that even the prisoners rattled the bars of their cells when they heard about it. The day before the paralysed soldier was to be discharged, however, Iron Gustav decided to go up and see this strange person who was leaving Torgau in such an irregular fashion.

With the peak of his cap well down over his eyes he silently entered the ward, and stood looking at the paralytic, who in a few seconds, at the very sight of Iron Gustav, had become even more paralysed than he was before.

Iron Gustav's lips parted and fired three words at the paralysed Unteroffizier:

'Attention! Qui-ick *march*!'

What an entire medical commission had not been able to cure, with all their medical knowledge, Torgau's Hauptfeldwebel cured in thirty-one seconds.

The completely paralysed man sprang out of bed like a mountain goat, ran out of the ward, across the parade ground and into the prison office, where he cracked his paralysed feet together and shouted in a loud voice:

'Prisoner 226 reporting k.v.* from the infirmary!'

Since then Iron Gustav has always visited the incurable cases, which the doctors have given up.

Iron Gustav can not only cure human beings. He can also get horses and mules back on their feet, when the veterinary surgeons are helpless.

When the punishment companies return to Torgau late in the evening Iron Gustav is waiting to meet them, dressed in a pure white tunic. He wears this tunic, winter and summer. A soldier is never too cold or too warm, he says. The weather is of no consequence to him.

They say he never notices whether it *is* winter or summer.

The punishment companies have always to finish the day's duty by marching round Iron Gustav, singing loudly:

'Es ist so schön, Soldat zu sein!'

It is the only song Iron Gustav is fond of.

On Saturday morning their stay at Torgau is ended for Oberst Frick and Oberleutnant Wisling. They are collected

* k.v. = Kriegsverwendungsfähig (German) = fit for (war) duty.

while the punishment company is on duty.

Three military policemen are waiting in the prison office. Silently they leave Torgau. In the evening they arrive in Berlin, and are handed over to the military armed guard on the station.

The Rail officer, a Rittmeister, considerably older than Oberst Frick, feels at something of a loss. If they had been other ranks he would have known what to do with them. Into the cells until they were picked up. Instead he offers them cigars and a glass of wine, even although hospitality is against regulations.

At 22.00 hrs the air-raid signal sounds. Everybody goes to the shelters. Ill at ease, and obviously embarrassed, the Rittmeister tells them that in the case of an attempt at escape he will be forced to fire on them.

'I'm sorry, but those are the orders,' he explains, showing them his weapon, a 6.35 dress pistol hardly capable of hurting anything at a distance of more than half a yard.

Right over the railway station a target marker blooms like a Christmas tree, and the air shakes with the sound of bomber motors.

They move closer to one another in the shelter. The Rittmeister has placed himself between the two prisoners and addresses them as 'comrades'.

Then the bombers arrive. Railway lines are twisted into unrecognisable shapes, heavy goods wagons fly through the air like tennis balls. A railwayman is thrown clear across the goods station and is smashed to pieces against the 1914–18 War Memorial.

Burning phosphorous flows down the streets. Human flesh melts away in it. People are stifled in cellars. There are many casualties in Berlin that night.

The Flak-guns roar and bombs explode. Now and then a bomber is hit and explodes in the air in a giant rain of stars high above the city.

In the air-raid shelter the Rittmeister is telling Oberst Frick what he likes about the music of Sibelius.

Oberleutnant Wisling sits with his eyes closed and dreams of the past. He thinks about his time at Potsdam, when he was attending War School I, and remembers the pretty, and willing girls on the benches at Sans Souci. He shivers and curses himself. Now everything is over for him, and merely for disclosing his real feelings that ice-cold night up on the Arctic Circle.

He should have kept his mouth shut like Major Pihl and the others, and then he might have had a chance of living through the war. Now there was no chance for him. The stupidest man in the army even, would know where this was leading. The only uncertain thing was whether they would shoot him or hang him. They didn't often behead military personnel. Only civilians. Shooting or hanging was better, anyway.

Oberst Frick, who had been given his monocle back when he left Torgau, polishes it thoughtfully, before replacing it in his eye. He inspects the Rittmeister, who looks very old and does not seem to fit his uniform.

'Sibelius is, of course, a great composer, but I am afraid I have little understanding of that. I am a professional soldier. I was fourteen years of age when I entered the Cadet School, and I have never had time to occupy myself with music.'

A long, piercing howl breaks into their conversation. The air raid is over. It is the All Clear sounding.

Round about in Berlin fires are burning. An acrid, evil-smelling smoke rolls down over the city.

'There they go, those bloody air-gangsters, back home again,' rages an elderly Home Guard with the party insignia on his chest. 'Kill innocent women and children, they can do that all right!'

Nobody bothers to answer him.

C'est la guerre, the little Legionnaire would have said.

For a brief instant Oberst Frick thinks of escaping. It would be the easiest thing in the world to knock the old Rittmeister down. There is panic everywhere in the burning city. There would be time enough to get safely away before they could pull themselves together enough to come in pursuit. He had many friends in Berlin, and even if discovery might cost them their lives, he felt sure that they would help him. Just one night at each place, down to Osnabrück and into Holland, then contact the Dutch Resistance. One of his friends had done it. He deserted from Germersheim during outside duty. Once a man can get out of sight with the Dutch Resistance he has a good chance of surviving.

He looks around for a weapon and decides on the Rittmeister's desk lamp.

Oberleutnant Wisling looks at him with slitted eyes. They understand one another immediately. There are no guards between the Rittmeister's office and the great station hall, which is crowded with hurrying people. If they can get that far, they're safe. It would be like jumping into a swamp, the mud would close around them and hide them.

Then out of one of the exits and away into the burning streets.

Over the back of the chair hangs the Rittmeister's belt and pistol holster. We must take that with us, the Oberst thinks. He nods to Wisling, who gets up as if to stretch his legs. He reaches for the lamp shaking with tenseness. He has his hand on it when the door flies open and a young, steel-helmeted Leutnant enters, followed by five infantrymen armed with machine-pistols. They come with all the soundlessness of a Tiger tank on the attack.

The Leutnant is energetic and active. His pale-blue eyes shine from a dirty smoke-blackened face. He salutes carelessly with two fingers to the brim of his helmet and nods towards the two officers who are staring at him in amazement.

'This them?' he snarls, brutally.

'Yes,' answers the Rittmeister, crushing his cap on to his head in sheer confusion. 'These are the two gentlemen who are waiting for you.'

'Gentlemen, that's a good one!' grins the Leutnant, pulling out his heavy P.38 and pointing the muzzle at the two prisoners. 'But if that's the way we're doing it. Okay by me! Gentlemen,' he trumpets through his nose, weighing the pistol in his hand, 'it is my duty to warn you that on any attempt to escape this will go off! Do *not* think that you can commit suicide by attempting to escape from us! You would not be the first I have hit in the lower end of the spine.' He smiles like a snarling wolf. He is obviously accustomed to dealing with prisoners.

Odd that he's not with the Military Police, thinks Oberleutnant Wisling, looking at the Leutnant's white infantry lanyard, but then he recalls that the infantry is home for both the best and the worst of officers. If you are looking for a true gentleman you can always find one in the infantry, and if you are looking for a thoroughgoing scoundrel you can always find one of those there too.

'Shall we be getting along,' grins the Leutnant, bobbing impatiently at the knees.

'In all friendliness, of course! Double up now, gentlemen! Let's get this over with. We prefer not to be in your company longer than necessary.'

Outside the railway station a lorry with a tarpaulin cover is waiting for them.

'Into the coach,' orders the Leutnant, harshly.

'Where are we going?' asks Oberst Frick.

'Shut it,' snarls a young soldier, giving him a blow with the butt of his weapon.

At a breakneck pace the lorry drives through Berlin. It swings through the gates of the pompous General Command building in Bendlerstrasse, where they are taken down into a cellar. An Oberfeldwebel greets them with rough kindliness. He is also an infantryman. They have to hand in all their personal property: Belt, braces, bootlaces. It wouldn't do for them to hang themselves and cheat the court martial.

'Open your mouths an' we'll smash 'em in for you,' promises a brutal-looking old soldier with an S.A. emblem on his breast pocket.

Ten minutes later they are fetched again and taken upstairs.

A fat major of *Jägers*, sitting arrogantly behind a desk, introduces himself as prosecuting officer at their trial. He eyes them for a moment as if they were cattle he was thinking of buying. He flips over a few pages of the documents which lie in front of him and leans back in his chair with a satisfied expression.

'Gentlemen, I have decided to do everything in my power to ensure your being sentenced under paragraph 91a.' He snaps his fingers. 'That means to say that we intend you to be executed, and that I feel almost certain that I shall be able to see to it that you swing. You have been responsible for the perpetration of an infamous crime up there on the Arctic front. If the rest of the Army were to follow your example we'd soon lose the war. But, thank God, there are only a few of your kind in the great German Army. Hang you will!' He passes his hand gently over the gold party badge on his chest.

'Did you know that a man can take up to twenty minutes to die on the end of a rope?' he asks with a sardonic grin. 'Where you are concerned I hope it will take twice as long. It is my duty to attend every execution with which I am concerned as prosecuting officer. I do not normally attend but in your case

74

it will be a very great pleasure, Guard!' he roars, in a voice that rings through the office.

Startled, the two infantrymen tramp into the office, convinced that the prisoners must have attacked the prosecutor.

'Remove these two scoundrels from my presence,' yells the Major, hysterically. 'Get them out of here, throw them in the worst cell we have!'

The cells in the cellar at Bendlerstrasse resemble cages at the zoo. Thick vertical bars separate them from the corridors, along which guards perambulate continually.

'Pigs, dirty pigs,' whispers an artillery Hauptmann in the cell next to Oberst Frick. His face is beaten up and swollen. One eye is completely closed.

'What in the world has happened to you?' asks the Oberst, quietly. His body begins to tremble.

'They beat me,' whispers the artillery officer. 'Smashed my teeth in, sent an electric current through me. They want me to confess to something I never did.'

'Where are we?' asks Oberleutnant Wisling, curiously.

'Third Army Court Martial Unit, section 4a, directly under the jurisdiction of the J.A.G.,' a Stabszahlmeister replies. 'Don't expect anything good! Its short and not sweet here. I've been here three weeks. It's like living in a railway station. You get the impression that half the Army's up for court martial. There'll be nobody left soon. They say we're short of soldiers and yet we're shooting our own quicker'n the Russians can.'

'What have you done?' asks Oberst Frick, looking at the supply officer.

'Nothing!' answers the Stabszahlmeister.

A muffled laugh comes from the cell opposite them.

'There's no place like a gaol to meet innocent men,' jeers an Obergefreiter.

'Why are you here?' the Oberst asks a naval officer, the captain of a corvette, who is sitting in his cell, humming, seemingly without a care in the world. His left eye has been shot away leaving only a raw hole.

'For singing,' smiles the naval officer, amusedly.

'Singing?' asks the Oberst, doubtfully.

'That's what I said.'

'They can't gaol you for that,' says the Oberst.

'Can't they, though,' answers the sailor. 'They can gaol you for a lot less than that.' He begins to sing, softly:

75

Wir werden weitermarschieren*
wenn Scheisse vom Himmel fällt.
Wir wollen zurück nack Schlicktown,
denn Deutschland ist der Arsch der Welt!
Und der Führer kann nicht mehr!

'The gentlemen with the oak leaves on their collars didn't like my lyric. So now they'll probably have me hanged.'

'Impossible,' cries the Oberst, unbelievingly. 'People do not get hanged for such nonsense!'

'In this case they do,' smiled the naval officer. 'I sang it standing on the bridge of my submarine when we came back from a foray and ran into the U-boat base at Brest. They'll hang my first officer, too. He asked a high-up officer in the SS who had come out to welcome us back, whether Grofaz† was still alive.'

'Was he drunk?' asks Oberst Frick, wonderingly.

'No just inquisitive. What a party we'd have had if somebody had put a bomb under Hitler while we were out fighting the Jack Tars.'

The piercing howl of an air-raid warning siren breaks off the conversation.

A Feldwebel rushes down the corridor.

'All prisoners on the floor with hands folded at the back of their necks! When you're lying down you're safe from shrapnel. Anybody getting to his feet will be shot down without mercy!' he roars.

Immediately after, the building is shaken by an explosion. The lights go out and the whole prison is in darkness. Every so often the light from a flare illuminates fearful ashen faces.

An oppressive silence descends on the prison. Then the roar and crash of exploding bombs. It sounds as if they are dropping them in quick succession in the neighbourhood of Spree. Plaster rains from the ceiling. It is almost as if it were snowing. There is a tinkling of broken windows. Flaming phosphorous gutters.

* (Freely) We're marching merrily onwards;
    Shit's falling for all it's worth!
    We want to get back to Schlicktown,
    For Deutschland's the arse of the earth!
    And the Führer's all shagged out!

† Grofaz: Grösster Feldherr aller Zeiten = greatest military leader of all time, a jeering reference to Hitler.

Berlin groans in its death throes. The heavy Flak-guns on Bendlerstrasse thunder incessantly.

'Help, help, let me out! Mother! Mother!' it is the shrill voice of a child.

'Shut up, you little bastard,' roars a harsh, commanding voice. 'Stay down on the floor!'

Two shots are heard. A lamp flames. A suppressed oath, and all is quiet again.

It is the hour of death. Death outside the walls. Death inside them. Everywhere death is hastening by. In movement, or crouching in a corner, one can feel his cold shadow pressing close to one.

Some get accustomed to it, become phlegmatic. Others break down under it and end in the melancholy madhouse. Some again are silenced by a rifle shot. Throughout the city nerves are tautened to breaking-point, in prisons, infirmaries, air-raid shelters, streets, submarines, in the oil-stinking interiors of tanks, in training barracks. Wherever one may look, death and fear rule supreme.

A long howl on the siren proclaims the end of the raid, but the respite is only for a few hours. Then the bombers, with the white star or the red-white-and-blue rings, are back again.

Berlin is burning.

Fire engines thunder through the streets. Their task is hopeless. Day in and day out the Berlin fire services fight the flames lighted by the incendiary bombs.

An uneasy, irritable noise is heard from the corridor. Keys jingle. Iron strikes against iron.

'Damnation! The lousy bastard's hanged himself!'

'Save us the trouble,' says another voice, harshly. 'We ought to put the lot of 'em up against the wall and knock 'em over with an SMG!'

At eight o'clock the first of the prisoners go before the court martial. Late in the afternoon a platoon comes to remove the prisoners who have been sentenced. They are taken away never to return. Nobody knows what happens to them.

One morning Oberst Frick and Oberleutnant Wisling are called for. Escorted by four soldiers they are taken to the court and each of them is locked into a closet.

Before they are taken into court they are allowed a short interview with their defending officer, a friendly, elderly Oberstleutnant.

'I can't do much for you,' he smiles, pressing their hands. 'But the rules say I have to be present. And as you know we have a great reverence for good order and *correctness*.

'Is this a preliminary hearing?' asks Oberst Frick, hopefully.

'What a sense of humour,' laughs the Oberstleutnant, loudly. 'Preliminary hearing? Not part of the procedure and particularly in cases such as yours. Everything is quite clear, and the result has been decided long ago. I'd be very much surprised if your sentence hasn't been signed by the Kriegsgerichtsrat*. You have disobeyed an order of the Führer's and have confessed to having done so! I would like to see the defending officer who could do anything for *you*! Do you smoke?' he pushes a gold cigarette-case towards the Oberst. 'The court will convene at ten o'clock.' He looks out of the window. Rain is pouring down. 'The prosecuting officer wants you hanged. But I suppose you know that? I shall attempt to get the verdict changed to a firing-squad. In view of your many decorations I believe I shall succeed. There is still some respect for that sort of thing although we *are* beginning to get prisoners who have been awarded the Knight's Cross. Unbelievable only six months ago. Good God, look at you! Have you had no opportunity to shave and straighten up your uniforms? You look as if you had come straight from the trenches. It will make a bad impression on the chairman of the court.

'We can neither shave nor wash,' remarks Oberleutnant Wisling, dismally.

'I'm sorry,' says the Oberstleutnant. 'Everything's going all to hell. Sometimes we have up to twenty death sentences in the course of a single day. Yesterday it was three generals. Don't think *I* like it! But I *have* to! And I'm a soldier!' He slaps his leg. It sounds hollow. False. 'The Kiev Cauldron,' he smiles, sadly. 'I had a battalion in a motorised infantry regiment.'

'Line officer?' asks Oberst Frick, without interest.

'Yes, indeed,' sighs the Oberstleutnant, 'there soon won't be any of us left.' He looks out again, at the rain whipping against the windows. 'Take more than Grofaz to win this war.'

'A tragedy,' says the Oberst, quietly.

'Tragedy? Why?' asks the Oberstleutnant. 'We Germans are like hungry dogs, running after a sausage dangling in front of

* Kriegsgerichtsrat (German) = JAG.

78

our noses. We keep biting at it, but we never get hold of it!'

'How long will the legal proceedings take?' asks the Oberst nervously.

'Ten, at most twenty minutes. They're busy people. And there are a lot of cases to get through today. Yours isn't particularly difficult. If regulations didn't require it, it would hardly be necessary for you to come into court. A guard Feldwebel could have told you what the result would be days ago.'

'Then we might as well go back to our cells now and do without all this theatrical business,' considers Oberleutnant Wisling.

'No there you're wrong. You forget regulations. No German transgresses regulations. Regulations and paragraphs are a necessity of life,' says the defending officer, seriously.

A military policeman opens the door and clicks his heels with a sufficiency of noise.

'Let's get it over with then,' sighs the defending officer, rising to his feet.

The courtroom is as cold as the board of officers. From the wall, Adolf Hitler stares down on the accused. It is not promising. It is as if the large portrait is alive and sends out an emanation of pitiless self-justification.

The prosecuting officer takes his seat at a little table to the left of the chairman. He spreads a few documents out in front of him. Not many, but enough for a sentence of death.

The three officer judges enter. They give the Hitler salute.

The prosecuting officer starts to scream straight away. It is what is expected of him. His face goes purple. His voice rises to the highest octave.

'These traitors,' he roars, 'have attempted to sink a knife in the backs of our fighting men in the front line. They have committed a monstrous crime. They are not merely traitors, but also common murderers, who have handed over wounded German heroes into the hands of the Soviet *untermensch*, and this infamous crime they have committed merely to save their own miserable lives. They have also attempted to persuade other German soldiers into taking part in their criminal activities. When their sick suggestions were refused, this scoundrelly Oberst ordered these brave Germans to take part in the crime and to leave the wounded like a heap of offal. I demand that both the accused be sentenced to death in accordance with paragraph 91a: Defiance of orders and aiding the enemy, paragraph 8, sub-paragraph 2: Treachery against the people and security of the state, paragraph 73 and 139, sub-paragraphs 3 and 4: High Treason. I do not request the taking into consideration of paragraph 149: Desertion. I regret that there is no heavier punishment than the death penalty. In this case it is too humane.'

The three judge-officers doodle on the paper in front of them unconcerned with hiding the fact that they find the trial boring, and only attend to the prosecutor with half an ear.

The prosecuting officer sits down and gives a smiling nod to the defending officer.

The defending officer turns over his documents for a few moments. Then he gets to his feet slowly, pulls down his tunic, brushes a well-manicured hand over his grey hair, and smiles a comradely smile at the prosecutor and the presiding officer.

'I ask the court to take into consideration the accused officers' decorations and the attention to duty shown in their previous service records. I ask the court to consider their crimes with mercy.' He sits down again, avoiding the Oberst's reproachful glance.

'Do the accused wish to make any statement in their defence before sentence is passed?' asks the Kriegsgerichtsrat, looking impatiently at his watch.

Obertst Frick rises and begins to explain the hopelessness of the situation in that Arctic hell.

'You are wasting the court's time,' the Kriegsgerichtsrat cuts him off, sharply. 'Did you or did you not leave wounded German soldiers at the mercy of Russian troops, yes or no? Did you give the order for your unit to withdraw, yes or no?'

The Oberst realises that it is impossible to combat this kind of cold logic.

'Yes,' he replies, sitting down heavily.

'And you,' the Kriegsgerichtsrat nods at Oberleutnant Wisling, 'stated clearly that you were in agreement with your Commanding Officer?'

'The whole proceedings are a mixture of truth and falsehood, an infamous juggling with the facts,' screams Wisling in a piercing voice. 'I refuse to recognise this caricature of a court! It is a slaughterhouse! Any respectable judge would be ashamed to sit in it!'

'Sit down and be quiet! You are the worst villain we have

ever had in this courtroom,' shouts the prosecuting officer, sulphurously, purple in the face.

The Kriegsgerichtsrat nods and whispers for a moment to his two assisting officers. In a low, pleasant voice he begins to read from a document which has lain in front of him throughout the trial:

'For cowardice, contempt of the Führer, the Commander-in-Chief of the Greater Germany Army, aiding the enemy and sabotage of orders, the accused, Oberst Gerhard Frick and Oberleutnant Heinz Wisling, are condemned to death by shooting. Their rights, civil and military, are lost to them for life. Their entire property is to be confiscated on behalf of the state. Both of the accused are reduced to the rank of rifleman and all decorations they may have received are withdrawn from them. The sentence to be carried out as soon as possible. The accused are permitted, in view of previous bravery, to seek pardon from the General High Command, Defence Area III, Berlin/Spandau.' The Kriegsgerichtsrat removes his gold-rimmed spectacles, looks at the condemned men with icy indifference, and gives a sign to the military policemen at the door.

With practised movements the shoulder-straps and decorations are ripped from the condemned men's uniforms. Last the eagle on the right breast.

'Lead them out,' snarls the Kriegsgerichtsrat, flapping his hands as if he were waving away two flies.

'You blokes were lucky, remarks one of the MPs, when they are back in the cellar again.

'Lucky? How do you mean?' asks Oberleutnant Wisling, blankly.

'You've been allowed to apply for a pardon,' grins the MP Unteroffizier, amusedly. 'That'll keep you alive for a few more days, even weeks maybe. Otherwise you'd have been knocked off within the next two days. We're a bit short of room in the cage, so we carry out orders as soon as we get them! Well, you'll probably have plenty of time to think about things. The responsible general is somewhere in Russia just now, so it'll probably be some time before he gets your application and who's to say he's got the time to bother with it when he *does* get it? He's sure to have more to worry about than you two heavenly tourists, and by the time your papers get back who knows what the hell mightn't have happened here? Things are moving fast these days. Ivan's gettin' a move on!'

'Heute sind wir roten*
morgen sind wir toten.'

he murmurs, softly. 'Infantryman Frick and Infantryman Wisling reporting back from court martial,' he reports to the duty Unteroffizier, cracking his heels together.

'I presume they are not reporting for release?' grins the duty Unteroffizier, sarcastically, marking a large red cross beside their names in the guard report book. The death sign.

'In a way, yes,' answers the watchdog, jovially. 'Nappers off, and down to the moles!'

'Children, children,' says the duty Unteroffizier, handing them a cigarette apiece, 'be glad that you have been allowed to apply for pardon. Otherwise you'd have been given a post to lean on tomorrow morning already. We're collecting a large party of tourists together. Don't tell me us Prussians aren't a humane lot. Hold your hands out, lads. You have to have irons on. That's regulations. Those who have lost the right to carrying heads on top of their shoulders, have to be chained up.'

Wisling nods tiredly. The truth is beginning to soak through to his brain. His stomach contracts and his mouth fills with bile.

'There's a bucket over in the corner,' says the duty Unteroffizier, who knows the symptoms.

Wisling gets to it in time, and throws up.

Early the next morning they are taken from their cells and chained tightly to one another with their hands behind their backs.

The lorry is full of prisoners, sitting crosswise in the back. Two muscular MPs with Mpis at the ready, climb up on to the tailboard. They shout at the least movement amongst the prisoners.

At the Air Force Law-courts, at Tempelhof, they pick up three airmen and a flak-soldier. One can see the three are officers, by the finer material of their uniforms. Their decorations and shoulder-straps have been removed.

They continue through Berlin, past Plötzensee, where the State Executioner is busy every day with his guillotine.

* Heute etc. = Today we are red,
       Tomorrow we are dead.

82

The lorry rumbles over Alexander Platz. Police head-quarters is blackened with smoke.

They pick up two condemned SS officers at the SS barracks Gross-Lichterfelde.

'Come on get your arses moving! We're in a hurry!' the watchdogs shout, angrily helping them up with blows from their Mpi butts.

The prisoners stare longingly at the streets, full of people hastening along. A tram rattles round a corner. The clang of its bell sounds like the music of freedom.

'Where are they taking us?' whispers Oberst Frick to the prisoner alongside him, the demoted naval officer.

'Shut up, swine,' screams an MP from the tailboard, 'or I'll knock your teeth down your throat!' He lifts the muzzle of his Mpi, as if he were ready to carry out his threat on the spot.

The lorry bumps and shakes its way over the uneven paving. Burned-out ruins grin up at the rain-filled clouds. Several are still smoking from the night's fires. Everywhere bodies are being dug from the caved-in cellars.

Heavily-armed SS patrols sneak through the smoke-blackened streets on the watch for looters. If they catch any they are given short shrift. They carry ropes with them and there are plenty of lamp-posts in Berlin.

A group of women outside a butcher's shop gaze inquisitively after the lorry, which has to take to the pavement to avoid a bomb crater in the middle of the road.

The watchdogs on the tailboard seem to enjoy the trip. Escorting prisoners is considered a light job. It is a duty like any other duty, like training recruits, delivering ammunition, or clothing and equipment. Some get guard duty for years outside GHQs, barracks, depots and airfields. Countless soldiers fight at the front as infantrymen, artillerymen, tankmen. Shoot, kill, execute in one way or another.

The MPs escort prisoners. A much pleasanter job than slogging around in mud-filled trenches.

Oberleutnant Wisling watches them through half-closed eyes. He is thinking again of escaping. It would be easy enough to tip those fat, self-satisfied policemen over the tailboard and run for it, but the problem was to get to the tailboard. He would have to get over three benches. The prisoners were closely packed and the watchdogs would have shot him down without compunction before he got past the first of these. He thinks of crawling under the benches between the legs of the other prisoners, and begins to slide down to the floor of the lorry. His neighbour understands immediately what he is trying to do and covers him, but it is harder than he expected to crawl with his hands handcuffed behind his back. He has only reached the second row when the lorry swings through the barred gates of the Gross Deutschland Infantry Regiments' barracks. This has been converted to a military prison because all the regular prisons are packed. Even though Germany is second only to Russia as the country in the world which has the most prisons, there is now a shortage of them. But since there is also a catastrophic shortage of recruits the authorities are able to use the empty barracks for the purpose. Nothing is impossible to God and the German nation.

The lorry stops with a jerk, and the prisoners fall from their benches. This saves Wisling from being discovered. He is almost weeping with disappointment when fellow-prisoners help him to his feet.

'Out of it, you villains,' scream the MPs swinging their Mpi butts, brutally. 'Double up, you bastards! Think you're in a rest-home, do you?'

Everywhere, screams and shouts, threats and oaths. Above everything the guards must be tough with prisoners. Otherwise the pleasant life in barracks may soon be over. It's only prisoners who're getting the rough end of the stick, anyway, and they're the scum of the Third Reich.

They rush, chains jangling, across the parade ground. The dust whirls up around their hurrying feet.

'Double up, double up, one-two, one-two!' screams the MP Feldwebel, swinging his long wooden stick at the nearest of the prisoners.

A few old infantrymen peer inquisitively from the open windows. Not because there is anything new in this sight, but something out of the way just might happen.

Oberst Frick falls forward and smashes his face into the parade ground dirt, unable to break his fall with arms chained behind his back, but kicks and butt-strokes soon bring him to his feet again. A prisoner in a military gaol in Germany learns amazingly quickly the way to get to his feet again without using his hands. With shouts and screams they are chased round the parade ground. Yet another prisoner falls on his face and smashes his head into a sharp rock. He receives a deep slash in his forehead, and blood pours down over his face.

'Up, you rotten sack!' roars the MP Unteroffizier, giving him a brutal kick. 'Who the hell ordered you to lie down? Double man, double you dog! You can lie down when we've filled you with lead, you swine!'

An MP-Leutnant with a lipless mouth receives them. He is hardly more than a boy, with down still on his cheeks. But his eyes shine with fanaticism. A Himmler product of the worst type.

The Oberst looks at him with foreboding. From bitter experience he knows that these half-grown boys are the worst. They are afraid of not appearing tough enough and go headlong at everything and everybody merely to anaesthetise their own fear.

'Who are you?' asks the youthful Leutnant in a dangerous voice, pointing at one of the wretched prisoners in the ranks.

'Major von Leissner, 460th Infantry Regiment.'

With all his weight behind the blow the Leutnant strikes the older officer full in the face, so that he sways for a moment as if about to faint.

'What is your name?' howls the Leutnant, his voice breaking.

'Infantryman von Leissner!'

Again the clenched fist crashes into the face of the demoted Major, who is old enough to be the Leutnant's grandfather.

'Herr Leutnant, you sad sack! Can't you see my rank? Fifty knees-bends! Double to it!'

'Infantryman von Leissner, Herr Leutnant, fifty knees-bends as ordered!'

The Leutnant struts on to the next man as if the episode with the Major had never occurred.

The next prisoner also feels the Leutnant's fist. He always finds something to provide him with a reason. The prisoner may shout too loudly, or not loudly enough, or has answered incorrectly. When he has been through the ranks there is not one of the prisoners without a bloody face. Then he places himself in front of the ranks, and claps his gloved hands together gently.

'Those who are entitled to apply for a pardon, two steps forward, *march*!' he screams in a high, boyish voice. He counts them and compares the tally with his list. 'Block 4,' he orders, brusquely.

A party of snarling Unteroffiziers moves them to Block 4.

They fall on the prisoners like hungry beasts of prey. Hysterical commands, roars and screams echo around the barrack blocks.

The young Leutnant struts like a cockerel around the remainder of the party. Those who do not have the right to apply for pardon!

'Enjoy the sun,' he jeers at them. 'Tomorrow morning we're going to blow the rest of you out of this world! Any man due to get shaved by the big razor, step forward!'

An artillery officer steps forward. He is a big man running to fat with a sickly face.

The Leutnant looks at him like a snake looking at a rabbit.

'Reserve officer,' he comments, with a sly grin.

'Yes, Herr Leutnant.'

The Leutnant butts him in the face, the brim of his steel helmet smashing the bridge of the nose. Blood spouts.

'Damned if this criminal swine isn't standing there trying to fill me full of lies,' he shouts, throwing his arms out in indignation. 'Giving himself titles he's not entitled to! On your face, ape!'

Like a falling tree the former artillery officer falls forward, his unprotected face smashing into the dirt.

'He's *good*!' laughs the youthful Leutnant, pleased.

The watchdogs laugh with him, dutifully. The whole barrack square bubbles with happy glee. Even the inquisitive infantrymen in the company block are amused.

'Gunner Schröder, demoted Oberleutnant of the reserve, condemned to death for sabotage of orders, reporting for duty as ordered, Herr Leutnant!'

'See now, that's better,' smiles the Leutnant, and with sadistic friendliness. 'And what does Gunner Schröder do in civilian life?'

'Schoolteacher, sir.'

'Well, well! A schoolteacher!' a dangerous glint appears in the Leutnant's pale-blue eyes. Without any kind of warning he kicks the prisoner between the legs, and smashes the back of his gloved hand into his face. 'Gunner schoolteacher dares to stand easy, does he? The villain thinks he's back in his village school, where he can do what he likes with the Führer's defenceless children. No, my fine friend, he's in death's ante-room now, waiting for his turn to be shaved by the big razor! Get that heap out of here,' he orders an Unteroffizier. 'I'm sick of the sight of it!'

The young Leutnant amuses himself by tormenting the prisoners for another hour until his macabre display is stopped by a Major coming back from his daily morning ride in the Tiergarten. The Leutnant gets a terrific dressing-down. He has to stand to attention and stare into the eyes of the Major's nervous horse. He is one enormous miserable human inferiority complex. All his arrogance has disappeared.

The Major does not move away until the prisoners have been sent off to Block 2, hell's antechamber, where those who have not the right to apply for pardon are sent to await the firing squad.

The Major looks down at the Leutnant again, and bends forward slightly over the horse's neck.

'Your second button is missing, Herr Leutnant,' he trumpets, slashing his shiny boots with his riding whip. 'At 15.00 hours you will report to the company due to march off. They are short of a platoon officer. Do you think the posting will suit you?'

'Yes, Herr Major!'

'I thought you would,' snarls the Major, flicking his boots again with the whip. 'On the Southern Front you will find ample use for your surplus energy. Do you know where the March Battalion is due for?'

'No, Herr Major!'

'They are being flown into the Circassion encirclement. See to it that you do your regiment honour, and earn yourself an Iron Cross.' The Major spurs his horse, which jerks nervously and splatters foam into the Leutnant's face. The horse seems to be smiling to itself as it trots across the parade ground. Military horses develop a fine degree of instinct which their civilian counterparts never attain.

Not until the Major is out of sight does the Leutnant dare to stand easy and wipe the foam from his face.

'Blasted Jew horse,' he swears, 'hope it gets the gaschamber!'

He trudges over to the company quarters and packs his kit. What there isn't room for he throws in the fire, rather that than give it away.

At the March Battalion he is met by a bony Oberleutnant who immediately gives him a tongue-lashing and prophesies an unpleasant future for him. He is placed in charge of the supplies section, an obvious down-grading. The other officers, who are all front-line veterans, ignore him.

Three weeks later a dugout collapses and buries him. Nobody

bothers to dig him out. His duty period in HKL* lasted twenty-five minutes.

The prisoners hand in their uniforms at the QM stores, and are given uniforms of scarlet drill. They are manacled hand and foot with short steel chains. Then all their hair is shaved off, to bring them to a full realisation of the miserable state they are in. Even the guard-dogs seem to disdain them and growl and show their teeth as soon as a red jacket comes near them. The ankle manacles are deliberately so short that the prisoner has to hop like a sparrow. The stairs are the worst thing. They are pure torture. And still the permanent guards continue shouting:

'Faster, faster, double up, double *up*!'

Oberst Frick is the first to fall while climbing the steep staircase. Kicks and butt-strokes rain pitilessly down on his back and kidneys.

'Damned if he isn't lying down on it!' roars a Feldwebel, pressing his Mpi muzzle, brutally, into the former Oberst's neck. More dead than alive he reaches a cell, where there are already eight other fellow-sufferers in scarlet drill with yellow numbers on their chests.

In the cell his wrists are unmanacled, but not his ankles.

'And these men are fellow-countrymen,' groans the Oberst, falling heavily on to a wooden stool. He looks at his red-clad fellow-sufferers, depressedly.

'Hugo Wagner,' the eldest of them introduces himself. He is an upright man with a severe face. 'Gunner, former General-leutnant and Divisional Commander, condemned under paragraph 91b. I imagine that tells you everything. And yourself? Hanging or shooting?'

'Shooting,' replies Frick with an indifference which surprises even himself.

'Then you have been fortunate. I am to hang! I still hope, however, that they will change the sentence to the firing-squad before it is too late.'

The door is opened with a great clatter, and a Feldwebel throws a sheet of paper and a pencil on the small table.

'Here,' he growls, unpleasantly, looking at Frick as if his very presence were an insult. 'Write your application for pardon. I'll be back to get it in twenty minutes' time. See that it's finished by then! Understood? It's not the story of your life

* HKL (Hauptkampflinie (German) = The front line.

you're writing! And don't you forget it, Gunner Shit!' He bangs the door shut so forcibly that plaster falls from the ceiling.

'Thank God,' mumbles Oberst Frick, in relief. 'At last I can explain what really happened. This whole business is a tissue of lies and has been turned round completely.'

'I would not recommend your writing in that tone,' warns the former Divisional Commander. 'It will serve only to annoy them, and before the General has got half-way through your application he will have refused it and signed the order for your execution. Nobody is in the least interested in you or your particular case, and if you are pardoned, which I doubt – your rank is too high – it will be purely because you can be used in some very smelly business. Absolutely *not* for *your* sake. Write as follows: Demoted *Jäger* Oberst, full name and birth date, and address it to General responsible for Pardons, No. 3 General Command. Begin two fingers in from the side, do *not* forget *that*. Thereafter, date, time, sentenced to death by Higher Field Courts Martial, Berlin. Thereafter request that the sentence be reduced to penal servitude. Finally, three fingers lower down on the page: Infantry Barracks, Berlin-Moabitt, date, Heil Hitler and your signature.'

'Heil Hitler?' asks Frick, wonderingly.

'Do you think that this form of salutation has been changed by your having been sentenced to death?' smiles the former Generalleutnant.

Exactly twenty minutes later the sour Feldwebel is back. He runs his eyes quickly down the application, nods in satisfaction and leaves the cell without a word.

'Do you think I have some small chance of a pardon?' asks Frick, with hope in his gaze.

'Naturally not. People *do* get pardoned, but so infrequently that it is a sensation when it does happen. In your particular case I would consider it to be out of the question. If you had been a private soldier, an ordinary conscript, you might have had a tiny chance, dependent upon the General's temper that day, but as a line-officer sentenced under 91b, no! You will be shot!'

'Heavenly powers, then, it's a mere waste of time to send in the application,' says Frick, a feeling of despair rising within him.

'Are you so eager to let go of life?' asks the General, sarcastically. 'The application will keep you alive longer. Nothing will happen to you until it comes back. You will not be taken from here at 08.00 hours tomorrow morning, as may be the case with any of the rest of us. During the next eight days you will not lie in terror throughout the night.'

'Do they fetch you at 08.00 hours in the morning?' asks Frick, his voice shaking. He feels the cold hand of death upon him already. The whole cell breathes fear. It exudes from the walls, drips from the ceiling, rises up from the floor.

'Yes, each morning at exactly 08.00 hours you will hear marching feet and the rattle of arms in the corridor. You will hear cell-doors open and close. At exactly 11.00 hours, on the stroke of the barracks clock, there is nothing more to fear for that day. We have almost another day in which to live and the entire prison breathes again. Fear envelops us again when darkness falls and we again lie in our beds. The worst period comes in the morning between 04.00 and 08.00 hours. That is the time you hear screams coming from other cells. Some succeed in committing suicide, but God help them if their attempt does not succeed and they are revived again! The guards take such attempts very personally. They are sent to the front-line if a prisoner succeeds in cheating the firing-squad.'

'Is there no possibility of escape?' asks the Oberst, his face livening up.

'Completely impossible,' the General rejects the suggestion with a sneer.

'What about air raids?' asks the Oberst, stubbornly. 'When everything is in confusion.'

'Not here,' smiles the General. 'Here they double-lock the doors of the cells, and sit down to play cards. If a bomb or two should happen to score a direct hit, what then? The enemy has merely carried out sentence on us. We are temporary and highly expendable. If we are expended a day earlier or a day later what difference can it make. It is important only that our lives *are* taken and the sentence can be reported as carried out! Put all thoughts of escape out of your head. Accept what is your fate. It will make things easier for you.'

'It's a fearful thing,' says the Oberst, running his hand over his cropped head, 'to try to become used to the thought that one is to be butchered like an animal.'

'I agree with you,' admits the General.

'Where do the executions take place?'

'Where *have* you been, Oberst Frick?' asks the General, sarcastically. 'Are you not aware of how things are done these days in Germany? In the Morellenschlucht people are shot in groups. Most of them for small offences.'

'Do the hangings also take place there?' asks the Oberst, shivering.

'Of course. The gallows stand in rows. Decapitation is the only sentence the military authorities have requested not be carried out on army premises. These are carried out by the civil authorities at Plötzensee. The work is done by the Chief Executioner. Those who are to go under the big knife have already been dismissed from the army and are to be regarded as a kind of civilian.'

Shortly before bedtime Oberleutnant Wisling is shoved into the cell. His face is bloody and swollen. He sits down on the floor and regards the occupants of the cell with empty eyes.

Almost all his teeth have been knocked out and one of his kneecaps gapes open. Several ribs are also broken. He complains of pain when he draws breath.

'I jumped the duty officer and tried to strangle him,' he explains, quietly.

'That was foolish,' says the General. 'It hurts only yourself, and often other innocent prisoners.'

'Yes, it was foolish,' admits Wisling, feeling his bruised body gently.

'It isn't so bad here,' explains the General, making himself comfortable for the night on the damp, mould-blotched seaweed mattress. 'I have been in many places which were much worse: Torgau, Germersheim, Glatz, Fort Zittau, Admiral Schröder Strasse. They were hell in the deepest meaning of the word. Here we are at least left in peace in our cells, and are given the same food as the soldiers. You should have seen what we were given at Germersheim!'

'How long have you been in prison?' asks the Oberst, wonderingly.

'Fourteen months, but it will soon be over. I expect to be taken out any morning. The only chance I have is for the war to end suddenly, and the gentlemen from the other FPO to come and let me out.'

'That'll be a while yet,' considers a fellow prisoner, pessimistically.

'In Peenemünde they are busy experimenting with a new

91

weapon,' comes from the corner. 'It is a kind of weapon so terrible that nothing like it has ever been heard of before. If they get it finished they'll win the war.'

'I've heard of that weapon,' remarks the Oberst. 'Something to do with heavy water they get from Norway.'

'I've worked on it,' reveals the red jacket in the corner. 'I'm a chemist, but unfortunately one who never learnt how to hold his tongue. That's why I'm here. It was a lovely evening with too much cognac and beautiful girls. The girl I went to bed with was working for the Gestapo. They turned up the very next day while we were still nursing our hangovers. Polite young men in long leather coats and with turned-down hat-brims. *Geheime Staatspolizei,** an oval tin shield on a chain, and a politely communicated order: 'Be so kind as to accom-pany us! We would like to clear up a small matter!' The chemist in the corner laughs cheerlessly and points a finger at his chest.

'The "small matter" was me! They treated me relatively gently. Everything was over in about an hour. Interrogation completed! One month later a ten-minute court martial and here I am!'

At 06.00 hrs there is a clatter of tin buckets in the corridor. A key raps loudly on the door. This is the signal to get out of bed and to pile mattresses.

Soon after, breakfast comes along. A slice of bread, a pat of margarine and a mug of thin, lukewarm ersatz coffee.

Then there is the waiting. The prison stinks of fear and terror. The minute hand on the tower clock moves in tiny jerks. The clock strikes eight times and exactly on the hour iron-shod heels sound in the corridor. Sharp orders are rapped out. Steel sounds on steel.

In the cells all talk ceases. Eyes stare fixedly at the grey doors. The first party has already been escorted away. March-ing feet make echoes which disappear down the corridor.

A demoted assistant M.O. breaks down in heart-breaking sobs.

'Pull yourself together, man,' General Wagner scolds him, harshly. 'Crying won't help you. It will only make things worse. That sort of thing irritates the guards. It is too late for regrets now. You should have realised sooner that a nonentity of a naval surgeon like you cannot criticise Adolf Hitler unpunished.

* Geheime Staatspolizei (Gestapo) = Secret Police.

What would *you* have said if some criminal had called you a quack? Would you have laughed at the joke?'

A crushing silence falls on the cell. Close by the jingle of keys and shouted names can be heard.

The youngest prisoner in the cell, a Gefreiter only seventeen years of age, sneaks over to the door to listen. The red drill tunic, the robe of death, hangs loosely on him.

A former Leutnant sits petrified on the cot next to the General's and stares as if hypnotised at the door. Will it fly open any second now? Will a tough-looking face beneath the rim of a steel helmet call out one or more names?

He begins to sob, completely loses control of himself, and collapses into a shaking heap. He has gone through three weeks of waiting – every morning.

The General, who is old enough to be his father, looks at him for a moment.

'Stop that nonsense! Straighten up, man! Remember you're a soldier – an *officer*! Up with you, chest out, stomach in! Yes, it's foolish, but it helps! They taught it to you in school and in the HJ. Now you've a use for it! What's going to happen *will* happen. Crying won't make any difference!'

The Leutnant begins to scream. Horribly! Shockingly!

General Wagner grabs the chest of his tunic and slaps his face resoundingly several times.

'Stand up, man, pull yourself together!' he commands, sharply.

The Leutnant stands to attention. He is pale as a corpse, but collects himself. The glaze disappears from his eyes.

Outside the steps of the death squad can be heard approaching. They are not far away. Rattling screams are heard from a cell close by.

The post Feldwebel curses and scolds. 'I can't stand it,' whispers the chemist. 'I'll go mad!'

'What are you going to do, man?' asks General Wagner, mockingly. 'Throw yourself down in front of the firing squad? Tell them you are innocent and that they mustn't kill you?'

'Oh God, I wish they'd fetch me today,' groans the chemist, in despair. 'Then it'd be all over.' He gets up. His mouth is a red hole in his face. Before the others can get to him, he screams: 'Fetch me, you bloody murderers! Kill me! Shoot me, you Nazi bastards!'

They throw him to the floor, and cover his mouth with their bodies to muffle his screams.

They listen fearfully at the door. Will the guard come with their long staves? Noise in the cells is strictly forbidden. Screams count as noise.

Quite soon the chemist is quiet again. He sits down in a corner, his lips trembling like those of a terrified rabbit.

'If one of you should, against expectations, live through this,' says the General, softly, 'I would like to ask you to greet my wife, Margrethe Wagner, Hohenstrasse 89, Dortmund, from me. Tell her that I died well. It will be a help to her. Explain to her that everything I own is forfeit to the German state treasury. For this reason I could not even send her our wedding ring.'

All the prisoners repeat the address to imprint it in their memory: Margrethe Wagner, Hohenstrasse 89, Dortmund.

The General looks up at the frosted window. For a while he is silent. His thoughts are far away in Dortmund in Westphalia.

'I have a feeling they are going to come for me today,' he says suddenly, smoothing down his red tunic.

But they did not come to fetch the General that day.

The clock in the staff company tower struck eleven times. The whole prison gave a gasp of relief. Until 08.00 hrs the next morning is a long time.

'Yard exercise, march, march!' Whistles shrill through the prison blocks. A storm of noise and unrest raises itself from all sides.

Manacles clash. Keys jingle, and boots tramp. The red-tuniced prisoners hop breathlessly along. The unlucky ones who fall are beaten remorselessly with rifle butts.

A machine-pistol barks wickedly and long. A prisoner who attempts to speak to one of his fellow wretches slumps down in a pool of blood. He is dragged like a sack back to his cell. His head bumps hollowly against the steps of the staircase.

'Dirty dog, swine,' the guards scream at him. They can think of nothing better in their fury.

A medical Feldwebel comes running with his Red Cross bag. He eyes the badly wounded prisoner wickedly.

'Throw the shit on the floor,' he snarls. 'I'll get enough life in the bastard, that we can carry him to the execution post!'

'Don't you dope him,' says one of the guards morosely.

'Wouldn't dream of it,' answers the medical Feldwebel. 'I'd cut his prick off if I had *my* way!'

All three laugh loudly.

The parade ground is filled with men. The condemned in their red uniforms mixed with ordinary grey-green prisoners, who feel like kings in comparison with the 'reds'.

'Form up in column of threes,' roars the Duty Feldwebel. 'Column of route, forward march! Keep your bloody distance, you sacks! Let's have a song!'

> 'Ich bin ein freier Wildbrettschütz*
> und hab' ein weit' Revier,
> so weit die braune Heide reicht,
> gehört das Jagen mir ...
> Ich bin ein freier Wildbrettschütz ...'

Yard exercise always ends with various kinds of 'bull-dozing', depending on the duty feldwebel's humour.

The afternoon passes quickly. Slowly the long shadows creep across the parade ground and creep up the wall opposite the window. Evening comes, then night. Whispered conversations; voices that stammer fearfully. Their death hour approaches on rapid feet.

Breakfast is eaten in silence. Only a few have any appetite. From the clock-tower eight death strokes sound again.

Confident voices are heard echoing from the walls of the barracks and penetrating to each and every cell.

The execution squads march in step down the corridors. Heavy boots approach cell 109

The nine prisoners hold their breath. Open-mouthed and wide-eyed they stare at the door. They know that the squad has come to a halt just outside their cell. Heavy keys jingle. Startling as a gunshot the heavy key is pushed home in the lock. Click, click, it says, as it turns twice.

The heavy door flies open. A steel helmet gleams warningly from the door opening. Rifle butts scrape on the concrete. Silence, silence, waiting silence.

---

* Ich bin etc.: (freely) I *am* a free hunter
> And roam far and wide.
> O'er the heather-clad heath
> A'hunting I stride.
> I *am* a free hunter ...

A tough face peers into the cell from under the helmet brim. Whose will be the name that comes from those thin colourless lips?

General Wagner takes a half-pace forward, his face like chalk. His lips are almost inky. The terror of death creeps icily up his spine. He is certain his name will be called.

The chemist and the Leutnant push themselves deeper into the alcove. The little Gefreiter stands behind the table, his mouth half-open as if he were about to emit a scream.

The door bangs shut. It was a mistake. The candidate to be taken to his death is in the cell next door.

A long ululating scream of terror tears the expectant silence apart. A body is dragged along the concrete floor of the corridor. Three of the iron bars of the window throw a shadow now. When the fourth appears as a pencil-thin line, it will be 11.00 hrs, and life can begin again.

The atmosphere becomes almost cheerful.

Now, now, thinks the Oberst. The shadow has almost reached the washbowl. Heavy, marching steps can be heard coming from the far end of the corridor. They approach rapidly.

'They can't possibly manage any more,' whispers the Leutnant, staring in horror at the spot where the shadow of the fourth bar will appear.

'We'll soon see,' answers the General, quietly, taking two steps towards the door.

The young Gefreiter begins to sob, spasmodically. Nobody pays any attention to him. Everyone is thinking of himself.

'Come, shadow,' implores Oberleutnant Wisling. It cannot be more than a few seconds to 11.00 hrs.

The marching steps approach pitilessly. No military boot in the world has the ominous sound of the German jackboot. It is built to inculcate fear and horror into those who hear it.

The marching feet pass by. A short way further along the corridor a sharp word of command is heard. The steps are returning. Crash! Crash! Crash! Exactly opposite cell 109 they come to a halt.

Something is wrong. The fourth shadow is plainly visible.

The prisoners glare at it, clutching at it as drowning men at a straw. After 11.00 they don't take people. It's *never* happened. Why should it happen today?

Strike clock, for God's sake *strike*! Give us another day of

96

life! Life is so short, one more day is a wonderful gift, even in prison.

The key jingles. The sound as it enters the lock is nerve-shattering. The sound a guard who is fond of his work can produce.

Even before the door swings open eleven strokes sound from the HQ Company clock-tower. The key is withdrawn from the lock. Orders forbid executions taking place after 11.00 hrs.

Sharp commands ring through the prison.

'Shoulde-e-r *arms*! Le-e-ft *turn*! Qui-i-ck march!' Crash! Crash! Marching steps recede and disappear down the corridor.

'Lord Jesus Christ,' pants the chemist, from his corner. 'I'd never have believed a man could stand such things without losing his mind. Have they no pity for us at all?'

'Pity does not exist in Germany,' laughs the General, sarcastically. 'But we can be sure of one thing, at least. One of us will be taken between 0.800 and 11.00 hrs tomorrow.'

'Who?' asks the Leutnant, in a quivering voice.

'If you are a very brave man you can knock on the trapdoor and ask,' smiles the General. 'But I can assure you that if it is you, you will not be able to walk to the post unaided tomorrow morning!'

'The vile devils,' whispers the Leutnant, furiously.

'Devils,' the General emits a jeering laugh. 'And you have attended the War Academy! My dear young man they are no more devils than you or I. Merely a product of military education in the Third Reich. Be honest, now! Were you not an admirer of it, until you came to know the German court-martial system?'

The Leutnant bows his head and agrees silently with General Wagner. He could just as easily have been one of the guard officers here. Instead, by a trick of fate, he is a condemned prisoner.

Oberleutnant Wisling looks towards General Wagner. Is the man made of teak and iron he thinks? It was certainly he they were coming to pick up this morning. He has long since passed the normal time limit for wearing the red tunic, and he must be aware of it.

' '34 was the last time I took part in the sharpshooter contest in the Morellenschlucht,' remarks Oberst Frick, casually, looking up at the grey window. 'It was in August and hot. We filled

97

ourselves up with overripe morellos,* which lay in a thick yellow carpet under the trees. The blast from the mortar bombs had knocked them down. We got stomach-ache . . . '

The door opens with the usual crash, and a new prisoner in red enters fearfully.

'Feldwebel Holst, 133rd Infantry Regiment, Linz, Donau,' he introduces himself.

'Oberst Frick, 5th Grenadier Regiment, Potsdam,' smiles the Oberst, sadly.

'The aristocrats with the pretty hats,' says General Wagner, sarcastically. 'I am not from such a high-class outfit. 11th Panzer Regiment, Paderborn.'

'I've been to Paderborn,' says the seventeen-year-old Gefreiter. '15th Cavalry Regiment.' He clicks his heels. He is still speaking to a General, even though a demoted and condemned one.

'Leutnant Pohl, 27th Artillery Regiment, Augsburg,' the frightened young Leutnant introduces himself.

'How formal we all are, suddenly,' laughs Wisling. 'Very well then: Oberleutnant Wisling, 98th Mountain Jäger Regiment, Mittenwald.

'You'd know Schörner?' asks the General. 'He was, I believe, in command of your regiment?'

'Yes, he was Oberstleutnant. He is now Generalfeldmarschall and not less hated than formerly,' smiles Wisling, bitterly.

'When we had sharpshooting trials in the Morellenschlucht,' continues Oberst Frick, 'hazing was forbidden. It was important that we were not nervous when our turn came. We enjoyed ourselves in the Morellenschlucht but only in the summertime. In the winter it was damnably cold and windy. It was as if the cold was coming all the way from Russia and in amongst those crooked trees.'

'And now you are to end your life in the Morellenschlucht,' comes drily from the General. 'Did you know that in the Kaiser's time they also used to execute soldiers there?'

'No, I had no idea.'

'It's one of the most remarkable things about we Germans,' sighs the General, apathetically. 'We never know *anything*. We are a nation in blinkers. God knows how many innocent people have been shot in the Morellenschlucht.'

* morellos = golden cherries.

'Does it hurt to be shot?' breaks in the young Gefreiter, suddenly.

His fellow prisoners look at him in astonishment. None of them has considered the matter. The horror of death itself has been so overwhelming that nobody has thought about the possible physical pain involved.

'I do not believe you will feel anything,' answers the General, confidently. 'A single bullet can kill instantly. The state is generous and gives you twelve!'

'I don't think they'll ever shoot me,' says the Leutnant, with a note of hysteria in his voice. 'I'll be sent to a specialist unit. I feel it in my bones. I *know* it. When they discover what my speciality is they'll realise how useful I could be in a specialist unit! I give you my word I will visit your wife and give her your last message, Herr General. I look up to and admire you!'

'Don't do that,' sighs the General. 'It is a great fault in us that we Germans always need somebody to look up to and to kill for.'

The food wagon is heard rattling along the corridor. The clock strikes eight.

Orders, the rattle of weapons, screams and oaths, jangling of keys. Many are taken that morning. The prison buzzes with nervousness.

Now there are again three shadow bars on the floor. Soon the fourth will arrive. The door crashes open.

'Paul Köbke,' snarls the Feldwebel.

The chemist, who could not keep his mouth shut, gets to his feet.

'No, no,' he groans. 'It's a mistake. I've not been here very long. It must be you, Herr General!'

'Shut up, Köbke,' rumbles the Feldwebel irritably, taking a step into the cell. 'The General'll get his turn, just like the rest of you. Today it's your turn, and quick about it! Your travel group's waiting.' He pushes Köbke so that he falls into the arms of two Unteroffiziers who manacle his hands with practised ease.

'See you soon,' grins the Feldwebel, banging the door to.

The Fatherland has the right to demand that the people sacrifice everything for it. Therefore, I command that every person who is capable of holding a rifle be called, immediately, to the colours and sent into action against the enemy without consideration of age or health.

Adolf Hitler, 25th September, 1944

'The devil take you,' says the Old Man, angrily, as he enters the cellar and sees us lying there amongst all the bottles.

'Not so loud,' groans Tiny. 'There's a imp inside me bonce knockin' in tent-pegs for all 'e's worth!'

'Dirty lot of swine,' scolds the Old Man.

'You're dead right,' hiccoughs Gregor. 'It's not right sitting down here in a damp cellar getting pissed.'

'Holy Agnes,' drools Porta. 'If we go on like this we'll risk turning into alcoholic wrecks, and burnin' up our livers!'

'Oh my head,' groans Barcelona, worn out. 'Let's go outside and see if they've declared peace while we've been drinking up the Red Army's schnapps.'

The Old Man keeps on nagging at us and doesn't stop until we turn in amongst the fruit trees and catch sight of a round helmet slowly appearing from behind the road-block.

A shot cracks and the helmet disappears. We throw ourselves down in the wet grass and take aim at the spot.

Shortly after another round helmet appears.

Heide's automatic carbine spits fire and the helmet rolls down on the wrong side of the barricade.

It takes almost twenty minutes before the next helmet appears.

This time it is Porta who fires, the shot smashing the enemy soldier's face.

Again a long period of waiting. Then another round helmet appears.

'Are they piss-barmy?' mumbles the Old Man, slapping his forehead.

As he speaks Tiny's sniper's rifle roars.

The helmet flies up into the air and falls rattling upside down.

101

After a while, when no more helmets appear, we sneak round behind the barracks.

There they lie, faces blown in.

We go through their pockets and provision pouches and slouch carelessly on again.

THE EXECUTION

Chief Mechanic Wolf is holding court, at the large round table in No. 5 Company canteen, with his two snarling wolfhounds on either side of his chair, ready to tear anybody to pieces at the slightest sign from the Greater German Mafia boss.

The two Chinese bodyguards are placed, each on his stool, behind their master's chair. They view everybody who enters the canteen as an enemy to be rendered harmless as soon as possible.

Round the table crowd a mob of admiring yes-men, Wolf's temporary errand boys, who only remain in the garrison as long as it suits the big boss.

Porta stops and slaps his forehead in assumed surprise.

'What, you still alive, you stinking piss-stall?' he shouts, happily. 'Anybody ever tell you, you look like a banged-up arsehole? Let's have some air in this place. It smells like a sewer!'

'You gonna take that?' asks an armourer, bending obsequiously towards Wolf, who is rocking his chair back in imitation of the big-shots he has seen in American films. He gives Porta an evaluating look, and does not feel in the least insulted. That is a luxury which can cost money, the only thing Wolf loves and respects. He is first and foremost a business man. You can spit right between his eyes, as long as you are willing to pay for the privilege.

Tiny grabs the armourer by the front of his tunic and lifts him up as if he were a rabbit to be slaughtered.

'What the hell!' screams the armourer, in terror, kicking his legs about.

'Shut it, louse,' growls Tiny, who is in the mood for breaking things, bashing people, ruining something or other, in short possessed of the normal, healthy impulse, to do something which other people will take notice of.

Chief Mechanic Wolf laughs with satisfaction at the prospect of this miserable grey day livening up. His sycophants laugh noisily with him. They simply daren't do anything else.

'You dare to lay hands on an Unteroffizier!' shouts the armourer, trying to kick Tiny in the face.

'Unteroffizier!' grins Tiny, contemptuously, swinging him round in the air like a windmill. 'You're nothin' but a bleedin' rifle-fucker!'

'Kill him,' suggests Porta, philanthropically, emptying a large mug of beer in one long noisy gulp. He gives a pleased belch and orders a refill.

Cook-Oberfeldwebel Weiss comes rushing in with a P-38 in his hand.

'Let go of that man,' he shouts, pointing the pistol at Tiny. 'Don't imagine you're still pissing about amongst the Eskimos and can carry on how you like. In my place there's discipline, and particularly in my kitchen. Let go of that man! That's an order!'

'What man?' asks Tiny, lifting the babbling armourer higher above his head.

'The one you've got in your hands, bastard,' roars the Oberfeldwebel, losing control of himself completely.

'That ain't a man, it's a rifle-fucker,' answers Tiny, swinging the armourer around in the air again.

'Let him go,' screams Oberfeldwebel Weiss, waving his pistol at the rest of us, as if he were shooing hens.

'All right then,' sighs Tiny, resignedly, and throws the armourer straight through the closed window so that glass and wood splinters fly around our ears.

For a moment the Oberfeldwebel stands undecidedly, staring at the remains of the window through which the armourer has disappeared.

'Herr Oberfeldwebel, sir! Instructions carried out!' grins Tiny, saluting.

Weiss draws a deep breath, purple in the face. He opens and closes his mouth several times without a sound crossing his lips. He looks like a balloon from which the air has escaped.

'I won't have you spoiling my canteen,' he whines, tamely. 'Drink up your beer and pay at the desk. Sing good German songs, pray to God for victory and otherwise keep your mouths shut! If you don't abide by the regulations out you go on your ear!'

'Count on us, we're on the side o' religion,' Tiny assures him, putting his head out of the broken window to see where the armourer has got to.

The yes-men are chased away from the round table like a flock of sparrows from a newly sown kitchen garden.

'Deal the cards,' orders Chief Mechanic Wolf, amicably. 'Double stakes!'

Weiss pushes himself to a place at the table, and arrogantly demands cards.

'Who the hell invited *you*?' asks Porta, highly surprised, laying heavy emphasis on the '*you*.'

'Just you watch yourself,' warns Weiss, importantly. 'What are *you* then? I'm a whole lot above a shitty little Obergefreiter.'

Porta regards him condescendingly.

'Well, I'll be damned! Don't you know that I am of the same rank as the Commander-in-Chief, Obergefreiter Hitler?'

'Piss with all that,' breaks in Wolf, categorically. 'Deal the cards, Porta and you, Weiss, shut your face, or you'll be out on your arse, smartish!'

'Thrown out of my own kitchen?' shouts the Kitchen-General, excitedly. He looks as if he is ready to start something.

'*Own*? You don't *own* nothin',' states Wolf, with assurance. '*I* ordered Hauptfeldwebel Hofmann to give you that kitchen because I reckoned you was one of mine. But maybe I'm wrong about that?'

'Course I am. I'm with you all the way,' crawls the Kitchen-General, sweat breaking out on him at the thought of going back to the ranks.

'Want more than four cards?' asks Porta with a crooked smile, as his hawk's eye catches Weiss letting a card disappear.

'If you should happen to be tryin' to twist us,' roars Wolf, with false pathos, 'then us two've been pals as long as neceesary, and you will be out of your nice warm kitchen an' into an ice-cold trench fightin' the good, but hopeless, fight for Führer an' Fatherland, quicker'n knife!'

Weiss sulks. It is the end of the month, and his lack of money is catastrophical. He *has* to win a few hundred marks. He cannot let any more supplies slip out on to the black market. The Catering Officer has expressed surprise, three times now, at the pilferage rate. It will not take much more for his house of cards to collapse.

'You look as if you were thinking of Napoleon's hurdles race to Moscow,' grins Porta, examining Weiss's pallid face with savage pleasure.

Wolf wins the first two games and the three following. He is in noisy good humour.

'You wouldn't be cheating now, would you?' asks Porta, inquisitorially, looking greedily at the considerable pile of money in front of Wolf.

'I reject such insinuations with the contempt they deserve,' replies Wolf, arrogantly.

Gregor swears ill-humouredly. He has already lost a large amount. The Old Man is silent and nervous, having lost 200 marks he had intended to send home to Liselotte.

Weiss is on the verge of tears. He asks for a small short-term loan. He is still optimistic that the piles of money in front of Wolf and Porta can be made to change owners.

Generously Porta pushes 500 marks over to him.

'Just sign this piece of paper, please!'

Weiss runs his eyes over the writing.

'Eighty per cent!' he howls, outraged, 'it's usury! How dare you make an offer like that to a higher rank, to a Chief Cook? Don't you know it's piss against regulations and a civil crime even?'

'Are we going to have a discussion on illegalities?' asks Porta with a crafty look in his deep-sunken eyes. 'What about an Oberfeldwebel who borrows money from ORs?'

'A kick up the arse and off go his bleedin' stripes,' whoops Tiny, taking the opportunity of secreting two cards. He regards Weiss's borrowed money as already his.

Weiss gives up and signs the note with a sour expression. He puts the 500 marks in his pocket quickly as if he were afraid someone would steal them.

Porta hawks noisily. A gob of spittle lands in a bucket by the door.

'Stop that filthiness,' admonishes Weiss, darkly. 'That's not a spittoon, that's No. 3 Company's coffee pail.'

'All right then,' answers Porta, readily. 'Next time I'll spit in your face!'

Wolf whinnies with laughter and wins again.

Gregor takes a loan from Porta, but naturally on the eighty per cent man's terms.

Weiss lays down his cards. He cannot understand how it is possible to have such bad cards all the time. He is pale as a corpse. For a moment he thinks of suicide, but gives up the idea. After the third hand in which he has not taken part, he begs, in a whisper, for a new loan.

Porta looks at him doubtfully, but after a long pause he pushes 300 marks over to him and solemnly unfolds a new I.O.U.

'What the hell?' roars Weiss, red-faced as a lobster. 'Payable within twenty-four hours! Why?'

'Because you're a bad risk,' grins Porta, shamelessly, continuing to deal the cards with practised fingers.

'A bad risk?' mumbles Weiss, despondently. 'What do you know about that?'

'More than you think,' smiles Porta, knowingly. 'Soon as the figure-boys come to take your stock, you'll be on your way out into the ranks of the great unknown heroes.'

Weiss goes dark blue in the face.

'Are you insinuating that I'm a thief?'

'I didn't think you were slow on the uptake,' grins Porta, shamelessly, and almost jumps when he finds he is holding three kings.

Wolf whinnies again and slaps Porta on the shoulder with assumed friendliness.

'You're probably right, Porta. You an' me can smell a pork pincher a mile off. Weiss just stinks of rancid innocence and armpit sweat!'

'I hope your sense of humour can stand the sight of these,' grins Porta, slapping his three kings down victoriously on the table.

'Same to you,' smiles Wolf, blissfully, putting down two aces and a queen. His hand is already out to rake in Porta's money.

''Old it then,' shouts Tiny, throwing down two aces and a king. He has quickly exchanged a deuce with one of the aces he was sitting on.

'*You* aren't cheating, are you?' asks Porta, staring hard at Tiny.

'Never in all my life,' bawls Tiny, insulted.

Porta looks round the table. He knows Tiny has cheated.

107

The three he is sitting on and has exchanged for a king feels red-hot and he is in no doubt that Tiny is sitting on a card he has switched. He can, of course, demand that Tiny stand up and he will then be exposed, but if Tiny has one of his rarer, bright moments he will demand that everybody stand up and Porta himself will be exposed. On the other hand it is probable that there were others sitting warming cards. This would mean that play would be started again from the beginning and all winnings would have to be handed back. He does a lightning calculation in his head and decides to let things go on as they are. With his eighty per cent loans and his winnings he has had a good day. But he decides to watch Tiny like an Alsatian dog watching a stolen meat-bone.

Porta wins the next five hands.

Weiss withdraws from the game and goes down to the cellar to eat bread and sugar. He has heard that sugar is an energy source. Porta gives him a new loan, but this time he has to give 50 kilograms of coffee as security. What the company is going to do for coffee tomorrow morning doesn't worry Weiss. It's a long time to breakfast, and a lot can happen before then.

The door flies open with a bang, and in marches Staff Quartermaster Sieg with a large, threatening, black briefcase, adorned with the Reich eagle, under his arm. Fat and wobbling he drops into a shaky armchair which creaks under his weight.

Weiss goes quite green in the face.

'What the devil do you want?' asks Wolf, without attempting to hide his disgust at this unexpected visit.

'Now *then*, now *then*,' Sieg stops him with a conceited mien and bangs the briefcase down on the table, where it lies with the threatening look of a time-bomb. 'It'd be cleverer to go a bit more easy, don't you think?' He snaps his fingers and bares a row of tobacco-stained teeth in an unpleasant grin.

'Maybe it'd be cleverer for you, too, son,' says Wolf, grinning like his namesake, in a way that doesn't promise anything good for Sieg.

Sieg looks at Wolf through narrowed eyes.

'If it's the last thing I ever do,' he hisses, 'I'll see you and Porta full o' bullet holes before this man's war is over!'

'You poor dope,' grins Porta, superciliously. He picks up the brimming glass of vodka in front of Sieg and empties it in one long happy swallow. Then he fishes a cigar out of Sieg's tunic pocket, and asks for a light.

In amazement Sieg hands him his gold cigarette lighter.

Porta takes his time lighting his cigar, but finally he is successful. He blows enormous clouds of smoke towards the ceiling and puts the lighter in his pocket.

'That wasn't a bloody present,' protests Sieg, weakly.

'You said, here you are, didn't you?' Porta cuts him off, condescendingly, 'and now I say thank you! Presents are always welcome.'

'I'm not *standing* for this,' shouts Sieg, furiously. 'I'll put you on a charge, Porta, I'm a Staff Quartermaster, I am!'

'You are a stupid man,' states Porta. 'Keep on an' I'll kick your arse ten feet up in the air!'

Sieg jumps up in a rage and knocks over Gregor's mug. The table swims with beer.

Gregor looks at him reproachfully.

'Mind you don't wash yourself away, old son,' he warns and wipes the beer up with Sieg's officer's scarf.

'My scarf!' roars Sieg raging.

'My *beer*,' smiles Gregor, throwing the soaking-wet scarf on to the floor at his feet.

'What the hell do you think you're up to?' shouts Sieg, clenching his fists in powerless rage. 'You'll get paid out for this! I'm not your old buddy any more. I'm the Staff Quartermaster now. And I've got friends big enough to crush lice like you lot!'

'You remind me of a randy buck rabbit on heat,' says Porta, contemptuously. 'Staff Quartermaster! The arsehole of the Army!'

'You've had it now all right,' shouts Sieg, threateningly waving the beer-soaked scarf above his head.

'We have decided to release you from the heavy burden of living,' Porta grins, diabolically.

'I'd kick you straight up the arse if I wasn't scared of losin' me boot,' says Wolf, waggling a hand-made officer's boot out in front of him admiringly.

'You're under arrest,' roars Sieg, drawing his Mauser. With murder in his eyes he cocks the gun and releases the safety-catch.

Like lightning the Old Man knocks the pistol out of the enraged QM's hand.

109

'Now you can choose whether or not we settle this here and now or whether I make a report on it! In the latter case you've been a kind of an officer for a good long time anyway!' says the Old Man sharply, putting the Mauser in his pocket.

'What do you mean settle it here and now?' asks Sieg, uncertainly.

'*You* are a stupid fool,' the Old man nods in confirmation of his own words. 'You haven't changed a bit since you were a saddler with our lot.'

'I was an Oberfeldwebel,' Sieg corrects him, inflating his chest. 'And now I'm an officer!'

'Rubbish,' the Old Man rebuffs him, coldly. 'You're some kind of civil servant in uniform and nothing more! How'll you have it? Want us to beat you up here or will you have it out with Porta behind the cook-house?'

Sieg rocks uncertainly, thinking furiously. He is both bigger and stronger than Porta and he was one of the best boxers in recruit school. On the other hand you never know what kind of underhanded dodge Porta can get up to.

After a minute or so he nods sharply.

'I'm ready to bash the bastard's face in!'

Porta gets up from his position in cover behind Wolf, and removes his tunic ceremoniously.

'I'm ready to get my face bashed in, if that wobbling lump of jelly thinks he's the man who can do it.'

Wolf bends over and whispers something in his ear which makes him shake with laughter.

Soon after, we are standing in a circle behind the cook-house waiting for the fight to begin.

Porta and Wolf put their heads together, and look Sieg over like a couple of old, knowledgeable tom-cats.

'Can we wear gloves?' asks Porta, obsequiously. 'I'd hate to spoil my manicure on a face like that.'

'You can wear boots on your hands, far as I'm concerned,' shouts Sieg, contemptuously. 'You ain't gonna hit anything anyway, before I've splattered you up against the wall.'

'Did you know the QM officer is fucking your wife while you're out counting sacks of spuds?' grins Barcelona, cheekily.

'Fuck you,' screams Sieg, furiously. 'My wife never went to bed with nobody but me. She was a virgin when I met up with her.'

'If she 'adn't of been, she'd never've took you,' shouts Tiny, provocatively.

'I'll look after you when I've finished with this one,' Sieg promised him, darkly.

'Get them bloody gloves on,' he shouts, moving towards Porta who is still fumbling with a pair of black gloves.

'Ready when you are,' grins Porta, happily, pulling the gloves well up on his hands.

'First round,' orders the Old Man, bringing his hand down.

Sieg charges forward like a bull elephant in musk.

Porta steps to one side and Sieg rushes past without hitting him. Instead he runs into Gregor who is thrown up into the air and ends in the withering potato rows.

'Hey, I'm over here,' shouts Porta, who has moved back a couple of paces. 'What the hell you knockin' Gregor about for when it's me you're fightin' with?'

Snuffling, Sieg gets back on his feet, rubbing his left fist.

'I'll trample you into the ground,' he snarls, bitterly. 'By God, I'll smash *you*! I've been waitin' for this for seems like a century!'

'I'm impatient,' smiles Porta, amiably. 'I feel the same way. I shoot my load thinking about bashing you up.' He dances towards Sieg, keeping his gloved hands up to protect his face.

Sieg tries a straight left but Porta isn't there any more. He turns and sees something black coming towards him. It hits his face with a force of about 2800 joules. The force of the blow lifts him up and deposits him several yards away on top of a dustbin. His face looks as if it had been on the receiving end of a dum-dum bullet.

'Get hold of a medical orderly,' says the Old Man, brusquely. He goes quickly into the canteen. He doesn't want to know what has happened.

Wolf laughs loud and long.

'Next time he won't be so easy about lettin' a bloke wear gloves, will he?'

'He'll have learnt something then, won't he?' laughs Porta, punching a dent in a heavy plate of steel standing by the door.

'Lovely grub,' shouts Tiny, admiringly, 'loaded gloves!'

Porta removes the black gloves. They are lined with lead, Russian loaded gloves, an heirloom from a fallen NKVD lieutenant.

'*Merde, ca va barder*,' says the Legionnaire, warningly. 'In

111

a couple of weeks' time, when he begins to be able to think again, he'll realise there was something fishy about those gloves!'

'Couldn't care less,' says Porta, carelessly, banging the loaded gloves against the wall. 'In this world war's difficult moments, I've so far been able to keep a clear head and to get by without damage.'

'What if 'e was to backshoot you, then?' asks Tiny, well knowing that Sieg is a dangerous and pitiless enemy.

'*I'm* the one that shoots people, not the one that *gets* shot,' boasts Porta. He goes into the canteen and empties a large mug of beer.

'Christ but it's rainin',' says Tiny, shivering, as we fumble our way back to the company lines in the dark.

Z.b.V. duty* is on the board for No. 2 Section. It annoys us. Z.b.V. could be anything.

At 07.30 hrs on the dot, we scramble up into the big Krupp-Diesel which has come to pick us up.

'Now you men, remember I expect you to be a credit to your company,' roars Hauptfeldwebel Hoffmann as we move off. 'It's a great honour for sad sacks like you to be chosen for this kind of special duty. The eyes of the Führer are upon you! Chests out, chins in, you lot of vultures!'

At Spree we turn the corner and drive alongside the river in the direction of Spandau.

'I thought as much,' says the Old Man, tiredly. 'An execution!'

'Well, let's be glad it'll soon be over, and we'll have the rest of the day off,' says Porta, and begins to plan his afternoon.

'If I'd known it was an execution,' says Barcelona, angrily, 'I'd have gone sick.'

'That's why they never tell you,' explains Gregor, testing the bolt of his rifle.

'Why can't they leave that shit to the SS or the MPs?' protests Barcelona, resentfully. 'We're soldiers not bloody executioners!'

'*C'est la guerre*, you are the slave of the rifle just like the rest of us,' the little Legionnaire admonishes him. 'Yours not to reason why. It is your duty when you live on the military dungheap – where you in all probability will also die.'

'You lot'll addle your brains thinkin' too much,' says Tiny,

* Z.b.V. (Zu besonderer Verwendung) = Special duty.

carelessly. 'What do you care what they tell us to do? When I knock one o' them off all I think about is it's the same as it was in the Reeperbahn when you're sendin' the bleedin' clown off 'is perch down into the water.'

'You've played that clown's part yourself before now,' remarks Porta, sarcastically.

'In time o' need,' sighs Tiny. 'I'd not more'n got meself up there on the perch, like some bleedin' lovebird or other, than down I was again in the drink. After I'd been shot down 169 times I'd 'ad just about enough. Three marks an hour I was gettin' for it. So off I went but not before I'd give the last two as shot me down somethin' to remember me by.'

Below the Morellenschlucht, out in the sand between rows of wind-bent fir trees, the lorry stops.

Chilled to the bone we jump down. An icy wind carries a cloud of tiny snow crystals into our faces and makes us all pull up the collars of our damp greatcoats.

'We could've passed all that crazy polishing up,' says Porta, crossly. 'Look at my boots! Muddied up already. Hell, now I'll have to polish 'em again before I go down to meet the bints in "the Crooked Dog".'

Grumbling we move along the hard-packed path along which thousands of soldiers have tramped before us.

The Old Man rolls along in front of us, shoulders hunched and far from regimental in appearance. The heavy P-38 dangles from his belt. It contains eight cartridges. Mercy shots.

A bony, wicked-looking MP Major is waiting for us. Silently he inspects our equipment. He is particularly interested in our rifles. He rates us and calls us bad names – a herd of filthy swine not worthy of the honour of wearing the German uniform. He does not try to hide the fact that he is sick at the very sight of us. Only Julius Heide gets praised.

'Stand at ease and pay attention to me,' shouts the Major into the sleet. 'We are using target cloths even if they aren't necessary. And the reason we're using them now is that I've had trouble with some squads who didn't use 'em. Now pay attention: I want to see all twelve bullets in that target. God help you if I find holes anywhere else! The other day two fools hit the man's sexual organs. That's sheer laziness! Clean misses will cost you something. Target practice night and day for three weeks.' He bobs up and down from the knees and looks at us with wicked eyes. 'I want you men on your toes today,' he continues in a shrill voice. 'There will be witnesses present! Not the usual after-birth from the court-martial authority, no, higher-ups from the party, the press and the civil administration. They have asked permission to be present. They want to see blood, the perverse bastards! The section will detail two security squads and nobody, not even the Reichsmarschall himself, is to be allowed inside the safety lines. I don't want any more corpses lying about than necessary. You, Oberfeldwebel,' he barks, pointing at the Old Man, 'are responsible to me that only people who have been sentenced to death are executed. Once I've gone and am no longer responsible for what happens here, you can mow 'em all down as far as I'm concerned! They're no loss. But just let one observer get hit while I'm responsible, by God I'll have your guts for bootlaces, the *lot* of you! We are here to carry out an order and we are going to do it, and do it properly. I hope there are no weaklings amongst you who might faint. Should one of you go weak at the knees, I will look after him personally when the job is over and I'll kick his backbone straight up through the top of his head! What the hell are you doing with your helmet?' he shouts viciously at Tiny, who has pushed it down on to the back of his neck so that it resembles a Jewish skullcap. 'What's your name?'

'Creutzfeldt,' answers Tiny, blinking the snow from his eyes.

'*General* Creutzfeldt, perhaps?' roars the Major, irately.

'Not yet, sir,' replies Tiny, wiping a blob of half-melted snow from his face.

'Are you mad, soldier? Keep your filthy paws away from your face, when you're standing to attention! Charge that man!'

The Old Man rolls over to Tiny and makes the motions.

'The PK* people will want photos of the bodies,' the Major continues, irritably, 'but I don't want to see anybody breaking through the cordon before the echo has died away. It's happened before. Some silly bastard lets go after the rest of the squad and shoots some fool of a spectator. I'd get a laugh out of it if I wasn't responsible.'

Heide and I get the job of tying the victim, the worst job of the lot at an execution. We look at one another unhappily, weighing the short pieces of rope in our hands. We move towards the execution posts. Two of them will be in use, the Major has told us.

* PK (Propaganda-Kompanie) = War Correspondents.

The ropes go through holes in the posts, which are old railway sleepers. The holes where the rails were attached can easily be seen. There are twelve of them standing in a row and it is obvious that a great number of executions can be carried out quickly when necessary.

We stand, freezing with cold, in front of the execution posts, then we are given permission to fall out but to stay close by in readiness.

None of the special observers have arrived yet. There is plenty of time. The condemned men always arrive at least half an hour late. The witnesses are here already.

We are pleased to see that they too are shivering with cold. A crow watches us sadly from a crooked tree. The wind sends rain and snow along the length of the earthworks. The ropes on the poles flutter as if beckoning to the condemned.

'What weather to die in,' sighs the Old Man, depressedly, putting up his coat collar, against all regulations.

'Better'n sunshine,' considers Gregor. 'It's that cold here the thought of a nice warm grave's comforting.'

'Why the 'ell don't they bleedin' well get a move on, then, so we can get 'ome an' get at them bints,' says Tiny, slapping the slush from his body. He throws a rotten apple at Heide who ducks like lightning so that the soft fruit sails past him through the air and hits the MP Major right between the eyes.

Everyone watches the Major in expectant silence as he scrapes the remains of the rotten apple from his face. He takes the highly-polished personally-owned helmet from his head and looks at it for a moment with narrowed eyes. It, too, is covered with pieces of rotten apple. Life comes back into him. Wild-eyed and with his close-cropped hair bristling like the ruff on a mad dog, he goes at Tiny with a torrent of oaths and threats.

'I'll pull your guts out through your arse, you miserable swine! What the hell do you think you're playing at?' He is aglow with rage and looks as if he were ready to eat Tiny, who stands stiffly at attention and stares out towards the horizon with an empty look in his eyes. 'Swine, madman, how dare you throw rotten apples at a Major? Are you out of your mind? I'd like to tie you to one of those posts in place of one of the condemned men.' Curses rain on Tiny for a full quarter of an hour.

The crow in the crooked tree croaks vociferously. It sounds just as if it were laughing. The Major seems to think so too. He throws a stone at it, but it merely lifts into the air a few inches and drops back on to the branch, where it begins to preen its feathers in order to conform to regulations, when the execution takes place.

Muttering curses the Major moves over to a hut where a telephone is ringing irritably. It will take him some time to forget No. 2 Section, 5 Company.

A dispatch rider splashes along the road and asks for the Major.

The soldiers straighten up. Something is about to happen.

The Major comes out of the hut.

'Execution postponed three hours,' he barks.

We receive the order to pile arms, in the way waiting soldiers have always done since firearms were first invented.

The rain is heavier and the howling wind colder.

'Keep yourselves neat,' orders the Major, before driving away in the Kübel. 'I'll be back soon!'

The compulsory witnesses stand shivering by the hut. For some reason nobody is aware of, it is not permitted to enter the hut.

The chaplain is blue in the face. He is the only one present without a greatcoat.

This is our ninth execution since we came together in 5 Company. Formerly it was the Pioneers who supplied personnel for the firing squads but now it is often the condemned man's own unit.

The wind turns our spines to ice. Freezing, we blow on our red, swollen hands.

The Major returns and gives the orders for food to be distributed. Some fool has neglected to close the lid of the container properly, and the food is only lukewarm.

'Damn it,' swears Porta, 'we've a *right* to hot food. This shit,' he bangs his spoon viciously into the mess-tin, 'is cold as a monkey's bollocks in the rainy season!'

The dispatch rider comes back again. The execution has been postponed for a further two hours.

'Means it'll be twilight when we have to knock 'em off,' decides Porta, sourly. 'Hope to Christ we don't have to do it in artificial light. I've tried that before. Not pleasant. They had to carry the candidate to the post and when they put the lights on we could see it was a Blitzmädel.* That did it. Two of the

* Blitzmädel = Signals girl.

116

squad threw down their rifles. The Leutnant went starkers. He snapped his sword over his knees and threw the pieces at the JAG officer. They dragged him away, of course, and an MP officer took over the squad, so we finished the girl off but not till another of us had keeled over flat on his face. Rifle, helmet, the lot rattled right up to the girl's feet, and she screamed so that we were close to getting put behind bars, the rest of us. The Leutnant wound up in Torgau and came back to us a rifleman. A year later they knocked him off in Sennelager as a deserter. I don't look forward to shooting in artificial light!'

'I took part in the execution of a girl once myself,' Gregor tells us, 'but it came off in brilliant sunshine. It was when I was with 1 Reiterregiment at Königsberg. We'd been told in advance it was a wench.'

'They filled us up with schnapps so we were half-cut when they brought her on. She was that white in the face we thought she was dead already. When we loaded she spewed up so hard it spattered on us. I lifted my sights so the muzzle pointed well above her head. Shoot a bint, I couldn't *do* it! Seemed to me she sagged a bit before we fired and she hung funny on the ropes, not like the way they usually do when they've had the wind knocked out of 'em. The MP officer went over, looking a bit pale, to give her the mercy shot. Three times his Walther bangs. We stood at ease and watched the medical orderlies cut her down. Along comes the M.O. and starts to bawl and shout, as if he'd gone round the bend. Not one bullet-hole in the lady! My eleven buddy-buddies had had the same idea as me and shot to miss. The MP officer, who was new to the game, had shot into the ground.

'The JAG fellow, the chaplain and everybody else, were all shouting at the same time. What a caper, and not even *planned*. The Blitzmädel had pissed on 'em too. She'd dropped dead of a heart-attack.'

'They gave *us* a trip all right. With the MP officer in the lead we wound up in a 500 battalion at Heuberg. Later on we were split up all over the place. Far as I know I'm the only one left alive out of that squad. I'd have been dead too and long ago if I hadn't overtaken my General in a ten-tonner. I didn't know it was a General's car I was passing. Found it out when I'd got by him and two MPs come racing after me. I speeded the ten-tonner up and braked so suddenly that both the MPs took a mud-bath in the ditch, but the General had a telephone in his Horch so that when I got to the crossroads at Kehl there was a whole army of MPs waiting to greet me and the ten-tonner.

'With his horsey service grin, the General asked me if I could drive a car as well as I drove a lorry. I couldn't deny it. He wriggled inside his General's uniform so that his oakleaves shot light-beams right over to France.

'After he'd felt me out a bit, he got the idea I'd been born on an engine block and conceived by a couple of valves. Two days after that I was a General's driver and if it hadn't been for Oberst Warthog I'd've been one still. And that'd have meant I'd have been certain of living through the war. Being a General's driver is pure life insurance. You never go anywhere where you can risk getting even a scratch.'

'But how did you get all that tin to hang on you?' the Old Man wonders.

'Staff work,' answers Gregor, proudly. 'When they hung something on my General there was always a little thing for me too. When he got the Knight's Cross with vegetables they gave me the Iron Cross. Later on I got the Fried Egg in silver,* so I could flash messages too.'

The Major drives back to town again.

We begin quietly hoping that the whole thing has been called off.

When the Major's back is turned, Porta lifts his arm and slaps the inside of his elbow to show what he thinks of him.

'Can't you wait with that sort of thing till I've given "stand easy"?' snarls the Old Man, sourly.

'No fun in that,' grins Porta, disrespectfully, 'the shit'd be gone by then!'

'There goes our afternoon off,' sighs Tiny, despondently. 'The others'll 'ave been in town long ago, an' all the cunt'll 'ave been took.'

'I remember once when I was doorkeeper at the "Tomcat",' laughs Porta. 'One afternoon, late, a crazy sod comes in looking for somewhere to strain his 'taters. He was a traveller in pots and pans and looked it. He disappeared into the green room with Birgitte the Cock-Swallower from Höchster. "Pots an' pans" started off biting her ear. She punched him and told him

* Fried Egg in silver = The German Cross in silver (Fried Egg because of its shape).

118

to stop that. A little later he bit her in the left breast.

'"Stop that bitin'," she shouted, nervously. "If you're hungry I'll get you a bag o' nuts. This is a knockin' shop you've come to not a bloody sausage bar, an' I ain't on the menu. I'm here to be fucked not to get chewed on!"

'"Now it better be a nice, good little girl," says "Pots an' pans", with a weak-minded expression on his face, "or Daddy'll have to smack it, won't he?"

'He threw his arms round her and this time he bit her in the other breast. She went bonkers and tried to kick his balls up into his throat, but the strength he had developed from carrying all those pots and pans around with him stood him in good stead, and he turned her over his knee and gave her a few hard slaps on her bare buttocks.

'Jesus, you should've heard her scream and howl. But the more she fought the happier grew "Pots an' pans". Her arse was red as a well-stoked stove before she managed to twist herself free. She hissed and spat, and when she saw her ill-used backside in the big mirror she started in swearing like a docker on a cold morning after a night on the booze. She showed him her breasts, which carried the imprints of his teeth.

'"You bloody, bastarding cannibal you," she raged, beside herself. "You've fucked this night up for me all right. Who'd want a girl with goddam shark-bites all over her tits? I'll introduce you to 'Big Willy,' I will! He weighs twenty-two stone an' he ain't too heavy for his height. He'll nip your goolies the way they nip suckin' pigs!"

'"No, I don't want to meet him," "Pots an' pans" gave in, nervously. "It was only a bit of fun!"

'"Oh you're a *real* funny man, *you* are, you lecherous bastard you," she shrilled, resentfully. "My breasts are my bank-book, boy!"

'"Pots an' pans" swallowed a couple of times, and even though his think-tank's a bit leaky he doesn't have to knock his head on the wall to get it working. And the thought of "Big Willy" resting and building up his strength somewhere under the roof of the "Tomcat" made him think faster. He pulled 500 marks from his pocket and asked if they couldn't help the tooth-marks to go away quicker.

'"You a Yid or somethin'?" asks the "Cock-Swallower". "Circumcised, are you? I don't want no trouble with the bloody race coppers!"

119

' "Pots an' pans" looked insulted and whipped out his John Thomas. It was an ordinary sort of German prick. Then the "Cock-Swallower" started moving towards the door and he got the message. A new 500 mark note appeared in his hand.

' "Took you a while," she smiled, pushing the note under the washbasin. The thought of it being slush money never crossed her mind. She crept willingly into bed with "Pots an' Pans".

' "*Bon appetit*, little cannibal," she trilled. "Chew all you want an' for another 200 you can smack too. I give my customers what they want. But everything's got its price tag!"

'She screamed with pleasure as he belaboured her buttocks with his belt, and when he bit her on the inside of her thigh she meowed like a she-cat being gone over by two experienced toms.

' "I'll be back soon," he promised as he left, but she soon realised that had been a lie when the cops picked her up in the savings bank for trying to pass the two forged 500 mark notes. She, of course, denied any knowledge of it being slush but it made matters worse when they found a dud 200 mark note in her room. She went inside for quite a while and "Pots an' pans" was never heard of again.'

'It's hardly worth while living in Germany any more since we got this special kind of Socialism,' says Gregor. 'It used to be you could tell a rozzer to stand on one side and play cops an' robbers by himself. Nowadays they turn up in the middle of the night an'll tear you right off the top of a throbbin' quim. And if you don't confess immediately they flatten your face till you look like a bulldog, and you're nearly ready to start barking!'

'Outside Germany they call that a police state,' Porta grins, broadly. 'Constitutional and civil rights you can stick straight up a pensioned-off Reeperbahn whore's arsehole!'

Tiny, who is eating bread and sugar, swallows a huge bite with some difficulty, and washes it down with a schnapps and a draught of beer. He lets out a long, rolling belch.

'Whatever 'appens,' he says, apathetically, 'you end up in David's Station, where they set you on a stool that's been polished to a 'igh gloss by 'undreds of tremblin' arseholes. Then they tell you what you can refuse to answer accordin' to paragraph piss an' shit. Also you can 'ave a defendin' lawyer, they say, but before you've got a soddin' line on what it is you've got a right to, they start up interrogatin' you enough to make God an' Mary's son Jesus confess 'e'd planned the latest bank robbery on Adolf 'Itler's Platz and shot the bonce off of the cashier because 'e was wearin' a red tie. Citizen's rights,' he hisses, contemptuously, 'much truth in 'em as in the bleedin' Bible! If your address is Sanct Pauli both the police and the citizens count *you* as bein' a dirty crook an' if they beat you up enough they might get a confession as to who it was committed the latest unsolved crime they're still playin' about with. *And* if you're really up shit creek in one of them sidestreets to Bernhard Nocht Strasse, there where the pros can only get theirselves fucked in total darkness, they don't even read the book to you but just set their fuckin' dogs after you to give 'em a bit of a lesson in rippin' out arseholes. Did you 'ear the latest? Wolf's 'ounds've chewed up another poor sod as couldn't pay up to that Mafia bastard!'

'They're wicked, those dogs. Chew on your arse without a second thought,' says Porta, disgustedly. 'I wouldn't *own* curs like that! Even if they spoke twelve languages and could write Sanscrit and knew the British and the Prussian drill-book for mounted troops forwards and backwards.'

'Them dogs are *devils*,' says Gregor, with hate in his voice. '*All* dogs are stupid. Just look at 'em. One of 'em starts to bark because some Jew-boy fly has pissed on his nose. Straight away some other four-legged dope answers him and then a third starts up. And they go *on*. All night if need be. And there's nothing *to* bark at. Just keeping everybody awake. God how I *hate* dogs! Every one of 'em ought to be poisoned, stuffed an' mounted on wheels so's the bloody dog-lovers could pull 'em round after 'em without them shittin' all over the streets.'

'Tell me,' Porta turns to Tiny, 'did Sieg pay up?'

' 'E laughed in me face and give me the message that *you* were on your way to the glass 'ouse and would only come out again in a 'orizontal position with twelve bullet 'oles in you,' answers Tiny, with a melancholy look on his face. 'If there'd not been four crooks alongside 'im at the time I'd 'ave smeared 'im all over the wall.'

'I'll smash that bastard's kneecaps,' rages Porta, savagely, 'and then his elbows just to make a job of it. I'll stuff him back up into his mother's German cunt before I've finished with him!'

'Let's knife the sod, an' shoot 'im afterwards,' suggests Tiny, wickedly. 'I *can't stand* untrustworthy people!'

Porta lifts one leg and lets a huge fart, which makes all the gentlemen over by the hut look at us reproachfully.

'Make sure you secure them properly,' the Old Man warns us, conscientiously.

'We had an execution in Grafenwöhr where the ropes hadn't been secured properly and the condemned man ran round the execution ground like a chicken with his head cut off. What a scandal that was! Everybody panicked. The chaplain got the shock of his life when he saw the firing squad chasing the condemned man all over the execution square.'

'Good God,' cries Barcelona, aghast. 'Did he escape?'

'As I said, like a headless chicken flapping on the ground when you let go of it,' says the Old Man, impassively.

'Old man Attila would've rolled around in his saddle,' grins Porta.

'Ordinary people'd never ever understand it,' admits Tiny, shaking his head. 'It's unbelievable what can go on in the bleedin' Army. When I was post Gefreiter at Torgau, one Thursday mornin' we got the job of blowin' out some kind of a sailor. A queer sod 'e was who'd done a lot of *very* peculiar things in 'is lifetime. 'E'd started school at the age of seven an' managed to spend three years in the first class an' another three in the third. 'E went out in the fourth. 'E broke the German law as if 'e was workin' to a plan, 'is crime sheet was that long it'd've took a person six months to get through it. The court martial said to 'ave 'im shot but bein' a unusual sort of bloke they changed it to 'angin'. There was a staff Feldwebel from Torgau who was an expert at strangling people with a bit o' rope an' they give 'im the job. *Then* they found 'e'd got no neck to speak of. Shoulders an' 'is neck was all one an' 'ow *can* you 'ang a man with no neck? Why else'd God *give* people necks, I ask you? Well the executioner an' the condemned man talked it over an' agreed to get the Navy to make a special rope for the job. An' the Feldwebel promised 'im 'e'd make a good quick job of it, without 'urtin' 'im.

'But that's where 'e made 'is mistake. The first try went wrong 'cause the rope wasn't tightened properly. Least that's what they *said*. The sailor slides out of the noose an' straight down through the trap when it opened. Not a scratch did 'e get. Bang 'e goes down to the bottom of the pit an' sits there cursin' an' swearin'.'

'He didn't hurt himself, I hope?' says Porta, solicitously.

'No, no more'n 'e could climb up on to the scaffold again on 'is own. 'E was the least disturbed of the lot of us. Bawled out the staff Feldwebel for a clumsy fool who'd no idea 'ow to 'ang people. Next time the noose is pulled real tight an' even the condemned man 'imself says 'e's satisfied. But it didn't do no good. 'E slips out of it again like a fuckin' eel.

' "This lot's enough to kill off the strongest nigger as ever lived," shouts the sailor, as 'e climbs up on to the scaffold for the second time.

'The staff Feldwebel is full of excuses, an' the JAG man promises the sailor if it goes wrong a third time 'e gets a pardon. And believe it or not, 'e slips out again on the third go. The Feldwebel goes barmy an' runs around on the scaffold as if 'e was tryin' to bite 'imself in the arsehole. And before we could stop 'im 'e puts the noose round 'is own neck an' jumps gracefully down the 'ole. 'E was dead as a nit when we got to 'im. A beautiful, a perfect 'angin', carried out on 'imself.

'The chaplain talked in Latin to Gawd Almighty an' the JAG, the prosecutin' officer an' the defence officer went into a legal 'uddle, that nearly ended in fisticuffs. The sailor 'ad only been condemned to death once an' they'd already executed 'im three times in a row. It was contrary to regulations, said the defending officer. They agreed to send it to the JAG's office for decision. Carefully forgettin' they'd promised the sailor a pardon if it didn't work third time.

'All the witnesses left. They couldn't take it any more. 'Angin' the same man three times in one day was too much for the strongest stomach.

'When they'd gone all us guards went over to the 'ole to get 'im out, but 'e wouldn't come up. 'E'd lost all patience.

'The duty NCO told us to go down after 'im but nobody felt much like it.

'So we got 'old of a Navy AB from out of one of the cells. 'E'd sold a cutter to the locals while on service in Norway, and was a nice, friendly sort of bloke, as understood 'ow to talk convincing-like to people. 'E got that sailor up out of the 'ole with no trouble at all.

'Well, there was a dreadful lot of discussion went on in a

dreadful lot of different kinds of courts, but in the end they made up their minds to let 'im go back to the Navy so they could shoot 'im, though there was some as thought the bullets'd just glance off of him 'e was that bony.

'Some clever bleeder in Kiel found out the only certain way o' gettin' rid of 'im was to drown 'im, so they decided to give 'im a trip under a warship, the way they used to do in the good old days. As you know people condemned to death ain't allowed to travel by train so off they takes 'im to Kiel in a Kübel. That saved 'is bleedin' life for 'im. The Kübel never got to Kiel where they 'ad a old-fashioned keel-'aulin' all ready for 'im.

'A bit outside Celle a British fighter-bomber is stragglin' along and sees this Kübel an' 'as a go at it, so the three 'ead-'unters get sent upstairs. There was only their tin 'elmets and their badges left, but the sailor never gets a scratch. Death wouldn't 'ave anythin' to do with a bag o' bones like 'im. 'E disappeared and 'as never been 'eard of since.'

'*Sacré nom de Dieu, ça commence à bouillir.* How I wish I was on my way to France with everything I own on my back,' sighs the little Legionnaire, lighting a *Caporal*. 'France, a glass of good wine and a big bowl of *bouillabaisse*! *Mon Dieu*, homesickness is tearing me to pieces!'

'You wouldn't be thinking of taking off, now, would you?' asks Porta, worriedly. 'The headhunters'd pick you up quick as a monkey picking a flea off his bollocks.'

'If you *do* do it,' says Tiny, 'go that way,' and he points to the west.

The witnesses over by the hut walk about impatiently. The rain has turned to a slush which cakes on their clothes. The telephone inside the hut jangles irritably. Everyone looks towards it.

'Departure has been put off for another two hours,' shouts a JAG aide to us, as if he were announcing a change in a train time.

'Damn it all to hell,' the Old Man curses, 'artificial light.'

'Maybe they've been pardoned,' says the Westphalian, optimistically. 'It'd be the first time I'd be really happy at having wasted so much time waiting around.'

'Nobody gets pardoned any more,' answers the Old Man gloomily. 'They're that far gone they can't afford to.'

'They cut the heads off two girls in Halle the other day just

124

for buying butter coupons on the black,' Gregor tells them, feeling his neck tenderly.

'Rather eat marge, at that rate,' says Tiny, shuddering.

'What about fetching up dinner?' shouts Porta from a bush, behind which he is squatting with his trousers round his ankles.

'The Major didn't say anything,' says the Old Man, thoughtfully, 'but to hell with it. Off you go!'

Tiny and Gregor are off towards the truck like well-oiled streaks of lightning.

'You touch any of that pork and beans before you get back and I'll mow you down,' shouts Porta from the bush, wiping away with a large chestnut leaf.

The food container smells beautiful. The bean soup is thick as gruel. There is half a crate of beer too, and we get into quite a party humour.

'The departing guests can't be getting better than this,' thinks Porta, joyously, shovelling food into his mouth.

They have forgotten to give us a knife, so we have to pass the pork from hand to hand and bite it off in chunks. It doesn't taste any the worse for that.

'They ought to have rubbed a bit of garlic on it,' continues Porta, taking a large bite.

'I'll be glad when this war's over,' says Heide, 'so we can go out on proper manoeuvres again.'

'You must have shit where your brains ought to be,' shouts Porta, shaking his head. 'Soon as one war's over you bastards want to get out on manoeuvres and before we know where we are you've started a new war to see if what you've been manoeuvring about is right or not?'

'There will be no more war,' says Heide, decisively. '*Our* world war will be the last!'

'What the devil will we need the Army and manoeuvres for, then?' asks the Old Man in wonder.

'Because the Army is as natural a necessity as prisons and policemen,' says Heide, with an airy gesture.

'There's something in that,' Gregor agrees, stroking his chin thoughtfully. 'A country without an army's like a man with no balls!'

'Here, want some?' the Old Man says to the JAG clerk who has sat down by us.

'No thanks, I've no appetite,' says the clerk, an elderly man.

125

'*Tu m'emmerdes*,' says the Legionnaire, with a short laugh. 'The chap's frightened at seeing people get shot!'

'It isn't a pleasant sight, either,' the Old Man admits, quietly.

'Everybody who shouts and screams about the death penalty ought to be made to see what it's like knocking a man off,' says Gregor, blowing on his cold-reddened hands.

'In Madrid we did not make so much fuss about it,' Barcelona explains. 'We put them up in a row against a long wall and let them have it with an SMG. Always from left to right. It was like a mower going through a cornfield. Afterwards they hosed away the blood, so it was all clean for the next lot. Witnesses and all that, we didn't bother with. Some of 'em we didn't even try.'

'Let's have a cup of milk o' madness, to drive away our uncontrollable fear,' says Porta, with a little laugh, filling up our mugs.

'Have you got schnapps?' asks the clerk, in surprise.

'I can hear this is your first outing,' laughs Barcelona. 'There's always firewater at these parties!'

Porta pushes forward his mess-tin for a new helping. His stomach seems to expand visibly. He takes a big bite of pork, chews, swallows and washes it down with beer and schnapps.

'God, the way you can *eat*,' says the Old Man, wonderingly. 'Where d'you *put* it all?'

Porta licks his spoon clean and pushes it down into his jackboot, where he can get at it quickly if he becomes hungry again.

He falls on to his back in the heather using his steel helmet as a pillow.

'Pass the pork,' he orders Tiny. 'Soon as I see it I get hunger pains again,' he sighs. 'I've *always* been like that.' He lifts up his backside and blows a thunderous fart which echoes over to the hut where the witnesses stand freezing.

'Have you ever really eaten your fill?' asks the Old Man, with an indulgent smile.

'Never! No, never *really*,' Porta admits, without having even to consider his answer. 'There's always been room for a little bit more. At old Mr Porta's place in Bornholmerstrasse there were two huge padlocks on the pantry to keep his best son from taking it over completely. My appetite got me into trouble too, at the greengrocer's where I worked. He found out I used to take a sample of all his delicacies.' He pulls his piccolo from his jackboot. Tiny's deep bass joins him:

126

'Sie ging von Hamburg bis nach Bremen*
bis dass der Zuz aus Flensburg kam.
Holahi-holaho-holahi-holaho!
Sie wollte sich das Leben nehmen
und legt sich auf de Schienen dann.
Holahi-holaho-holahi-holaho.
Jedoch der Schaffner hat's gesehen,
er bremste mit gewaltiger Hand.
Holahi-holaho-holahi-holaho.
Allein der Zug, der blieb nicht stehen,
ein junges haupt rollt in den Sand . . .

The staff-chaplain came raging over towards us.

'I forbid you to sing that filthy song,' he screamed in a voice which cracked several times. 'Can't you keep order here, Feldwebel?'

'Yes,' says the Old Man, remaining seated on the heather.

'Such horrible filth,' splutters the padre. 'You are carrying on like street-boys!'

'Just what we are,' grins Porta, shamelessly. 'Bornholmerstrasse, Moabitt.'

'*Heyn Hoyer Strasse, Sankt Pauli*,' echoes Tiny, cheekily.

'Request the padre to tell us please,' smiles Porta, putting his heels together in the attention position whilst remaining seated. 'Has the padre ever been in "The Crooked Dog" in Gendarmenmarkt? Best bunch of crumpet in the whole of Berlin, sir.'

'Impertinent man,' spits the staff-chaplain, disgustedly, withdrawing to the other witnesses over by the hut.

'The new CO's wife's a nice bit of stuff,' says Porta, pursing his lips.

* 'Sie ging, etc.'
  Freely translated.

> She walked from Hamburg on to Bremen,
> Where the Flensburg train was due to pass.
> Hola-hi, hola-ho, hola-hi, hola-ho!
> This life she wanted soon to leave, then
> Across the rails she lay, poor lass!
> Hola-hi, hola-ho, hola-hi, hola-ho!
> The brakeman, who was never faulted,
> Braked mightily – but, Oh! Alas!
> Hola-hi, hola-ho, hola-hi, hola-ho!
> The train rushed on could not be halted
> A sweet, young head rolled in the grass . . .

127

'Something queer about her,' says Gregor, thoughtfully. 'She's got prick in both her eyes, and she's always showing everythin' she's got!'

'She's a war widow,' states Barcelona.

'She's married to the CO,' the Old Man gapes at him uncomprehendingly, 'and he was alive this morning when we left!'

'Nevertheless she's the widow of a Kapitänleutnant who's at the bottom of the Atlantic with his VII B U-boat,' Barcelona enlightens them.

'Maybe she's interested in science and is studying prickology,' laughs Porta noisily. 'First the Navy, then the Army and when our Oberst flies off to Valhalla she'll move on to the Luftwaffe or the SS!'

'She's still an eyeful,' says Gregor, his own shining. 'Longlegged, round-arsed and high-titted! She wouldn't need to ask me more'n once. Me and my old man'd be into that like a knife into a pound o' butter!'

'I'm afraid you'd be disappointed,' Porta considers knowledgeably. 'She smells a mile off of the Party and the BDM.* Shouldn't wonder if she'd got a swastika up her cunt rotating the wrong way, and no prick outside the Party'd fancy running into that!'

'Swastika bints ain't the worst to get down on their backs,' Gregor corrects him. 'They're trained at the bridal schools, so they can fix up the happy warrior husband when he gets back from the wars with a tattered swastika banner and a deepfrozen prick!'

'Bridal schools?' asks the Old Man, rolling the words round his mouth. 'Are there really such places? I thought it was only a joke.'

'Jesus on the Cross, man,' shouts Gregor, indignantly. 'They teach these BDM bints all the tricks of the bloody trade, *and* they don't get taken on if they aren't well prepared in advance. For example they put a piece o' chalk up their arses and get taught how to write with it while they're swinging 'em in time to: *Ein Reich! Ein Volk! Ein Führer!* That exercise makes 'em that supple they can make a Party member ninety years old remember he's still got a set o' rattlers danglin' between his creaky old legs.'

'I once knew a countess who was so high-bred she could only come on if you bit her in the arse and filled her cunt up with

* BDM (Bund deutscher Mädels) = German Nazi Girls Association.

128

champagne,' says the Westphalian in a quiet, confidential tone of voice.

'Them kind also get into *Café Keese*,' says Tiny, importantly. 'Met a real Duchess there once, 'Ohenzollern of the blood, she was. On the Reeperbahn she used to go incognito and called 'erself Ina von Weinberg. She'd got opera on the brain. Every time a John Thomas with a roll-collar got into 'er she used to start screamin' out Wagner. Everybody in the 'ouse knew when she was gettin' it in 'er old box-office.'

'There are far more exotic ways than getting bit in the arse and singing Wagner,' grins Porta lasciviously. 'After we'd liberated Paris we ran into a couple of bits of stuff sitting, on the lookout for occupation prick, outside the *Café de la Paix*. One of 'em had to have a champagne cork with a violin string attached stuck up her arsehole. When she began to pant, you had to pull the cork out slowly. You can't imagine the way that arse of hers could go on thrumming and twanging. It was nothing more nor less than the Marseillaise at full pressure.'

'Couldn't be more complicated, I should think,' considers the Old Man, lighting up his silver-lidded pipe.

'I *have* heard,' continues Porta, 'that it's even better with a nail in the champagne cork. It should be one of the square kind with ridges on it, but it can only be done of course with bints who have *not* got piles.'

'An arsehole can be used for a lot of things,' grins Tiny, blissfully. 'The Jew furriers boy, David in 'Ein 'Oyer Strasse could, usin' a tinwhistle, play the opening of *Deutschland, Deutschland, über alles* with his arsehole. But it *'ad* to be just after we'd filled up with pea soup.'

'With his *arse*?' asks Heide, doubtfully.

'Course,' says Tiny, proudly. 'That Yid boy David could 'ang on to 'is wind long as 'e wanted. Once 'e drove the coppers down at David's Station 'arf barmy by goin' round with a police whistle up 'is arse. They arrested all the ventriloquists in the Reeperbahn, thinkin' it was them as was imitatin' police whistles. Some way or other we'd got into an exhibition of paintings and goin' down a narrow corridor the Yid lets off a rip-snorter of a fart so all the paint fell off the paintings an' made 'em into valuable functionalistic works of bleedin' art!'

'My wife's made a terrible fool of herself,' says the Westphalian, pulling out a letter. 'She's pregnant and doesn't know who she's got the prize from.'

'She must bloody know,' says Heide in disgust. 'All German women know who the father of their children is.'

'You must have been born in a gasworks and mixed in a bucket with a hole in it,' the Westphalian says, irritably. 'Try pushing your arse up against a circular saw and pointing out afterwards which of the teeth it was that tore the cheeks open.'

'Is your wife one of that kind?' sniffs Heide, contemptuously.

'Of course she is,' says the Westphalian, proudly. 'Think I'd marry a homebody who could only have it off with a broom-handle?'

'Soon be Christmas again,' says the Old Man, thoughtfully, and lights his pipe again. He is having difficulty in keeping it going. 'It seems more than a century since I spent Christmas at home with Liselotte and the nippers.'

'Maybe we'll have as crazy a Christmas as we had last year,' says Porta, expectantly. 'Somebody or other's sure to hit on something quite mad.'

'Yes, something always happens at Christmas,' laughs Gregor, heartily. 'I'll never forget once when I was with my General. I didn't spend it *with* him, of course. I was sent over to the *Unteroffizier* mess. It wasn't boring by any means. In the middle of the meat course Feldwebel Berg, the Divisional Chief Clerk, pulled out his P-38 and pointed it straight between his eyes so that everybody could see he really meant to be on his way for ever and ever. We who were close to him could see he'd taken the magazine out. He was a great man for a joke, that Chief Clerk was.

' "Good-bye, comrades," he shouted, and pressed a couple of beery tears out of his eyes. "Give my regards to the Führer," were his last words. Then we heard a bang and half his face flew over and landed in the lap of our Chief Mechanic, looking like a used carnival mask. Feldwebel Berg was well-known for his carelessness. He'd taken the magazine out all right but forgotten there was one up the spout and that was too bad for *him*. The cartridge case landed in my pudding. I'll never forget the silly look on his face, just before he slipped under the table.'

'New Year usually costs a few lives, too,' puts in Tiny. 'I was in Bamberg last year. What a new Year's Eve we fixed up! We'd a bloke with us was dumb as the droppin's of a cow, and 'im they'd set to look after the explosives store. Pokin' about there 'e'd turned up some of them old signal bombs as looked just like Brazilian cigars. You lit 'em same road, with a match

130

or a live coal. The first of 'em 'e threw out the window just before dinner. It wasn't that easy to light 'em so the Kitchen Feldwebel'd give 'im a cigar. 'E got it goin' an' lights the next bomb all right. After a bit 'e went amok an' was throwin' bombs out of the windows for dear life. Then things went wrong for 'im, drunk as 'e was by now. Out of the window went the cigar an' into 'is mouth went the bomb. The whole bleedin' mess was covered in blood an' bits o' flesh. The explosives dope stood there a bit swayin' without a 'ead. Then somebody shouted " 'Appy New Year" an' 'e laid down on the floor.'

'Smoked his last cigar then, hadn't he?' remarks Porta drily and pours himself an extra large schnapps.

In a loud voice he begins to sing:

> 'Liebe Leute, wollt' Ihr wissen,*
> was einem Fähnrich einst gebürte,
> ja, für die Nacht ein schönes Mädel
> oder fünf und zwanzig Flaschen Bier . . .'

The witnesses by the hut stretch their necks like hens who have caught sight of a hawk.

The padre is on his way over to us, but when he has got half-way he gives up and turns back.

It is almost completely dark when a Kübel, followed by a lorry and a closed troop-carrier, rumbles down the hill.

Three MPs in a motorcycle and sidecar follow in the rear.

'Here they are,' says Porta, stretching his neck like a goose who gets a sight of the farmer's girl coming to feed him.

'Devil take 'em,' grumbles the Old Man, viciously, pulling at his equipment. 'Up on your feet. Helmets on! Get hold of your rifles! Into threes! Get a move on now! That goddamned Major might chase us all the way down the Morellenschlucht! Look at your bloody self, Tiny!'

'Look?' asks Tiny, in surprise, with his steel helmet on the back of his neck. 'I know I ain't *pretty*, but I never 'ave been!'

'Get your equipment and your helmet on straight,' shouts the Old Man, angrily.

The talk between the witnesses over by the hut stops. Every-

---

* Liebe Leute, etc:
> Dear friends now would you know
> What happened to an ensign:
> A night with a lovely girl
> or twenty-five bottles of beer . . .

body stares at the vehicles which have stopped a little way into the heather.

'Party, atten-tion!' orders the Old Man and salutes the Major.

'Everything in order, Feldwebel?'

'All in order, sir!'

'Have the propaganda people and the rubberneckers arrived?' asks the Major, looking over towards the hut.

'No, Herr Major, I've not see them.'

'Bastards,' snarls the Major, spitting angrily. 'The condemned men are here now. They'll drop dead of fear if we keep them sitting alongside their own coffins, waiting! What a bloody day!' He shivers in the cold rain, and points at the lorry. 'The lights are in there. Get 'em set up, on the double, Feldwebel! We've got three of them to turn off!'

'Three?' cries the Old Man, fearfully.

'I said it, three!' The Major shows his teeth in a snarling grin. 'They're to be shot one at a time, so there'll be no risk of having to do any of them over again. They all go to the posts at the same time. That's the easiest way. We'll take 'em from left to right!'

'And the mercy shots?' asks the Old Man, with fear in his mind.

The Major looks at him searchingly for a moment.

'Feel it in your guts, do you, Feldwebel? Don't worry! I'll look after that part of it. You command the squad, no breaks between orders. Keep it moving! One clip to be issued to each rifle, reload and secure immediately after the first round has been fired. Then aim again. Understood?'

'Yessir!' answers the Old Man in a low voice, swallowing spittle.

Three powerful projectors are directed at the upright railway sleepers used as execution posts.

The Major throws two ropes to Gregor, who is to be the third member of the roping party.

'Should anything happen outside the normal programme,' says the Major, fiercely, 'this party is under *my* command, and if *I* give the order to fire you fire no matter if it's straight in the face of a chaplain or a General or whoever.' He takes a deep breath, wipes the slush from his brutal face and looks over towards the hut again. 'You never know what witnesses can get up to!'

Two dark-grey Mercedes saloons, luxury cars with command flags on their wings swing across the heather. Their lights flicker over the ambulance-type personnel transport. Red and white general officer's tabs show in the melancholy twilight.

'Save us,' groans the Old Man, nervously. 'We *are* in good company. Who can we be sending off on the long trip this time?'

'*Nacht und Nebel*,'* answers Gregor, gloomily.

The Generals and those with them are conversing audibly. The aroma of expensive cigars wafts over to us.

The propaganda men take photographs. Flashes go off blindingly.

The spectators over by the hut disappear. Some of them are laughing loudly. An Oberst lets a hip-flask go round.

The Major comes over and hands four pieces of white cloth to the Old Man.

'Here are the marks,' he says shortly. 'As soon as the criminals are tied to the posts you will hang these around their necks!'

'There are *four*?' the Old Man breaks out in confusion.

'There comes the fourth,' grins the Major, pointing to a prisoner transport-vehicle, swaying down the hill.

The Old Man goes pale. Four executions for one squad! That's a pretty rough assignment!

'What hellish weather,' says the Major, looking up at the threatening, low-hanging clouds. 'Has it been raining all the time out here?'

'Yes, Herr Major. Snowing and raining and still getting colder,' says the Old Man, looking out over the heath.

The Major pulls his coat-collar up around his ears, nods morosely, and watches the propaganda squad still taking photographs.

'*If* I wasn't responsible,' he says softly, 'I'd love to see you knock those pigs off.' He looks at his watch and turns to Heide. 'Now you do know how to secure them? In ten minutes time we'll be bringing on the leading actors!'

Why it will be in ten minutes time, he doesn't tell us.

The telephone inside the hut rings.

'If they've decided to send any more,' says the Old Man in a low voice, 'they can get themselves another squad commander!'

* Nacht und Nebel (German) = Night and mist (slang for secret liquidations).

'*En avant, marche!* No foolishness!' the Legionnaire warns him.

With long strides the Major returns from the hut.

'Securing party, quick march,' he orders in a loud voice.

Heide marches smartly over to the prisoner transport, a proper four paces behind the Major. He holds the two pieces of new hemp in his left hand as laid down in regulations.

'He's enough to make you sick,' says Gregor, with contempt, stuffing his ropes in his belt.

'Shouldn't we go too?' I ask, when Gregor stays where he is.

'Let him give the order again,' says Gregor. 'The slower we are the longer those poor sods stay alive!'

'I don't think they'll give you much thanks for that.'

'What the hell, you men?' roars the Major, turning round when he finds that Gregor and I have not moved. 'Think it's bedtime, do you? At the double!'

We trot over in something resembling a double. I am carrying the ropes in my left hand. I daren't put them in my belt like Gregor.

The Major unlocks the back door of the vehicle with a special key. Two Pioneer Unteroffiziers stand off a little with Schmeissers cocked and ready.

The three prisoners sit chained to one another on the cross seat inside the vehicle. The floor is covered with a thick layer of sawdust. To one side lie three paper sacks of the kind butchers use to pack sides of meat in.

The door bangs to on the Major's finger and he lets out a wild string of oaths. The rain splashes from his steel helmet and streams down his leather coat.

'Bloody *shit*,' he growls irritably, twisting his body sideways through the door.

He unchains the three prisoners.

'Get out,' he orders hoarsely, almost pushing them.

The three condemned men tumble headlong out of the van and look about them nervously. The cold, raw air cuts through their thin red drill clothing.

I have difficulty in keeping from vomiting. Suddenly I am longing to be back at the front and away from all the hypocrisy of the safe zone.

The Major fetches the fourth prisoner himself. He is an elderly man, and pale as a corpse.

The Major is polite and servile.

'This way, Herr General,' he says, pointing to the execution posts.

We look curiously at the prisoner. A General to be executed! We straighten our backs.

Respect for such a high-ranking officer is deep within our bones.

Heide inflates his chest, lays his hand on the shoulder of the youngest of the prisoners and screams in a cracking voice:

'If you attempt to escape I shall use my weapon!' He cocks his gun noisily and waves it about.

'You crazy cunt,' whispers Gregor, spitting contemptuously.

Heide sends him a wicked look and raises the P-38 slightly. For a moment it looks as if he is going to shoot Gregor down.

'Can't you save your private battle until this is all over?' says one of the prisoners softly.

We recognise him. It is our Oberst from the Arctic front.

Heide bows his head and puts his pistol back in its holster.

Close together we cross the wet heather.

Curious eyes follow us from over by the hut. We can smell cigar smoke.

The propaganda party ready their cameras. They push for position, cursing one another.

I am walking alongside a Feldwebel from the *Luftwaffe*. Gregor and the Oberst are behind us.

'Go on, if you can, Herr Oberst,' says Gregor, shoving him gently. 'Run like the devil. It's only a hundred yards to the cherry trees and none of the squad'll aim to hit you!'

'You've got a lively imagination, Unteroffizier,' mutters the Oberst in a low voice. 'Where'd you have me run *to*?'

'What a lot o' *shit*,' sighs Gregor, dejectedly. 'Until today I *liked* the Army. Up the lot of 'em from now on! From now on it's me or them!'

'It'll be them,' smiles the Oberst, almost humorously.

'The bloody Army'll find out,' hisses Gregor furiously, kicking at a clump of heather which flies amongst the witnesses.

'Have you got a cigarette?' asks the *Luftwaffe* Feldwebel.

I light one and hand it to him. I offer him the packet.

'Nice of you, but I won't have time to get through it!'

It is strictly forbidden to give the prisoners cigarettes, but I couldn't care less. I can't even be bothered to look round to see if the Major has noticed. They can only give me six weeks inside and I'd probably live through it.

The Old Man sees the Oberst, goes over to him determinedly and presses his hand firmly.

'Get a move on,' shouts the Major, nervously. 'Let's get this over with!'

'That bastard ought to come over to us,' snarls Gregor, contemptuously. 'He'd soon be looking like a sieve.

'Backs to the posts,' orders the Major, kicking at the *Luftwaffe* Feldwebel's feet to get his heels close in to the post. Roughly he pulls the Feldwebel's arms behind the post.

'Tie here,' he orders me.

I vomit, all over his shiny boots. With a wild roar he jumps back.

'You'll *lick* those boots clean, as soon as we've finished here!'

With shaking hands I tie the Feldwebel's arms behind the execution post.

'Tighter,' shouts the Major, infuriated. 'What sort of a granny knot's that?'

He snatches the other rope from my hands, and ties the Feldwebel's feet himself.

'You're the wickedest bastard I've met yet,' says the Feldwebel, angrily, and spits straight in the Major's face.

'Are you mad, man?' screams the Major. 'This'll cost you – !' he stops, realizing that there is nothing he can do to the Feldwebel.

'You know, you're really funny!' says the condemned man, with contempt. 'Sooner or later somebody'll be tying *you* to a post!'

'That's where you're wrong,' snarls the Major, raging. 'That sort of thing only happens to nothings like you.' He turns on his heel and goes over to the next post where he helps Heide with the private soldier.

Then he examines the Oberst's bonds. Gregor has not tied him particularly well. He is obsessed with the idea of the Oberst making a run for it. The Major shouts and fumes at Gregor.

The condemned General he takes care of personally.

'Target cloths,' he shouts impatiently at the Old Man. 'Target cloths, man!' He is now so angry that he wants to do everything himself.

He snatches the cloths from the Old Man's hands and hangs them round the necks of the prisoners.

136

'Chaplain,' he shouts towards the witnesses, 'where the devil's he got to?'

The staff-chaplain comes tripping effeminately from the hut with a Bible in his hand.

'What the devil do you think you're here for?' shouts the Major, at white-heat.

Nervously the padre drops his Bible, picks it up and wipes it off. He mumbles something incomprehensible to each of the prisoners. Then he stumbles back into the hut as if wishing to hide himself.

'Ready, Feldwebel,' growls the Major, opening his pistol holster.

'Party! Ri-ight *dress*!' orders the Old Man, hoarsely.

Noisily they dress off. Tiny drops his rifle. He shrugs his shoulder and smiles apologetically to the Major who is red as a lobster.

'Eyes front! Standing aim!'

Another rifle rattles to the ground and the Westphalian falls forward, flat on his face.

'What a crowd of nervous old maids!' the Major rates them viciously. 'Weaklings! Pansies!'

'Fire!' orders the Old Man. The explosion sounds like an earthquake and shakes the entire Morellenschlucht.

The propaganda men's flash-bulbs go off like tiny streaks of lightning.

The infantry private sags against the ropes, his chest a mass of blood. The Westphalian lies unnoticed in the heather in a faint. The steel helmet has fallen from his head and is filling up with rain.

'Rifles – *load*!' orders the Old Man, looking away from the posts and out over the heath.

Locks rattle and a new cartridge is pushed home.

'Ta-ake *aim*!'

The spotlights turn on to the next post.

The Luftwaffe Feldwebel looks white as chalk in the sharp light. Even the blood-red drill of his prison uniform looks white.

'Fire!'

The rifles crash again, and the echo is thrown back from the earthwork at the opposite end.

The Feldwebel is tied so tightly to the post that he remains upright against it. His face looks horrible. A bullet has cut away

137

part of his upper lip and smashed his teeth and gums.

The lights go off, and for the third time the command sounds through the rain.

'Load! Ta-ake *aim*!'

The fingers of light settle on the Oberst, who stares into them with a jeering smile on his face. In that blaze of light he cannot see his executioners.

'Forgive us our trespasses,' mumbles the chaplain, hypocritically.

'Fire!'

The shots roar.

The Oberst sinks forward, hanging like a broken branch against the ropes.

It is getting darker. The lights go out and the rain is getting heavier. The wind whirls withered leaves across the execution place.

Tiny curses, a long vicious oath out into the rain.

The Major turns his head sharply and looks at him.

Tiny merely shrugs his shoulders.

The JAG officer goes over to General Wagner and says something to him, inaudible to anyone else.

The Major gives a sign to the Old Man.

'Ta-ake *aim*!' orders the Old Man.

The lights go on again.

The General smiles proudly.

'Fire!' the Old Man's order cracks above the sound of the rain.

The rifle muzzles swing about. Four in a row is too much. The shots come raggedly.

The General screams. Not one shot has been mortal. A couple of rifles clatter to the heather. Two men have fainted.

The Major shouts hysterically.

'Fire! Fire!'

The Old Man looks at him uncomprehendingly, doesn't know what to do. The whole squad has gone to pieces.

Porta and Tiny turn on their heels and go quietly off, with their rifles across their shoulders, like two duck-hunters on the way home.

Some flashes cut the night.

'Turn off those lamps,' screams somebody or other.

An Oberstabsarzt arrives at the double. The badly wounded General cries out nerve-shatteringly.

'Do some bloody thing, then,' shouts Barcelona, beside himself.

The Major looks confusedly at him. He is deathly pale. Then he pulls himself together, tears the blue-black Walther pistol from its holster, runs to the post and presses the barrel against the wounded General's neck. There is no shot, only a click.

The Major reels, staring at the pistol. His eyes have taken on a strange sheen. This is too much to bear, even for a hard-boiled MP officer.

The Old Man straightens up suddenly.

'Take *aim*!' he roars, madly.

The half-dazed squad takes aim.

The post can only be vaguely distinguished in the darkness. Nobody thinks to turn on the lights. The Old Man has his back to the post and is looking at the squad.

'Fire!' he shouts in a piercing voice.

The shots sound, but irregularly.

The Major gives out a long shrill scream and falls to the ground.

There is wild confusion amongst the witnesses. A group of staff officers with two Generals in the lead rush forward.

'Clear rifles, safety on, order arms!' orders the Old Man with well-trained Feldwebel precision.

The Generals come to a halt directly in front of the squad. They look confusedly first at us, then at the executed General hanging against his bonds, his chest shot to pieces. Then at the Major collapsed in a great pool of blood by the side of the post. His face is smashed and a large part of the neck has been blown away.

The Old Man cracks his heels together and carries his hand to the brim of his helmet.

'Herr General, orders carried out!'

'Thank you, thank you,' pipes the Infantry General, in confusion. He is still not quite certain what has happened.

The other General looks at the dead Major again.

'It was entirely his own fault,' he shouts defensively. 'According to regulations it is forbidden to walk in front of a firing squad! This must be regarded as a regrettable accident!'

'What about the mercy shots?' asks the medical officer.

An Oberstleutnant suddenly has a pistol in his hand. With firm steps he goes from post to post. Each time he stops a short wicked report is heard. The last is the General.

139

The Oberstleutnant looks down at the Major for a moment, before returning his pistol to its holster.

Two medical orderlies arrive with paper bags under their arms. With difficulty they push the bodies into the bags.

'Give us a hand, can't you?' they shout, irritably, to Porta and Tiny, who are standing talking to two Pioneers by the nearest lorry.

'Not our job,' Porta refuses sharply. 'We aren't garbage men!'

'Arseholes,' the orderlies shout at them.

'Want to try your luck?' asks Porta, cutting the pack into four in front of the Pioneers.

One puts down five marks, carefully, the other two marks.

'What the hell?' shouts Porta, contemptuously. 'Think this is a sewin' bee or somethin'? No bets under a ton here!'

'You must be nuts,' answers one of them, but puts down a hundred mark note as he says it.

Porta turns over the talon.

'You see,' he grins, as the Pioneer wins, 'easy ain't it?' He pushes two hundred marks over to him.

When they have won four times in a row, Porta suggests they put the lot in. 'Five hundred to one I'm offering,' he says with a false grin.

But the Pioneers daren't. They put down four hundred marks and win again.

'Sorry you didn't now, ain't you?' says Tiny slyly, patting a hundred mark note.

'Too bloody right I am,' says one of them, disappointedly, throwing everything he has in. Much more than he has already won.

'You goin' to, as well?' asks Tiny, giving the other soldier a shove.

He nods darkly and empties his pockets.

'What about you?' he asks, looking at Tiny.

'I feel funny about it,' says Tiny laying down a hundred marks.

Porta turns the pile. Ace of Spades.

The pioneers have a ten and a five. Tiny has a king.

'That's the way it goes,' sighs Porta, raking in the money. 'Why didn't you take a chance the round before? You'd have been rich men now. Well so long, then!' he says going towards the other lorry into which the squad is scrambling.

140

The orderlies throw the last of the bodies into the prison wagon. Doors bang and soon the vehicles have disappeared over the hill.

As soon as we arrive back at the barracks we are issued schnapps and a special food ration.

Chief Mechanic Wolf comes over to us. With his usual big boss manners he lights a huge cigar and blows the smoke into our faces.

'Wish it'd been you we'd turned off today,' says Porta in a friendly voice. 'I'd have shot your balls off personally!'

'Windy, are ye?' grins Wolf, wickedly. 'I'd be too, in your boots. Seems you lot've all got bonces full o' sawdust, you probably ain't realised yet how far you are up shit creek! When this war's over an' they reckon up accounts you lot'll most likely wind up gettin' shot!'

'What are we to understand by that?' asks the Old Man sharply. 'Who'd want to shoot us?'

'The Yanks maybe,' grins Wolf, happily, 'not to mention Ivan!'

'Shut up you wicked sod, you've got an imagination like a sick rat,' shouts Porta, uncertainly.

'Those bastards do the same thing themselves,' protests Gregor, angrily.

'Course they do,' smiles Wolf, devilishly, 'but who's gonna tell 'em that when they've won the war. Winners are always in the right. The losers've got hold of the shitty end of the stick! Wait and see! They'll tear your *balls* off for not refusin' to carry out that execution!'

'They can't do that,' protests Tiny loudly. 'I'd like to see where I'd be if I was to've told that Major I wasn't goin' to do it.'

'He'd've shot you up,' grins Wolf pleasantly.

'The other side knows that too,' says Barcelona uneasily, shivering already at the thought of peace which was turning from being a longing hope into a terrible threat.

'Course they know it,' answers Wolf maliciously, showing his strong well-cared for teeth in a broad smile. 'But *that* won't worry 'em. They've got to have somebody to take revenge on an' superfluous bastards like you are just right for the job!'

'They're not *like* that,' protests Gregor, with fear in his eyes.

'Heard the enemy radio?' smiles Wolf, knowingly, 'if you *had* then you'd be prayin' for this war to last a hundred years!'

141

'They must be crazy,' says the Old Man, worriedly.

'No more'n we are.' Wolf screams with laughter. 'I'm just glad I ain't been an executioner. Christ Almighty! But, if it's any consolation to you sons, I'll *be* there when they shoot you! I'll feel sorry for you, but you wouldn't ask me, would you, to break down *al*together when they send you to Valhalla with twelve orifices in your bodies!'

'Looks like we're going to have to do all we can to *win* this bloody war,' says Barcelona thoughtfully, pushing away his food.

His appetite has gone.

'From the day of my bleedin' birth, I've 'ad a kind of a intuition that life was as crazy as it was soddin' *wicked*,' says Tiny with conviction. He orders beer and schnapps and promises the canteen Gefreiter a beating up if he isn't back with them in two shakes.

We drown our fears in buckets of beer and vodka. Then we start mixing red wine in our beer and get there quicker.

It is late when we leave and walk singing across the barracks square.

Tiny leads us in the beeriest bass anybody has ever heard.

'Er wollte mal, er konnte nicht, ar hatt' ihn in der Hand,
da ist er voll Verzweiflung die Stube lang gerannt.
Er wollte mal, er konnte nicht, da Loch war viel zu klein ... *

---

* Er wollte etc.
  Freely translated.
  He *wanted* to, he *could* not, he *held* it in his hand!
  He *ran* around, and *up* and down, the *room* so fine and grand!
  He *wanted* to, he *could* not, the *hole* was much too small ...

142

By order of OKW* the delinquent was shot 27.12.1944 at 06.55 hrs. The sum of 100 reichsmarks was paid to Mrs Vera Bladel for assistance in the arrest.

Reinold, Major, Geheime Feldpolizei.

Two medical orderlies hold the bloody body firmly against the table. They press a first aid pack over his mouth to stifle his cries. All narcotics have been used up long ago. The Russian nurse hands the surgical instruments to the staff doctor.

'Hold the leg tightly,' he orders in a hollow voice.

Soon after the amputated leg is thrown on to a heap of other amputated parts.

'Dead,' the medical Feldwebel confirms, and looks up at the corpse-pale staff doctor, who makes a curt hand movement. The dead armoured corps soldier is thrown out, like a sack of garbage, on to an already sizeable pile of bodies. Early tomorrow morning they will be buried in a mass grave amongst the fir trees.

An ambulance column stops outside the *kolchos* which has been turned into a main first-aid post. A horrible smell, like that arising from a slaughter-house, billows around the ambulances. Groaning soldiers are dragged into the *kolchos*. A medical NCO sorts them out. The hopeless cases are pushed to one side. The others are carried into the operating room. But the majority *are* hopeless.

* OKW (Oberkommando der Wehrmacht) = Army High Command.

FLIGHT

In the course of the night the majority of prisoners, both the red and the green, are taken from their cells and marshalled in long rows.

Again and again a count is taken. The guards become more and more hysterical when the numbers do not agree with the books.

'Do you think they're going to mow us down in rows?' says an Unteroffizier in a whisper to the man alongside him.

Nobody answers. Nobody knows. Everyone fears the worst.

From all over the huge prison, prisoners stream, chased along by sharp orders, which echo back from the walls. After a long night of nervous waiting they are led at the double to the regimental stores where a dirty uniform without badges is thrown at them.

A demoted Unterfeldwebel grins sarcastically as he points to twelve roughly patched holes.

'The former owner died suddenly,' he states, drily.

'Punishment battalion,' mumbles a former Oberfeldwebel in green drill, as he accepts a uniform with large bloodstains on it.

'Death battalion,' a former Artillerie-wachtmeister in scarlet corrects him. 'Grave unit at the front line. The ones Ivan doesn't knock over are shot for fun!'

'For fun?' asks a green-clad Leutnant, narrowing his eyes.

'I said it, for *fun*,' answers the artilleryman. 'Their papers say – shot whilst attempting to escape – of course!'

'Those three chaps who escaped – last week were brought back by the "watchdogs" yesterday,' explains a Staff-Feldwebel, running a finger across his throat. 'They were crucified on the fence last night.' After a short pause he goes on. 'Nails through their hands and ankles, and they were left hanging

145

there to argue about which of them was Jesus and which the robbers!'

'Is that true?' asks an Oberstleutnant, who only missed being condemned to death by a hair.

'I saw it myself,' answers the Staff-Feldwebel, with a dry laugh. 'They made us march past them singing "Edelweiss". The sight of them was enough to make *us* lose any desire to make a try for it.'

'That crucifixion's the reason we're here,' says an SS officer in scarlet. 'Somebody's passed it on to the little doctor, and he doesn't like it. He knows how it'll be used if it gets to London. Propaganda soup! Even the SS Reichsführer's had to stand to attention before the little doctor cripple. The crucifiers were shot this morning, and we're being moved out at top-speed, so they can invite a commission of neutrals to inspect the place. They'll open the doors and show them nobody's being crucified *here*. Lies, all lies, the doctor'll say.'

'Preserve us,' mumbles a Leutnant in scarlet. 'How will it all end?'

'The thousand year Reich's complete downfall,' answers the Staff-Feldwebel, convincingly. 'But none of us are going to see it. They'll knock us off at five minutes to twelve, and they don't even trouble to conceal it.'

'Why don't you escape?' asks a rat-faced Gefreiter.

'You try, grins the Staff-Feldwebel, eyeing him up and down, contemptuously.

'Shut it, you dirty lice,' screams a guard Unteroffizier, throwing a bundle of equipment at a former Oberst.

'You'll soon've shut up, for ever an' ever amen,' grins the weapons Feldwebel, diabolically, hitting a former Major in the stomach. 'Believe me, you nothing, fourteen days from now your arse'll be cold as the balls on a dead polar bear.'

The permanent staff whinny happily, not because they are particularly bad men, but simply because they are glad to have their safe job at the depot.

'The whole lot's gonna get liquidated,' states a beery Oberge-freiter, kicking out at the nearest prisoner, an elderly man whose hair is quite white. 'What kind o' shithouse were you 'fore you got here?'

'Herr Obergefreiter, sir, I was a Generalmajor!'

'Did you hear him?' howls the fat Obergefreiter, enthu-

146

siastically. 'He was, God help us, a Generalmajor! But now you're only a shitty private, son, so get movin' off an' get yourself shot for *Führer Volk und Vaterland*!'

'My tunic's too small,' protests a former Rittmeister from over by the window.

'Cut down your rations the next three weeks,' the depot Feldwebel suggests, practically. 'Then you'll fit it!'

'He ain't gonna live that long,' grins the fat Obergefreiter. ''E'll've been off to Valhalla this long time, ridin' a blind nag.'

The Rittmeister pulls in his stomach despairingly, and manages with great difficulty to get his tunic buttoned. But he is unfortunate enough to lose two buttons in the process and to run into the arms of the duty officer without them.

'Hell man!' screams the young Leutnant. 'What're you doing, you missing link you, running around half-naked so even a blind vice squad cop'd be ashamed. Knock the wind out of him,' he orders the duty NCO.

Twenty minutes later the old Rittmeister drops dead of apoplexy.

In the course of the day the newly-uniformed unit is taken to Stettiner Bahnhof and locked into two large warehouses close to the goods yard.

An SS-Sturmbahnführer with the T-Division death's-head embroidered on his black collar-dogs tells them that they will be shot down without mercy if they make the slightest attempt to escape.

A little later they all realise where the trip is taking them. SS-Sonderbrigade Dirlewanger, the most infamous and horrifying military unit that has ever existed. Its commander, SS-Brigadeführer Dirlewanger, a former sexual criminal, was taken out of gaol and given command of this death unit, which operated mainly in Poland and the Ukraine under such sadistic circumstances as to be completely indescribable.

A cordon of heavily-armed SD* guards surround the warehouses. Every so often vicious machine-gun bursts rattle across the goods yard.

Shortly after the tower clock has chimed four, an air-raid signal sounds, and several bombs fall close to the railway area.

'Let's get to the cellars,' shouts a former Feldwebel, hysterically, 'or do you *want* us to get slaughtered here?'

* SD (Sicherheitsdienst) = Security Service.

147

'Why not?' grins the guard, swinging his machine-pistol round in a way which cannot be misunderstood. 'Swine like you don't deserve any better!' He is a very young soldier, the most dangerous kind, particularly for prisoners. 'On your back, dung. Get your thievin' fingers behind your neck! Move an inch an' I'll let the shit out of your head for you!'

The Feldwebel obeys the order to lay down, certain that the young hooligan would be only too happy to make his threat good.

Oberleutnant Wisling glances at his neighbour, a demoted staff M.O.

'What about making a run for it?' he whispers without moving his lips.

'How could we?' answers the M.O. staring straight in front of him. 'Try to go out of that door, and your escape'd be over before you'd gone two steps!'

'We don't use the door,' whispers Wisling. 'We'll wait till the transport moves off, when there's always some confusion.'

Dr Menckel draws a deep breath.

'It's hopeless. But if it's to come off at all it's got to be here in Berlin.'

'You're right. When we get to the Dirlewanger Brigade, escape'll be impossible,' says Wisling. 'There we couldn't even desert. The guerrillas make a quick end of anybody coming from Dirlewanger's murder brigade.'

'Fall in!' roars a Feldwebel in a ringing voice, rolling the heavy door to one side. 'At the double, you wicked lot! *Move*, you bastards!' Those who are closest to him get a blow from the butt of his weapon.

Unteroffiziers chase up and down the column of threes counting away for dear life. Three companies have been made up to make things easier but, as usual, the tally doesn't agree. Now there are a couple too many. Then there are a few missing.

The SS-Sturmbahnführer from T-Division rages and swears. Prisoners who get in his way are felled brutally to the earth.

A little way off a locomotive shunts and whistles along, hauling a long train of cattle wagons. The openings are blocked with heavy barbed-wire. Through the open doors the floor of the wagons can be seen, covered with a thin layer of straw. Typical prisoner transport wagons of the new era. They even move horses better.

'Our train, I think,' mumbles the Staff-Feldwebel with a death's-head grin.

'Muss i denn, muss i denn
zum Städtele hinaus,'

hums a tall, powerful Obergefreiter with a face covered with the scars of shell splinters.

'Fifty men to a wagon,' orders an SS officer, pointing to the cattle trucks.

The Unteroffiziers tally the men in. The first party is already on its way across the tracks, covered by machine-pistol muzzles.

'There's our chance,' whispers Wisling, pointing guardedly towards the fence to the right of the warehouse. 'It's a six or seven foot jump. Then we'll be under cover. Come *on*,' he hisses, pushing the doctor roughly, as the two guards turn round, called back by the SS-Obersturm-Bahnführer by the water tower.

Like lightning they go down and crawl in under the warehouse.

'Bloody quick thinking!' cries the big Obergefreiter with the scarred face. 'It'll cost you your coconuts though, when they get you again!'

But they don't hear his remark. At breakneck speed they cross the coal heaps and crawl under a shunting train. Menckel stumbles, but Wisling pulls him back before the wheels can cut him in two.

A railway shunter looks down at them from his brakehouse, swinging a lamp up and down. The wheels scream and whine. The train stops with a rattling crash and begins to back. Shortly after the locomotive passes, spurting steam, and they disappear in the heavy mist.

'We're saved,' whispers the doctor breathlessly. 'God in heaven! We're saved!'

'Not yet,' mumbles Wisling, beginning to run down towards the canal.

Shouted orders are heard not far behind them. They go rigid with fear. Are they on their track already, these blood-thirsty carnivores.

Shouts sound in the dark. An Mpi rattles viciously in two short bursts. Shadowy figures hasten down the rows of goods wagons.

'Quick,' pants Wisling, catching Menckel by the arm.

They jump over a low gate, and sneak along the subway terminus. Some railwaymen look at them curiously. From the block station somebody shouts something, but when an express comes thundering along they realise that it was merely a warning to them to get off the line before they were crushed under the hurtling train.

'That would have been the right train for us,' says Wisling with a smile, pointing at the destination boards on the coaches. BERLIN–WARNEMUNDE–GEDSER–KOPENHAGEN. 'From Copenhagen to Sweden is only a short journey.'

'The Swedes would send us back as deserters,' says Menckel, gloomily. 'In Fort Zitta there were three the Swedes had turned over.'

'We could say we were Jews,' thinks Wisling, optimistically. 'Many do. They don't send *them* back.'

When they turn the corner by the double turntable they see a chilly SS guard, leaning up against the door of a warehouse.

'That's our man,' says Wisling in a hard voice, picking up a piece of rail from a heap of scrap.

The guard is half asleep on his feet with his collar up around his ears. The wind whistles past the brim of his steel helmet. He shivers and sinks deeper into his greatcoat. It is a cold, wet night.

A cigarette glows revealingly in his cupped hand. Each time he takes a draw at it he turns his head in towards a corner so that the glow will not betray him to anybody sneaking around checking on the sentries.

Under cover of the heavy darkness Wisling creeps silently closer to him.

From the other side Menckel comes tip-toeing with a piece of wood as a club in his hand. As the sentry turns again into the doorway, and the cigarette glows brighter, Wisling brings the steel rail down with all his might.

The SS soldier slumps down with the back of his head smashed in. Not a sound comes from him. Killed on the spot. The cigarette rolls along the wall and the wind sweeps it away over the tracks, where it fizzles out in a puddle.

'God preserve us,' groans Menckel, pulling the dead man's greatcoat away from his face and revealing a boy not more than eighteen years of age. 'What times we live in!'

'He'd have shot us dead on the spot if he'd seen us first,' answers Wisling, roughly.

Menckel puts on the greatcoat and the steel helmet. Wisling takes the tunic and buckles the belt carrying the 08 around his waist.

Menckel slings the Mpi on his shoulder. The absence of a belt is not too noticeable. Sometimes a soldier will wear his greatcoat loose over his uniform without a belt, especially in rainy weather like this particular night.

'There'll be the devil to pay when they find him,' says Wisling, nervously. 'There'll be a hell of an alarm set off immediately!'

'Wouldn't it be better to drop him in the canal?' suggests Menckel, shuddering. 'Then they'll think he's deserted. It could be several days before he turns up in one of the locks. There are so many bodies floating around just now.'

They take one end each, swing him a couple of times to and fro like a sack, and send him flying out into the muddy waters of the canal where he disappears with a loud splash.

'I've got friends here in Berlin,' says Menckel, as they cross Uhlandsstrasse. 'We can hide with them and get some civilian clothing before we continue our flight.'

'Yes, we need civilian clothing more than anything,' says Wisling. 'Uniforms are no good when you're on the run.'

The air-raid warnings begin to howl again. Even before they have finished sounding, flak is going up and nervous fingers of light waver across the gloomy heavens.

An air-raid warden shouts at them in a rough voice, but becomes servile at the sight of the SS uniforms.

Explosions shake the houses, and yellow-red flames lick up towards the sky. A fire engine roars through the dark, deserted street. An entire wall crashes down across the road.

A stick of bombs falls in a neighbouring street, splashing fire over the walls.

'Phosphorus,' confirms Wisling, covering his eyes.

By Lüneburger Strasse an amphibian with four MPs turns the corner. The flames of phosphorous reflect from their shiny headhunter badges.

Wisling springs lightly into a doorway, pulling Menckel with him. They cock their weapons, fully determined to shoot their way free, if it comes to it. Capture means certain death, and in all probability a slow and horrible one.

The amphibian's motor purrs like a wheedling cat, and comes slowly closer. The spotlight by the windshield searches along the walls of the houses, down cellar steps, in gateways. The MPs know where to look for their prey.

Restraining their breathing, and with weapons ready, Wisling and Menckel press themselves up against the soot-blackened wall, and stare in terror at the amphibian which has stopped right outside the gateway in which they are hiding.

One of the 'watchdogs' swings his boots over the side. His grey raincoat is shining with water. He cocks his Mpi noisily, switches on the field lamp on his chest, and is half-way to the gate when a shouted order recalls him. In one jump he is back in the amphibian which swings round and with motor roaring races back in the direction of Lüneburger Strasse.

An Mpi barks, long and wickedly. A scream echoes between the dark houses. A few short, shouted orders, a loud, satisfied burst of laughter and everything is quiet again.

A carpet of bombs falls over by Charlottenburg. Phosphorus spurts towards the sky. The ghostly ruins throw long shadows in the cruel light of the flames.

The covered bus-stop at Litzenburger Platz is thrown high into the air, balancing on the tip of a tongue of flame, and two human bodies are thrown fierily from the traffic control kiosk as the rest of it falls, in a rain of pulverised brick dust, back to the ground.

A writing-desk sails through the air, completely unharmed, and is shattered to tiny pieces against the Hercules Bridge. A red telephone flies onwards. A conductor's black cape glides across the street and lands, softly as a bird, on the murky waters of the Landewehr-Kanalen. Bombs carpet the Lüneburger Strasse, where Wisling and Menckel stand in hiding. The shrill whistle of their stabilising fins cuts into the very marrow of their bones.

'Let's get out of here,' gasps Menckel. 'If we stay here we're finished!'

As fast as they can go they run across the Spree Bridge at Helgoland-Ufer. An aerial torpedo falls in front of them and sends a whole row of houses up into the air.

Through the roar of the explosives the strange grating sound of the incendiary bombs can be heard. It ends with a sound like a tin full of paint hitting a concrete yard.

In seconds the whole street is ablaze. Phosphorus flows down into the cellars. People run, burning, panic-stricken, through the night directly into the sea of flame. They sizzle and shrink to charred caricatures of humanity.

High above the burning town rumble the heavy Wellington bombers. Inside them, youthful airmen work like automatons unloading their deadly cargo. Not one of them thinks for a moment of what is happening down there in the blacked-out city, where thousands of human beings are burning to death. They are looking forward to getting back to their bases, somewhere in Scotland, where bacon and eggs and a nice hot cup of tea are waiting for them.

As soon as the first bombing wave has released its load, and turned noses towards the north, a new wave of Wellingtons comes in from the north-west and again Berlin is carpeted with bombs. Fifteen–sixteen-year-old boys serve the flak-guns. They work until they drop or until fragmentation bombs or incendiaries put an end to them.

The queen of the guns, the 8.8 cm flak gun, thunders unceasingly. One attack in depth silences the four flak batteries by the Zoo. Nothing is left of them. They are reduced to dust. A few moments ago they were spitting out shells defiantly. Now a great bonfire of phosphorus roars in their place, engulfing everything.

An SD patrol turning in from the riding path is thrown into the air and disappears into the furnace.

An old man with two artificial legs lies under a bridge and watches the terrible scene through a crack in the concrete. When he is found the heat has melted him down to the size of a monkey. There is nothing left of his artificial legs. They throw him up on to the corpse wagon in company with other shrivelled-up mummies, as they do every morning in Berlin.

'We'll be there soon,' mumbles Menckel hoarsely, pushing into a half-collapsed ruin.

They catch sight of an SD patrol at the far end of the street, slinking along the walls of the houses in search of victims.

'Where the devil did they get to?' whispers Wisling, furiously. The patrol has disappeared as if it had sunk into the earth.

'I think they're in that gateway over there keeping an eye on us,' Menckel says, pressing himself hard against the wall.

'If they cross the street and come towards us, we open fire,' says Wisling, going down on his knees. There is a narrow niche in the wall into which he can press himself.

'We'll never make it,' stammers Menckel, holding his Mpi at the ready.

'Think we ought to put up our hands and let them hang us on the nearest lamp-post,' growls Wisling, jeeringly. 'Those boys won't give us a chance. They ask one question: Papers! And if you haven't got any you get it in the back of the neck or get to dangle from a lamp-post with a card on your chest saying:

ICH HABE DEN FÜHRER VERRATEN!*

'They're nothing but crazy murderers,' whispers Menckel in a voice shaking with rage.

'What's it matter?' smiles Wisling. 'I do believe every one of us is more or less crazy just now. Even our escape is crazy!'

A stick of bombs falls with a roar in the street next to them. The flame of the explosions lights up clearly the faces of the SD patrol across the street. They look like faces chiselled in stone.

'Get on,' snarls a voice accustomed to giving orders and being obeyed, and the death patrol moves off hugging the smoke-blackened walls. One hand holds the magazine firmly, the other is at the neck of the butt with a finger on the trigger.

The patrol has not gone more than a few yards down Leipziger Strasse when a series of shots crack through the dark, followed by a brusque, metallic command.

'Halt! Hände hoch!'†

Two women step out in the middle of the road and lift their hands above their heads.

Greedily the SD patrol surrounds them. They laugh, and sound like a party of satisfied hunters who have just brought down a long-sought-for animal.

'You ladies been out plundering?' asks the patrol commander, squeezing one eye shut slyly, as if he had said something amusing.

'Herr Oberscharführer,' stammers one of the women.

He smashes the back of his hand brutally across her face, knocking her over backwards.

Her shopping bag slides across the asphalt and two packets of butter and a bag of flour fall from it.

Practised hands search her friend. Two rings, a necklace and

* Ich habe etc. (German) = I have betrayed the Führer.
† Halt! etc. (German) = Halt! Hands up!

a packet of ration coupons are found in her pockets. Explanations and excuses pass unheard.

'String 'em up,' orders the Oberscharführer, and points to an ancient lamp-post from the time of the Kaiser.

'Come on, girls,' grin the two young SD men. 'Up you go and enjoy the view.'

A long-drawn female scream echoes down the street, back and forth from the houses in Spitaler Markt.

'Shut up, you bitch, cut that screaming *out*!' scolds an SS man.

Soon the two women hang kicking alongside one another from the antique lamp-post.

Nonchalantly the Oberscharführer hangs a card around their necks:

ICH HABE GEPLÜNDERT*

The SD patrol sneaks on its way across Spitaler Markt, and stops for a moment outside 'DER GELBE BÄR'.† One of them tries the door but it is locked.

'Damnation,' he swears viciously. 'I could have done with a couple of cold beers an' a shot just now! One of those bitches pissed on me!'

'They always do. Fear!' says one of the others.

They do not hear the bomb on its way. It is one of the small ones which do not make much noise. The just have time to flinch from the enormous flash of flame before the blast throws them straight through the wall behind them.

The Oberscharführer does not die immediately. He looks down in surprise at his legs, torn off and lying beside him. He opens his mouth and screams. A long howl like an animal. Then he is dead.

'That's where my friend's wife lives,' says Menckel, as they pass Alexander Platz just at dawn. 'We were in the same regiment. He was the OC. Let's hurry there.'

'No,' says Wisling. 'It's too late now. We must wait until it gets dark again. If the caretaker sees us we've had it. He *has* to tell the SD if strangers enter the house.'

'Those bastards,' groans Menckel, 'they've got their spies everywhere!'

* Ich etc. (German) = I have been looting!
† Der etc. (German) = The Golden Bear.

They move instinctively closer to one another when the sirens blow the all-clear.

People come up from cellars, hastening along with grey, tired faces. Their eyes are bloodshot, their faces smudged with smoke and dust.

'Let's get away from here,' says Wisling, pulling Menckel after him into a maze of small backyards.

In the middle of the labyrinth of tunnels and corridors they find an ancient half-timbered house. A low door, half rotted away, leads down to a cellar.

For a moment they stand listening in the darkness. Far inside a cat miaows. Silently they creep forward, feeling their way through the dark. The cat miaows again.

Wisling bangs his head against one of the low beams. He curses viciously, biting his lip in pain.

A long way off a faint light flickers.

'Look out,' whispers Wisling, stopping so suddenly that Menckel runs into him. 'There's somebody there. Stay here and keep me covered with the Mpi!'

The cat miaows again, complainingly. It's eyes shine in ghostly fashion in the dark. It comes slowly towards them, looks up at Wisling, purrs and rubs itself against his legs.

In the flickering light they catch sight of an old woman lying on a heap of sacks and straining her eyes to see them in the dark. An acrid stench of damp and half-rotted wood reaches them.

'Anybody there?' cries the old woman in a piping, asthmatic voice. '*Is* there anybody?' she repeats.

'Yes,' says Wisling, stepping forward.

The woman stares at him suspiciously.

'What do you want?' she asks and goes into a violent attack of coughing which for a moment seems close to choking her.

'Can we stay here until it gets dark?' asks Wisling, when her asthma attack is over.

'You're welcome,' she smiles tiredly. 'There's nobody here but me and my cat.'

Wisling looks around the stinking cellar, which has formerly been used for coal and coke. Now there is no coal and only a bucket of coke a day to a flat.

'Do you live down here?' asks the doctor, in amazement, looking down at the old woman. Her skin is the horrible blue-grey colour which people get who stay too long in the dark.

'You could say that,' answers the old woman, with a tiny smile. 'I lived in the house above for seventy-six years, but when they'd taken all my family, and I was the only one left, I took shelter down here. Now they haven't been here for a long time. One of the neighbours told me I'd been declared dead. He's a soldier, too old to be sent to the front, so he's been put on service in Berlin. He's one of the few who aren't frightened to bring food down to me.' She collapses in a new violent attack of coughing.

Menckel helps her, and wipes the sweat from her face.

'Don't you get any medicine?' he asks, naïvely.

'No,' she smiles sadly. 'Can't you see? I'm a Jew! There's no medicine for us. It's no wonder people are afraid to help us. They kill people who give us food. These are *bad* times.'

'Yes, they are indeed bad times!' agrees Menckel. 'Sick times!'

'God of my fathers,' she cries in a muffled shout, as she realises that the strangers are wearing SS uniform.

'Have mercy on me, poor thing as I am!' The words come in stammering bursts. 'God is my witness I never did a bad thing to anyone, dead or alive.' She strains for breath. Her chest whistles; her lungs wheeze. 'Both my daughters' men fell at the front and the rest of my family you have taken from me long since.'

'Easy, easy,' says Menckel, 'we are not SS. The uniforms mean nothing. We are escaped prisoners.'

Steps sound from the street. All three listen, wild-eyed with fear.

'The dustmen,' says the old woman, after having listened for a time in silence.

Berlin is awake again. People throng the streets on their way to factories and workshops. Between air-raids they work hard. To stay away from work without valid reason is regarded as sabotage. Twice in a row brings the death penalty.

'Are you the only one of your family left?' asks Wisling, looking compassionately at the old woman.

'Yes, all the rest are gone. Whether they're dead or not I don't know. I've never heard from them since they were taken.'

'It is terrible to be a Jew in Germany today,' says Menckel.

'I don't suppose there are many left,' sighs the old woman. 'The soldier who brings me food says that there used to be long goods trains filled with Jews going east. Now they've stopped.

So maybe there are no more Jews to be sent. And what are we anyway? Just ordinary Germans like yourselves. My family has always been German and lived here. My parents. My grandparents. Many of them were officers in the army of the Kaiser. My husband was in the 1st Grenadier Guards Regiment and fought for Germany from 1914 to 1918. Three times badly wounded. After the war he worked in a Ministry until they said he was an *untermensch* and sacked him in 1933. Then he shot himself. When they came for him that evening there was only a body. They spat on him. Called him "cowardly Jewish pig!" They crushed the medals the Kaiser had given to him under their jackboots. Yes, we are Germans. From Berlin. We have always lived here. I love this town,' she says, and smiles dreamily. 'It was such a *happy* city, but now it is sick and will die. As will I. Before we used to sail on the Spree every Sunday and dance in the Grünewald. Then that was forbidden to us.'

For a while there is silence. They listen tensely to the many sounds which filter down from the street.

'I think you would do best to get rid of those uniforms,' says the old woman suddenly. 'I know a man who hid in such a uniform. When they caught him they killed him slowly, smashed every bone in his body. His terrible screams could be heard all over the house. Nobody dared to go to his aid. We heard them hitting him, until there was no more life left in him. And he was such a handsome young man. A man we all liked. It was stupid of him to come back here. They caught him in the yard. Perhaps they would not have killed him if he had not been wearing that SS uniform. They were like wild beasts when they saw it. You must get rid of those uniforms. Do you not know anyone who will give you civilian clothes?'

'I hope so,' says Menckel. 'We shall make a try when it gets dark.'

'If they had not taken my boys' clothes you could have had them, but they said they were confiscated for the use of the state.'

Menckel knocks his helmet off. It goes clattering across the floor. The cat spits and arches its back.

'In gaol?' she says, seeing his shaven poll.

They both nod. That is where they have been.

'Get out of Berlin,' she says. 'Yes, best out of Germany altogether. Here they will soon catch you!'

'She is absolutely right,' mumbles Wisling. 'We *must* get

hold of some civilian clothes, even if we have to strip somebody in the street.'

Shortly after noon the air-raid warning sounds again. Now it is the Americans coming over in their Flying Fortresses. The bombs rain down close by. Explosions roar. The old house shakes and shivers. A thick cloud of mortar dust covers them.

For a moment they think the house is falling in on top of them. A few hours later it is over and the sirens sound the all-clear.

Up in the street a company of soldiers marches by singing:

> Die blauen Dragonen, sie reiten
> mit klingendem Spiel durch das Tor . . .

They hear sounds from the street and the cellar door is kicked open noisily.

'Anybody here?' shouts a hoarse voice.

They can see him clearly in the open door, an air-raid warden in blue overalls and black steel helmet.

'Answer up, damn you! Anybody here?'

The cat gives out a loud, long miaow.

'What was that?' asks another warden, taking a couple of steps down the cellar stairs.

The cat goes miaowing towards them. Then it sits down and begins to wash itself.'

'A cat, a bloody, bleedin' cat,' says one of them and bangs the cellar door to.

Wisling thinks it is best for Menckel to visit his friends alone. It is important that he is not observed. His friends may not live there any more. Anything is possible in Berlin at present. The flat can have been taken over by the party. It wouldn't be pleasant if a golden pheasant* were to answer the door. Displaced persons might have been quartered on them, leaving the family only one room to themselves. Long columns of refugees are continually entering the town. They must be given a roof over their heads and those without connections within the party are soon merely accepted in their own homes.

'If I'm not back inside two hours,' says Menckel, 'you'll have to consider I've been caught and get out as fast as possible.'

As soon as darkness arrives Menckel is on his way. Adroitly he avoids the patrols out on the hunt, moving quickly from gateway to gateway. He holds the Mpi cocked and ready, firmly

* golden pheasant = High-ranking Nazi party member.

159

determined not to allow himself to be taken alive. He curses the SS uniform. It makes his task ten times more difficult.

The house is an old, patrician building from around the turn of the century. In the gateway is a board with brass nameplates. It is an upper-class residence.

For a while he observes the house from a gateway across the street. He can see down into the porter's basement room where a middle-aged woman, who resembles a watchful rat, is sitting. Her pointed nose moves continually from side to side. She is one of those horrible people who seem to have eyes in the back of their head. No help can be expected from her. Before 1933 she was certainly as red as she is brown now. And it wouldn't cost her a minute's consideration to change back to red again tomorrow. Always on the side of the ruling class, ready for any kind of dirty business as long as it is to her own advantage. There are thousands and thousands of her kind around.

When she disappears for a moment into a back room he slips rapidly through the gateway and up the carpeted staircase. Arriving at the second floor he knocks gently on the door. He is about to press the bell but thinks better of it. It could be connected to an alarm system in the porter's basement.

After some time a woman's voice asks, in a low tone, 'What do you want?'

Nobody opens their door in Berlin any more without knowing who is waiting on the other side of it.

'Who is it?' repeats the woman.

'Albert Menckel,' he whispers, his mouth close to the door.

For a moment there is a heavy silence.

'Frau Peters, I have a message from your husband,' he whispers impatiently, throwing a nervous glance back down the stairs, as if expecting the portress's rat-like face to appear. If it does he has only one choice. To kill her. Quickly and silently so that none of the dwellers in the building observe anything.

'Frau Peters, open the door! It's very important.'

The door is opened a little, but is still held by two chains.

A pale, female face appears behind the narrow opening.

'Menckel! I thought you were dead long ago!' Then she sees the SS uniform, and stiffens.

'Open the door, hurry *up*, and I'll explain everything,' he whispers, desperately.

'No, go away, go!' she stammers, in almost a shout, 'I don't want to get mixed up in anything!'

'You *must* let me in. My life is at stake. You are my last hope.'

She makes to close the door, but his foot blocks the opening. For a moment he considers forcing an entrance by putting his shoulder to the door.

She begins to cry.

'What do you want here? You'll get me into terrible trouble! Take away your foot or I'll give the alarm!'

'Open the *door*! Just for a moment! I promise you I'll leave immediately. Hurry, let me in before anybody sees me!'

She stares at him, terrified, and opens her mouth as if about to scream. Suddenly she nods.

He takes away his foot. The chains jingle, and the door is opened just enough to allow him to enter. With shaking hands she locks the door again and puts up the chains. She stares at him with fear in her eyes. The rain-wet steel helmet, the slate-grey SS greatcoat, the machine-pistol with its long magazine.

'You said you had a message from my husband?' she asks, doubtfully, pulling her kimono more tightly around her.

'No, I only said that to get you to open the door. I haven't seen Kurt since I was arrested.' He looks across the room, at a painting of his friend Kurt Peters, carried out shortly before the commencement of the war.

'Then it *is* a long time since you have seen him,' she whispers. 'It is almost two years since we heard you had been executed. Did you know your wife is soon to be married?'

He shrugs his shoulders. What does it matter now? What does Gertrud matter? She's let him down. Witnessed against him, said whatever they wanted her to say. They had threatened her, of course. They did that to everybody, even the children. You didn't have to spend long in the cellars at Prinz Albrechts Strasse before you were softened up. They always had something ready there which could drive a witness into a state of terror.

In a few words he tells her what has happened, begs her to shelter him and Wisling until they can continue on their way.

'I daren't,' she stammers. 'Here the walls have eyes and ears.'

'Nobody saw me come in,' he states confidently.

'We don't *know* that,' she says, nervously, looking despairingly at the carpet, as if she were trying to count every thread in it.

'Just for one night,' he pleads. 'We'll leave as soon as we've got hold of some civilian clothes.'

'I dare not,' she repeats. 'If you and your friend are found here, it means a death sentence for me. It has just happened to another woman who lived a little further along the street. She was beheaded,' she added, shivering.

'I know we are putting you in great danger,' he says, gently, 'but you are our only hope. We shall go as soon as we have civilian clothes.'

'Have you any papers?' she asks, nervously.

'Not yet. I know where I can get some, but I can't go there until tomorrow. If you will take us in, until we have got hold of papers and civilian clothes, I will never forget you for it.'

She shakes her head.

'I have three small children. They will take them from me and put them in an NS-camp* where they will teach them to hate their own mother, tell them I was a traitor to the people, and have received a well-deserved punishment.'

She takes a few steps up and down the floor, thinking, looks in at the children, then sits down on a chair in front of an antique writing-table.

'God in Heaven, what shall I do,' she moans, her hand going to her throat. 'I cannot hand you over to those devils!' She looks at him for a long time in silence, fingers a paperknife shaped like a bayonet, gets up, goes to the blacked-out windows and parts the black curtain slightly and stares down into the street. An amphibian drives slowly past. Four steel helmets, shiny with rain, gleam from it.

She turns round quickly, after having seen to it that the curtains are closely drawn. The least trace of light will bring a patrol thundering on the door.

'Will you give me your word of honour to leave here tomorrow morning, before it becomes light? And if you are caught will you promise never to tell that you have been in touch with me?'

'I give you my word. I have been tortured before, and I know what I can stand.'

'Very well, you can stay here tonight. Fetch your friend, but for heaven's sake be careful not to be seen! The portress here is

* NS-camp = Nazi Children's Camp.

162

a devil. I'll turn out some of Kurt's clothes for you whilst you are gone.'

'Thank-you,' he mumbles and slips quickly through the door. Like a shadow he moves down the stairs and out of the gateway.

Some way down the street he catches sight of an MP patrol, and jumps into hiding in a cellarway. The three MPs pass by with heavy tread. The half-moon badges on their chests glint warningly.

A few yards further on they check two soldiers on their way on leave with pack and slung rifles. Their uniforms are faded and still smell of the front line. Meticulously the MPs examine their papers, dates, stamps and unit designations. The photograph in the small grey identity book is carefully compared with the soldiers. The identity tags round their necks do not escape the punctilious examination of the MPs. Live rounds are counted. Does the date on the delousing certificate agree with the date of departure on leave?

Almost twenty minutes pass before the 'watchdogs' are satisfied. None of the people in the street take any notice of them. Everyone has enough to do looking after himself. If those two are deserters then it's *their* bad luck.

'*Hals – und Beinbruch*,' grins the MP Feldwebel, bringing his hand up to the brim of his helmet.

The two soldiers smack their heels together resoundingly and salute rigidly. They know the MPs can ruin their leave if they are not satisfied with their appearance.

'Bastards,' whispers one of them and the MPs. 'When this bloody war's over, I'll smash in the skull of every "watchdog" I meet!'

'Like buggery you will,' says the other. 'They'll always be there. The new bosses'll have a use for "watchdogs", *and* for the stinking coppers too.'

Menckel goes on down the street a little easier in his mind. Tomorrow they'll have civilian clothes and papers and in twenty-four hours they'll be a long way from Berlin. With luck out of Germany. After the war he will make sure Frau Peters is rewarded for her bravery.

Outside the artist's restaurant on Kemperplatz there is a long queue of soldiers and civilians. It is an oasis in Berlin where the war can be forgotten. In the street the sound of the weeping violins can be heard. But Menckel has no ears for gipsy music.

Twice more he has to take cover from police patrols. He almost runs into the middle of a big raid. With shouts following him he disappears through several backyards and over a couple of fences. Before he realises it he is on Alexander Platz. A well-dressed gentleman with a monocle throws a cigarette butt away. Thoughtlessly, Menckel picks it up.

A street-sweeper looks at him in amazement. SS men don't usually scavenge for butts. He waves violently to a *Schupo*** who saunters over to him. The arms of the Reich glitter menacingly from his helmet.

Menckel notices the street-sweeper pointing after him and talking to the policeman. Quickly he turns down the first side street and runs for all he is worth. Panting he reaches the street where Wisling awaits him.

A grey Kübel is parked outside the house. An SS soldier in slate-grey uniform leans up against one of the fenders.

'God in Heaven,' he groans. 'What's up now?' In terror he presses his body into a niche in the wall. Is it the two in the cellar or somebody else from the house?

The sirens begin to howl. Air-raid. Almost immediately bombs begin to fall. But the SS man leaning against the Kübel seems not to notice them. Carelessly he lights a cigarette and puffs out a cloud of smoke. He does not even look at the heavens from which bombs are raining down. He is accustomed to it.

Four slate-grey uniformed figures with black collar-dags come from the gateway. Laughing, they throw a bundle into the back of the Kübel. An arm dangles over the side. The four soldiers jump aboard and it disappears with a roar into the darkness.

As soon as they are gone Menckel dashes headlong into the yard and down into the cellar.

'Wisling,' he shouts, fearfully. 'Where are you?'

The cat comes miaowing from the darkness, and rubs itself lovingly against his leg. He picks it up and strokes its soft grey fur. It purrs happily, and sniffs his face in recognition.

'What's happened?' he asks, scratching behind its ears. 'You've seen it, but you don't understand it. You still think all human beings are good.'

He goes on searching along the dark cellar corridor, falls over a plank, finds the stub of a candle on the floor and lights

* Schupo (Schutzpolizist) = Civilian police.

164

it cautiously. The sacks are spread about all over the cellar. A dented blue enamel pot, containing some remnants of food, stands in a corner. The old woman is lying over by the wall. Her face has been kicked out of recognition and one arm is broken. The bone sticks out, sharp as a needle.

Further down the corridor is an SS side-cap. Wisling must have thrown it there without them seeing him. Now he knows what has happened. The thought paralyses him. It seems as if this whole devilish world has fallen in on him. He hopes Wisling is dead. It is impossible to imagine what the SS men will do to him. An escaped prisoner in *their* uniform! An unforgiveable crime! And they will certainly find out to whom the uniform belonged.

He puts the cat down on the ground. It follows him all the way to the door. Then it miaows and disappears into the cellar and creeps close to the old woman's body.

The brilliant white light of a flare breaks out like a Christmas tree straight up above the half-timbered house. He looks up and shudders. Slowly the marker approaches the ground swaying slightly with the wind. Bombs fall where there are Christmas trees. He hears the piercing howl of stabilisers and throws himself back into the cellar, falls, and crawls desperately further inside. The cat jumps, spitting, out of the way.

The explosions thunder and roar incessantly. A beam breaks and splinters spray the room. Half the ceiling falls in in a cloud of dust. The yard door flies inwards like a piece of paper in a storm. He coughs and feels as if he is suffocating. There is smoke and dust everywhere. He listens fearfully. Through the noise of the bombs a strange, hollow roaring sound can be heard.

He knows what it is. It is the heat, the all-destroying heat which precedes the flames of the phosphorus bombs.

The house sways like a ship in a hurricane. The cat is crushed under a beam, and its blood spurts over his face. The old woman's body is buried under a heap of bricks. A cloud of brickdust rushes at him like a clenched fist. The fire-wall between this and the neighbouring house has been blown away. He looks inside. A number of bodies lie in a twisted heap. There is blood everywhere. Flames come licking through the cracks in the walls. Then comes a wave of heat, roaring like a giant vacuum-cleaner. He is sucked up and thrown straight

165

through a board wall into the flat next door. He goes unconscious for a moment and then slowly comes to.

He looks around him confusedly, wipes his hand across his forehead and finds it full of blood. The steel helmet is gone but he still holds Wislin's side-cap in his hand. Dizzily he gets up and goes into the kitchen. He pushes his head under the tap and drinks like a thirsty animal.

Hot air, searingly hot air, throws him to the floor. A hellish noise roars all around him. There is no fire, only an awful heat.

What has happened now has happened often before. Another bomb has blown away the fire started by the first.

He stumbles over a dead Hauptmann. The body seems to move, but it is the heat. He looks down at himself. An SS greatcoat without a belt. He has lost the Mpi. In the stifling heat and hellish noise he pulls the uniform from the dead man. He is an elderly man with a belly and the uniform is far too large. The cap falls down over his ears. He pushes some half burnt cloth under the sweat-band. In the left tunic pocket are the dead man's papers. Hauptmann Alois Ahlfeldt, 5 Geheime Feldpolizei-Bataillon. He cannot help smiling despite his fear and agitation. Everywhere he runs into policemen. He buckles the yellow officer's belt and the pistol round his waist. Anybody can see the uniform is not his but it is still better than the SS uniform. It is an officer's uniform. All Germans respect an officer. Most patrols were commanded by an Unteroffizier who would think twice before stopping him.

Quickly he jumps down to the next landing where a wall of flame rages at him. Doors and walls are already blackening, the paint blistering and burning with small oily flames. He rushes headlong down a long corridor. The flames follow him hungrily up the stairwell enclosing him in a furnace of fire, but a colossal vacuum sucks him out of the house.

Bodies burn with blue and yellow flames. The street is an inferno. The curious scraping sound of the incendiaries raining down from the skies can be heard continually. The heat comes up through the soles of his boots. Asphalt boils like lava.

He dashes past Nadolny, where the dead lie in rows waiting to be trucked away to their last great bonfire. The victims of the air-raids are no longer buried. There are far too many of them.

Nobody takes any notice of him as he crosses Blücher Platz. A dust-covered Hauptmann with a wild look in his eyes. What does it matter? Who isn't sooty? Who isn't more or less crazy?

A tramcar is thrown from its tracks. The seats burn with small dancing flames. The tramdriver hangs half out of a smashed window. His head has disappeared. The inside of the tramcar is filled with mutilated bodies.

A new rain of bombs falls on the city. Houses collapse in great clouds of dust. After the explosives come the incendiaries. Splashing and smacking against the ground. Hell rages in the streets.

Two old men in the uniform of air-raid wardens catch at his arms.

'Herr Hauptmann, help us,' they plead. 'It's fallen in our cellar. We can't get them out!'

'Get away from me, you fools,' he shouts, furiously, pushing them away from him. 'Get them out yourselves! That's why you're wardens!'

He runs on, taking long strides and moving from house to house. His burns are hurting, every step he takes pains him dreadfully. He feels as if he is running on red-hot steel sheets. He has lost his cap. One of his silver shoulder-straps is dangling loose. He looks like anything but a Prussian officer. He jumps quickly to one side to avoid a rattling column of fire-engines coming noisily up from Blücher Platz.

The firemen are hanging from the engines. Faces black with smoke and dirt. One of them falls off as the engine corners and the next drives over him. They continue without stopping. What is a dead man more or less? What does it matter?

At Burgstrasse an MP patrol shouts at him to halt but he merely puts on pace and runs on towards the Landewehr canal. One of the 'watchdogs' aims an Mpi after him but the patrol commander, an Oberfeldwebel, knocks up the barrel.

'Let the fool run,' he growls. 'It's an officer and bomb-happy like as not!'

All three of them watch him running, laugh loudly and go on their way with heavy, confident policeman's steps.

At last he reaches the patrician house which is his destination, looks both ways quickly, and as a car appears round the corner throws himself headlong through the gateway. In a few rapid strides he is up the stairs. Desperately he presses the bell. When the door is not opened immediately he keeps his finger on the button.

'Have you gone mad?' asks Frau Peters, as she opens the

door and pulls him into the flat. 'Where is your friend?'

'The SS have taken him!'

'And you come here!' she cries, going white as a corpse. 'Get out! I'll scream if you don't leave immediately!'

'Don't worry,' he calms her. 'Nobody has seen me!'

'How can you *know* that,' she says, in a shaking voice. 'For God's sake *go*! I can feel something terrible is going to happen! They'll be here soon! I pray you, *go*!'

He goes slowly towards the door.

'What's that uniform you're wearing?' she asks, as his hands are on the chains.

'Taken from a dead man,' he says quietly, looking down at himself.

'That too,' she groans, looking at him with terrified eyes. 'Did you kill him?'

He shakes his head.

'Come here,' she says, with decision in her voice. 'I'll give you some civilian clothes!'

He changes rapidly.

The filthy Hauptmann uniform is thrown under a kitchen cupboard.

She almost pushes him out of the door.

'Good-bye,' he says, but by then the door has been slammed and the chains are on.

Carefully he tiptoes down the stairs. Two steps more and he will be in safety on the street.

In the gateway he runs into a Staff-Feldwebel. As if through a mist he sees the half-moon hanging from a heavy chain around the Feldwebel's neck. Three other headhunters stand a few paces behind him.

The portress leans against the wall with a triumphant smile playing around her mouth. Her small rat-like eyes seem to glow with pleasure. In spite of air-raids, fire and death she has got in touch with the MPs, who move fast when they are hunting humans.

The muscular Staff-Feldwebel, with the headhunter badge, takes his hand to the brim of his helmet in a polite salute.

'Papers,' he smiles, coldly, holding out a demanding policeman's hand.

Menckel shrugs his shoulders carelessly.

'I have no papers,' he says quietly, fumbling in his pocket for the pistol. To his horror he finds he has forgotten it.

The Staff-Feldwebel smiles unworriedly. It is not the first time he has met a person without papers.

'When he went up there, he was wearing an officer's uniform,' babbles the portress, excitedly.

'Up where?' asks the Staff-Feldwebel, without looking at her. He would like to have kicked her. Hard. Not because he feels any pity for Menckel, but because she disgusts him.

'Peters, second floor,' she pipes up, anxious to be of service. 'There's been something funny going on up there for a long time. She's a stuck-up bourgeoise bitch she is. Never gives you the time of day like a proper National Socialist ought to do!'

'Second floor, Peters,' says the Staff-Feldwebel, and begins to ascend the stairs heavily.

'No!' Menckel protests in a piercing voice. 'She's lying! I haven't visited anybody! Nor was I here in uniform!'

'Oh wasn't you, you sneaky traitor to the people, you?' screams the portress, furiously.

'Come along,' says the Staff-Feldwebel, pleasantly, drawing Menckel along with him.

The iron-tipped boots echo on the stairs. Treads creak. Fearful ears listen behind closed doors. Everyone knows what those steps mean.

'It *was* the second floor,' boasts the portress in a triumphant voice. 'I saw it on the board when he rang the bell.'

The Staff-Feldwebel knocks on the door, a hard, commanding knock which only the police of a dictatorship are able to produce.

'Open, in the name of the Führer!'

He knocks again. Harder this time.

'Who is it?' asks Frau Peters from behind the closed door.

'Military Police! Open up immediately!'

Chains jangle. The door is opened a little.

'Frau Peters?' asks the Staff-Feldwebel with his hand at the brim of his hat. He is polite and formal, but icily cold. Arresting people has become a matter of course to him.

She nods, realising that all is over.

'You know this gentleman?'

She nods again.

'Where is the uniform?' he asks and pushes her away from the door.

'In the kitchen cupboard,' she answers, hoarsely.

He jerks his head to one of his men, and soon after the uniform is found.

The Staff-Feldwebel emits a prolonged whistle of understanding when he sees the officer's uniform and the yellow holster. With a wolfish grin he looks at Menckel.

'Was this the uniform you were wearing?'

'Yes.'

'Is it yours?'

'No.'

'Where did you obtain it?'

'From a dead Hauptmann.'

'I can see it wasn't from an Oberst!' He takes the pistol, removes the clip, and counts the bullets. There are five. Two missing. He sniffs the muzzle and looks again at Menckel with raised eyebrows. 'Not so long since this iron was used! You shot the Hauptmann, didn't you?'

Handcuffs close on Menckel's wrists. The steel cuts into the flesh.

'And you look such a nice, pleasant sort of chap,' grins one of the 'watchdogs', 'still you don't *have* to look like Frankenstein to be a murderer!'

'Murder an officer!' says another. 'That's rough stuff! And pinch his holster! Jesus, man! They'll have your nut for this! You can count on *that*!'

'You're wrong, I didn't murder anybody,' protests Menckel, in horror. 'He'd been killed by an aerial bomb when I found him.'

'See that now,' grins the Staff-Feldwebel. 'Killed by a *bomb*! Don't leave much of a man, as a rule, those things don't. But, of course, strange things *can* happen! The uniform, now, was lying folded neatly alongside the shattered body, I suppose, and the Herr Hauptmann had been practising pistol shooting just before the bomb dropped on his head? That would explain the two expended bullets. Now tell me plainly, do you think we are simple-minded? What are you? Jew, Communist, deserter? Out with it! Sing a little song, please do! You'll sing before long anyway, so why not save us all trouble? Your head'll roll anyway! You might as well get used to the idea!'

'Stabsarzt* Albert Menckel, 126 Infantry Division.'

'Well, well,' answers the Staff-Feldwebel, with heavy irony, 'why not Generalarzt? You *are* a funny chap! German M.O.s

* Stabsarzt = Staff M.O.

in their right mind don't go running around in stolen uniforms. Why should they when they've got one of their own? What *is* the uniform of a Stabsarzt, anyway?'

'I have escaped from a prisoners' transport column,' confesses Menckel, looking past the Staff-Feldwebel. 'But I give you my word that Frau Peters knew nothing about that. I told her that I was on leave.'

'There now,' grins the Staff-Feldwebel. 'It seems as if you *still* think we are simple-minded.' He turns to Frau Peters. 'I would be interested to know if officers on leave *usually* come here and throw their uniforms into the kitchen cupboard? No, you'll never get anybody to believe *that* one. You are also under arrest and it is my duty to inform you that if you attempt to escape we shall make use of our firearms.'

'My children,' whispers Frau Peters, horror-stricken.

'You should have thought of them sooner,' answers the Staff-Feldwebel, taking a pair of handcuffs from his pocket. 'Your bracelets, Madame, to avoid any foolishness on the way. Now we must be going!'

'There's one born every minute,' says one of the MPs, as he takes Frau Peters by the arm and leads her down the stairs.

'Heil Hitler!' screams the portress, loudly, and raises her arm.

They drive down to the Spree, their way lighted by countless fires. They swing into the great, grey building on Prinz Albrecht Strasse and the cellars swallow them up.

At exactly the same moment in time, our newly reorganised unit goes on board JU-52 transport carriers, at Tempelhof airport, to be carried back to Finland.

The feeling amongst many officers is that they have quite definitely said good-bye to life and now wish to sell it as dearly as possible.

Political officer to Hitler, April 1944.

Through the dirty windows of Heino's Bar, Porta sees a Finnish corporal rush from the bank with a pistol in one hand and a grey box in the other. Close on his heels two other soldiers emerge from the revolving doors. They run down the street as fast as they can.

'Rubber cheque, d'you think?' asks Tiny, interestedly.

'Something like that,' says Porta, thoughtfully. 'It's not the *usual* way of leaving a bank, with a pistol in your hand!'

'Jesus, a bank-robbery,' cries Gregor, happily, putting his head out of the door to see where the three soldiers with the pistol and the grey box have got to.

'I know where *they* are,' says Tiny, with a sly grin. 'Come on, let's go down and ask 'em what they made out of it.'

They find them in the illegal speakeasy.

'What did we get out of it?' asks Porta, in a fatherly tone, touching the nearest man lightly on the forehead with his P-38.

The corporal, a huge man with a wicked cast of countenance, spits on the floor and asks Porta if he is tired of life.

'I said how much?' repeats Porta contemptuously, releasing his safety catch.

'We haven't counted 'em yet,' answers a sergeant who closely resembles a fieldmouse.

'Then let's do that,' grins Tiny, pleased, reaching for the box. 'It ain't no fun 'avin' coppers if you don't know 'ow many of 'em you've got!'

The lid flies open with a crash.

'Now I've seen it all,' shouts Gregor, hoarsely, tossing a bundle of papers with a Finnish lion decorating them, into the air.

The sergeant who resembles a fieldmouse throws himself across the table, racked with sobs. For lack of anything better the big corporal smashes three chairs to kindling.

'What a super bunch of crooks,' says Porta, with a grating laugh. 'Pinching War Bonds that haven't even been issued yet!

173

And the paper that stiff you couldn't even use it to wipe your arse on!'

The following day all three of them are shot as a warning to all and sundry. The execution takes place on the parade ground of the Artillery Barracks. They line them up against the wall of the bath-house. A squad from the Sissi *Jägers* takes care of the execution. They arrive on bicycles which they lean against the fence outside the old car repair shop.

Since Tiny has always wanted a bicycle he steals two of them whilst their owners are shooting the bank-robbers.

We enjoyed the use of those bicycles for a long time.

THE SPURIOUS GERMAN

The silence of utter boredom envelops No. 5 Company office in Titowka.

Heide has been detailed for temporary service as Company Chief Clerk. I have been put on indoor duty sorting out personnel records. In between, Hauptfeldwebel Hofman uses me as a runner. It hurts when I put weight on my leg but that doesn't worry *him*.

'Exercise,' he states, 'gives a man a healthy soul in a healthy body. You should be thanking God, and some Russian's bad marksmanship, for having any leg left at all!' He grins, and blows a cloud of cigar smoke in my face.

The shell splinter went straight through the calf of my leg. A year earlier I'd have been sent straight into hospital, and might, with luck, even have got sick leave. But those wonderful times are a thing of the past. Two or three weeks indoor duty and you're declared 'fit for service' again.

Hauptfeldwebel Hofmann has acquired an American chair which can both swivel and rock. He sits in it as if it were a throne. His big feet are up on the desk. A huge cigar rotates between his teeth. He throws a superior glance at us and pours himself a big shot of vodka.

'If you sad sacks should ever get to be Hauptfeldwebel, then you too will be able to allow yourselves a little eye-opener in the mornings!'

The telephone interrupts him, loud and jangling as only an army telephone can sound. Nobody takes it. We look at it in silence.

'Unteroffizier Heide! Why the hell don't you answer that phone?' roars Hofmann. 'What the devil do you think you're here for?'

'Five Company, Unteroffizier Heide speaking!'

He listens for a moment, then hands the instrument to Hofmann.

'Paderborn, Werhkreiskommando,' he whispers secretively.

'Hauptfeldwebel Hofmann, Five Company,' roars Hofmann, self-confidently. 'Jawohl, Herr Oberstleutnant,' he whines in a servile tone, jumping up from the American chair and going white and red by turns. 'There must be some mistake,' he says weakly 'Unteroffizier Bierfreund died long ago. Fallen for Führer and Fatherland. Half-Jewish? Impossible, Herr Oberstleutnant. There can have been no mistake. That bastard was dead as a Jew after a trip in the gas-chamber! I beg your pardon, sir! Yes sir! I'll watch my tongue Herr Oberstleutnant!' Hofmann would be wagging his tail if he had one. 'No sir, no! Unteroffizier Müller is alive and well. Serving here with the company. In charge of accounts, sir! Very good man, recently recommended for promotion to Feldwebel. Yes of course Herr Oberstleutnant. A photograph, sir? I'll send one immediately. I'll have him photographed from every possible angle, sir. I will look after it personally, Herr Oberstleutnant.' He listens, for several moments, in dismay, shifting his weight from one foot to the other. He concludes with a weak: 'Jawohl, Herr Oberstleutnant, the possibility of any such monstrous crime having occurred will be closely investigated.'

He replaces the telephone on its hook as carefully as if it were made of glass. He glares at it uncomprehendingly as if he cannot believe his own ears. With a resigned movement he falls into the American chair which rocks back under impact and deposits him on the floor.

'Bloody foreign Jewboy shit!' He swears at it viciously, rubbing his rear. He sorts feverishly through the papers on his desk. 'Get hold of Porta and Wolf,' he roars at me. 'Fast! Get your fucking legs *moving*, man! There's hell to pay! If we ain't quick about it, quick as all hell, we'll be on our way to Torgau before the week's over!'

I go off at a trot to carry out his orders. I find Wolf in a storeroom, banging away at an adding machine.

'Beat it!' he roars, as I open the door. The wolfdogs get up from the floor and show their teeth.

'It's important,' I shout, backing nervously towards the door, followed by the hungry eyes of the two great dogs.

'Important? For who?' asks Wolf, without looking up from the adding machine. 'Not for *me*, I'll be bound!'

'They've rung from Paderborn! They've found out something or other to do with Bierfreund and Müller!'

'None o' my affair,' decides Wolf, brusquely. 'Give Hofmann my love and tell him if he wants anything from me to come over here! A Chief Mechanic doesn't jump for a shit of a Hauptfeldwebel.'

Porta is in the sauna with three girl soldiers.

'Paderborn,' he grins carelessly. 'Wehrkreiskommando! Up them! Never *heard* of anybody called Bierfreund! All the Jews I know are either on their travels or in a concentration camp queuin' up for the gas chamber. Müller I've known for *years*. A good solid German if ever there was one. Got a pedigree that goes back to the times when caving skulls in with a club was the regular pastime on Sundays!'

'Are they coming?' asks Hofmann, shortly, when I get back.

'Herr Hauptfeldwebel, sir, they say they are *not* coming!'

He stares at me uncomprehendingly, and his face takes on the look of a man who has just been shot.

'D'you mean to tell me those two bastards refused point-blank to get over here? On your way, man!' he roars in a voice like the baying of a giant hound. 'I'll tear the guts out of you if you don't come back with those two sons of whores!'

Porta comes to meet me, with long, well-considered strides.

'Where's he hiding, this chap who wants to see me?' he asks superciliously, straightening his yellow topper.

I point silently to the closed door of the company office. Without taking any notice of the sign: KNOCK AND WAIT, he thunders on the door and enters the office as noiselessly as a T-34 crashing its way through a tinware factory. He cracks his heels together and roars at the top of his voice:

'Herr Hauptfeldwebel, Obergefreiter Porta, Five Company, Number Two Section, Number One Group, reporting for service as ordered!'

'Stop playing the bloody fool,' hisses Hofmann. 'And don't shout like that! Anybody shouts here it's *me!*' He leans back in his American chair. Through the window he sees Chief Mechanic Wolf on his way across the muddy parade ground, jumping from dry spot to dry spot to avoid dirtying his hand-sewn, 550 mark, officers' boots. 'Oh God,' he prays, silently, 'let him fall on his arse in the middle of all that mud!'

But God is not on Hofmann's side. Up on his toes Wolf

jumps, picking his way safely to dry ground, where he stops, standing on a large stone.

Wang, the Chinese, comes running with a cloth to polish the 550 mark boots carefully. Chief Mechanic Wolf considers his boots to be an important part of his image. Highly polished, hand-sewn boots are the outward sign of a big boss. Only *untermensch* and suckers go around in issue boots. He straightens his tailor-made, non-issue, slate-grey uniform, unnecessarily.

'Heil Hitler!' he says, ironically, as he enters the company office. He helps himself to one of Hofmann's cigars without being invited.

Hofmann does not try to hide his feelings. There is nothing he would rather do than knock the cigar down his throat.

'I don't remember your turning up with interest and repayment for the last quarter on that loan of yours,' begins Wolf, holding out a greedy hand.

'We have more important things to discuss today,' Hofmann cuts him off superciliously.

'Can't think what they could be,' answers Wolf, perching himself on the edge of the desk. 'But perhaps you'd *like* a visit from my collector?'

'How much?' asks Hofmann, sourly, scratching himself behind the ear.

'You know very well how much,' smiles Wolf, slyly, 'and you've also heard all about what happened to Staff-Wachtmeister Brinck, who was two weeks behind with interest and payments!'

'Usurer,' snarls Hofmann, the muscles of his face twitching nervously. He knows the story of how Staff-Wachtmeister Brinck lost his ear under mysterious circumstances and got it back in a parcel sent through the FPO. The story went it was the partisans who had done it but it was in reality the 80 per cent men. And not for the first time.

Hoffmann opens a drawer and hands Wolf a large grey envelope.

The notes are counted carefully, and every one of them is held up to the light.

'D'you think I've made 'em myself?' asks Hofmann, bitingly.

'No you're too stupid!' answers Wolf, cheekily. 'You're the kind that gets it passed on 'em!'

'They've called me from Paderborn,' says Hofmann, sadly. 'The shithouse is on fire!'

'Send for the fire engines then,' suggests Wolf, unworriedly. 'Ought to be their job!'

Porta doubles up with laughter, and bangs both fists on the desk.

'Funny men, ain't you? In a minute you'll be down to earth again, though,' predicts Hofmann, threateningly. 'It was "Arse and Pockets"* himself on the blower. Falsifying personal documents is a serious business. It can cost a man his head! The *least* you can get is a long, long spell in the cage.'

'We'll send you a Christmas parcel every year long as you're in Torgau,' promises Wolf, '*and* we'll give you a letter to take with you to Iron Gustav, so he won't be too hard on you.'

'*If* I go to Torgau,' bawls Hofmann in a stentorian voice, looking for all the world like an overheated boiler which needs a valve opening, 'then you go too. The lot of you! I'll tell 'em everything I know and what I don't know I'll guess at and tell 'em that too! Did you know, by the way, that the penalty for selling on the black is death?'

'You *don't* say!' smiles Wolf, merrily.

'Herr Hauptfeldwebel knows somebody, perhaps, who sells things on the black market?' asks Porta, with a hypocritical smile.

Wolf gives out a neigh of enthusiasm.

'Don't you get me worked up, Porta!' threatens Hofmann, letting himself fall back into his American-made chair. 'I'll blow you off the face of the earth like the shit you are!' He takes an oily revolver from a drawer in the desk and waves it back and forth from Wolf to Porta.

'Why not start by shootin' yourself?' Wolf baits him. 'Be one problem less for the company!'

'A Hauptfeldwebel doesn't have to take that kind of shit,' shouts Hofmann, beside himself. 'Insult me one more time in the presence of subordinates and you're on the hook! You're Chief Mechanic in Five Company, but I *am* Five Company!'

'May I touch you?' asks Wolf with assumed awe, putting out his hand. 'You're a big man, but things *can* happen to big men, too, you know!'

'He could, for example, get blown up,' breathes Porta, exposing his single tooth.

* See 'Wheels of Terror'.

'Are you threatening to take the life of your Hauptfeld-webel?' roars Hofmann, hammering the desk with his pistol. 'I could throw you lot to a court martial easy as winkin'! Take a look at your crime sheets. They'd make any lawyer fall arse over bollocks backwards.' He flicks through Porta's. 'After three months' service at the Army Ammunition Depot at Bamberg you were sent to the military prison at Heuberg because they'd come to the decision that you ought to be chained up. Larceny and arson! Several times. All the way through: deceitful, untrustworthy, mendacious and so on.' He throws Porta's record back into the drawer with an expression of disgust. 'Here, you can read your own,' he says, pushing Wolf's record towards him.

'I've seen worse,' grins Wolf, proudly. 'Here, see! Here they say I am an excellent organiser.'

'The devil take this company of thieves, swindlers and habitual criminals,' cries Hofmann, furiously, rustling through the pages of a pile of personnel records. 'Here's that bastard of a Yid's sheet,' he shouts, throwing it across the desk. 'I'll wrap his circumcised Jew cock round his neck for him, an' make him understand a German ain't made just by changin' a Yid name to Müller! I've *always* been *against* this fucking falsification business. I warned you! Now the shit's hit the fuckin' fan!'

'So, that's what it's all about,' Wolf grins noisily. 'Don't forget that though it *was* us that changed the papers, it also *was* you that put your silly great sprawling signature under the whole bloody swindle.' He waves the record sheet above his head jeeringly.

'Says here: Above corrections confirmed. Hofmann, Haupt und Stabsfeldwebel. Couldn't mistake that signature. Lovely, clear handwriting.'

Hofmann seems to take up less space in his American-made chair. He looks as if he is being rendered down slowly.

'It's falsification of documents,' he says in a voice which is hardly audible. 'We've turned that Jew, Bierfreund, into Müller, a pure German! My God this is *serious*. You could just as easy turn SS-Hein* into a Yid. If this ever gets out . . .'

'Who says it *will* get out?' asks Wolf, '*You* weren't thinkin' of puttin' it in the papers were you?'

* SS-Heini = Heinrich Himmler.

'No falsification of records has occurred before somebody's proved it. For example by a plain confession,' declares Porta, airily. 'But who'd be nutty enough to confess to a thing like that? Bierfreund, the Yiddischer German, alias Müller, he'll keep *his* trap shut all right. Let's think this through!'

'Yes, let's think, for Christ's sake *think*,' shouts Hofmann, hope awakening in him. 'What d'you say, Wolf? You can make black look white when you want to!'

'Don't know a thing about it,' says Wolf icily. 'Never even heard of it!'

'Me neither,' says Porta, smiling cheerfully.

'What do you mean by that?' asks Hofmann, doubtfully, feeling like a man who is walking on thin ice and has to move extremely carefully.

'It's not so difficult,' says Wolf, with a sly look in his fishy green eyes. 'You're the one who's turned a Jew into a German with a stroke of the pen. *And* you've put him in for promotion to Feldwebel. A Jew *Feldwebel* in the Greater German Army! That's *something*! The boys in Prinz Albrecht Strasse'll be movin' that fast when they hear about it you'd think somebody'd put gunpowder up their arseholes!'

'Who's gonna tell 'em, then?' asks Hofmann, with fear in his voice.

'The boys who rang you up from Paderborn,' smiles Wolf, sarcastically.

' "Arse and Pockets" can't *stand* the Gestapo! He hates 'em,' says Hofmann, with certainty.

'Anybody say he likes the Yids?' grins Wolf, maliciously. 'Particularly one of 'em who's goin' to become Feldwebel on forged papers?'

'I don't like Jews either,' admits Hofmann. 'So why the hell should I have helped one of 'em to become a German?'

'He's good with figures,' answers Wolf, jeeringly. 'If you hadn't got him here you'd've been court martialled a long time ago for embezzlement. It's no secret you can't count to twenty without takin' your boots off! A figure-wise Yid's like manna from heaven to *you*!'

'Those papers in Paderborn are going to have to disappear,' states Porta, tearing a copy of Army Regulations in two.

'How?' says Hofmann, seeing a straw to clutch at.

'This way,' says Porta, rubbing thumb and forefinger together, the international sign for money changing hands.

'Shit, Porta. You can't buy Oberstleutnant von Weisshagen!'

'Don't need him,' Porta waves the objection away. 'He's only an Oberstleutnant. We've got a pseudo-German here and I know there's more'n one of *that* particular race in Paderborn. If those boys get their scimitar-shaped noses together then they'll move over that poor German Oberstleutnant like a steamroller!'

Hofmann looks at Porta admiringly.

'You'd make a *good* Unteroffizier, Obergefreiter Porta. What do you say to signing on for a twenty-four?'

'Herr Hauptfeldwebel, I only wish I had the time. But they're expecting me in Berlin!'

'Let's get hold of this pseudo-German bastard,' roars Hofmann. 'he ought to be able to sort this out. It's him it's all about, anyway. On your way,' he chases me, pushing me out of the door.

The Moses dragoon is sitting with one of the cooks, Unteroffizier Balt, gnawing on a shank of reindeer which he dips repeatedly into a bowl of garlic sauce.

'Hofmann is sighing with longing to see you,' I say, accepting a piping-hot chunk of reindeer.

'What's *he* want?' he asks, casually, biting off a large mouthful of meat.

'They've been on the blower from Paderborn asking how it comes about you're a German? Hofmann's fallen out of that American chair of his several times already.'

'My papers are gilt-edged,' says Müller, knocking back a large glass of beer. 'Permit me,' he says to Unteroffizier Balt, dipping a piece of bread in the garlic sauce. He champs like a hungry pig. Fat runs down from the corners of his mouth and down over his chin.

Unteroffizier Balt fetches more beer and a pack of cards. It'll do Hofmann good to cool his heels a bit. Anyhow, who's to say how long it's taken me to find the Moses dragoon? An accountant Unteroffizier might be anywhere.

'Took your time, then, did you?' roars Hofmann, in an acid voice, glowering at us suspiciously, when we get back to the company office an hour later.

'What the hell've you been eating, man? You've got fat all over your dirty synagogue face? Don't you know Yids ain't *allowed* to eat German pigs? German pigs are for Germans! What the hell've you been wasting your time at all morning?'

'Been round taking stock,' answers Müller, carelessly.

'*What* stocks?' growls Hofmann, unbelievingly. 'You've counted 'em all long ago! You've been counting stocks now for the last two *years*!'

'Ammunition count's wrong,' answers Müller, as if that were something unheard of. No ammunition count has ever been right since the first German soldier began to use firearms.

'Ammunition count wrong?' roars Hofmann, furiously. 'Are you mad? What the hell do you think I've got you and your Yid snout for?'

'We're short of ten boxes of rifle ammunition,' answers Müller, pleasantly, 'and forty grenades have disappeared without trace!'

'What *kind* of grenades?' snarls Hofmann. 'Express yourself properly! You're not fartin' round in the synagogue with a skull-cap on now!'

'Potato-mashers,' sighs Müller, tiredly. 'Must've been pilfered!'

'Have you checked Chief Mechanic Wolf's stores?' asks Hofmann, accusingly.

'Just let him try,' suggests Wolf, with a threatening undercurrent in his voice. 'Then it won't be just the skin on his prick he'll be short of but a lot more of it all over his body!'

Hofmann drops back dejectedly in his American-made chair. He has forgotten he has released the catch and almost goes arse over tip again.

'Fucking Jew shit!' he reviles it, as he recovers, with difficulty, his balance. 'Listen to me Müller or Bierfreund or whatever your fucking name is now. You know damn well that if it wasn't for me you'd've been a pile of ashes and three pieces of cheap soap a long time ago! They've been looking at your personal record in Paderborn. At the moment it's got no further than to an Oberstleutnant. Oberstleutnant von Weisshagen, it's true, but still no further. Now *you* are going to ring the Feldwebel i/c personnel up. Bernstein his name is, and with a name like that I'll lay money there's desert sand still sticking between *his* toes! Light a fire under his fat arse. Tell him you're in trouble and he's got to help you. There's not only Jew blood at stake but valuable German blood too! And it's *your* fault! Get that through your calcified brain. Now get on that blower! Don't worry about what it costs. The Army's taking care of that. Just *talk*! What comes of it's what matters

183

and for your sake it'd better be something good!'

It takes Müller a long time to get through to No. 11 Panzer-satzabteilung in Paderborn. Finally he manages it.

'Want to talk to Bernstein, eh?' says a squeaky, happy voice on the line. 'You're just one hour too late. He's gone! Try again in three weeks' time!'

'Ask where the hell he's gone to!' snarls Hofmann, who is listening in on an extension.

'Do you have his address?' asks Müller, politely.

'Of course we have. Don't you think we know what we're doing here?' chortles the happy voice. 'What do you want his address for?'

'I want to get in touch with him.'

'You can't! He's not there!' comes a happy shout from Paderborn.

'Well then where is he? You must know where he has gone to? If everything collapses, you'd want to know where to get hold of him, wouldn't you?'

'If everything collapses he won't come back anyway,' laughs the Paderborn voice. 'Think he's an idiot? He's gone on leave. He *may* be taking the cure at Bad Gastein. He mentioned it as a possibility. Ever been to Bad Gastein?'

'No, never,' groans Müller, ready to give up the whole business.

'Supposed to be a wonderful place,' states the jolly Paderborn Unteroffizier. 'You lie in warm mud all day long and get up your strength by eating. Here's the boss coming. Ring again in three weeks' time, mate, and if Bernstein's not been suffocated in the mud he'll probably be here.'

The telephone buzzes. The connection in broken.

Hofmann shoots up out of his American-made swivel chair, and takes a kick at the company cat. As usual he misses it.

'So it's gone that far,' he screeches madly. 'The Jewboys go on leave, wallowin' about in Bad Gastein havin' mud baths and takin' the waters, whilst we Germans are refused leave, because the Fatherland is in peril. That's the worst thing I've ever heard of. *Now* I begin to *really* believe we're not gonna win this war!'

'God knows what the Reichsführer will say to it,' comes wonderingly from Julius Heide.

'Shut your trap, Unteroffizier Heide. This is something your pygmy German brain'll never understand! Müller *you'd* never do that would you? Go to Bad Gastein and make the mud baths dirtier'n they were before? Heavenly Father! This is the *top*! Well, back to work! We'll take care of that scoundrel in Bad Gastein later. How many more pseudo-Germans do you know in Paderborn? Use your loaf! Think! Think hard as if you had to remember the whole of the Talmud and write it down! Get on that blower, man, get the synagogue moving!'

'*Could* perhaps try ringing Wachtmeister Sally at Wehrkreiskommando,' suggests Müller, thoughtfully. 'He's a very nice chap.'

'Shit on how nice he is, or ain't,' shouts Hofmann, beside himself. 'He's got to help us. It's our lives and liberty that's at stake, man. Explain that to him!'

Porta is leaning over the washbasin humming the prisoner's chorus from Nabucco, and examining himself intently in the mirror.

'Stop pissing about there,' roars Hofmann, 'and stop staring into that mirror! It'll only give you bad ideas! I only said stand easy, I didn't say you could look at yourself in the glass!'

It takes almost an hour for Müller to get a connection to Wachtmeister Sally.

'Remove a personnel sheet?' says Sally, when the matter has been explained to him. 'Could be done, but what's in it for me?'

'What times we live in,' groans Hofmann, with the extension pressed to his ear. 'Now that son of the sodding desert wants to make something out of helping people in distress!'

'What can we offer him?' asks Müller, looking at Wolf and Porta.

'Ten tins of pork,' suggests Porta, largely.

'No, *no*!' says Hofmann, 'the Yids don't *eat* pig meat!'

'I've got some ugly-looking Russian typewriters,' says Porta. 'Think he'd like to write on Russian machines? They're sure to be all the rage after the war!'

'He's got all he wants of typewriters at HQ,' Hofmann rejects the idea, irritably. 'German ones. Think again, Porta!'

'Polish eggs,' suggests Porta, lifting one eyebrow. 'He might be one of those dopes who loves eating omelets because they think eggs make 'em more virile!'

'That's a thought,' Hofmann brightens up. 'Let the bastard have ten boxes of eggs so's his limp prick can get a hard on a bit more often.'

'Ten boxes of eggs,' offers Müller largely.

Wachtmeister Sally laughs long and heartily.

'Do you realise just how comic you are?' he asks, when he has got his breath back. 'We've got so many eggs here we've begun hatching 'em out ourselves. Just to help your thinking processes along a bit, there's an information sheet in triplicate just come in the door: Two Feldwebels were executed last Saturday for falsifying documents. So what are you offering now? But not those eggs again!'

Müller looks unhappily at Wolf.

'It's blackmail almost,' snarls Wolf, with loathing.

'What do you expect of a Yid?' says Hofmann. 'Adolf's *right*. All they want is to keep us Germans down.'

'Offer him a case of Scotch whisky,' mumbles Wolf, unwillingly. He knows instinctively that Wachtmeister Sally can't be bought cheaply.

'You can have a case of real Scotch,' Müller transmits the offer over the telephone.

'That's okay,' grins Sally, satisfied. 'Wolf or Porta aren't anywhere near are they?'

Hofmann shakes his head in negation, and winks one eye.

Müller understands.

'No, what do you want with 'em?'

'When you see 'em, ask if one of 'em'd like to buy a wildcat. I've got one of the devils here. If either of 'em is interested I can send the monster by the mail plane. The freight charges are paid.'

'What the devil would anybody want with a wildcat up here at the Arctic Circle?' asks Müller in wonder.

'If you've got any enemies it'll fix 'em in two shakes. If it gets any madder than it is now it'd put an infantry division to flight. Wait here and keep your ear to the phone!'

A little later the sound of hissing, spitting and snarling comes through the earpiece. 'What d'you think of it?' asks Sally proudly. 'Hear how mad he is? And that's just his normal temperament. Tease him a bit and I'm the only one who dares to stay inside HQ. If he once got out of his cage there'd be no garrison left in Paderborn before we knew where we were. Shall I send him up to you lot? Save you placing guards at night!'

'We don't want any wildcats here,' shouts Hofmann. 'Tell him we're sending the whisky today!'

'*We?*' growls Wolf, condescendingly. 'As if *you* had any whisky to send!'

'Wildcat,' says Porta, rolling the world around his mouth. 'Is that one of those beasts with the pointed, triangular ears?'

'Right,' replies Wolf, 'good animals to stay clear of. Throw one of 'em into Hell and the Devil and his grandmother too'll take it on the lam and leave the place to the wildcat!'

'I think I've got an idea,' says Porta, looking even more intently at his reflection in the mirror. 'Wildcat! Not so bad, not so bad!'

'No wildcats,' shouts Hofmann, nervously. 'Did you understand me, Porta? That's an order!'

'Very good, Herr Hauptfeldwebel,' barks Porta. 'Wildcat,' he whispers to himself a little later and looks at Wolf, who winks back at him.

'Got any other hook-nosed friends in Paderborn, Müller?' asks Hofmann, marching nervously up and down the floor. 'Then ring up and get them together. You know the doctrine. Don't disperse your strength. *Klotzen, nicht lockern,* as Panzergeneral Guderian has taught us.'

The whole of the afternoon and most of the evening goes by on the telephone. But despite all the activity their only hope remains Wachtmeister Sally.

Hofmann sits down in his swivel chair and puts his feet on the desk.

The following day a heavy silence hangs over the company office. Every time the telephone rings we all jump. Black and menacing, it stands in the middle of the desk in front of Hofmann.

'Even if the Führer wants to speak to me personally on any subject,' roars Hofmann, 'I'm not here! You don't know where I am and you don't know when I'll be back. D'you understand me, you dogs?'

Just before midday the telephone rings loud and shrill for the umpteenth time.

'Fifth Company here,' I answer it.

'How's everything with you?' asks an oily voice, which I feel I ought to recognise.

'Who is calling?' I ask.

'Can't you guess?'

'No, but I know your voice.'

'I'm glad to hear you can recognise the voice of an old

187

friend. Is Hofmann there? Tell the shit there's somebody wants to talk to him.'

I point to the telephone and look inquiringly at Hofmann, who shakes his head violently and points out of the window.

'No, the Hauptfeldwebel isn't here. Is there any message?'

'Yes, tell him that your arses may be burning now but if I don't play the part of a good comrade and keep my mouth shut about what I know they'll be that hot you could fry eggs on 'em!'

Suddenly I realise who it is I am speaking to. I'd know that laugh amongst a thousand. Staff QM Sieg!

Hofmann goes white. He has obviously guessed who it is on the telephone.

'Is that Staff QM Sieg?' I ask, uneasily.

'Inspector, Field Security Police,' he corrects me. 'I have been posted to Gefepo*. That is what happens when a man is good at his work and pulls in criminals to receive their just punishment. How are my old friends, Wolf and Porta, getting on? Still falsifying papers in cahoots with Hofmann are they? I hear they've changed your flashes to the Star of David!'

Hofmann bangs the desk silently several times. He is almost green in the face from suppressed rage.

'I don't understand what you mean.'

'Oh yes, you do! You understand me very well. Don't you think I found out what kind of games were going on while I was serving with your stinking company? You can tell the others, if they don't already know it, that it's the death penalty for letting a Jew stay alive on a dead German's papers!'

'What's this to do with us?' I ask, with dreadful forebodings.

'Don't play silly buggers!' Sieg grins, wickedly. 'You know damn well you're on thin ice! If I pass that story on you'll be lucky if they only let you keep your heads! In any case you'll be permanent inmates at Torgau!'

'What's it cost to stop your tongue from wagging?' I ask, sharply.

Hofmann slaps his forehead, and looks as if he could eat me.

I offer him the telephone but he recoils from it as if it were red-hot.

'Now you're being sensible. I want fifty thousand Reichs-marks to forget my duty to National Socialism, and I want them inside twenty-four hours. One of you'll meet me with

* Gefepo (Geheime Feldpolizei) = Secret Field Security Police.

the dough on the little path behind the fort. But don't try anything!'

I look inquiringly at Hofmann, who is whispering conspiratorially with Porta and Wolf.

'Now then, what's it to be?' asks Sieg, impatiently. 'Will you pay up? Or do I come and pick up the circumcised prick?'

I appeal to Hofmann again. He nods with unconcealed distaste.

'Okay,' I answer him. 'You'll be informed when we'll be there with the ducats. We've got to collect them first!'

'You'd be wise to get hold of 'em *fast*!' Sieg rings off with a demonstrative clatter.

'That dirty jackal,' bawls Hofmann, banging his fist on the desk so hard that the telephone dances. 'That wicked shit's got to be put out of the way! He's *dangerous*!'

'Herr Hauptfeldwebel, sir, now we must bite on the bullet and keep our heads clear,' shouts Porta. 'Perhaps we *do* need a wildcat,' he says, thoughtfully. 'A creature like that can make mincemeat of a man, before you can say Jack Robinson!'

'Wouldn't it be wiser to pay him?' says Hofmann. 'We can scrape fifty thousand together!'

'*I* can, but *you* can't,' says Wolf, superciliously.

'Don't forget I'm in this too,' remarks Porta, drily. 'If there's money to be put out I'm going to get stuck for half of it. But in principle I don't *like* paying out blackmail. That Kaffir bastard'll not be satisfied with the fifty thousand. He's insatiable. We'll wind up being his slaves!'

'Emil Sieg is a wicked old rambag,' shouts Tiny, indignantly. 'Let's go an' shoot 'oles in 'im now! These kind of things've got to be fixed quick!'

'The sneaky rat thinks he's smart,' says Porta, spitting on the floor.

Hofmann has difficulty in controlling himself. Nobody has ever dared to spit on his office floor before. In helpless rage he kicks out again at the company cat, but as usual misses her.

'He was a shit then, when we were encumbered with the bastard in this company,' continues Porta, taking one of Hofmann's cigars without being invited.

'That's enough,' growls Hofmann warningly, locking the cigar box in a drawer of his desk.

'What if he was to tell Sieg as how old men are sometimes better off dead,' grins Tiny, smoothly, 'then maybe 'is better

189

judgement might make 'im ask for a postin' to some far-off spot?'

'All this nonsense for the sake of a shitty *Yid*!' says Hofmann, bitterly. 'Porta! For Christ's sake find a way out. You're quick enough on the uptake as a rule!'

'Let's have a cup of coffee,' suggests Porta, and without being asked goes and finds Hofmann's valuable reserve of beans.

'Coffee clears the brain!'

Tiny hands round the cups. He salutes Hofmann as he goes past him.

Porta takes a long swig of coffee and looks around him, pleasantly.

'We could invite Emil out some evening. One of those places with Lapland girls. You know 'em. Up with your glass an' down with your trousers! On the way home after the party we knock him on the head and push him down one of the sewers. That does for him and his corpus delicti at one fell swoop!'

Tiny bends over, roaring with laughter at the thought of Emil down a sewer.

'On the Reeperbahn we'd a nose by the name of Emil. Emil the Dwarf we called 'im, 'cause 'e was one! We put Emil down a sewer in Davidstrasse. We'd thought of droppin' 'im in the river first of all but one of the bints 'ad the bright idea of usin' the sewers. When 'e went down there was a great big suckin' noise like when a stopped-up water closet goes loose.'

'You seem to know all about that sort of thing. What about you and Gregor doing the job?' suggests Wolf, insidiously.

'Why don't you go along?' asks Gregor, rocking nervously on his chair. 'How'd you think it ought to be done?'

'The sewer idea ain't bad,' says Wolf, rubbing his chin thoughtfully. 'You could, of course, go straight into his pigsty and let off at everybody in sight. You'd be certain to hit Sieg together with all the rest.'

'Count me out,' decides Tiny, categorically, ''ow do we get away when the shooters are empty?'

'Something'd turn up while you're doin' the job,' Wolf rallies him.

'No good,' Gregor rejects the idea with decision. 'Dangerous as all get-out.'

After a long conference Tiny and Gregor agree to go into Petsamojoki and do the job quickly and efficiently.

'Every evening Sieg leaves his place of duty, and returns to his quarters in Starja Street,' Porta explains. 'The shit's usually on his own. It'd be the easiest thing in the world to knock him off when he's on his way down Jyväskulä Alley. If both of you let go at him at the same time one of you's sure to blow his candle out!'

'What about if he's got one of these Lapland whores with him?' asks Gregor, worriedly.

'If she's in the way, knock her off, too,' decides Wolf, loftily. 'Women like that have got to learn it's dangerous to run around with Germans, and particularly dangerous if they're MPs. It might even be of preventative value, so the MPs can't get hold of cunt any more, and *that* I would be happy to see.'

'I don't like it,' says Gregor, uneasily. 'My primitive instincts tell me it's wrong. What if there's a lot of trigger-happy types around? Bullet's ain't choosers. They don't give a sod who they perforate.'

With some anxiety they scramble into an amphibian, which Wolf has organised for the job.

'Take him when he turns into Starkaja Street,' suggests Hofmann. 'It's black as the inside of your hat there. You can knock him off easy as a cannibal pickin' a banana!'

'*Do* cannibals eat bananas?' asks Tiny, with a simple look on his face.

'Don't ask silly questions, Creutzfeldt,' says Hofmann, sharply. 'Off you go and reduce our load of troubles by one!'

As they swing down Tölö Street, they catch sight of Emil Sieg.

'Holy Mother of Kazan, there's our mark,' screams Gregor, excitedly. In a colossal jump he is out of the vehicle and goes at Sieg like a tank aiming to run over a frog.

Tiny swings the amphibian up on to the pavement immediately in front of Sieg, who has to jump quickly to one side to avoid being crushed against the wall. The amphibian crashes into the wall.

'Why don't you stand still, you cowardly sod?' shouts Tiny, indignantly.

Sieg lets out a hoarse scream and looks round despairingly for help.

'Oh Cripes!' roars Tiny, jumping from the amphibian with his pistol ready in his hand.

Sieg whirls round. He knows what is happening and tears

191

at his holster, but it is one of the new, elegant types which is not easy to get open.

Tiny lifts the Nagan and stretches his arm towards him.

'Now you're goin' to die, you twisted son of a bitch,' he screams, murderously.

Sieg drops down like lightning and rolls under a parked lorry.

'Send for the undertaker, he's a corpse already!' howls Gregor enthusiastically, going down on his knees to liquidate Sieg whom he thinks is under the lorry. But all he sees is Sieg's officer's boots, drumming through the half-melted snow so that it spurts to all sides.

Without regard for passers-by Gregor fires at the boots, but only succeeds in hitting the tyres of a Finnish artillery lorry. The whole street is in an uproar. Three MPs drop down and open fire in the wrong direction.

Some Supplies Corps soldiers say they have seen five Russian paratroopers running through the streets pulling a German General after them on the end of a rope.

Tiny and Gregor jump into the amphibian and drive after Sieg, who is now a good distance away.

He runs down an alley which is too narrow for the vehicle to enter.

'Now we've got him,' howls Tiny, looking like a bulldog which has found the bone somebody had stolen from it.

On foot they go after Sieg, who is in no doubt that he is running for his life. He curses himself for having gone into the blackmail business.

Behind him come the two assassins, thundering down the alley like a couple of express trains on their way through a tunnel, and ready to spread death and destruction around them.

'Come out, you crooked dog, so I can put a bullet in you,' Tiny bawls. 'We're gonna fix you *right*! Count on *that*!'

A couple of shots crack down the alley and bullets ricochet from the walls of the houses. The alley is a long one, but some way down it there is an elbow, with a little passage into which a man can disappear if he knows where it is. Sieg knows. A few days ago he caught a deserter in that same passage.

He checks and almost flies through the air as, at the last minute, he turns the corner into the passage.

Two and a half seconds later Tiny and Gregor blunder past, splashing melted snow up the walls from their boots.

Sieg just catches sight of Tiny's pale-grey bowler, which is pressed firmly down on his head.

The alley ends in a wall, the end wall of a five-storey building. They brake to a halt, their studded boots striking sparks from the stones, and stare in amazement at the impassable wall.

'Where'd that cow get to?' asks Gregor, open-mouthed.

''E ain't climbed *that*,' says Tiny. 'Even a Finnish cat couldn't get up there. They do say as fear can put wings on people, but that's a load of bull like a lot of other things. That bastard's sittin' around 'ere somewhere waitin' to get shot. God 'elp 'im when I get my teeth in 'is arse. I'll tear 'is eyes out, I will, and then I'll rip 'is bleedin' ears off. What a rat! Runnin' away like that when *we're* comin' to shoot 'im up!'

They creep up some backstairs and almost frighten the life out of an old woman coming down with a pail of garbage.

Tiny asks her if she's seen a man who's going to be shot and she throws the pail at his head. He falls over backwards and takes Gregor with him a good way out into the yard.

'You sure that wasn't him?' asks Gregor, brushing potato peelings from his uniform.

'That was an ugly Lapp woman,' snarls Tiny, picking eggshell out of his ears. 'She thought we were the dustbin!'

'Do we *look* like dustbins,' asks Gregor, insulted.

'In the dark it's easy to make that mistake,' considers Tiny, 'but Emil's goin' to pay for this too! I'll tear 'is bollocks off, I will, and stuff 'em straight up 'is stinkin' arsehole!'

Soon after, they catch sight of somebody, standing close to the wall, further down the alley.

'Holy God's mother, that's *him*!' roars Gregor, and empties the magazine of the Nagan so fast it sounds like an Mpi.

The shadowy person disappears into a gateway leaving a respectably sized pool of blood. The spots of blood lead into a house, but tail off little by little.

'We made a 'ole in 'im any road,' says Tiny, with satisfaction, spitting contemptuously at the blood spots.

'He'll bleed to death like a sick rat,' says Gregor, pleased.

'*Should* that bastard survive all this, *we* ain't gonna be sittin' so pretty, though,' says Tiny, worriedly.

'Jesus, no,' says Gregor, blackly, wiping sweat from his forehead.

'I reckon we can go back 'ome and tell 'em we've punctured that lukewarm turd,' says Tiny, resolutely. 'The blood can't

193

leak out of the sod if there ain't a 'ole in 'im, can it?'

'They'll strangle us if they ever find out we're taking the piss out of 'em,' says Gregor, pessimistically.

'Stop your cryin', then,' says Tiny, calmly. 'If we ain't made a big enough 'ole in 'im, then we'll come back an' do it better next time. But 'e *must* be dead. 'Ell, 'e must've lost at least five gallons of 'is rat's blood, which is more'n God give anybody to lose!'

'It's odd,' Gregor admits, 'let's have another look. I'd *rather* go home and be able to say I'd taken a kick at his body. But the body *we* saw, ran bloody off, didn't it? And it's not often bodies do that sort of thing!'

'Maybe we've frightened him enough to make him keep his mouth shut,' thinks Tiny.

'It's not impossible,' agrees Gregor, 'and then he'll get himself a posting to some place a long way away where we can't get to him, and the others'll never find out he's still breathing. We're the only two who *do* know, and *we* don't even know for sure. Let's be true believers. We believe he's dead!'

'Tell me, now,' says Tiny, nervously, pushing the bowler to the back of his neck. 'You don't think it's some other silly cow we've 'ad a bang at and who's lost all that blood we saw back there?'

'I think that's it,' Gregor nods, with conviction. 'That sod we shot was too big to be Emil. And I think he was wearing a Finnish uniform!'

'Jesus, Jesus,' shouts Tiny, clasping his hands as if in prayer. 'Let's not 'ave any more to worry about! If we've shot one of them polar blokes they'll be complainin' to the German authorities. Emil knows we were close to 'avin' 'is arse in that alley an' the case'll go to 'is section. Ain't no Sherlock needed to sort out who it was 'ad a crack at an arctic 'ero!'

'You're right,' says Gregor, weakly. 'It's a black outlook. But no matter what, we stick to it that we've fixed him good. We didn't leave the body till it was full of blue-bottles, understand?'

'I 'ope you know what we're doin',' mumbles Tiny with a grimace, 'but don't forget Porta an' Wolf! Those two treacherous sods'll be askin' questions all over the shop, and if the rat's still alive they'll find out for sure!'

The same evening a happy wake is held in Hofmann's quarters, with Tiny and Gregor as the guests of honour.

'That's the way to treat blackmailers,' shouts Barcelona, enthusiastically. 'No talk. Lightning-fast action!'

The beer is laced with Slivovitz, and the gaiety of the party rises to unprecedented heights. The singing can be heard all the way over in the Russian lines:

> 'Denn wir wissen, dass nach dieser Not*
> uns leuchtet hell das Morgenrot!'

'We 'it 'im right between the eyes,' lies Tiny, with practised ease, believing it for a moment himself. 'The bullets went "smack" as they went into 'im!' he boasts, bringing both hands forcefully down on the table.

'And the blood *spouted* out of him,' grins Gregor, happily. 'There was blood all over! It went *streaming* down the gutters! It was like the Stockhold bloodbath!'

'I put three shots straight up 'is jacksey 'fore we got out,' states Tiny, impudently, crooking his forefinger.

'*Merde alors!* What did you do with the body?' asks the Legionnaire, practically.

'We slung it down into a 'ell of a deep cellar,' explains Tiny, eagerly. 'Should've 'eard 'im splash when 'e 'it bottom.'

'I suppose you could find that cellar again?' asks Porta, with a suspicious gleam in his eye.

It is Hofmann who exposes them next morning.

'There was a lot of blood yesterday?' he asks sarcastically, and stands in front of Tiny.

'That's right,' Tiny assures him. 'Four or five gallons at least!'

'And the body you threw into a deep cellar?' continues Hofmann.

'Word of honour,' Gregor gives the guarantee solemnly. 'We heard the thud when it hit bottom.'

'Then perhaps it would interest you to know that I have just spoken to the body on the telephone, and that the body has promised to give us his very special attention!'

Tiny is about to turn and run for it, when the muzzle of an Mpi is pushed against his stomach.

'Stay put,' smiles Porta, dangerously. 'Or I'll show you how lying bastards like you get blown off the face of the earth!'

* Denn wir etc. (Freely translated)
> Since we know that after all our pain,
> The sunrise will shine clear again!

'There must be some mistake,' stammers Gregor, confusedly.

'Sure! One of the big ones,' snarls Hofmann, grinding his teeth. 'But one thing's a certainty. It was Emil Sieg I talked to. It may also interest you to know that an attempt to murder a Finnish sergeant has been reported, and that Sieg has been given the case!'

'Doesn't sound so good,' sighs Tiny, in a small voice.

'Let's have the story,' demands Porta, narrowing his eyes.

'Well it was black as a cannibal's arsehole,' explains Gregor. 'We shot some silly bleeder, but it doesn't seem it could've been Emil when the Herr Hauptfeldwebel here's talked to him on the phone today. It doesn't often happen the dead ring up!'

'There is simply no other way,' says Wolf, decisively. 'We've got to chill the bastard!'

'You're telling me,' says Porta. 'He's dangerous as a cobra in a warm bed, and now he's mad on getting back at us!'

'Can't we report him to the police?' suggests the Westphalian, naïvely. 'It's a crime to blackmail people.'

'You're that stupid it's a wonder you know enough to stay breathin'!' shouts Tiny, contemptuously. 'Only the feeble-minded ask the rozzers to 'elp 'em!'

'I suggest we storm his lair and shoot his head off,' says Gregor, filling up the glasses from Wolf's stock.

'It'd be difficult to get in to him,' says Barcelona, doubtfully. 'He's sitting pretty there right in the middle of the old fort. The gates are strong as them in a prison.'

Porta picks up his beer and drinks deeply, then bites off a chunk of hot pork.

'I know that bloody fort. The only way we'd get in there'd be with a big, big load of TNT. That'd send the lot of 'em up, but it could mean sudden death for us too if we made a balls of it. Gimme a cup of coffee, and I'll think of something else!'

'I got a plan,' says Tiny, twirling his Mpi. 'Let's invite the silly sod out to us an' give 'im the treatment. I know a way as'd make a nice, considerate citizen of 'im.'

'No good,' says Porta. 'He's a crook, and he won't stop until he's taken us for everything we've got.'

'I can turn 'im into a Sunday School teacher,' shouts Tiny, cocksure of himself. 'Listen! It's a great plan. When 'e arrives we give 'im a welcomin' glass for old times' sake. Then we attend to 'is personal comfort. 'E'll no doubt be in need of a pedicure. I pulls out me battle-knife an' amputates the little toe on 'is left foot, so there'll be more room in them narrow officer's boots of 'is. If 'e still won't come to 'is senses we explain to 'im as 'ow both parties are wastin' their time talkin' an' might as well go 'ome. On the way out of the door we notice the poor bleeder is limpin', because 'e ain't got the same number of toes on both feet. Now what do old friends do to 'elp the louse?' asks Tiny, looking around and proud of himself.

'Hit the back of his neck with an acid drop,' suggests Porta, large-mindedly.

'No, no! No brutality,' Tiny turns the suggestion down. 'We leave that sort of thing to Nazis and Commies. We are 'umane. We don't shoot a man just because 'e limps. No, we take off 'is right boot, and 'elp 'im off with 'is right little toe. Then the boots fit 'im, and 'e don't get corns!'

'I don't think he'd like that,' says Barcelona, looking tenderly down at his own feet.

'Nobody's askin' 'im to,' says Tiny, companionably. 'But I'd expect 'im to stay with us a bit after that to discuss things. At any rate 'e'd 'ave the thought that 'e still 'ad eight toes, ten fingers, two flappin' great ears an' a big, ugly nose in the middle of 'is kisser, as we could 'elp 'im off with one by one.'

'Don't forget he's got a prick too,' whoops Porta. 'We'd cut that off an' stick it in his mouth so's he'd think he'd come to a fairies' party!'

'No good,' says Barcelona, gloomily. 'If we can't *pay* the bastard to keep quiet there's only one thing to do: Liquidate him like the rat he is! Be the first sensible killing in this whole war!'

'My feeling too,' agrees Hofmann.

We agree to get things moving right away.

Inspector Sieg is not feeling too well when he leaves his office. He leaves early. He goes cold, and begins to sweat at the same time, when he hears that ten kilogrammes of TNT have been stolen, in the course of the night, from an ammunition store close by. From what he knows of Porta it can only be he who has stolen it to use in an effective liquidation.

With all his senses working overtime he walks along, keeping close to the walls and taking cover behind other people the whole time. Every time he sees an amphibian he stops in

197

terror. He realises suddenly that blackmailing is a very dangerous business.

He gives a terrified start when a vehicle brakes hard out on the road and takes cover behind a perambulator containing a pair of wailing twins.

With his hand on his pistol butt he sneaks along. He stands still for a long time, watching the house in which he is quartered. He enters it only when he is satisfied that nobody is lying in wait for him.

He changes to civilian clothes and congratulates himself on having had a really clever idea. Those fools will be looking for a man in a uniform of a poisonous-looking green colour. Civilians will be about as interesting to them as a bunch of carrots to a well-fed dog.

Part of the way down Hollanti Street he again thinks he has caught sight of Tiny and Porta and pulls the pistol from his pocket. To his huge relief it turns out to be a couple of ordinary infantrymen, who are trying to hit it off with three Finnish girl soldiers. He has realised long ago that he cannot follow the usual service procedure and hand over the case to a colleague. If he does, he himself will end up behind bars.

'The devil!' he curses, thinking with longing of how pleasant it would be to be living a boring civilian life, paying taxes and rent, and going to bed at ten o'clock every night with a wife in hair curlers.

With these melancholy thoughts running through his mind he sneaks into Hurme's Bar for a cup of coffee and a large cognac. That should pull him together a bit. If there is anything he needs now it is clear thinking.

There are only a few people in the long bar-room. The barmaid is leaning, half-asleep, on the bar. Without a word she shoves a cup of coffee and a glass of cognac towards him. He squeezes into a dimly lit stall, and swears viciously when he scalds his tongue on the hot coffee. Carefully he pours it into the saucer and blows on it. He slobbers it down, noisily, and begins to feel a little better.

With a satisfied expression he smooths down his black tailor-made suit. Black is stylish, the tailor has told him, not having anything else in stock. His shirt is white. His tie scarlet. The national colours, red, black and white. He enjoys looking at his smart 200 mark, patent-leather shoes. Not everybody could give himself a pair of shoes like that.

The third cup of coffee goes down and another cognac. He dreams rosy dreams of the whole of 5 Company being mowed down by a firing squad.

'I'll get those criminals,' he says, half-aloud.

By now there are only two guests left beside himself. Two Finnish ski soldiers look in but leave immediately. One of them, a sergeant with partisan badges, takes a suspiciously long look at him. Had that murderous pack joined up with the Finnish allies? He shudders and gets up to leave.

A Nagan pokes his spine brutally.

'You're dead, you crooked son of a bitch,' says Tiny, sharply. 'Take a deep breath and that dog's 'eart of yours'll get blown through the wall! And, as you know, it's difficult gettin' along with no 'eart left!'

Porta bursts noisily through the revolving-doors, with Gregor at his heels. The last two guests disappear quickly, and the dozy barmaid wakes up suddenly. It's not the first time she has seen an armed business meeting.

'So there you are, you rheumaticky old bug,' says Porta, in a friendly tone, patting his cheek. 'If there'd been a bit more up there you'd have kept your fingers off us, and then you wouldn't have died so young!'

Fear has made Sieg dumb.

'Let me kick 'im a bit, before we knock 'im off,' pleads Tiny, drawing back his enormous boot.

'Start the player-piano,' answers Porta. 'We need a theme song for this little drama.'

'You've got to put money in it,' says Tiny, fumbling around over by the piano. 'A mark a time!'

'Then put some in,' orders Porta.

'Ain't got a sou,' answers Tiny, looking in all his pockets.

'Give us some marks,' Porta turns to Sieg and reaches into his pocket. He comes up with a handful of coins.

The player-piano begins noisily:

Eine Frau wird erst schön durch die Liebe ...

'You wouldn't believe where we've been, looking for you,' says Porta, reproachfully, pulling a thin rope from his pocket. With a practised movement he slips it round Sieg's throat.

'Now you're off on your travels,' he says, pleasantly, tightening the cord.

'I don't like that song,' protests Gregor. 'When people are

going on a trip it ought to be something with: Boom-da-da-boom!' He studies the selection and pushes button number eight: 'Prussian Glory' roars through the room.

'Strangling is said to be the quickest way of saying good-bye to life,' Porta comforts him, opening his mouth as if he himself were being strangled.

'You can't kill me like this,' chokes Sieg, terrified. 'It's murder!'

'Piss and galoshes!' Tiny cuts him off, impatiently. 'Be a man! We all 'ave to go *some* time!'

'Prussian Glory' ends, and exactly at that moment Sieg screams shrilly for the first time.

'Music, dammit!' roars Porta, looking round nervously.

Tiny clumps over to the piano and pushes button five: 'Finnish Cavalry March.'

Sieg screams again. A long, strangled scream, like that of a man being dragged to the scaffold.

'More music,' demands Porta. 'Lots of music! And give it more gas!'

Out in the kitchen the barmaid knocks back her third schnapps and sucks violently at an Army cigarette.

Sieg babbles and screams like a sick cat.

'Now the're beating him up,' shudders the barmaid. 'As soon as they've gone,' she thinks, 'I'll get the janitor's wife to help me drag the poor sod out into the gutter. Then the police can take over! That's what they're for!'

'The coin's stuck,' shouts Tiny, kicking the piano impatiently. 'That monkey had dud money on him!' He hammers at the piano with his fists. 'Play, sod you, that's what we've paid for,' he roars furiously.

'Now we're going to strangle you slowly, the way they do it in the American deep south, when they've got a black monkey on the end of the rope,' sniggers Porta. 'That'll teach you not to pass false money another time.'

Sieg opens his mouth and screams. There is death in it. It penetrates to the very marrow of the bones.

Passers-by stop and try to peer in through the dirty windows. A Lapp woman thinks there is a revivalist meeting being held and wants to come in.

'Beat it,' shouts Gregor waving his hands, as if he were shooing off a flock of pigeons. 'It's nothing to do with you what's going on here. On your way!'

'You certainly *are* a noisy chap,' says Porta, reproachfully, to Sieg. 'It's time we stopped your breath altogether!'

Tiny is almost going amok. He calls the piano every name he can think of. Then he lifts it up on end and lets it fall back to the floor with a terrific bang.

'The Finnish Cavalry March' starts up again with a roar. It sounds as if a whole mounted division was galloping through the bar.

Tiny opens the window and roars at the crowd in the street. 'Move along there! *Geheime Staatspolizei!* Back in your igloos and get to bed, you Polar bastards!' The last of them gets a snowball in the back of the neck and breaks into a run.

Sieg throws himself on the floor, and screams like a slaughter-house pig being butchered. He kicks out with both feet. His arms jerk spasmodically.

'You sound like an Indian bint who's losin' 'er maiden'ead,' says Tiny, kicking him. 'Be a German! Show us you can take leave of life as a member of the *Herrenvolk* ought to do! He taps Sieg's gold Party badge. 'Don't forget you're one of the old warriors!'

'Limp prick's what *he* is,' says Porta, contemptuously, looking up for a hook in the ceiling. There is none. It is obviously not so easy to hang a man as you'd think from the American films.

'Why not shoot 'im an' 'ave done with it?' suggests Tiny, emptying a tankard of beer in one go. He tugs a large army pistol from his pocket and aims it at Sieg. 'When one of these 9-mm chaps 'as made its way from the back of the neck, through the brain at a angle of forty degrees an' out again, the whoreson who's been in the way don't usually 'ave much more to say about anythin'!'

'Makes too much dust,' says Porta. 'And can't you see what a lot of nonsense could come out of one shot? His fuckin' mates'd soon be chasing about, and who d'you think'd be the first to be suspected when they find his punctured corpse? Obergefreiter Joseph Porta! The Army's done its best to ruin my reputation. The swastika cops and me have never been able to hit it off properly.' He snaps his fingers and his face lights up in a pleasant smile.

While he has been talking he has hit on an amazing idea. For several minutes he wonders why it has taken him so long

201

to find the answer, which is so simple an innocent nun could have thought of it.

He gives Sieg, who is lying groaning on the floor with the rope around his throat, a friendly kick.

'Stop that whining! You ought to be happy when you find out what we've thought up for you! You'll die laughing when we start! Stand up man! You're the star performer!'

Porta places Sieg in the middle of the room and tightens the rope round his neck.

'You stand here,' he orders Tiny, 'and hold tight to this end of the rope, and when I say run you take off for all you're worth! Out through the kitchen until you're stopped by the rope!'

'Sounds easy as fallin' off a log,' says Tiny, brightly, scraping his foot like a racehorse ready to start. 'What about shit'ead 'ere? Does 'e go out in the kitchen with me?'

'Don't bother with him! According to my plan he stays here.'

To the final tones of 'The Finnish Cavalry March', Porta moves over to Gregor with the other end of the rope.

'When I shout "Run", you beat it towards the revolving doors fast as you can! You, Emil, you stay where you are and don't move. You two take the command from me: "Ready-set-go!" on the word "*go!*" you start running in the direction I've told you!'

'Does that bastard's body stay in the rope?' asks Gregor, with a worried expression on his face.

'Of course,' Porta assures him.' The trick is that Emil stays inside the rope!'

Sieg moans and begs for his life.

'Oh shut up! My method is so quick you won't even know you're dead. By the way, before you go, do you know anybody who might be interested in a shipment of Polish eggs or some ugly Russian typewriters?'

Sieg shakes his head sadly. He does not know anybody who wants to make omelets or to tap away on Russian typewriters.

'Well then, good-bye,' says Porta, shaking his hand heartily. 'Ready!' he shouts, moving over to the revolving door to be ready for a quick getaway when the business has been concluded satisfactorily.

'Holy Mother of Kazan,' whispers Gregor, admiringly. 'His

nut'll be nipped off like the top of a radish. You could sell this idea to any dictatorship!'

'Well, some are born clever!' says Porta, modestly.

The only person present who is not amused is Sieg. His brain is working so hard you can almost hear the rope vibrate.

Both the rope-pullers take up position with their backs to one another and cannot see what is happening behind them. Porta, standing in the bright light by the revolving door, can only see Sieg as a shadowy form in the dimly-lit restaurant.

In some way Sieg gets one foot up over the rope, so that he is hanging like an ape from a liana, and with the strength of desperation he also manages to free one hand.

'Go!' shouts Porta, and Tiny and Gregor dash away from the prisoner as fast as they can go.

Sieg brings his free hand down on the rope with all his force, with the excellent result that it flies from Tiny's hands. With the speed of a runaway artillery section he crashes through the closed door of the kitchen and straight over the barmaid, who thinks for a moment she has been killed. Tiny goes on through the wall, out on to the staircase, and down head-over-heels into the cellar, the noise sounding as if one of the greatest battles of the war was being fought inside the house.

Gregor, who is holding tightly to his end of the rope, flies at full speed through the revolving door. Goes round in it four times, together with Porta, until they are ejected with the force of a bomb from a mortar, roll straight across the roadway and end up in a baker's shop. Bloody and confused they come to their feet again.

Tiny digs himself, groaning and dizzy, from a heap of coal in the cellar, crawls up the stairs and out through the bar without bothering about Sieg who has been thrown over behind the piano. His hand-sewn, 200 mark shoes can be seen sticking out.

Porta wobbles back into the bar and bows politely to the barmaid, who is still sitting on the floor laughing like an imbecile.

'*Fantastic,*' shouts Tiny, proudly, as they race out of the town in the amphibian. 'I've never seen anythin' like it before in all my war!'

'His whole head flew off!' laughs Gregor, enthusiastically. 'His face smashed into the ceiling and stayed hangin' on the lamp!'

'Lovely, lovely grub,' groans Tiny, between two spasms of laughter. 'That's the way to treat bleedin', blackmailin' sods!'

'You must admit, my ideas aren't bad,' boasts Porta, puffing on one of Sieg's cigars. 'I know *exactly* how to fix little matters like these!'

It is Hofmann again who discovers that Porta's method of execution has not been effective enough. The criminal is still alive and in hospital. He cannot speak but he can, unfortunately, still write. For some strange reason he has not told anybody that he has been the victim of a murderous attack, but has told the doctors that he felt a sudden pain in his throat and lost his voice. The red marks on his neck he tells them, are birthmarks.

'That lame police-dog can't be given time to get over this and start barking,' says Hofmann, bitterly, staring straight in front of him. 'If he does we've not only got a serious race-falsifying charge hanging over us but also two attempted murders and one that nearly succeeded! That's more than enough to lose you your nut three times over, with a twenty-year sentence on top of it. Besides the other things that go along with being court-martialled.'

'There's no way out,' shouts Wolf, with decision. 'That Nazi louse has got to be got out of the way, if we're going to be able to enjoy the short life the God of Germany has endowed us with!'

'The wildcat!' says Porta, thoughtfully, looking up at the beams which cross the ceiling. 'Let's make a signal to Paderborn!'

Hofmann soon has Wachtmeister Sally on the telephone. He hands it over to Porta.

'Remember I know nothing. Never *heard* of wildcats,' he whispers, warningly.

Porta gets straight to the point.

'I'd like to have a closer look at this wildcat of yours. I'd suggest you send him up here to the cold regions as a sample.'

Wachtmeister Sally laughs long and loud.

'Tell me, Porta, do you think I was born in a gasworks and dried out on a canal barge? Send the wildcat as a sample?' He bursts out laughing again. 'No, soon as I receive one thousand marks in cash, he'll be on the way to you by the mail plane!'

'I can't go to Paderborn just to pay for a bloody wildcat,' protests Porta, indignantly. 'Don't you know I'm one of the more important participants in this world war?'

'Don't go on so! I know all about your connections with Panzer-Ersatz-Bataillon. It'll be easy for you to transfer a thousand bananas to me here at HQ.'

Porta takes a swig of coffee to help him think.

'Did you say a *thousand* jimmies for a lousy roof acrobat? D'you think the Lapp women have sucked my brains out?'

'Roof acrobat?' says Sally, scandalized. 'Wait till you see him! When he goes amok he's like a million ordinary cats all rolled up into one!'

'Five hundred,' says Porta, shortly.

'Eight,' Sally demands.

They agree on seven hundred, freight paid.

'Don't you try to take me,' Porta warns. 'I'm a deep-frozen Obergefreiter up here for the present, and it is possible there won't be many of the German Wehrmacht left in the end, but one of us'll live through it and that, by the grace of God, will be Obergefreiter Porta. If I don't get that bloody cat tomorrow morning by first-class mail you can go to mass and prepare yourself for a very quick death!'

'I've never done anybody down on a deal,' lies Wachtmeister Sally, shamelessly. 'You'll have that wicked monster tomorrow evening with the last mail plane, and it'll be sent first class. Ask for the chief pilot, but be careful not to open the cage, because he'll go straight for your face and for anybody else near you. He doesn't care if it's coolies or generals. I'm sending a little apparatus with him. It sends out sounds which drive him quite crazy. If you want him to tear some bastard to bits just put the little apparatus close to the victim and that devil of a cat will look after the rest. I've used him that way before with a bloke and in twenty-one seconds he'd gone into shock.'

'Jesus,' cries Porta in surprise. 'That's just what we need. What does he eat?'

'I usually give him the same as we eat, and he sucks it up like a vacuum cleaner.'

'Does he drink coffee?' asks Porta, wonderingly.

'Yes, and beer,' answers Sally.

'What's his name?'

'Dynamite!'

'Sounds promising,' chuckles Porta, deep down in his stomach. 'Tell him we've got some interesting work for him!'

Tiny and Porta go out to the airstrip to pick up Dynamite,

205

who arrives, angry and vicious, on board a JU 52 mail plane.

'I'd be careful with that wicked bastard, if I were you,' says the pilot, looking nervously at the wildcat's cage.

'Hello, puss,' says Porta, bending over the cage.

The wildcat replies with a mad burst of spitting and snarling, and bites furiously at the bars of the cage.

'Jesus, Jesus, 'e's a mad 'un ain't 'e?' says Tiny, admiringly. 'Let's get 'im 'ome an' lay our plans!'

Everybody keeps well away as they haul the cage containing the snarling wildcat across the air-strip. An elderly Leutnant, who is fond of cats, comes across to them.

Before Porta has time to warn him he puts his hand between the bars to scratch the cats neck. He pulls it back with a scream. It is streaming with blood.

'Dynamite, you devil! You mustn't *do* that,' Porta admonishes him. 'Ask the Herr Leutnant's pardon, now!'

There is a terrific row when they get back to the company lines. One of Wolf's wolfhounds gets its nose slashed to pieces when it tries to sniff a welcome to the new arrival at 5 Company.

'Visiting time at the hospital it between 11.00 and 13.00 hrs,' Hofmann informs them. 'No more than two visitors to each patient.'

'That'll be enough,' answers Porta. 'Tiny and Dynamite!' He takes the sonic apparatus from his pocket to test it. The result is beyond all expectations. The wildcat spins madly in its cage, biting and scratching like a mad thing. There is no doubt at all that it wants to get at Porta who is holding the apparatus. 'This is *it*!', says Porta, happily, throwing a piece of meat into the cage. 'Tiny and Dynamite enter the hospital tomorrow, shortly after they've opened up for visitors. Tiny pushes the apparatus quietly under Emil's arse and lets Dynamite loose. Then I'll be very much mistaken if things don't get very lively, and we'll get rid of that leprous son of a bitch once and for all!'

'I ain't too keen on this,' protests Tiny, weakly. 'Dogs an' cats don't like me much!'

'Piss!' says Porta, decisively. 'You do as I say!'

'An order's an order, Creutzfeldt, and don't you forget it,' shouts Hofmann, harshly.

Dyamite is put in the Kübel's trunk. We can hear him, spitting and snarling with accumulated rage, even through the noise of the engine.

'He's right on top form,' says Porta, with satisfaction. 'You'd almost think he *knew* who he was going to visit!'

An aged, slow-moving, medical Gefreiter shows us the way to Emil Sieg's ward.

A little way down the corridor we are stopped by a forbidding matron, who has caught sight of Dynamite.

'What is *that*?' she asks, pointing indignantly at the cage.

'Matron!' answers Porta, clicking his heels smartly. 'That is a cage!' She ranks as an officer.

'I mean what is inside it?' she snarls, irritably.

'A pussy-cat, which is longing to visit its sick friend,' Porta smiles, sycophantically.

'Cats are not allowed in the wards! It must be left outside!'

Tiny pretends to go outside, but as soon as the sour matron has disappeared he runs down the corridor with the cage rocking after him.

'You're a hard man to get rid of,' says Porta, extending his hand to Sieg. 'But we've got rid of eight million Russians and we'll get rid of you too! You'll see!'

'Get out!' whispers Sieg, fumbling for the bell, but Porta is quicker and pulls it out of the wall.

'Why ring?' asks Porta with false friendliness. 'Let's enjoy ourselves. We've got a friend with us you'll be interested to meet. *He'll* help you to pass the time!'

'A wildcat,' whispers Sieg, in terror, staring with frightened eyes at the snarling animal.

'As you no doubt are aware, cats have nine lives,' explains Porta, 'and, after what's happened so far, you seem to be almost as immortal! We have decided to carry out a scientific experiment: Cat against man! If you are as lucky as you have been the other two times then you should *be* able to fix Dynamite too. Scratch him under the left ear and he'll purr like a house-cat lying under the stove!'

'Listen now,' whispers Sieg, beside himself with fear, and pulling the blankets up under his chin. 'I only wanted to have some fun with you and see how you'd react.'

'You've *seen* how we react,' grins Porta. 'What we're doing now is only in fun!'

'I swear I've never even heard of your Jewish Germans,' whispers Sieg, hoarsely, 'and you will never again have any trouble with me!'

'I know all about that,' grins Porta. 'But now I'd like you to meet Dynamite and after that we'll bury the whole thing.'

'Bury?' whispers Sieg, hoarsely, struggling to get out of bed. Tiny catches him by the hair and pushes him back.

'Stay where you are,' he orders gruffly. 'The poor animal might suffer loss of breath if 'e 'ad to chase after you!'

Sieg opens his mouth to scream, but only a weak rattle leaves it.

Tiny starts the acoustic machine, and the wildcat goes mad. His movements knock the cage over and the door opens. Like a furry rocket he shoots from the cage and springs to the table in the middle of the ward, where he crouches ready to attack. Warning sounds come from his throat.

'No, no!' shouts Tiny, his eyes glaring wildly, as Dynamite flies through the air towards him. He has forgotten he still has the acoustic apparatus in his hand. 'It's not *me!*' he screams, as he falls to the floor with the wildcat on top of him. He feels as if his skin is being pulled, in one long movement, up over his head. In some strange way he lands on Sieg's bed, with the apparatus clutched in his hand.

Fear has given Sieg his voice back. A long, guttural roar comes from his wide-open mouth.

The beds fly round in the room. The table is smashed to bits. Cupboards fall with a deafening crash. Glass tinkles. Feathers from ripped eiderdowns float in the air in clouds.

Tiny rushes towards the door with blood streaming down over his face and his uniform in tatters. He is in such a hurry to get away from the wildcat that he takes the frame of the door with him.

'The sound machine,' shouts Porta, warningly, as Tiny comes running, with the wildcat at his heels.

Tiny stops for a second. The wildcat catches up with him.

'The machine!' shouts Porta, desperately. 'Throw it away for God's sake!'

At last Tiny understands him and sends the apparatus rattling down the corridor. The hospital superintendent, with his assistants at his heels, turns the corner at the same moment.

Dynamite whirls around on his own axis a few times to discover where the hated sound is coming from now. He crouches, and turns his bloodthirsty eyes on the matron, who has picked up the sound machine.

'What *is* that thing?' asks the hospital superintendent, interestedly.

There is no time for him to receive an answer. The wildcat is on top of them. Never in her life has the matron been undressed so quickly. The superintendent goes head over heels down the staircase, and the party with him fly to all sides.

'Let's get out of here,' shouts Porta. 'This is getting *hot*!'

But we have only got a little way down the corridor when the machine comes flying after us.

'No!' Porta manages to scream. Then the wildcat has caught up with them.

Nobody knows how we get away, but one of us must have kicked the apparatus back to Sieg's ward because all hell is loose there.

Bloody, shaking and shocked we crawl back into the Kübel, where Wolf sits waiting for us impatiently.

'What the hell's happened to *you*?' he asks open-eyed. 'You look as if you've been in a fight with a whole panzer division!'

'No more wildcats for *me*!' moans Tiny, who is practically unrecognisable.

'My arse, what a sight you are!' says Wolf. 'What about Dynamite? Aren't you going to take him home with us?'

'Forget *him*,' groans Porta, trying to get a torn-off tunic arm to stay in position. 'That bastard's going to empty the whole hospital before he's done!'

As we turn out of the grounds we hear the tingling sound of broken glass. Sieg sails through the window, followed by two medical orderlies. Before they land, the wildcat is on top of them. They are hidden in a cloud of snow.

'Holy Mother of Kazan,' mumbles Porta, through swollen lips, 'what energy there is in an animal like that!'

'Did you fail again?' asks Hofmann, despairingly, when he sees us.

'Take it easy. It's only just begun,' Porta comforts him.

The following day Hofmann brings us the happy news that Sieg has been declared unsuited for any kind of service and has been transferred, a shaking wreck, to the Army Psychiatric Hospital at Giessen. Nobody takes any notice of his disconnected babbling of murder, racial falsification and wildcats. They merely laugh at his crazy accusations.

'He'll never get out of Giessen,' grins Porta, well-satisfied. 'He'll be seeing wildcats everywhere.'

Hofmann snatches up the jangling telephone. It is Wachtmeister Sally from Paderborn.

'You can sleep easy, lads,' he laughs, jovially. 'Bierfreund-Müller's papers've disappeared for ever and ever! It'll cost another case of whisky though!' he adds. 'If anybody, in the future, catches sight of his half-naked prick, he can say some bloody Jews cut it off of him and it won't even be a lie!'

With a sigh of relief Hofmann puts the receiver back on its hook.

'For safety's sake we'd better leave here for a time,' says Hofmann. 'Actually it's Number Four's turn to go up front, but maybe we'd better take their turn for them. Section leaders and group leaders to me in an hour's time!' he orders, and he is the Hauptfeldwebel again.

The same night we sneak through the front line.

I never dreamt that I would ever have to lead such a mélange of ill-equipped troops as No. 5 Panzer Army.

Generaloberst Balck in a letter to Generaloberst Jodl, September 1944.

Without thinking I bring my right hand back over my shoulder. The edge of it is stiff, from the little finger to the wrist.

I throw my hand forward, straight at his Adam's apple.

Gregor has already killed the other one by hitting him with the edge of his hand from behind between the shoulder and the neck. I heard the crackling sound of bones breaking quite clearly.

Porta jumps neatly to one side to avoid the long bayonet and, like lightning, thrusts the tips of his fingers into the Russian sergeant's throat with such force that the blow knocks him backwards, and the head breaks away from the spine with a cracking sound.

My stroke was perfect. Our Japanese instructor would have been pleased. I crushed his throat and perforated his windpipe. The blow was so powerful that my hand cut into the throat and did not stop until it struck the vertebra which connects the head with the backbone. I made one bad mistake. I looked into the face, saw the twisted mouth and bloodshot eyes.

It was a woman!

I remained sitting in the snow for a long time, vomiting. Our instructor was right: Never look at them! Kill them and move on!

It took me a long time to forget her distorted face.

NOVA PETROVSK

'Get your arse off the ground, you red bastard,' shouts Feld-webel Schröder, with a hard look on his face. 'Run, you louse, run!'

'*Nix Bolsjevik*,' shouts the prisoner, with fear in his voice. With a quick movement he pulls off his fur cap and bows. '*Nix Bolsjevik*,' he repeats, throwing both hands up. 'Heil Hitler!' he screams, confusedly.

'Must be one of their clowns we've got hold of,' grins Unter-offizier Stolp, prodding the prisoner brutally with his Mpi.

'Sod off, you lazy bastard,' hisses Schröder, with a mur-derous gleam in his eyes.

'*Nix Bolsjevik*,' cries the prisoner, beginning to run clumsily through the deep snow.

'He looks like a wet hen,' says Stolp, laughing loudly.

'Jew bastard,' snarls Feldwebel Schröder, lifting his Mpi.

Stolp laughs wickedly and throws a snowball after the prisoner, who has got a good way down the hill. Then the Mpi rattles and the prisoner turns a series of somersaults.

Schröder moves towards the body with the sure steps of a hunter going to pick up a pheasant he has shot down. He prods the dead man, tentatively, with the muzzle of his Mpi.

'Dead as a nit,' he grins back, proudly.

'If the Old Man gets to know about this,' says Gregor, coldly, 'I wouldn't be in your boots!'

'The Old Man can kiss my arse,' says Schröder, with assurance. 'I'm following the Führer's orders. Liquidate the *untermensch* wherever you find them!'

'Your Führer didn't tell you to murder prisoners of war though, did he?' comments Porta, turning the muzzle of his Mpi towards him.

'You can report me if you want,' grins Schröder, super-ciliously. 'I'll manage all right!'

'I hope so, for your own sake,' answers Gregor, contemptuously, going into the woods where the remainder of the section is resting.

The Old Man is grumpy and irritable. The section has been saddled with two guests. A Finn, Captain Kariluoto and a German, Leutnant Schnelle, who are to observe us on these long trips up towards the White Sea. There are also some new men who have taken the interpreter examination in Russian. Comically enough they do not understand a word of the language spoken up here at the Arctic Circle. Both Porta and Barcelona get along much better with the local language.

The officers are shocked by what they have seen already, and there have been several clashes between them and the Old Man. But they can do nothing about it. Oberst Hinka has told them, in no uncertain fashion, that the Old Man is in command and that Barcelona Blom is next after him, irrespective of what happens.

Grumpily we collect our equipment. Porta is ready to fight Unteroffizier Stolp over the murdered prisoner and the Old Man has to speak plainly to Leutnant Schnelle. For no apparent reason Tiny knocks Feldwebel Schröder down.

'Don't follow the road,' shouts the Old Man to Tiny, who is marching in the lead.

'Why not?' shouts Tiny, in a voice which raises echoes in the forest.

'Because we'll run straight into the enemy if we follow the road,' hisses the Old Man, irritably.

'Ain't that what we're lookin' for?' grins Tiny, pleased. 'If we keep on avoidin' one another the bleedin' war'll *never* be over!'

'Do as I say!' shouts the Old Man, gruffly.

'I'd court-martial that man,' cries Leutnant Schnelle, angrily, and has notebook and pencil out already.

'Leave that to me,' says the Old Man, passing the Leutnant quickly.

'The whole of the neighbour's fucking army's on its way towards us!' shouts Gregor, rushing out of the forest in a cloud of snow.

'I thought as much,' sighs Leutnant Schnelle, resignedly. 'Here it goes! That's what happens when they give a Feldwebel too much authority!'

The Old Man looks at him for a moment with stony eyes.

'You can report me, when we get back, Herr Leutnant, but until then I must ask you to refrain from criticising my orders. To put it quite bluntly, I am in command here!'

Leutnant Schnelle exchanges a glance with the Finnish captain, who merely shrugs his shoulders and wishes he was back in Helsinki and had never got himself mixed up with these operations behind the enemy lines.

Tiny is lying in the snow with his ear pressed to the ground, listening intently.

'How many?' asks the Old Man, brusquely, throwing himself down alongside him.

'By the noise the sods are makin' they could be a battalion at least! But if you ask me I don't think there's more'n a lousy company! They're probably out lookin' for snowdrops!'

'How far away?' hisses the Old Man.

'Ard to say,' answers Tiny, trying to look wise. 'These Commie forests can play tricks on you!'

'On your feet,' orders the Old Man, 'out of the marsh and down along the slope! At the double and no firing without my express orders! If we have to fight it'll be with knives and spades!'

Leutnant Schnelle has already his pistol in his hand and is looking very warlike.

'Put that iron away!' snarls the Old Man, irritably. 'If it goes off they'll hear it in Moscow!'

Looking insulted the Leutnant puts his pistol back in the holster, and assumes the look of a boy who has been sent to bed early.

We can hear them a long time before they come into sight. Arguing noisily, they turn the corner by the group of firs. Two lieutenants, with Mpis slung across their chests in the Russian manner, are in the lead. Behind them the company follows in a disorderly mob.

We lie silently in the snow and watch them over our sights. It would be an easy matter to knock them over, but they are not important. We are not interested in killing them. Our mission is of much greater importance.

'The enemy,' whispers Fähnrich Tamm, excitedly. 'Why do we not shoot them?'

'Violence is not always the best way,' Porta rejects the suggestion, scoffingly.

'But it's the *enemy*,' whispers Tamm, loudly, pressing the butt of the LMG into his shoulder.

'Mind you don't bend that finger too far,' Porta warns him, jovially, 'or you'll be a dead hero!'

Tamm loosens his grip on the LMG, and looks around in a lost manner.

'The Führer has ordered it that the enemy is to be destroyed wherever he is met with!'

'Why don't you report to Führer HQ, and spit an' polish his boots a bit for him,' suggests Gregor, with a broad grin. 'Just be the thing for you! You might even get some of Adolf's foot-sweat up under your nails!'

The noise from the departing Russian company dies away gradually. A long, grating peal of laughter is the last we hear of them.

The whole of the day and most of the night we continue marching. The wind cuts like sharp knives. Face masks are of little use when the thermometer is down to minus 50 degrees C.

The steely clouds hang low and move faster and faster. A storm is on its way. One of the feared polar storms which can blow an elk along over the snow as if it were a snowflake.

'Jesus'n Mary, but it's piss cold,' moans Tiny, knocking his hands together. 'What the hell's Adolf *want* in this bleedin' country? We're only doin' the neighbours a favour by pinchin' it from 'em!'

Just before dawn the Old Man allows them a short break for a cold meal.

'Why the pace?' groans Leutnant Schnelle, worn out and throwing himself flat on the snow.

'Because we have to get to the lakes before the supply planes,' answers the Old Man, grouchily. 'We have a very tight time schedule. If you are not able to keep up, Herr Leutnant, you can stay here! You are not assigned to my section, but only with us as an observer!'

'Ready to move,' shouts the Old Man and turns his back contemptuously on the Leutnant.

From the top of the heights they can see out across the White Sea where great waves lift towards the gloomy heavens. On the horizon they can just make out a dark line, resembling a distant coastline.

'Think it's America?' asks Tiny, interestedly.

An animated discussion commences immediately. Only the two observer officers keep out of it.

'Holy Agnes,' cries Gregor, hoarsely, 'it's no further off'n we could piss over there, an' if that's America I'd say let's shit on Adolf and move on out of his shitty war!'

We lie on our stomachs in the snow, and stare dreamily at the dark shadows, while we try to outdo one another in fantasy. Tiny imagines he has met the furrier's boy, David, in New York, where he is passing the time waiting for Hitler's defeat.

On the fourth day, late in the afternoon, we reach the lakes, and have only just stretched out the long red cloth marker for the planes when the first JU 52 roars through the clouds. It swoops low over the snow and we almost think for a moment that it is going to land.

The Old Man sends up a flare, and containers begin to fall from the machine.

Two other aeroplanes come roaring out of the snow-haze, circle for a moment above us, and literally shovel their containers out one after the other.

'They seem in a hurry to get away again,' says Porta, sarcastically, banging the inside of his elbow.

The last of the planes swings about uncertainly. One of its motors splutters and backfires. The next moment it hits the earth, ploughs through the snow and turns a somersault. One of the wings flies off and flames spring up from the wreck.

'Leave it,' says the Old Man, shortly. 'We couldn't get 'em out anyway!'

A huge explosion drowns his voice, and pieces of the wreck are thrown far and wide.

'That bang must've made 'em get up off their arses far away as Murmansk, says Tiny, shocked. He throws a piece of the wing away from him across the lake.

We have just managed to finish collecting the dropped material together when a volley of shots comes from the forest. We rush to take cover and get ready to fight.

The shots go off in volleys, but oddly enough we do not hear the whistle of the bullets.

'It's only the frost,' grins Porta, 'cracking the trees.' He gets to his feet. 'Adolf wouldn't like seeing his heroes get frightened at such a little thing!'

The Old Man chases us and shares the heavy stores between us. The officer guests accept their burdens unwillingly.

Suddenly we stop and look in fear towards the north, where the whole of the horizon seems to be on fire. Thin streaks of flame shoot in bunches across the sky and change in a moment to green, red, white tongues of light, which die out and then grow up again. Each second we expect to hear the roar of explosions but not a sound reaches us.

Even Porta's reindeer snuffles in surprise and looks, blinking, towards the northern sky.

In slow-motion the lances of light change to long, gleaming, glassy rods, like those which hang from an antique chandelier.

The glittering rods dance all around the horizon, turning slowly from white to red-gold, then change suddenly to waves of fire which chase one another across the heavens. Far out over the White Sea new lightnings flash. It seems as if the whole world is coming to an end in a volcanic explosion of colour. Around us it is as light as on the brightest of sunny days.

Suddenly everything goes black. It is as if a black velvet cloak had been thrown over us.

The reindeer snuffles and stamps the ground with its fore-feet.

The lights come rushing across the sky, even more violently than before, and directly towards us.

Quickly we take cover in the snow. The strange phenomenon wheels away from us and disappears out over the sea. The snow gleams and glitters as if strewn with millions of diamonds.

'Fantastic,' mumbles the Old Man, fascinated.

'What's doin' it?' asks Tiny, with respect in his voice.

'It's quite natural,' says Heide, who, as always, knows all about it.

'If that's God playin' games, a man could easy go and get religious,' mumbles Tiny, uncertainly.

The Old Man orders an igloo to be built. Nobody protests. Everybody is looking forward to getting under cover and having a few hours' rest. The moon hangs in the sky like a huge glowing disc in the midst of all the green and red. Its light is pale, but bright as an acetylene lamp which is about to explode. On the horizon clouds appear. At first they are the steely blue of icebergs then, suddenly, they light up as if studded with sapphires. The snow becomes a sheet of crackling silver foil, completely blinding us.

'This on its own's worth the whole trip,' cries Barcelona in amazement.

'It's the Northern Lights,' explains Heide, instructively.

'Makes me think of a pub in Davidsstrasse called "The Northern Lights",' says Tiny. 'The nobs used to come there to take a gander at the natives. Part of the round trip they used to call "*Hamburg bei Nacht*". Me 'n' old "Bannister Monkey" ran into three 'igh-class bints as was sittin' waitin' for a real good Reeperbahn bang. We squeezed down between 'em an' begun to feel 'em up, the way we always used to in "The Northern Lights".'

'Can't you talk *anything* but filth?' hisses Heide, scandalised.

'Stick your fingers in your ears an' keep your mouth shut,' advises Tiny. 'It's accordin' to the spirit of your Führer! The one I'd fished up was named Gloria and she looked it too. On the way out to Blankenese we fell out with the taxi-driver, a spaghetti-German from Innsbruck, who didn't like us throwin' bottles out of the window. As we turned the corner into Fischermarkt we thought it was time 'e took a bath so we threw 'im into the Elbe. To save 'im the trouble of walkin', over on the other side, we pushed the taxi after 'im, after settin' the meter back to zero so's the ride was free.

'The last part of the trip we done in a police car a couple of Schupo's 'ad left parked in a side street. We give it the lot, siren, blue lights an' all. The bints was crazy with it. It was the first time they'd ever been for a ride in a police car.

'Gloria 'ad a smashin' place with a lovely big lawn with cows on it to keep down the grass. She said the cows was English and was more racially pure'n most Germans was. One of 'em tried to 'ook me, so I grabbed it by the 'andlebars and swung it round as if it wasn't no more'n a consumptive goat. Gloria goes into a Wagner act and sets a vicious, bleedin' Dobermann on me, but I got a 'old of 'im an' sent 'im on the longest airtrip 'e'd ever 'ad. Then *she* bit me. 'Avin' no dog any more, I suppose she felt she'd better do the job 'erself. Well after a bit we got 'er quietened down and nipped into 'er monkey's nest.

'We struggled up a spiral staircase an' down a long passage like the tunnels under an old fort. All over the place there was pictures of 'ungry-lookin' skeletons fuckin' away so 'ard steam was coming out o' their arseholes!

' "Classical reproductions from Pompeii," explained Gloria, as if it was the Kaiser's bollocks preserved in spirit she was showin' off.

' "Gawd! 'Ow long was you there?" I asked 'er, thinkin' it

was some sort of a brothel where perversions was their speciality.

' "Dope," she snarled, with the charm of an adder. "They're from the time of the Romans!"

' "Did they used to fuck then, too?" asks "Monk", showin' what a dumb shit 'e was.

'They started pourin' glasses o' port 'n' sherry, but me an' "Monk" didn't fancy it so we nipped down to the Elbe and got us a box o' Löwenbräu, and then we got goin'.

'Gloria was whinin', with passion runnin' out of 'er ear'oles, but just as I'm goin' to throw meself on to 'er she's over an' up the other end o' the bed like a shot. That bed was big enough to've took drivin' lessons on it in a lorry.

' "Why are you so *primitive*?" she sighed, slingin' down 'alf a port. Then she started takin' off 'er clothes bit by bit, like they do in Café Lausen when the peasants come in from the marshes of a Saturday. When she'd finished she pointed 'er legs at the ceilin' and started wagglin' 'er flamin' toes.

'I was on me way into 'er old gondola when she kicked me straight out o' bed and started givin' me a lecture on 'ow us Germans was a cultured people. It was that solemn I come near to standin' up an' givin' the Führer's salute with me prick.'

'Well did she hit you in the balls with a hammer? Or pour vitriol on your cock?' asks Porta, with a lascivious grin.

'No, better'n that,' answers Tiny, bursting into a roar of laughter. 'One of 'er eyes was a glass 'un, an' she could pop it right out so's you could see inside 'er 'ead.'

' "Like me to blink it off for you?" she asked, pullin' at me old pud.'

'Stop it, you filthy-mouthed swine,' roars the Old Man, with every sign of disgust.

'A pig like that to be allowed to wear the honoured uniform of Germany!' rages Heide, turning disgustedly away.

The two officer guests look at one another in silence, and think about the Army to which they belong.

'Did you *really* get it *blinked* off?' asks Porta, curiously, after a long, painful silence.

'She wanted to,' answers Tiny, without a sign of shame.

'You were taking a big risk,' muses Porta. 'Think if you'd got her pregnant and she'd had a kid with a glass eye in the middle of its forehead! They'd have charged you with racial pollution!'

In the course of the night the wind has dropped, and the sun, just above the horizon, is so big and red that it seems as if a man could touch it just by stretching out his arm.

The Old Man spreads a green army handkerchief out in a hollow in the snow.

'Piss on it,' he says to Porta.

'Why not?' grins Porta, and empties his bladder on to the handkerchief. Slowly it changes colour from green to white with a reddish tinge.

The Old Man stretches the handkerchief out on the stub of a tree, looks through the sighting mechanism of the special compass, twists the adjusting screw a few times, and finally presses both sides of the instrument. A narrow green tape appears at the top, by the adjusting screw. He tears it across, breaks off the top edge, makes a square frame of the tape, and lays the compass in the middle of the square. The colour of the handkerchief is now rose, like the piping on our uniforms. He notes some figures down from the compass, and looks up at the sun, which is about to disappear. Then he clips the handkerchief firmly to the frame.

'I'll be damned,' cries Porta, in astonishment. 'Is my piss so strong it can make a snot-rag go all different colours?'

Without replying, the Old Man twists the noses from two cartridges, and blows gun-powder across the handkerchief until it completely covers it. He waits a few minutes and then blows it away.

He places the compass in the top right hand corner and presses a tiny screw. The compass throws a sharp blue light over the handkerchief, which has now become a topographical map on which even the tiniest insertion can be read. When the material is lighted from below he can read the name of the objective for our top-secret mission.

'Nova Petrovsk,' he says, shortly, rising to his feet.

'Where the hell's that?' asks Barcelona. 'I've never even heard of it!'

'Plenty more haven't either,' says the Old Man, drily. 'Nova Petrovsk is so secret it's never officially existed. *Abwehr** has its information from Russian V-men.† There is no town, only a huge camp, camouflaged to look like a forest, with a defence zone 100 kilometres in depth. If you are found inside that area without permission it's good-bye to life. Our job is so

* Abwehr = Counter-espionage.
† V-men = (Vertrauensleute) = spies.

221

GEKADOS* that only the top officers on Canaris's staff know about it. The rockets the supply-planes dropped us are of a completely new design. Nothing concerning them must fall into the hands of the enemy. I imagine I have made myself clear enough?'

'Us Germans are a bright lot,' says Tiny. 'We rub our 'eads up an' down the wall an' out comes something like that 'andkerchief trick. I'll bet both my bollocks that if the neighbours catch us they'll blow their noses all over that snot-rag without ever findin' out they're wipin' their 'orn on the German GEKADOS job of the century.'

'Are there mines where we're goin'?' asks Barcelona, with fear in his voice. Since that time in the minefield he has been neurotic about mines.

'Course there's bloody mines,' answers the Old Man, gruffly. 'What did you think there'd be? Whatever you do, walk in the front man's tracks. Our lives can depend on a step an inch to the wrong side . . . If one of you treads on a mine it won't only be him that goes up but half the section with him.'

'Mines aren't nearly as dangerous as people think they are,' says Feldwebel Schröder, with a superior expression.

'You sound off like you knew what you were talking about,' Barcelona answers him. '*I've* been blown up three times, that high I could've tickled Jesus's footsoles, and *I* know what mines *are*!'

'And you they made a Feldwebel,' jeers Schröder.

Barcelona is about to go for him, but the Old Man steps smartly between them.

'When we've blown this shit away you can cut one another's throats all you want. Until then save your energy! This is the most dangerous and serious action we've ever gone on. Now there's three hours' rest, and stoke up on the rations. There'll be neither food nor rest from the minute we march out of here till we've smashed that bloody camp.'

We dig ourselves in in the snow. Away from the icy wind, which sweeps across the snowy waste with a long drawn out, melancholy sound.

Porta opens some tins and shares out the contents between us.

'The rockets'll be released with the help of a launcher which

* GEKADOS = (Geheime Kommandosache) = Secret Command Case.

222

is in that green case,' explains the Old Man. He holds up one of the new rockets, so that we can all see it. 'Listen closely,' he continues, 'you too, Tiny! If you make a balls of it with one of these there won't be as much as a button left. You turn this dial to the left and stop at the figure 5. Push it up until it clicks. Turn the dial to the figure 9. Push it in and turn it back to figure 5. Now the rocket is armed, and nothing can stop it exploding in five hours time. The rubber gadget on the top of the rocket is a suction cup, which attaches itself to the object hit. If anyone attempts to pull it loose the rocket will explode in that person's hands. As soon as all the rockets have been fired the launching apparatus will be destroyed. Nothing, not the slightest fragment, must fall into the hands of our neighbours! If you should happen to be surprised whilst preparing for the launch, pull out this pin and one second later you and the rocket will have been blown to atoms! Understood?'

'The bleedin' Army's got us by the balls all right,' says Tiny, apathetically. 'Now they've got us committin' suicide by numbers!'

'Life is a throw of the dice,' sighs Porta. 'We're shooting for a six every single day!'

'I won't pull any pin out,' says Gregor with certainty. 'The fellow who does that is, to my mind, the dumb cluck of the world. The safest way to live through a war is to meet up at the enemy's place with something top secret in your pocket!'

'Wouldn't it be a better bet to go straight over to Ivan and pass 'im the lot, an' fuck the Fatherland!' suggests Tiny.

'High treason!' howls Heide, furiously.

Leutnant Schnelle shakes his head, and moves pointedly away from Tiny and Gregor.

'Each group will be issued with three rockets and a homing device,' continues the Old Man. 'You will inform me, by radio, as soon as the rockets are armed and ready to fire, and I will fire them. Once more: turn only to the left and remember you must hear the click. If it does not click, or you turn the dial to the right, the whole lot'll go off in your hands! Did *you* understand, Tiny?'

'Completely,' Tiny assures him, knocking his knuckles on his forehead. 'It's chiselled into me bonce for ever an' ever amen! Instructions on explosives I *listen* to, mate!'

'I bloody well hope so,' laughs Porta, 'or it's good-bye for now, see you later!'

'Let's get going,' says the Old Man, working the bolt of his machine-pistol. 'No smoking whatever permitted!'

Every now and then a blue flash lights up the sky above the forest. The sound of engines grows louder and louder.

In the course of the night we creep past the outer A-A positions. We are so close to them we can smell their machorka.

'Mines,' warns the Old Man, lifting his hand as a signal to us to take even greater precautions.

The Legionnaire takes a mineprobe from his pack and offers it to Feldwebel Schröder with a sarcastic smile.

'*Peau de vache*, this must be just the job for you,' he whispers, wickedly.

Schröder shakes his head nervously, and withdraws a pace.

'I have no experience of that kind of thing!'

'Then keep your blasted mouth shut another time when somebody's talking about mines,' growls Barcelona, tautly.

'*Cuillon*,' snarls the Legionnaire, jeeringly, and works a wooden mine carefully from the snow. 'Come death, come . . .' he hums, while Tiny cuts the cables.

The Old Man turns on the blue compass light and measures the distance on the chart. 'The V-men's information's dead right!'

Step by step the section works its way through the mined area. The least mistake and a roaring explosion will tear us to bits.

Fähnrich Tamm nearly steps on a string but the Legionnaire grabs his foot and puts it down gently alongside the innocent-appearing cord.

'You bloody cow,' the Old Man rates him. 'My God, to think of being burdened with a moron like that!'

'*Par Allah*,' hisses the Legionnaire. 'Do that once more and I will take your life with *my* cord.'

Out in the darkness a dog barks furiously. Two others answer it from further away.

'Bloody dogs,' curses Gregor. 'I'll kick their curs' arses for 'em if they come here!'

A spotlight goes on. A finger of light searches over the snow, stopping at intervals. It sweeps round in a wide half-circle, turns suddenly back, and stops, just before it reaches me. Paralysed with fear I press my body into the snow and await a deadly MG salvo. The guards shout reassuringly to one another. We know how they feel. Sentry-go in the dark is frightening for anybody. When a sentry is killed at his post it happens so quickly that he hardly knows he is dead, before it is a fact.

We crawl the last part, and despite the heavy equipment we are dragging with us, we pass through the defences quickly. No sound of treacherous metal against metal is heard, to warn the sentries in the darkness.

Lorry after lorry rolls through the two great wooden doors of the fortress-like depot camp. Field lamps shine briefly as the NKVD guards check the lorries' papers. Nobody gets into this place without high-priority authorisation.

'Ivan's on his toes all right,' whispers Porta, tensely. 'They don't even trust their own coolies!'

'No bloody wonder,' answers Gregor. 'Take a sniff. Must be a million gallons of petrol inside there!'

'Yes, enough for another Thirty Years War, or more,' whispers Tiny, overcome.

'Was it to the left or the right we were supposed to turn those warheads?' asks Porta, nervously.

'To the right,' says Tiny, confidently. 'But I don't remember if it was 5 or 9 as come first! It's gotta go click though or else it goes off!'

Suddenly we are all in doubt. Tiny suggests, with his usual optimism, that we can take it in turns and see what happens. Then it would only be every second rocket that blew up.

'Jesus, man, don't *turn* that thing!' I warn him, in terror, as Tiny is about to turn the dial. 'We could get our arses blown off!'

'If it does, let's hope they've lit the landing-lights back home,' grins Porta, fatalistically.

The Old Man comes crawling over to us from behind a great stack of shell casings.

'What in the name of hell are you farting about here for?' he snarls, sourly. 'First and fourth groups have got theirs set up already!'

'Was it to the left or the right we were supposed to turn it?' asks Porta, holding a warhead out towards the Old Man.

'God in Heaven have mercy on us,' groans the Old Man, despairingly. 'To the left you mad sods! Ivan'd die laughing if he could see you now!'

'Give him a shout, then,' suggests Porta. 'Then the war'd be over, and we'd go down in history as Adolf's secret weapon!'

'An' turn it to 5?' asks Tiny, with his hand on the dial.

'Not *now*, you great shithouse, you,' hisses the Old Man, slapping his fingers. 'Set 'em up and aim 'em first! What do you want to blow up here?'

'Lorries,' says Tiny, happily. 'There's masses on 'em.'

'Piss off, man,' snarls the Old Man. 'And to hell with the vehicles. These rockets are to be used against the most distant targets. You don't seem to have understood anything of what I explained to you! First we hit the distant targets with the rockets, then you place Lewis bombs and radio mines in the square you've been assigned to. Even a dummy could follow that. Try, for Christ's sake, to *listen* when I'm telling you what to do. When you get to the big open area where the trains are standing, be on your toes. They've planted signal-mines there with trip-wires. *Don't touch the trip-wires!* Don't even *breathe* on 'em! If they go off they'll send up parachute flares and the whole damned enemy camp'll be lit up like daylight!'

'Don't be nervous,' Porta comforts him. 'We can skin a louse without it even noticing!'

'I was at the Jews' pickpocket school on the Reeperbahn,' boasts Tiny. 'I could draw the rags off the throat of a whore with 'em on an' she'd never notice it!'

'How dumb can you get?' snarls the Old Man, angrily, disappearing again.

Squabbling, we reach the place where the rocket launchers are to be set up. We assemble the parts. The firing base seems a primitive affair, almost like an unfinished wooden packing-case. The one thing it does *not* look like is a firing base.

At the lower end of one of the aluminium rails are three small wheels with dimly lighted, graduated scales. These are used to adjust the launching base.

Tiny puts the 52 centimetre tube in place, and I screw on the warhead.

Porta attaches the odd-looking cables, which look as if they'd been taken from the inside of a spring mattress.

'Think it'll work?' asks Tiny, doubtfully. 'I'd rather 'ave a spray-gun.'

'It'll work,' says Porta, with conviction, shading the spirit-level on the firing ramp with his hand.

'Group six ready,' I tell the radio, in a low voice.

'Stay by the launchers until the rockets are gone!' orders the Old Man. He and Heide are lying in amongst the ammunition piles, to receive readiness reports from the various groups.

'Turn the dials to figure 5,' orders the Old Man, looking attentively into the green box.

Tiny rushes at his rocket as if he were afraid one of us was going to beat him to it.

'Was it right or left?' he asks.

'Left, you fool!' growls the Old Man, irritably.

'This is gonna make a bang that'll make the devil's grand-mother jump with fright,' grins Tiny, happily, and turns the dial to 5.

The launcher shudders slightly, and there is a low fizzing sound, as if a bundle of matches had all been struck together. Soundlessly the rockets leave their mountings and fly through the night like ghostly bats. No muzzle-flame. No exhaust flame. Their course is precisely directed by the instruments in the green box.

Several of the rockets land in the far-off petrol depot. Others adhere to piles of ammunition and to workshops inside camp 3. After five hours they will explode with inconceivable force.

Rapidly we destroy the launching rails and the rocket mount-ings. The Old Man presses a white button on the oblong firing box. A boiling, bubbling sound begins to come from it immedi-ately. An acrid mist tears at the throat and palate, as a corrosive acid runs from the small glass phials inside it, destroying con-densers, spools and blocks. A remarkable piece of engineering is destroyed in seconds, an apparatus the like of which no other Army possesses. The odd-looking measuring antennae, which resemble mattress springs, we cut into small lengths and dis-perse far and wide.

'Now the Lewis bombs,' whispers the voice of the Old Man through the radio. 'You've got one hour. Not a second more!'

One at a time we rush over the wide, heavily-trafficked road, leading into the recesses of the enormous ammunition and petrol storage camp. The air shudders with the noise of motors, and hoarse, guttural orders sound through the night.

Several times we pass so close to Russian sentries that we can hear their breathing quite clearly.

'Smell the petrol?' asks Porta, in a whisper. 'What a spot for a pyromaniac!'

'Ivan Stinkanovitsch's gonna shit 'imself with fright,' rumbles Tiny, deep down in his belly.

We almost run into the twenty-foot high perimeter fence.

Tiny pulls out his cutters.

'Let's 'ope there ain't no current in it,' he remarks, as he lays it on the first wire.

'Then you'd know what the electric chair was like,' answers Porta, drily.

'Piss!' growls Tiny, cutting through the wire as if it were cotton. His strength is superhuman.

'Jesus,' cries Porta, as we stand surrounded by great stacks of petrol drums. 'I didn't think there was that much petrol in the whole world!' He bangs on a couple of drums. 'Wouldn't want to blow up a load of empties, would we?' he continues.

Tiny has filled his lighter and is about to light a cigarette.

'A lame monkey must've chewed on your arse,' Porta scolds him. 'We'll all go to the devil if you start blowin' sparks about in here!'

With every sense taut, we move slowly along the mountainous stacks of boxes and drums. Well into the camp, we turn off to the left and come out into a wide connecting path, which stretches off into the distance.

Porta stops so suddenly that I run into him.

'Ivan,' he whispers, in an almost inaudible voice.

As at a command we draw the wires from our pockets.

Two Russian soldiers in ankle-length greatcoats come towards us. They are chatting to one another.

'*Job tvojemadj,*'* one of them laughs, loudly.

Tiny tosses his head impatiently and lifts his wire. Porta holds up a warning hand. It is better to let them go.

As soon as we are round the corner we ready the first of the Lewis bombs. We set the detonators on four hours. Tiny bites into the glass phials, unconcernedly, and spits the pieces into the snow as if they were cigarette ends. If one of them is cracked it is certain death. The powerful acid would eat its way from a man's tongue down through his whole body. Tiny does not realise the danger. He spits glass splinters continually, and washes his tongue clean with vodka.

' 'Oly maiden,' he cries, as we stand looking at the mountains of shells. 'And Adolf wants us to believe Ivan's arse is 'angin' out! Germany ain't never '*ad* that much gunpowder!'

'Careful,' warns Porta, as we attach the sticky bombs. 'For God's sake don't bend that bloody pin! If this lot goes up while we're inside we'll end up on Postdamer Platz with such a bang

* Russian: Go home and fuck your mother.

we'll never be able to get up and go into "The Crooked Dog" for a quick 'un again!'

'Sssh!' whispers Tiny, excitedly, pressing himself close to the shell stacks. 'Ivan!'

'Steady!' whispers Porta. 'We won't take 'em unless we have to!'

Two sentries come creaking towards us. They are talking to one another quietly in a dialect we cannot follow. 'Mongolian apemen,' whispers Porta, whipping the wire from his pocket.

That strange front-line tension begins to creep up my spine. I tighten my grip on the wooden handle of the wire and search with my left hand for my paratrooper knife.

A third soldier emerges from a narrow passageway and begins to bawl the other two out for smoking. They stop five or six yards from us and begin to quarrel. They throw their arms about and shout angrily at one another.

The NCO stamps his clumsy felt boots in the snow and shouts louder than any of them.

Porta makes a wordless signal. We simply *have* to take them.

Noiselessly we close on the three Mongolian soldiers, who are standing with their backs to us shouting at one another.

Porta gives a sibilant signal, and we are on top of them. With sharp tugs we tighten the wires around their necks. Then we go down on our backs, each with a kicking Russian on top of us.

A weak gurgling noise is the only sound they can make. They kick a little more and throw out their arms weakly. The piano wires cut deeper into their throats. For a few seconds their bodies continue to shudder slightly. Then we loosen the wires and get to our feet.

'Let's get these three tourists under cover,' says Porta, taking a swig of vodka.

'Leave it to me,' says Tiny, eagerly. He disappears with two of the bodies and forces them in between the ammunition boxes as if they were no more than two bundles of dirty washing.

'He's going to frisk 'em,' says Porta. 'That's why he was so eager!'

By the big oil store we meet Feldwebel Schröder and Fähnrich Tamm. We agree to help one another to move some large boxes and drums in order to place the small radio bombs better.

We have almost finished moving the boxes when a sentry comes out of a narrow passageway.

'Who goes there?' he shouts, in a penetrating voice. 'Who goes there?' he repeats, swinging his *Kalashnikov* from his shoulder.

Paralysed with fear we stare at him, anticipating the burst of machine-pistol bullets which will knock us over.

Then Porta answers him in pure Ukrainian: '*Rabotschijs dvidatji porokh!*'*

With his Mpi at the ready the tall Russian approaches us gingerly.

'*Krass tjuk?*'†

'*Job tvoje madj, djaddja*,' grins Porta, walking slowly towards him. '*Papirossa, starschij serschant?*'‡ he asks, holding out a packet.

'*Spajisibo*',§ smiles the sergeant. He wears green NKVD shoulder straps.

Porta extends his lighter politely. At the same moment Tiny lunges with his paratrooper knife. It enters the man's body close to the spinal cord and continues up into the neck.

Without a sound the stabbed NKVD man sinks to the snow. Remarkably, the cigarette is still in place between his lips.

Porta takes it and puts it back into the packet. The dead man has no more use for it.

Tiny withdraws the knife and wipes it on the dead man's greatcoat. With practised fingers he runs through his pockets and finds some pornographic photographs, which he keeps.

A little later we come out on to the wide connecting path, where we are bawled out by a lieutenant for not saluting a passing NKVD company.

'Report to me after morning parade,' he barks, angrily, in parting.

'*Dashe, Mladschij lejtenant*,'** shouts Porta, loudly, and clicks his heels.

In between some large brick buildings a long row of JS tanks are parked. Their huge 122 mm guns point threateningly at the clouds.

'Odd,' mumbles Porta, looking down through the hatchway.

* Rabotschijs dvidatji porokh (Russian) = Workmen moving ammunition.
† Krass tjuk (Russian) = Are you stealing?
‡ Papirossa, starschij serschant (Russian) = Cigarette, staff-sergeant?
§ Spajisibo (Russian) = Thank you.
** Dashe, Mladschij lejtenant (Russian) = Very good, sir.

'They're all tanked up, full of ammo, and ready to go!'

'Let's blow 'em away!' says Schröder.

'If we put the bombs on top of the petrol tank cover,' says Porta, 'we ought to achieve a good result when they blow down into the petrol.'

In the course of a few minutes we have positioned the bombs on the petrol tanks. Singly we run across the large parade ground and take cover between the packing-cases.

I am almost across when I stumble over a rail and slide on my stomach across the icy snow with my Mpi rattling behind me. I am stopped by a pair of felt boots planted solidly like pillars in the snow. Automatically I grasp my paratrooper knife, as I rise, groaning, to my feet.

The Russian, who is twice as big as I am, lays his machine-pistol on the snow and helps me.

'*Spajisibo, spajisibo,*' I stammer, nervously.

As he bends over me I drive my knife deep into his throat. With a rapid movement I turn the knife and withdraw it.

He emits a rattling sound, falls to his knees, and tries to draw his pistol.

I kick him in the face and drive my knife into his chest. To my horror the blade snaps.

Breathlessly, the others come to my aid. Tiny smashes the heel of his boot with all his strength into the face of the dying Russian, whose pistol is half-drawn from the holster. Schröder stabs him in the stomach.

'Come on,' says Porta. 'Let's get out of here! All we've got left to do's to place the last of the bombs amongst the boxes of vehicle spares.'

Feldwebel Schröder climbs up on the boxes and sits astride them. Tiny hands up the explosive charges while Porta readies the detonators.

I have just passed the last of the radio bombs to Tamm when I hear a faint click. Tiny hears it too, and drops flat. Porta disappears, in one long, acrobatic spring, and I roll under some drums behind a tractor.

Tamm, who apparently has not heard the click, stares uncomprehendingly about him.

Before we can manage to warn him, the bomb explodes with an ear-splitting noise. He is thrown into the air by the blast from it. His entrails are torn from his body, as if he had been cut open lengthways, and his backbone splintered to pieces. Flesh and bone spurt out to all sides.

The breath is blown from my lungs. The next minute I am thrown high into the air. For a fraction of a second I see Porta hanging in the air alongside me with his arms spread out as if he had wings.

Tiny comes flying past, as if he had been fired from a gun.

Feldwebel Schröder drops back into the snow in a bloody rain of flesh and bone. His own!

I whirl round in empty air, high above the camp, and fall back towards the earth. I go straight through a thatched roof and land in a giant bath filled with icy-cold, oily water. I go down and down into it, and the chill brings me back to consciousness. For a terribly long moment I feel the strangling grip of the water at my throat. I strike out desperately with arms and legs to get back to the surface. Air, air is my only thought. At last I am up, and filling my lungs with ice-cold air. My breathing apparatus freezes and again I am suffocating. The water alongside me boils, as if a tank had been thrown into the water. Time passes, seconds, minutes, hours, I cannot tell, and then Porta's scruffy red head pokes up out of the water alongside me, spouting like a whale.

'What the *hell* happened?' he chokes, half-suffocated. 'I'm stone deaf and there's a lot of stuff in my guts that hasn't any business being there!'

In a state of shock we work our way back to terra firma. All around us explosions crash and roar. We run like madmen, our only thought to get away from the burning camp.

'Where's Tiny?' I ask, in a voice which is still shaking from the terrible shock.

'He flew thataway,' mumbles Porta, pointing to the northwest. 'He's probably reached Alaska already, and is telling the story of his air trip to the bears!'

Behind us we can hear excited shouts. Machine-pistols bark, viciously.

'I think it's high time we got out of here,' says Porta, firmly.

Behind a long declivity we run into the section, waiting for the stragglers.

Tiny is sitting in the middle of a huge snowdrift, wiping off blood and dirt.

'Where the devil did you get to?' asks Porta.

'Bleedin' 'ell,' Tiny pants, wrenching his broken nose back

into place. 'First of all I went straight up to the German God'n knocked 'is throne over. Then I sailed off through the air with about a ton o' explosives back o' me arse, and ended up in this 'ere snowdrift!'

'I've never seen anything like it,' Heide tells us. 'He came rushing down from the clouds like a spaceship and bored his way ten feet down into the snow!'

'You must've made a balls of it,' says the Old Man, reprovingly. 'Those radio bombs are foolproof!'

'Maybe we're bigger fools than they reckoned on,' says Tiny, modestly.

A colossal explosion cuts him short. A volcano of snow, ice, earth, stones and military material explodes into the air and flies in all directions.

In the middle of it all are hundreds of lorries and tanks.

For a brief moment everything seems to float high in the air, then the cloud breaks into millions of fragments which rain down on the earth. Two long barrack buildings fly into the air and look as if they are floating on a sea of flame. They fall and shatter in a cloud of blood, entrails, smashed beds and the gods know what else. A long, shrill, massed scream comes from the soldiers, who are blown from the building and fall back to earth in a spurt of blood and crushed bones.

For a few seconds a terrible silence reigns. Then flames rise with a roar from the great storage camp.

Searchlights begin to criss-cross the sky, and flak-guns fire from the batteries around the camp. They must think it is an air raid.

A series of gigantic explosions rocks the surrounding countryside like the shock of an earthquake. A huge column of flame reaches towards the heavens, growing and growing as if it will never stop.

Two great sheets of flame shoot up from the thousands and thousands of gallons of petrol the rockets have ignited. The heat rolls across the ground like a hot breath from hell itself. For miles around, the snow melts and lakes come into being. Up from the middle of the camp rises a flame so clear and white that it fills us with terror. Then comes the blast wave and everything, living or dead, is swept from its path. Trees are torn up by the roots or snapped off like matchsticks. With a deafening roar it sweeps over us, throwing us far out across the frozen lakes.

A lorry and trailer sail through the air as if they were driving along an invisible road. They fall into the snow a long way off in the forest, and become a heap of twisted metal.

Three days later we can still see the glow of the flames far behind us. The whole horizon is a hell of fire, and even though we are forty miles from it it still seems to be just behind us.

By now we are almost mad from exhaustion, and fights break out for the most ridiculous reasons. Tiny has been about to knock Leutnant Schnelle down twice because he continually threatens him with a court martial.

Suddenly I break through a thin skin of ice, and only Gregor's quick reaction saves me from disappearing into an apparently bottomless cleft in a glacier.

A strange roar can be heard through the noise of the storm, almost like a violent artillery bombardment. Our compass needle swings about crazily, and points in all directions.

Heide talks of magnetic storms, but cannot explain to us what they really are. Just mumbles something about them being a special kind of Polar storm which sends both men and instruments crazy. We can only agree with him. But, as often happens in the Arctic, the wind suddenly changes as if two storms are blowing in different directions. Snow and ice are sucked up into huge spirals.

Suddenly Unteroffizier Stolp lets out a loud, piercing scream and disappears into the snow as if he had been pulled down by the feet. Despairingly we peer down into the dark crevasse into which he has fallen in a cloud of ice and snow.

We shout, but only the echoes come back to us from the depths.

'He's gone straight to the devil,' shudders Porta.

'Fuck '*im*,' says Tiny. 'A rotten bastard when all's said an' done!'

'That is no way to speak of an Unteroffizier,' Leutnant Schnelle corrects him sharply.

'NO?' answer Tiny, looking him up and down contemptuously.

Soon after, Barcelona goes through but manages to hang on to a ledge. We get a rope down to him and haul him up. He is almost mad with terror and says the devil was sitting down there in the bottom of the crevasse calling to him.

Suddenly the storm drops. The silence that follows it frightens us. It feels as if the threatening, steel-grey heavens are

234

about to fall on us. After only a few minutes the storm is back again with increased force.

'*Down!*' roars the Old Man, but his warning comes too late.

Leutnant Schnelle is blown over the edge of the cliff, hovers like a bird in flight, turns over, is whirled upwards and falls straight down into the green waves below. We catch sight of him on the tip of a giant wave and then he is sucked down into the greedy white foam.

'Swimmin' on in advance, I reckon, so's 'e can get that court martial set up for me,' says Tiny.

'It's nothing to laugh at,' says Heide, shocked.

'You expect me to break into tears over that shit of an officer?' asks Tiny.

The storm increases in violence. The snow is now so thick that we can only see a few inches in front of us. The entire desert of snow has been whipped, by the storm, to a raging sea. The snow comes rolling down on us in great waves, which threaten to engulf us completely.

The temperature has fallen to around minus 50 degrees C. Even our breath freezes to ice. The short day is over, and the darkness has descended. We press on, as if fumbling our way through black velvet curtains. The only satisfaction we get from the terrible polar storm is that it is just as bad for the Russians as it is for us.

The strange, changeable winds blow the veil of snow aside for a moment, and Porta catches a glimpse of a party of soldiers who are coming straight towards us.

The Old Man orders us to scatter and dig ourselves in the snow.

'Where've they got to?' asks Tiny, in amazement, after we have waited for some time in our snow burrows.

'They must be somewhere close by,' considers Porta, looking cautiously up over the snowy ridge.

'That bloody snow! Can't even get a sight of your prick without a telescope!' scolds Barcelona, straightening his face mask.

A little way across the tundra the snow has been blown together into a tall saw-edged drift. A fur-clad head shows for a moment above the rim.

'Uncle Ivan,' smiles Porta, releasing his safety catch.

'I'll knock that bastard's teeth in for him, when he shows

235

himself again,' says Gregor, wickedly, laying his cheek alongside the butt of his Mpi.

Almost two hours go by before they come, one by one, crawling over the mountains of snow. One of them half rises and gives a signal with his arm. They split into two groups. One goes north in single file. The other moves directly towards us.

'Quiet,' whispers Porta, 'none of that crazy, scattered firing! Tiny'n me'll do it! We'll take the rear ones first. The noise of the storm will cover the shots.' He lifts his sniper's rifle and adjusts the telescopic sights.

Tiny draws a deep breath, and aims at the fur-clad soldiers to the rear.

Porta has the next to last of them in his sights.

Both rifles go off simultaneously.

The two soldiers go over as if they had been hit by a fist. When the next two fall the section leader turns round and sees what is happening. He stops, and gapes uncomprehendingly. Then he too drops, remains kneeling in the snow for a moment with his hands to his shattered face, and goes down. Those left throw themselves flat and begin to crawl backwards to cover, away from the firing.

A salvo of bullets bores into the snow with a strange splashing sound.

The Legionnaire throws his Mpi to his shoulder. Three shots sound singly, and the last of the enemy group jumps and dies.

'What fools to go over the top like that,' says Porta, shaking his head. 'If they'd crept along under cover of it we'd never've been able to take 'em!'

'Wonder what sort of a dope the leader was?' says Tiny.

'A poor devil like us,' answers Porta. 'The kind they always use for the dirty jobs.'

'Come death, come . . . ' hums the Legionnaire, into the howling of the Arctic storm.

We build an igloo in a deep valley. The Old Man didn't want to give the order to do it, but he can see our strength has almost run out.

'Listen,' says Porta, making himself comfortable in the igloo's best spot. 'When I was serving with Fifth Panzer-regiment in Berlin the CO once sent me to take a letter to his wife.'

'Did you know Staff-Feldwebel Giese from the unarmed combat school at Wünschdorf?' Tiny breaks in. 'I'll *never* forget *'im*, not if I live to be a 'undred. 'E left this world through a shortage of oxygen, even though *'e* was a specialist in pressin' the air out o' people. One morning early, right at the beginnin' of drill 'e pulled our company clown, who didn't understand a fuck what it was all about, out of the ranks. 'E kept on gettin' his wire round 'is own neck and comin' close to stranglin' 'imself.

'"Look here," explained the Staff-Feldwebel, "you put your sling round *my* throat and imagine I am a Russian who wants to kill you. Pull tighter man! Take a good grip on the handles and pull outwards!"

'Well this dope'd been in the shootin' club long enough to know an order was an order, so 'e pulled 'early on the two ends of the sling. The rest stood looking on, the way you always do when you're bein' instructed. We *did* think it a bit queer as 'ow Giese was makin' faces an' stickin' out 'is tongue at us.

'"Let the Staff 'ave a bit of air then!" somebody shouted from the ranks.

'By then it was too late already. Staff Giese didn't need air no more. 'E was dead. There was a 'ell of a bother about that instruction period. Three of them snap-brim fellers came an' talked about it with us, an' when they left they took Ernst with 'em. They 'ung 'im as a warnin' to the rest of the pupils.

'A bit later I was sent to the war dog school at Hof, where somethin' even nuttier 'appened. There they 'ad a grey Alsatian, which 'eld the rank of Obergefreiter . . .'

'Fuck you and your Obergefreiter Alsatian,' Porta breaks in, impatiently. 'Now it's *my* turn. Off I marched to the CO's crumpet. Course I was supposed to use the back door. The front door was for Leutnants and above. So in I go through the rose bushes and all the other shit there is in a CO's garden. I was just going to open the gate into the back garden, but banged it to again pretty quick when I caught sight of a bulldog about the size of a calf, with a yellow, bristly coat and a head as big as a motor-cycle sidecar. He barked like a whole pack of bulldogs whose voices were breaking, but much, much louder. Spittle drooled down his chops and he didn't even try to hide the fact that he was just waiting to get his English dog's teeth into the cheeks of a German soldier's backside.

'"You bloody English've already lost this war," I said to him, and moved off sharply to the front door and pressed the bell. No reaction. I rang louder. Perhaps the CO's wife was deaf. It was only when I rang for the third time that an attractive "fuck me quick" bint opened the door.

' "You rang, soldier,' she twittered, rolling her giglamps at me.

' "Reporting ma'am,' I roared, so loudly that the bulldog took cover behind the house. "Obergefreiter Joseph Porta, Fifth Panzerregiment, HQ Company, on temporary service with ordnance, has a GEKADOS letter from the Commanding Officer to his lady wife, ma'am!"

'She threw the letter carelessly into a corner, as if it were last year's newspaper.

' "You're new?' she asked, pursing her mouth as if she was sucking a nigger prick in the rainy season.

' "No, slightly used," I answered.

' "Would the Obergefreiter like a glass of wine?" she purred, staring intently at the place where my bollocks were swelling up behind my flies.

' "Thank you, ma'am," I answered, hanging my cap on a wooden nigger, one of those things classy people buy when they can't afford to import a real cannibal to take the guests' hats.

'We smoked for a while and talked happily about the great victories we were winning all over the world. She inhaled so deeply that at a certain point in the conversation I looked under the table to see if smoke was coming out of her cunt.

'After we'd emptied the bottle of livening juice and confided our passionate thoughts to one another, she let my good friend out of his cage and tickled him till I was about ready to start swinging by my army sandals from the chandelier. Not long after, I took the heights by storm and planted me old flagstaff. This happened five times, before the doorbell rang. Fortunately the CO's wife had remembered to put the chain on. For a moment I thought it was the bulldog that wanted to be let in.

' "Are you home, Lisa," whined my CO, pushing his nose through the gap the chain allowed.

' "It's the old idiot," she whispered, in a voice which sounded as if she'd been drinking sulphuric acid. "His prick's so tiny he couldn't even satisfy a humming bird!"

' "Lisa! Is anybody home?" whines the voice from the doorway again.

"Jesus, Mary and Joseph," I think. "And *that's* your CO!

Who the hell'd have gone out and put the chain on from the inside."

' "Course we're at home you bloody old prehistoric German pygmy prick," I nearly shouted. "Come an' dip your cock in Obergefreiter juice!" But before I really knew what was happening she'd pushed me out of the kitchen door and there was that bloody great English giant of a dog, sitting licking his chops at the thought of a nice chunk of German soldier meat.

' "Nice dog," I wheedled, staring it in the eyes, the way I'd heard animal trainers do when they go in to have a chat with a lion.

' "Hurra!" shouted the dog. At least that's what it sounded like.

' "Hurra!" I replied, and sprinted off with that English monster hanging on to my Prussian soldier's arse.

'Two days later the animal is picked up by two SD snap-brims. The new racial laws have just come into force. No non-Aryan dog was allowed in a German home. The Jewish bulldog went straight to the gas chamber.

'In replacement for him my CO got himself a spotted bird-dog, but that dog too, ran foul of the racial laws. It had the blood of French Jews in its veins. It went to the gas chamber.'

'Isn't it about time you turned in, Porta,' remarks the Finnish captain, acidly. '*We* are tired, at any rate!'

'Later on they bought a Great Dane,' continues Porta, without taking any notice of the captain. '*There* was a dog the SD could accept. They were attracted to it because of its colossal stupidity!'

The storm drops, in the course of the night, and an unreal silence lies across the tundra. The cold air strikes us with the violence of a tank, sucking every bit of warmth out of our bodies.

Nobody who has not experienced it, can judge where the borderline of physical endurance lies.

Generalfeldmarschall von Keitel, February, 1945

'A real minister,' shouts Wolfgang, the Communist leader, giving a shove to Hirtsiefer, the former Minister for Home Affairs, who has just been received as a prisoner in the concentration camp at Esterwegen.

'If that bureaucrat can stand on his feet tomorrow morning,' says SS-Scharführer Schramm, 'I'll look after you shits personally!'

Wolfgang looks at him and smiles sardonically.

'We'll look after him all right,' he promises, blackly.

An SS man shoves Hirtsiefer roughly, so that he knocks two prisoners over towards the bunks. They get to their feet and strike out at him.

'It was you, you lousy Social Democrat, who gave our hungry wives two cups in recognition of them having brought their twelfth child into the world.'

Growls are heard from the men surrounding Hirtsiefer. Even the SS men's smiles have disappeared.

'Comrades, you forget they also received two hundred marks,' he says, weakly.

'You shit! You deducted it from the dole money,' screams a mousy little prisoner from the far side of the table.

'And you kicked us in the arse, when we wanted an increase in the money for the kids,' roars SS-Sturmmann Kratz crashing his rifle butt on the ground.

'Your rotten two hundred marks was our lot,' rages a prisoner, 'and we could then die of hunger far as you were concerned. But now you're where you belong and you can feel how it is to starve!'

'Kick his balls up into his throat,' an SS man suggests, smacking 'Mouse' on the shoulder.

They took him at nightfall. They beat him and kicked him. They dragged him through the latrines. Night after night they repeated the process. When his wife came to fetch him, in a large Mercedes, he had to be carried out.

241

The SS guards and the prisoners were furious. They'd got hold of a bureaucrat, and now he was being let loose.

A few days later the Gestapo came and took three SS men and eleven prisoners. They were shot for having mistreated the prisoner Hirtsiefer.

THE RED ANGEL

'If the lousy *Germanskis* come to Kosnowska we'll knock their heads in,' yells Mischa, making his Cossack sabre whistle in the air. 'If I hadn't got run over by that rotten train and lost my foot I'd have shot thousands of the fascist swine by now!'

'Germans are no better'n reindeer shit,' shouts Nikolaij, contemptuously, throwing a half-rotten potato against the wall. He is still too young to be called up, but he has already worked two years in the mines. His left leg is stiff. It happened last year when a charge went off too soon. Carelessness, said the NKVD examining committee. His father was killed in the same explosion. They carried his remains out on a tarpaulin. When the NKVD inspectors left they took an engineer and two dynamiters with them. They never came back.

'I'll eat a dog if those Germans don't get here, soon,' says Shenja, the hostess of 'The Red Angel'. She bends down and her huge breasts almost touch the floor. She takes a double-barrelled shotgun from under the counter and aims it at Yorgi, the party's political worker. 'I'll shoot their tails off, soon as I get a sight of them!' she shouts, ready for a fight.

'Your drawers'd drop off from the bang,' grins Nikolaij, knocking back a vodka.

'They would, would they?' shouts Shenja, furiously. She puts two shells in the shotgun, cocks it and fires.

The sound is terrific. Those closest to her are almost deafened by it.

'Mad devils,' shouts Yorgi, who has fallen to the floor from pure fright. 'That crazy bitch could've killed the lot of us!'

'Anybody else think my drawers'd drop off?' howls Shenja, loading the gun again so as to be ready if the Germans do come.

'Germans are the cowardliest people on the face of the earth,' says Fjedor, banging the flat of his hand on the table

243

and making bottles and glasses dance. 'Yellow-bellies! Scared of losin' the little bit of life they've got in 'em. When I was at the machine school at Murmansk, one of the swine came to look at our machines. Run away from his own country. Only just managed to save his skin when Hitler took over. A real bastard *he* was. So bigheaded he couldn't make do with *one* secretary, but had to drag *two* of 'em round with him. Anybody could see what *they* were! Couple of high-priced whores from Moscow. Prick an' balls was all they'd been educated in. That rotten German had his nose so far into everything an honest *rabotschij** could never feel safe. Well, for our own sakes we decided we'd best get rid of him. So, late one night we pick him up coming rollin' out of the brothel *Mollnija*† and stuff him in a cement sack. Believe it or not he got free before we got down to the old part of the docks. Down the street he runs, shouting his head off for help. But who's goin' to help anybody, particularly a German, in Murmansk in the middle of the night? We caught up with him, anyway, and give him one in the guts with a club, and then we all kicked his head about a bit and he quietened down. But they're hard to keep calm, those German sods. We dragged him down to the Czar's slipway. *You* know, there where they've got the barges laid up. Lord, the way he kicked and struggled when we held his head under the water. Just wouldn't go off quiet and self-possessed like a man. Every time we thought he must be dead, and pulled him out of the water, off he goes again, howling and spouting water and beggin' for his rotten life. A couple of us started kicking him in the balls. We kicked him so hard they must've ended up in his throat. He offered us all his money, every single kopeck, if we'd let him stay alive, and swore he'd put in a good word for us in Moscow. Just shows you what liars the Germans are. Who'd put in a good word for anybody who'd been doing his best to kill him?'

' "I know you, Alexandro Alexejewitsch," he shouted to our foreman, between gulps of water.

'See, even at the gateway to death a German notices everything, so that he can tell the Evil one down in hell who it was who sent him there. Now every Soviet citizen knows that one thing's what he tells God and the Evil one, and another thing's what he tells the NKVD. Well, his recognising Alex meant he'd

* rabotschij (Russian) = worker.
† Mollnija (Russian) = The Light.

left us no choice. Now we'd *got* to do him in. But these Germans are tough. We jumped up an' down on him till every bone in his body must've been broken. Under the water he went on sendin' up bubbles and spitting like a forest cat in springtime, but death took him in the end even though he'd fought a good fight.'

'They're a pestilence, those devils,' shouts Pjotr, gripping the bolt of his Home Guard rifle. 'If they come here, we'll soon finish *them* off. Bang, this'll go, and there'll be one German less left in the world.

'I want a couple of 'em alive,' shouts Cholinda, the milkman's wife. 'I'd hang 'em from the beams, I would, and castrate 'em. Then we could sit an' enjoy their screamin', just like the Tartars used to do when they surprised a feller between their wives' legs.'

'We caught a couple of Finnish fascists in December '39,' says Sofija, happily. 'We hung 'em up by the feet and beat 'em between the legs until we dropped with exhaustion. It was a couple of officers with green stripes down their trousers and swastikas in their wicked eyes. When we was finished with 'em their grey trousers'd turned red. Before they died they were sorry a hundred times over that they ever attacked the Soviet Union an' put out the eyes of small children!'

'That's what I like to hear,' roars her husband, Vassia, fanatically. 'When I was serving in the Levtenow punishment camp we had that many ways of killing off the enemies of the people we sentries got mixed up ourselves. But when it came to the fascists, we just used to flay 'em like we skin reindeer. Our OC, a hellhound from Chita, collected gloves. His house was just like a museum. One day he discovered that he was short of one particular kind. He whistled up the whole camp, went round the ranks and selected a man and a woman of each nationality. The chosen ones were taken to the kitchen and made to put their arms into boiling water. Then our Mongolian OC skinned their hands and arms neat as you please, and had some gloves for his museum that nobody else had. Some shit must have talked in Moscow, though. What a row there was! I was lucky, I'd been on other duties that day and hadn't been in the kitchen. On a hell of a cold morning up turns a little commissar, who'd forgot how to smile before he was born, even. He was so little he could've walked upright under the belly of a horse! The heel-less Cossack riding-boots he wore

245

had legs no bigger'n thimbles but still came up to his knees. If his ears hadn't stuck out like bat-wings his tall pointed fur cap would have rested on his shoulders. It was so tall he could use it for a stool. It took him twenty minutes to sentence the glove collectors to death. Decapitation by sabre on the parade ground before sundown. He chose the executioner personally. A *kalorshnik** from Leningrad, a giant of a fellow, who could have hidden the Commissar from Tomsk in his open mouth. He was in for life for having murdered four women, chopped their bodies to pieces with a woodsman's axe, and thrown the remains in the Luma.

'All of us, both prisoners and permanent staff, were paraded to see it, so we'd all get an idea of what'd happen to any of us who might get the idea of collecting gloves for ourselves. It was a nasty execution. The woman-murderer from Leningrad was as nervous as a virgin with her backside pushed up against a red-hot stove. Every time he looked at the little Commissar from Tomsk, he shook like an aspen. He started by cutting an arm off the first one. The poor fellow bellowed like a bull, but not for long. In two shakes his head was rolling on the parade ground. The next one he did, he took half the man's chest off along with the head. That's how it went with all ten of 'em. That murderer from Leningrad was strong as a bear. When he swung the sabre it fair *whistled* through the air.

'The OC from Chita was the last of 'em to be done. Three strokes and he was gone. Then the Commissar from Tomsk pulled his Nagan and put a bullet straight between the eyes of the quadruple murderer from Leningrad. He swayed like a tree in a storm and down he went amongst the ten he'd cut the heads off. That's what we'll do when the Germans come. We'll pull their hides off an' hang 'em to dry outside Party Headquarters. No commissar'd bother just now *what* we did to Germans.'

His stream of words is interrupted by the opening of the door. A thick cloud of snow blows into the drinking-shop.

'Shut the bloody door,' everybody shouts at once, as the icy breath of the Arctic sweeps through the room.

A young woman, holding a three-year-old boy by the hand, leans back against the door. With a tired movement she pushes back her hood and wipes the snow from her face. She blows on her cold hands and stamps her feet on the floor to get some

* kalorshnik (Russian) = Criminal.

246

warmth back into them. Then she looks searchingly around the packed room, where the air is thick with machorka smoke.

'Looking for me, woman?' asks a skinny fellow with a white face full of pimples. His forehead is as low as that of a mental defective. His eyes gleam with animal ferocity.

'Come home now, Gregorij,' she begs him, in a low, quivering voice.

'Not a chance,' snarls Gregorij, emptying his beer glass with a long slobbering sound. 'Get off my back, woman! I can't stand the sight of you *or* that little whore's son of yours!' He takes a long swig of spirits and gives out a rumbling belch.

'You promised me this morning you would not get drunk today,' she says, complainingly, pushing a lock of dark hair back from her forehead.

'Would you believe that? Now this bitch of a woman says I'm drunk!' He hiccoughs, and grins foolishly. 'If that ain't an insult, I don't know what is! You're forgettin' perhaps, who's commissar in this town! Just you wait, you bitch! It's easy for me to fix you an' that whore's brat!' He refills his mug and drinks again. The beer runs down over his chin and chest as he drinks. 'Pruhhh!' he puffs, blowing the beer out over his face. Don't come here tellin' us what to do, you Kiev mare! There's plenty of room in Kolyma for Trotskyists like you! I know what you're *thinkin'*, you wicked counter-revolutionary bitch, you!' he slobbers drunkenly, and wobbles uncertainly towards her with his full tankard in his hand. With a cackle of laughter he empties the beer over her head and slaps her face. 'Fuck with the pretty officers all right can't you, you wicked devil! Don't think there's any of us here believes you were married to that shit of a captain! Fell in battle 'gainst the Finnish fascists, you say! Jew lies! The shit shot himself 'cause he was scared of goin' to the front! *I* know what's what, I do! Ain't I the *polittruk**?'

'You're dead drunk,' she says, quietly, wiping the beer from her face with her sleeve. 'Won't you ever grow up? Tomorrow you'll be sorry!'

He looks at her with a foolish, drunken look on his face, pushes her to the floor dragging her by the ankle, like a sled, across the floor to the grinning crowd at the bar. 'Here,' he shouts, ripping her clothing apart, 'help yourselves, anybody! I Commissar Gregorij Antenyew, give you my permission!

* polittruk (Russian) = political commissar.

Whore's are state property!' With a harsh laugh he forces her legs apart.

'Here, give her a candle fuck,' shouts Shenja, delightedly, forcing a thick wax candle up into the woman's exposed sexual parts. 'Conceited upper-class mare!' She forces her down, brutally, across the table.

'Come on boys,' grins Gilda. 'The gate's open! Give it to her! A bitch like her, that looks down on us, 'cause we don't understand books!'

'Mother, mother,' screams the little boy, striking weakly at the drunken mob.

'Let me get at it,' grins Yorgi, slobbering as he opens his trousers. 'Here, you bitch, there ain't one this big in the whole of Kiev! Stop screamin'! It's good for you!'

'I'm gonna have her from the back,' titters one-legged Mischa with his trousers down round his one ankle.

'Shut up you little whore' son,' shouts Kosnow, the muscular fur hunter, sending the little boy flying across the floor.

'Pull her down a bit farther,' gurgles Mischa, lasciviously. 'I can't get it all the way up. There, that's it! Take this in your rotten, Ukrainian cunt!'

Each time one of the drunken, slobbering men has finished, Shenja throws a bucket of water over the raped woman.

'We believe in cleanliness here,' she says, laughing harshly, 'but Kiev whores like you wouldn't understand that!'

'You don't fuck a whore for nothin',' Shenja roars with laughter. 'Costs a kopeck a go, boys!'

'Cheapest whore I've ever had,' howls Fjedor, happily, pushing three kopecks up between the woman's legs.

When they are bored with it, they roll her under the table. She cries desperately for her boy, who is lying unconscious under a bench.

'Listen to that mare howling,' shouts Yorgi, irritably. 'Throw her out!'

They kick her out, brutally, into the snow.

'My boy,' she screams, desperately, hammering madly on the heavy door.

Gregorij picks up the boy and throws him out of the door as if he were a ball. He lands a good distance away in a snow drift.

'These traitors to the people've got to be wiped out,' roars Mischa, banging the table. 'I read in *Pravda* the other day that

248

they are showing their horrible faces everywhere. Think, they fished out a Jew who had sneaked into the position of *sampolit**. They shot him,' he adds, after a short pause.

'If you stop and stand still you damn well die,' says Yorgi, for no reason, handing Mischa a full mug of beer.

On a sudden impulse Shenja announces a round on the house. All talking stops. Silence falls over 'The Red Angel'. The amazement is universal. Nobody can remember the fat hostess ever having been *that* generous.

'I'll push that whore kid of hers back up her cunt,' screams Gregorij, falling to the floor with a crash.

'Get your rotten fingers off my legs,' snarls Shenja. 'You're the last man'll ever get inside my drawers!'

'If you'd tried it once you'd never fuck with nobody else!' grins Nikolaij, foolishly.

'You little turd,' jeers Shenja. 'Me, as has sailed the Seven Seas and served diplomats and generals? Think I'd sink to a snow monkey like you? I once got fucked by a real lord in the middle o' the Atlantic Ocean!' She smiles, happily at the remembrance. 'He was a real Englishman with a proper castle where a Duchess used to walk every night when it was full moon! When he shot his load it was *blue*. Blue as the lamp outside the commissariat!'

'And since then you ain't never washed your cunt,' jeers Tanja, who has been sent to the village, temporarily. Not even the *polittruk* knows what she has done. It is whispered that an order will come, one day, for her to be liquidated. It has happened before. Others say she is an informer.

'I was a lorry driver on the Omsk, Moscow, Leningrad trip,' boasts Dimitrij.

'Now you only do the run from "The Red Angle" to the reindeer pen,' grins Cholinda, the milkman's wife.

'You don't know what you're talking about, woman,' Dimitrij spits contemptuously. 'Omsk, Moscow, Leningrad's the toughest route in the whole Soviet Union. By the time you roll down Newski Prospect you're half batty!'

'Suit you then,' Cholinda screams with laughter. 'You've never been anythin' else!'

'When I cracked up at last,' continues Dimitrij, refusing to be interrupted, 'I went on the tramp and've travelled by train free o' charge, over the whole of the Soviet Union. The good

* Sampolit (Russian) = Regimental commissar.

thing about trains is there's always a set of tracks leading away from where a fellow is. And if you get to some place in the winter where it's too cold to sleep outdoors, then you can count on it there's a gaol around where you can get a warm an' some grub.'

'Yes, that's a good thing about the Soviet Union,' shouts Yorgi, patriotically, 'we ain't got no shortage of gaols. Long live Stalin!'

'The day came when I had to give up that wonderful, free life,' smiles Dimitrij, sorrowfully. 'It was in Odessa. I was lying dreaming on a bench in the Park of the Proletariat, when I felt a knockin' on my think-box. There stood some dope of a *garadovoj**, grinning at me, and whirling his long truncheon like a wheel. He'd hit me across the soles of my feet with it and I felt it all the way through my body. Right out to the ends of my hair it'd gone.

' "I am leaving," I said, bowing politely. "I am lying here quite by mistake!"

' "You're not so dumb as you look," grinned this *garadovoj*, giving me one in the middle of the forehead with his truncheon so that I wouldn't forget too soon that people are not allowed to sleep in the Park of the Proletariat. I moved off at top speed, but hadn't more than put my nose outside the park before I was arrested. It was, unluckily, just in the false dawn, when the milk-carts come rumblin', an' it's the best part of the day for the coppers. I'd been looking forward to a cuppa coffee and a bite, too!

'Well, they drove me to *spjaetsyalniyi stamtsyja.*† There they gave me a goin' over which made me admit that work was a great blessing for all Soviet citizens.' He throws his arms wide and looks over the ice-covered windows. 'And now here I am in company with a bottle of vodka!'

Above the bar Captain Wasilij Sinsow lies in bed watching Tamara, who moves up and down the room, like an angry cat, with a cigarette between her sensuous lips.

'What the hell is there to do in this dirty hole?' she hisses. 'Fuck and get drunk! I'm tired of it! Why don't you ever go out with me?'

'Where the hell'd we go?' he asks, irritably. 'We went to the pictures last week!'

* garadovoj (Russian) = police officer.
† spjaetsyalniyi stamtsyja (Russian) = special station for vagrants.

'Pictures,' she snarls, angrily. 'D'you call that a cinema? Political shit! We've got to *do* something! We'll go mad else! We'll die and we won't even know it!'

'Let's go skiing, when the storm has dropped,' he suggests, weakly.

'Ski? Now I *do* believe you've gone mad! I'm cured of skiing for the rest of my life!'

He supports himself in the bed on one elbow and shows his beautifully white teeth in a big smile.

'As soon as we've won the war, we'll take a holiday in the Crimea,' he comforts her. 'We'll go sailing and make love on the deck with only the gulls to see us!'

And in the evening we'll have dinner at a restaurant!' She laughs, and her face lightens at the thought.

'And we'll stay all night. As long as we want to. And we'll fill ourselves up with caviare and Crimean wine,' he promises.

'When we've won the war,' she sighs, sadly, emptying the vodka glass. 'You've heard of the Thirty Years War, I suppose? Why shouldn't this one last just as long? Well, there'd only be twenty-eight years of it left.'

'Twenty-seven,' he corrects her, beginning to whistle.

'What's a year more or less?' she groans, resignedly. 'Oh, hell, Wasilij, I feel as if I were locked in a stinking prison! You lie there on your back all day, drinking. What the hell are you *doing* here anyway?'

'I'm training Home Guards, *you* know that,' he answers her, angrily. 'I'm also keeping an eye on enemy movements, and sending wireless information if they get here. It's a very important job and you know it!'

'Oh, shut up!' she laughs, wildly. 'They do say the Germans are stupid, but I'll never believe they'd be stupid enough to come here! Nobody'd be *that* stupid! Only Soviet citizens are dumb enough to live in a hole like this.' She passes her hand over his coal-black hair, kisses him on the lips, and passes her tongue over his. 'I'm bored! Four months alone with you! Everywhere snow, nothing but snow! It's driving me *mad*! We can't even be bothered to make love any more! We can do all the hundred and ten positions in our sleep! Find something *new* to do, you fool!'

'Maybe we could arrange a dog race,' he suggests, without believing it himself. 'There's a lot of sledge-dogs here!'

'Those village curs are too stupid to learn to race,' she

considers. 'Do you remember when we used to go to the races in Moscow and then to the Bolshoi in the evening? Give me a drink!' She holds out her glass towards him. 'Get up for Christ's sake! What do you think you're for?'

'Not so impertinent, woman,' he says, threateningly. 'I can soon have you back in gaol!'

'Maybe that wouldn't be so bad! I'd soon find myself a nice lesbian bitch!' She gets up and sits in a chair. She puts her feet on a crazy table, and her black chemise slides up her legs.

He gives a long whistle.

'Come here and let me fuck you! You've got the loveliest thighs ever, and your cunt's the world's best. Not even those capitalist bitches are as well-equipped as you are!'

'Shut up!' she snarls, lighting one of her long, perfumed cigarettes. 'Let's get away from here, Wasilij! Moscow people can't live in a hole like this! Our brains rot! Yesterday I caught myself talking to a reindeer, and what the devil have I got to talk to a crazy reindeer about?'

She jumps on to the bed, curls herself round him, let's the tip of her tongue run over his face while her fingers run down over his hairy body.

'You're a lovely man, Wasilij! You're a damned rogue but you can do everything a woman likes a man to do!' She draws back and looks searchingly at him. 'You said you had connections. The best anybody could ask for. Why the hell are we sitting here then? Isn't it about time you got hold of them and got us out of here?' She kisses him again, rolls on top of him and bites his ear. 'Let's go to Murmansk for a day! Spend a couple of days in the places the naval officers go to. Order them to get the dogs in harness and we'll soon be in Murmansk!'

'Are you mad?' he replies. 'You know we can't do it. This is a very responsible post I've been given here! Suddenly the Germans'll be here! Then I've got full responsibility and I'm the commander. It can mean promotion, decorations, and if we're lucky we'll be the only ones left and can pretty the story up a bit!'

'Tell me now, Wasilij, isn't there something wrong under that hair of yours? If we are the only ones left alive we'd better be pretty careful what we say in Moscow.' She looks deeply into his naïve eyes. 'Have you ever met a German? They're good shots! If they really come here I'll be interested to see how your drunken Home Guard'll function!'

A noisy banging can be heard from the bar-room below.

'Listen to them,' she says, contemptuously. 'God help us if the Germans arrived at this moment! What a lot of blood'd be spilt! Russian blood!'

'Be careful what you say,' he snarls, pushing her away, angrily. 'You don't know me!' With a wicked gleam in his eyes he pulls a Nagan from under his pillow and presses it against her temple. 'I'd liquidate you, if I wanted to!'

'You wouldn't dare,' she jeers at him, provokingly. 'You shoot me and all you've got to fuck with is that fat, greasy bitch down below. Noticed the smell of her? She hasn't had a wash since '36, when the Party started the "save water" campaign.'

He throws himself back on the bed, laughing madly.

'What a hell of a woman you are! Nobody could get really angry with you.' He throws her a grifa.

They smoke for a while in silence. Then she reaches lazily for the balalaika.

He jumps out of bed and dances wildly around the room in the Tartar manner. He points the Nagan at the ceiling and empties the magazine.

She laughs noisily and throws a crystal vase at the wall. Splinters of glass fly around their ears.

Naked he springs over the furniture and with a long jump ends in the bed. Brutally he pulls her down on top of him. She hits him on the head with the balalaika, and screams with pain when he puts out his cigarette on her naked shoulder.

'Shut up,' he shouts. 'Pain and erotic love belong together!' He catches her by the hair and forces her head down between his thighs. 'Suck it, you dirty whore!'

'Swine,' she mumbles, closing her lips around his enormous weapon.

'Get moving,' he roars, lecherously.

She looks up at his fat, stupid face and snaps her teeth together suddenly with all her might.

He screams with pain and kicks her off him.

She spits out the lump of flesh and wipes her mouth, which is smeared with blood.

He goes down screaming and presses his hands over his bloody crotch.

'Pig!' she hisses. 'You thought you could treat me anyway

253

you liked!' She lights a grifa coolly, and looks at him maliciously.

'You crazy bitch, you've bitten it off,' he shouts, despairingly, taking a few steps towards her.

'So what?' she grimaces at him and goes backwards towards the door. 'You didn't know how to use it anyhow. You always wanted it French, but you've never had it as French as you've had it tonight!'

'Get a doctor,' he pleads with her, beside himself.

'A doctor,' she laughs, contemptuously. 'The only doctor we've got here is the fat woman, who once took an eight-day nurse's course. She couldn't even help a pig to farrow!'

'You'll pay for this,' he groans, looking at his hands, which are covered with blood.

'You're dying,' she confirms, as if she is telling him it is cold outside.

'It's murder,' he sobs, falling to the floor.

'Murder,' she laughs, shrilly, 'and you're the one who says you don't even know how many you've sent in front of a firing squad! Try now what it's like to die yourself!'

'You're a devil, Tamara, but I warn you! If I die Moscow will get to know!'

'Really?' she whispers. 'Maybe some'll believe it. All they'll hear in Moscow is you've died, and they'll take your name off the list and forget you like any other louse.'

'Tamara,' he whispers, hoarsely. 'You must help me. I'm bleeding to death!'

'Wasilij,' she hisses, bending over him. 'You've not got much time left, but I'd like you to know I *enjoy* seeing you die!'

'Tamara, you're the devil's sister. They'll hang you! You've killed a Soviet officer!'

'I've butchered a swine,' she laughs shrilly. '*You* made me take it in my mouth! I got cramps and, you know, they put a piece of wood between the teeth of people with cramps so's they don't bite off their tongues. Without tongues they can't tell the NKVD what other citizens say, you see. *That's* why you sacrificed your prick! Maybe you'll be a Hero of the Soviet Union after your dead!'

A terrific noise penetrates from the bar-room. Furniture breaking. Glass breaking. Women screaming. Men shouting.

Captain Wasilij Simsow dies to the sound of this turmoil.

Tamara sits for a long time looking at him, lying there naked with only his NKVD cap on his head.

'If you could *see* yourself,' she whispers, contemptuously. 'The ones you sent to Gulag would be *glad*!'

She gets to her feet, puts a grifa in her mouth, takes a long drink of vodka and looks at herself in the mirror, consideringly.

'You've done a good deed!' she says to her mirror image.

She dresses herself in a long red dress of tulle, throws a black shawl over her shoulders, and goes down into the bar-room.

'Captain Wasilij Simsow is dead,' she states, solemnly, as she comes down the stairs.

'We all have to go that way,' hiccoughs Shenja, drunkenly, from the bar.

'Give me something to drink,' Tamara says, harshly.

Shenja pushes a full tankard towards her. She drinks half of it, greedily.

'The last night in Moscow,' she sighs, dreamily, 'we danced in "*Praga*" on Arbatskaya Square. They've got the world's best gipsy orchestra at that place. Have you been there?' she asks Shenja, who scratches herself, thoughtfully, between her full breasts.

'They'd put me in the box, if I was to put my nose in there,' Shenja grins, broadly.

'I bit his prick off,' says Tamara, with a satisfied smile. 'That was *his* last big bang!'

Shenja's jaw drops. 'Well now I've heard it all! Hey, listen!' she shouts, her voice piercing the uproar of the drunken crowd. 'Madama Tamara Alexandrovna's bit Captain Wasilij Simsow's prick off!'

'How'd it taste?' asks Yorgi, with a scream of laughter.

Gregorij gets to his feet with great difficulty and stumbles several times on his way to the bar.

Mischa hands him his green commissar's cap. Solemnly he buckles the Nagan round his waist. Now everybody can see he is on duty. With a crash he falls across the bar, smashing two bottles.

Shenja hits him on the head with a rolling-pin.

'Gregorij Mikhailovitch Antenyew, you're a drunken pig. Button up your trousers, there's ladies present. You're not with the reindeer now!'

'Gimme a drink,' he grins, foolishly. He empties the mug in one go, belches violently and swallows two salted herrings whole. He lets them go down his throat like a stork swallowing a frog. He scratches his head and discovers, to his surprise, that he has his cap on.

'*Tovaritches,*' he screams, in a ringing voice, 'why am I here on duty?' He pulls out the Nagan and swings it around. A shot sounds. The bullet hits Mikhail's ear and ploughs on through his fur cap.

'Careful now, comrade commissar,' he says, admonitorily, wagging a finger at Gregorij.

'You're under arrest,' roars Gregorij, waving his pistol about. 'Confess, you devils, so we can have a big trial! It won't help to deny it! The NKVD knows everything!' He picks up a huge piece of pork from a dish, and pushes it into his mouth like a peasant pushing straw into his clogs. The pistol falls into the soup. He scalds his hand when he tries to fish it out. Roaring, he dances round on one leg, blowing on his hand. 'You'll pay for this,' he screams, furiously. 'Nobody gets away with scalding a commissar's hands. You can think it over in Gulag!' He drops heavily into a chair and feels so sorry for himself that he begins to cry. He wipes his forehead, and again discovers his service cap on his head. 'Jesus, I'm on duty,' he howls, pointing accusingly at Sofija. 'You've been talking nonsense again to that ikon of yours, you holy bitch! You just wait! They'll nip that out of you in Gulag, easy as a Tartar nipping out a suckin' pig's bollocks!' Waveringly he gets to his feet and stumbles over Fjedor's legs. 'The world's a ball o' *shit!*' he groans, from the floor.

Yorgi helps him to his feet, and sits him on the narrow bench alongside the stuffed bear, with which he starts a conversation. 'Who do you think *you* are, anyway,' he says to the bear. 'The arsehole of the Soviet Union, that's what!' He strikes at it, and falls again. He lies where he is for a while, looking wickedly at the bear, which looks back at him, glassily.

'*Tovaritch,*' he says, with a stifled laugh. 'Let's get a court martial goin' an' have us a bit of fun! May I offer you a drink?' he asks the bear. When it doesn't reply he takes a kick at it, misses and falls full length on the floor. He gets up again with difficulty. 'Auntie Shenja, a double go of "The Red Flag's Victory". I'll see to it next pay-day!'

'Not a chance!' says Shenja, coldly. 'You owe me a year's pay already. You've drunk every kopeck of it up, and what security've *you* got? You're a bad risk, Gregorij Antenyew. If the Germans come they'll hang you *and* your green cap. And I think they *are* coming!'

'Then we'll work with 'em,' says Gregorij, with an airy gesture.

'You're a nice sort of Soviet commissar,' remarks Shenja, drily.

'Give us a drink, then,' he begs. 'You *know* how hard I'm workin' for victory!'

'Best thing you *can* do,' sniffs Shenja. 'You know what'll happen to you commissars if you *do* lose!'

'It's the Jews,' says Gregorij, gloomily. 'Them rotten hook-noses are all sittin' over in America keeping the fire goin'. You know what their plan is?' he asks, in a whisper.

'To cut off your head,' grins Shenja, bringing the meat chopper down on the bar like a guillotine.

'That's part of it,' admits Gregorij, feeling his throat tenderly. 'They've thought up a monstrous plan!' He hiccoughs several times and empties Mikhail's mug, which, by mistake, has been left within his reach. 'They want us an' the Nazis to slaughter one another. They're sending a Kaiser Wilhelm to Berlin an' a Czar Nicholas to Moscow, to put a stop to the people's thousand years of rule.' He hiccoughs again, and tries to drain a few more drops from the empty mug. 'I tell you! I receive secret messages from Moscow,' he whispers, looking important. 'Well, are you goin' to confess?' he shouts suddenly, pointing at Shenja. 'Or would you rather go through intensive interrogation?'

'I thought you wanted credit?' says Shenja, her eyes like slits.

'You're a *one*, you are!' he grins. 'You know just how to manage things in the Soviet Union. The next time I send a report to those pigs in Murmansk telling 'em about life in our little community I'll put you in for a Worker's Hero, so's you can give a big party for us. The case against you is rejected as bein' a load of unnecessary nonsense! Now, how about a little drink on the slate?' He takes off his *bulowka* and smashes it on to the bar. 'Now you can all say what you like! I am no longer on duty.' He knocks the *bulowka* across the room. 'Let's get on with criticising those bastards in the Kremlin. Madame, do you always bite your lover's prick off?' he asks Tamara, confidentially. He attempts to bow to her and falls to the floor with a thud, his face landing straight in a spit-pan.

'The whole thing's a revolutionary conspiracy,' screams

257

Stefan Borowski from the corner. 'They always twist you in the end. They promised me something quite different when I was serving in Moscow, and now the capitalist lackeys send me here! A conspiracy, that's what it is! But they won't get Stefan Borowski like that. Wait'll the Germans meet me. That'll make 'em think a bit! This war's goin' to take me to the top of the tree. What the hell's a world war for, else?'

'You don't know what you're talkin' about,' says Carol, emptying a bottle, with a long gurgling sound, as if his throat was a sewer. 'I'm the only one here who's ever *met* the Germans. It was in the little war in '39.'

'There weren't any Germans in that war,' protests Stefan. 'Only Finnish fascists.'

'You Moscow pig,' roars Carol, excitedly. 'When I say I've met Germans, I've *met* Germans. They had swastikas both in their eyes and in their arseholes, but I also met some Finns, real Communist-eaters, bloodthirsty as you wouldn't believe. They didn't give a spoonful of caviare if it was men or women they butchered. They were *wild*! They stabbed and slashed every which way and bullets came out of their arses an' mouths. I can tell *you*, all them fuckin' Finns act like they've been shot out of their mothers' cunts, with a machine-pistol at the ready an' a knife between their teeth. But the Germans you run into in this big war are like ten crazy Finns. You don't *realise* how mad they are till you've met 'em, an' then they've took your life before you know it's them! They slash everythin' Russian they meet to tiny pieces, man, woman or beast!'

'Keep your stinking reindeer claws away from me,' roars Stefan, striking out at Carol. 'Those Germans'll get to know *me*! They won't get round *me* with their machine-pistols and their swastikas.' He pulls the fur cap down over his ears and swings his hunting rifle over his shoulder. 'Now you can all fuck off. You're so stupid an intelligent man can't bear to stay in the same room with you!'

Singing loudly he staggers off down the long, wide main street of the village. The storm tugs at his ankle-length fur coat, as if it were trying to pull it off him. He bumps into a telephone pole, and recoils into a deep snowdrift.

'Get the hell out of my way, German shit,' he scolds the telephone pole. With great difficulty he works his way out of the snowdrift, strikes out at the telephone pole, misses, and lands in the snowdrift again. 'There, you *see*!' he roars, angrily. 'Always trying to twist a man who is doing his duty, but I've had enough!' With a volley of vicious oaths he attacks the telephone pole again. 'You rotten enemy of the people, you won't knock me on my arse again. You've stood there doing nothing for long enough. It's the next train to Gulag for you!'

Panting and swearing he continues on towards his house. Arriving there he has great difficulty in finding the door, and has to go round the house three times before he finds it. On the way he has a row with an old fence and kicks it to pieces. He gets the door open and falls into the house. Throwing his fur cap and coat on the floor, he kicks the cat and with shaking hands gets hold of a bottle.

'I'm that *mad*!' he explains to the stove, 'I could break up bricks with my prick!' He takes a long swig at the bottle. 'They always manage to twist you in the end,' he confides. 'Never trust a Nazi German, and don't trust a Soviet Communist either.' In some strange way he manages to get one foot in the garbage pail, and dirty water splashes over him. 'Help! Save me! The Germans've got me!' he screams in terror, and falls on his back with a deafening clatter.

'What are you doing, you drunken pig?' asks his wife, putting a sleepy face out of the alcove.

'*Job tvojemadj!*' he roars. 'I have been attacked, woman. Attacked! Here in my own service accommodation!'

'Who has attacked you?'

'The German swine've laid a trap for me right inside my own kitchen door!'

'Drunk as a parson, you are, and soaking wet too! Wipe the muck off you, you pig! There's a sack behind the door.'

'And that is all you have to say to your husband, who bravely risks his life for the Soviet Union, and one day will be a Hero of the Red Banner?'

'Oh come to bed,' she hisses.

'*Njet*, you understand nothing! You are cattle, stupider than a reindeer's arse. It doesn't matter to you that I have been half-killed. When were you at a political orientation meeting, which is the duty of all Soviet citizens, may I ask? You don't *know*, I suppose, that we are at war, and that the Germans are almost ready to move into our village?'

'You are drunk as a fart, Stefan Borowski. And for the fifth time this week.'

'Me drunk!' he protests, furiously. 'You are out of your mind,

259

you mare! I am the only sober policeman in the whole of the Soviet Union!'

She crawls out of the alcove, and sees the garbage pail he has knocked over.

'Was *that* what attacked you?' she asks, with a sarcastic smile.

'The counter-revolutionary swine had laid a trap in it,' he asserts, kicking out viciously at the bucket.

'Don't shout so, Stefan! Come to bed, so that you can sober up before morning!'

'Get your peasant fingers off my spotless uniform,' he roars, trying to strike her with a wet sack. 'Perhaps you do not know who I am? Get the hay out of your ears and listen, you peasant sow. I am a Soviet state servant, a learned man who knows all the service regulations by heart, and *you* are a miserable counter-revolutionary who wants to get her fingers on my hard-earned kopecks!' He throws a pot at her. 'To Gulag with you! The skis are there in the corner!'

She rushes into the sitting-room and throws herself on the couch, weeping.

'Howl, woman, sob all you can! That's an old trick. Even the stupidest Soviet civil servant knows that one! You think you can get away with it by wringing out your tear ducts, but you are quite wrong. We civil servants are as hard as the walls of the mines in Kazakstan, and *that* you are going to learn. You leave on the next train for the mines! Gulag is longing for you! Go! Shit on a parson's prick! *I'm* going to bed!' Breathing hard he crawls into the alcove, knocking his head so hard on the frame that the whole house shakes. 'Hit me again, you sow, and I'll shoot you,' he roars from the depths of the alcove. He rolls himself up like a wet dog.

'Stop it now, Stefan! Let me help you off with your trousers. You are soaking wet! You'll catch cold if you go to sleep with your wet clothes on!'

'Catch cold!' He howls insultedly, and hangs on to his trousers with desperation. 'Have you gone mad? Servants of the Soviet state do not get attacked by capitalist illnesses.' Suddenly he becomes confidential. 'Listen to me, Olga, we must all stand by one another until the war has been won, or it'll end with the American Jews coming here and raping our women.'

'But they are on *our* side,' she cries, in amazement, hanging his dark-blue riding breeches over the back of a chair.

'You think so do you, you Trotskyist bitch,' he screams, feeling a pleasant anger rising within him. 'Don't you know that Jew Trotsky ran off to America and lent the rotten American Army our Communist hammer to crush Russia with? But you don't know the Soviet people. We'll do *this* to them!' He tears the pillow to pieces. Feathers fly in clouds inside the alcove.

'Look what you've done now!' she weeps unhappily, attempting to gather the remains of the pillow together. 'Where will we get a new pillow from?'

'Have you nothing bigger to worry about. Now, when our fatherland is fighting for its very life?' He jumps out of the alcove, seizes the brown crochet work tablecloth and throws it into the fire.

'Have you gone mad?' she screams, attempting to save the tablecloth from the flames.

'No fascist coloured tablecloth shall lie on my official table,' he yells, raging, and poking at the fire to make it burn brighter. 'Get me my machine-pistol, woman! Quick about it! We must be ready! The Germans are coming this very night!'

'Drunken animal,' she sobs, going in to sleep on the couch. But first, from bitter experience, she hides the machine-pistol.

Next morning he feels terrible. His head buzzes like a beehive, and he has pains in his back. He sneezes and coughs continually. He blows his nose violently and wipes his fingers on the curtains.

In accusing silence she gets the breakfast. From experience she knows he will not say a word until well into the afternoon.

He puts on his fur uniform tunic with the broad shoulder-straps, swings the *Kalashnikov* over his shoulder, and knocks the *bulowka* with the red star down on his head.

'I'm just going out to see everything's in order and that there aren't any reindeer trying to beat the red lights,' he says, apologetically, doing his best to bring forth a reconciliatory smile.

He fights his way down the village street, against the howling storm, and vows solemnly to himself that he will not go into 'The Red Angel' even though his throat is screaming for a drink.

Just before he reaches the dog kennels, the Lapp Zoliborz rushes up in a sleigh drawn by a pair of reindeer.

'Fly, Stefan Borowski,' he yells, excitedly, 'get back to Mos-

261

cow as quick as your dogs can take you! The Germans are coming!'

'Let me smell your breath, Eskimo,' orders Stefan, putting his nose close to the Lapp's mouth.

'I'm not drunk, *Pan* Stefan. I'm as sober as God's son on the cross! Believe me, I have met the Germans! They said many things to me I did not understand, but I could see in their mad eyes that they were coming to kill every man born of a Russian woman!'

'If you didn't understand their language how do you know they were Germans?' asks Stefan, distrustful. 'They could be one of our own Siberian patrols. You couldn't understand *them*, either!'

'They *were* Germans, *Pan* Stefan. They only hit me once, and none of them kicked me, although they were very angry. If they had been Siberians they *would* have kicked me, and shot me too, afterwards. These people let me go. So did the people my brother met let him go.'

'When did you meet them?' asks Stefan, uneasily, looking out across the hills.

'It could be five hours ago. It was just before the storm changed to coming from the east.'

'How should I know when the storm changed. I'm not a weather prophet. I'm a policeman! Now you're not filling me up with lies are you, you seal-eater? I suppose you know where Kolyma is?'

'Know all about it. My grandfather was there!'

'Where are the Germans now?' asks Stefan, with bated breath, holding the *Kalashnikov* at the ready.

'Out on the steppe,' explains the Lapp, pointing to the northeast. 'Stefan Borowski, you are not thinking of shooting at the Germans? Then heaven be merciful to us! They are angry enough now when nobody is shooting at them. If somebody *does* shoot they will rip our village to small pieces!'

'Come on,' orders Stefan, with decision. 'Let's go to "The Red Angel" and discuss it. We must lay a plan so the Germans won't think we are stupider than they are.'

Shenja is lolling in the canvas chair which is her pride and joy. It once belonged to a film director from the State Film Industry. They forgot it, together with other things, when they made a love picture in the village eight years ago.

'The Germans are here,' shouts Stefan, with despair, as he enters the door. 'The Lapp and I have seen them!'

Shenja is so terrified that both she and the director's chair fall over. There is wild confusion in the bar. Even the ancient, rheumaticky bear-dog begins to bark as loud as it can.

Gregorij, who has been asleep under the table with two sledge-dogs, rushes to the window and fires excitedly into the snow, but little by little they all quieten down and begin to question the Lapp.

'Are you dead sure they were Germans?' asks Mischa, unbelievingly. 'You can't understand Finnish *or* German.'

'What does that matter,' shouts Gregorij. 'A German's a German even if he talks Hebrew, and you could expect even that of those treacherous swine!'

'What did they say to you?' asks Yorgi. 'Now no fairy tales, understand!'

'They said get out or come down here,' explains the Lapp. 'Bullets are no joking matter, and do not care who they hit!'

'If you don't understand German, how do you know what they were saying?' asks Shenja, wonderingly.

'They say it in Russian,' says the Lapp, stubbornly. 'They spoke a terrible lot of different languages. But you cannot be mistaken when you meet a German. Those devils are as well-read as Jews. They're not like our soldiers, who have only learnt enough to take a machine-pistol apart and put it together again.'

'Watch your mouth, Lapp,' Gregorij admonishes him, sternly. 'I am wearing my official cap, so there must be no criticism of the heroes of the Soviet Army! In Pravda it says the Germans are as stupid as a reindeer's backside. Are you sure it was not an NKVD border patrol you ran into?'

'No,' says the Lapp, firmly, accepting a big mug of vodka from Shenja. 'They had no *nagajkas* to whip all the madmen who go about loose on the tundra with!'

'What did their uniforms look like?' Nikolaij interrogates him, with a crafty look.

'Like all uniforms,' answers the Lapp, throwing his arms out to both sides. 'But believe me, they were Germans. They smoked capitalist tobacco and not machorka, and they had a reindeer with them who was as haughty as a Finnish general. It would not even sniff at my reindeer, although they were Finnish reindeer once.'

'I have seen Germans,' shouts Puchal, rushing into the bar with a great clatter. 'A whole army with guns and all sorts of murderous instruments.'

'Where?' asks Gregorij, objectively.

'Five versts away, and they will soon be here. They are moving fast!'

'Well, I'm off to the mill,' says Kosnov, nervously, buttoning his fur coat. 'I've got wheat to grind. Now the Germans are here who knows when I'll be able to get it done. Those devils can get up to all kinds of craziness!'

'You stay here,' orders Gregorij, sternly. 'You can grind your wheat with the cheeks of your arse or wait till the war's over! I'm the chief of the military here!' With considerable difficulty he climbs up on to a chair. 'Shut up and listen,' he shouts. '*Tovaritches*, the Soviet Union expects that every man will do his duty in this our district's finest hour . . .'

'Can that shit,' Fjedor interrupts him, disrespectfully. 'You're not showing off in Murmansk now! Get down off that chair! Take that cap off and talk like a human being!'

Gregorij takes off his cap and settles into a chair. The wind howls amongst the beams, as if it were going to lift the whole roof off. A shadow of fear creeps through the bar-room. They drink for a while in silence, and think their own thoughts. How best to manage things for themselves when the Germans arrive.

Shenja gets to her feet and scratches her big backside thoughtfully.

'Somebody come and help me boil some water!' she says, moving towards the kitchen.

'What the devil d'you want to boil water for?' asks Gregorij, in amazement.

'To throw at the Germans when they get here,' she answers, with decision. 'That'll make 'em think a bit. They used to do it in the olden days when they got too close.'

'Not any more,' explains Mikhail. 'Those devils start killing when they're two versts away. And even a big wench like you couldn't throw boiling water that far!'

'I'll lay in wait for 'em just inside the door with all the women,' explains Shenja, patriotically, 'and soon as the Germans put their wicked faces inside we'll throw a bucket of boilin' Russian water straight in 'em. That ought to teach 'em to come here without an invitation!'

264

'You don't know what you are talking about,' says Fjedor, seriously. 'They throw all sorts of hellish machines in, before they open the door. There wouldn't be as much as the hair round your cunt left of you!'

'Probably be best then to kill 'em outside in the snow,' suggests Sofija, who is sitting on the floor cleaning a double-barrelled shotgun.

'When it's over we'll pile all the dead Germans up back of here,' says Mischa, proudly. 'Then we'll send a message to Murmansk for somebody to come over an' count the bodies!'

'Shooting a German isn't difficult,' explains Fjedor. 'When you hit him he spins round like a top and doesn't know what to do. Even the cleverest get confused, when bullets start rattling around in their heads!'

'Where are you going?' shouts Gregorij, as Kosnow begins again to sneak towards the door.

'I'm going to grind my corn, man! We've got to think of tomorrow, not just the war today. A Russian Finn told me the Germans'll let us keep our flour, but take the unmilled grain for themselves. Them who don't get their grain milled'll starve to death for no reason before this winter's over!'

'Let's get up to the mill and get that corn milled,' says Polakov, cheering up. 'Gregorij, you're in charge of defence. You stay here and defend "The Red Angel". If we hear firing we'll come back and help you. We'll surround the Germans and take 'em from behind, the way we learnt it at the Home Guard school. It's easy as scratchin' your arse. Even the Germans haven't got eyes in the back of their heads. Keep on firing until you hear us shout "Cease fire!"'

'You stay here,' shouts Gregorij, hysterically. 'I *shit* on your corn! D'you understand!'

'Make no mistake,' says Shenja. 'The Germans are dangerous! Let's harness up the dogs, and get out of here quick. Then the Germans'll be disappointed, and there won't be a single Soviet citizen here waiting to get killed.'

'It is cowardly to flee,' protests Gregorij, weakly. 'Stalin has ordered that every fucking one of us, man or woman, is to kill the fascists wherever they are met with. And don't think of getting taken prisoner by the fascists. They'll cut out your liver, neat as anything and eat it raw. I've seen pictures of it at the Commissar School in Murmansk, so it's not just propaganda.'

'Then it's about time we got going,' thinks Shenja, pulling on her felt jacket. 'I'm too fond of my liver to let any whoreson German eat it!'

'You stay here,' says Gregorij, aiming his machine-pistol at her. 'From now on there's military law here, and *I'm* the law! You've enjoyed the good years under the Soviet system, now you've got to take the bad ones with 'em!'

'Boots and barbed wire to you, Gregorij,' she shouts, contemptuously. 'We know you! You'll run like a hare soon as a German shows on the horizon!'

For a while they sit in heavy silence, drinking to get up their courage. Some of them try to get the Lapp to admit he has dreamt the whole thing. But he is firm on having spoken to the Germans.

Gregorij declares a state of emergency, and from then on all drinks are free of charge in 'The Red Angel'. They split themselves up into small battle groups, and the Home Guard is on Red Alert.

'Enemy contact about to occur,' shouts Gregorij, pathetically, feeling the false courage in every fibre of his commissar body. Inwardly, he is hoping that the Germans will pass by the village, which lies in a valley cloaked in snow.

There is a violent knocking on the door. Everyone huddles close, in fear, but it is only Julia, who always knocks on doors, whether she wants to go in or out of them.

'You're to come home,' she shouts, waving to Gregorij, 'there's somebody who wants to speak to you!'

'I haven't time to talk to people,' shouts Gregorij, dismissively.

'Don't talk nonsense! Come home or I'll warm your ears for you! Don't think you're so much, just because you're wearing a uniform!'

Everybody is a little frightened of Julia. She is the village *babuschka*,* and can tell fortunes and cure sickness.

'Who wants to talk to me?' asks Gregorij, weakly.

'You'll see when you get home,' answers *Babuschka* Julia, laconically.

'So tell 'em they'll have to wait,' says Gregorij. 'I'll come home when we've killed the Germans!'

'You're not right in the head,' says *Babuschka* Julia, and knocks on the door before she goes out.

* babuschka (Russian) = grandmother.

Shenja hangs the Party Message on the board reserved for special notices:

> *Tovaritsch*, every step in retreat is cowardly
> and dishonourable. It means death!

The rattle of a machine-pistol is heard out in the storm.

In a moment everyone has taken cover under a chair or a table.

In some mysterious manner Shenja has managed to force all her superfluous pounds of fat on to the shelf under the bar.

Sofija rushes wildly out to the coal bunkers. As she runs she tears the Party badge from her blouse and throws it into the stove.

Fjedor's Home Guard amulet goes the same way as the Party badge.

'Hard times are coming,' they confide to one another, 'and nobody can yet be sure who is going to win this war!'

But, shortly after, it proves to be only the fur-hunter, Sanja, who has been firing with his new machine-pistol. He looms large in the door, and bends down to look under the table where Gregorij is hunched down with his hands covering both ears.

'Come out, comrade! The Germans are sitting out there in the snow waiting to get shot!'

Slowly they crawl from their hiding-places, and, after a few glasses, Gregorij again begins to feel himself the born battle-group commander. He decides to put out advance posts. After a long discussion, about where people are to go, they slouch off to the selected positions.

Two men drag the water-cooled Maxim machine-gun with them, but as soon as they get outside they are knocked off their feet by the storm. It is not very long before they arrive back at 'The Red Angel', and agree that they might just as well wait for the Germans there as risk freezing to death before they arrive. But Gregorij has learnt at the Home Guard course in Murmansk that it is most important to put out a sentry.

Nobody protests, when he proposes the Lapp as the right man for that important post. He is used to being outdoors, in all kinds of weather, and living close to nature as he does, his eyes and ears are well trained.

'If you do this,' says Gregorij, solemnly, 'I will recommend you for the Workers' Order!'

The Lapp rolls off, grinning, to keep an eye on the Germans, but the storm is too severe even for him, and soon he creeps into the reindeer stables. Before he goes to sleep he tells the reindeer to listen carefully, and to wake him if strangers come.

'The Workers' Order they can stick up the arsehole of a wild boar,' he mumbles, just before he falls asleep.

The whole day passes with no sign of any Germans, and courage is coming back to the villagers. 'The Red Angel' has been turned into a veritable fortress. An 80 mm mortar has been emplaced behind the kitchen. True there are only two practice bombs for it, but Gregorij feels that the noise alone will frighten the Germans properly.

Just inside the door the heavy Maxim MG has been placed. Nobody thinks of the fact that the water-coolant has frozen to solid ice. Even if it cannot be fired at the moment it is a wicked looking gun, and there is plenty of ammunition for it.

'Is there still a state of emergency?' asks Shenja, when they demand vodka and beer at the expense of the state.

'What do you think?' asks Gregorij, sarcastically. 'Even a stupid woman like you should be able to see that fighting will soon commence!'

'No skin off *my* nose,' she gives in, sourly, and fills the glasses to the brim.

'Neither the Germans nor the Finns'll take us alive,' roars Mikhail, happily, as he empties his fifth mug.

'They say that in war it is the best who die first,' shouts Kazar above the terrific din. 'What d'you say to that, Yorgi, you've been in it?'

'Nonsense,' states Yorgi. 'You can see I'm alive! War is natural to human beings, and a clever man can easily fool death. In the 809th Infantry Regiment, where I was a corporal, we had a sergeant who often warned the section of danger, as if he were an astrologer who could read tea-leaves: "Boys, don't enter that field! There are mines in it will blow your piles up into your throats!"

'But there were some clever ones in the section, who wouldn't believe what he said, and walked straight into the grass. Bang! Up go the mines, taking earth and shit with 'em. That sergeant taught us not to believe that everything was predestined, for example walking on a mine or stopping a fascist bullet with your own body. "If everything's gone wrong," said this sergeant, "and the enemy's boys are pulling your arsehole up over your ears, just bash on like a crazy man. Above all never hold back. Grab hold of your feet in your hands and keep going!" '

'When the Germans come,' decides Gregorij, 'you take the lead. You have the experience, and the rest of us can learn from you!'

Yorgi strikes his chest proudly, and swings the machine-pistol above his head, so that half a magazine goes off into the ceiling.

'You pay for what you break,' shouts Shenja, angrily.

She gets up on a chair to examine the beams.

'I only hope this war piss doesn't cause too much damage,' she sighs, worriedly, as the steps down from the chair.

By now the whole village is inside 'The Red Angel'. Everybody is talking at the same time, stifling their fears with words. None of the women scold their husbands for being drunk again.

A party is learning how to load and arm the LMG by the window. The unavoidable occurs. A whole magazine rips through the wall and across the kitchen, where Shenja and Sofija come close to getting killed.

'The Germans, the Germans,' comes a howl from the coal-bunkers, where some have taken cover.

Gregorij throws a hand-grenade out of the window. Mikhail sends a hail of machine-pistol bullets into the snowdrift on the far side of the road. Shenja fires her shotgun off, and hits the stuffed bear. She strikes out blindly with the butt, and knocks it over on top of Fjedor, who is lying behind the MG.

'Holy Raphael,' he screams, in terror, putting up his hands. 'I surrender! It was Gregorij, that Bolshevik swine, who made us shoot at you! Don't kill me, *tovaritsch germanski*!'

A little later things have quietened down and they begin to quarrel.

Nobody will speak to Fjedor who is still sitting, talking to himself in his own version of the Finnish language.

'You pointed me out to the enemy,' shouts Gregorij, incensed. 'You'll answer for that in Murmansk when the war's over.'

'I was only joking,' Fjedor excuses himself, laughing forcedly. 'Can't you take a joke, any more?'

Five snow-covered Lapps come noisily into the room, together with their even noisier dogs.

'The Germans are here,' they announce, with grins.

'*Where?*' screams Gregorij, terrified, throwing himself to the floor.

'Outside,' says the Lapp hunter, Ilmi.

'Put out the lights,' shouts Mikhail, blowing out the nearest.

'Damnation, there they are,' screams Yorgi, excitedly, firing single shots with the LMG.

The lights are extinguished quickly, and everything goes black as a coal-cellar.

Cautiously they peer out through the windows, but only the storm howls out there.

'Can't you be mistaken?' asks Gregorij, with hope in his voice.

'No chance,' answers the Lapp hunter, Ilmi, insulted. 'We were so close to them we could feel them breathing down our necks. They are coming in a long column from the north. NKVD troops we have also met. They are looking for some Germans who have blown the roof from over their heads in some place to the east, where no ordinary people who are born of women may go. I think it is these Germans we have met. Well, we just dropped in. We are going now, and if we were you we would go too!'

'When d'you think they'll get here?' asks Gregorij, his voice shaking.

'They cannot be far away, since we are here,' says Ilmi, with crafty logic.

'You stay here,' orders Gregorij, firmly. 'Every man and woman who enters this district belongs to my battle group!'

'Can't you find anything to talk about but *your* battle group?' jeers Fjedor. 'I'll be sick if I hear that word again. All the senile chaps in the country with a couple of celluloid stars on their shoulders are runnin' round these days making up battle groups, God help us!'

'What do you want me to call us?' asks Gregorij, looking lost. 'We're not enough for a company, and a section doesn't sound like much if the Germans get to hear of it. Those devils'll eat a section, like a Lapp woman swallows a herring!'

'Let's call it "The Red Banner's Barricade",' suggests Sofija, proudly.

A shot splits the darkness.

'I got him!' screams Pavelov, and fires again. 'God dammit, I knocked the bastard over!'

'Where's he lying?' whispers Gregorij and Mickhail, in

chorus, peering cautiously out of the broken window.

'Can't you see! There he is over by the shed!'

A little later they discover it is one of the dogs which has been shot. To make things worse, a lead dog. Fear turns to anger. Everybody has a go at Pavelov.

Somewhere out in the snow a machine-gun stammers.

Terrified, they stop fighting. The sound comes to them in short, wicked bursts, like somebody hitting a bucket.

Sofija begins to scream, wildly and hysterically. Mickhail strikes her across the mouth with the back of his hand.

The distant machine-gun goes quiet again.

'Put that lamp out,' scolds Gregorij, as Shenja enters with a lamp swinging in her hand. 'The Germans'll think we're *asking* to get shot!'

For a while they remain lying on the floor, listening tensely to the howl of the storm.

'You'll see, our boys've found those Germans they were out looking for,' says Mikhail, who is the first to get to his feet again.

'And killed 'em all in one long burst,' says Shenja, crawling out from behind the bar with the shotgun in her hand. She lights a carbide-lamp and pours herself a respectable-sized mug. She tips the contents down her throat in one long swallow.

'Come and get it,' she shouts, filling up glasses convivially.

Slowly they creep from cover, convinced that the Germans are lying dead, somewhere out there in the storm-whipped snow.

Under no circumstances must any general or private soldier consider the thought of voluntarily giving up a position. To counter such foul thinking we have the Courts Martial. It is my order that such defeatist *schweinhunde* shall be liquidated.

Adolf Hitler, August, 1944.

'It's nothing to laugh at,' the Finnish corporal admonished us, looking at us in annoyance. But we kept on laughing. It was the funniest looking body we had ever seen and we *had* seen more than a few. It was really two bodies, locked so closely together that we thought at first they were one.

'Stop *laughing*,' shouts the corporal, furiously. 'There's really nothing *to* laugh at!'

'If that's not something to die laughing at,' shouts Porta, half-choking with laughter, 'then I don't know what *is*!'

'Think on it! There 'e is, lyin' in bed in the middle of 'avin' a lovely bang, an' just when 'e's ready to let go, a bleedin' flyin'-bomb comes 'n' blows 'im straight out of bed,' grins Tiny.

An Unteroffizier from the motor cycle squadron tries to force them apart, but the girl's legs are locked so rigidly around the man's hips that he gives up.

'He was the only man I ever loved,' says the girl standing amongst us. There are tears in her voice.

'Bloody shame he had to die just when he was making love to somebody else!' says Gregor.

'And a German trollop too,' says the girl, breaking into a burst of sobbing.

THE WAR DOGS

The cold air strikes us, with all the violence of a battering ram, and sucks every vestige of warmth out of our bodies.

'Breathe slowly,' Heide advises me, as I go into a violent spasm of coughing. 'If you get frost in your lungs you've had it!'

I bury my face in my fur gloves, draw breath only cautiously, and fight the cough which tears at my chest. Even through the thick layers of fur, and the heavy camouflage cape, the icy air feels like glowing iron. The still air turns our breath immediately to ice, if we stop moving for only a moment. We could be choked by our own breath.

The moon shines brightly, and the stars are brilliant in the night sky. The air as icily cold and dry. The tundra takes on a strange, ghostly appearance, terrible, and yet, at the same time, beautiful.

To the north-east dances a great curtain of light, colours shifting and shimmering through the spectrum. In sheer fascination we stare at the electronic streamers, as they move across the heavens.

'Did you know, it's one of the great holidays today?' asks Porta. 'All the war-extenders are in church today singing hymns. And here we are, rushing around in the snow, and knocking in one another's heads!'

'It's one of the great German feast days,' Heide tells us, proudly.

'Yes indeed! A thousand years ago our German forefathers consumed a lot of crisp wild-pig on this day!' grins Porta, clicking his tongue.

'Is it *really* Christmas Eve?' says the Old Man, staring up at the flashing iridescence of the Northern Lights.

'Think the war'll be over by next Christmas?' asks Gregor.

Nobody cares to answer. We've said the same thing every

Christmas, and the war is still going on when the next Christmas comes.

'Come on! Up you get, you weary sacks,' shouts the Old Man, cheeringly. 'Only a little way now, and we're home and dry!'

'We'll *never* get through,' groans Gregor, pointing at the huge clouds of snow whirling in front of us. A new storm is blowing up.

An Mpi rattles, out in the whirling snow, and we hear the long, high scream of a woman. The Mpi rattles again.

'Down!' orders the Old Man, diving behind a great wall of snow.

A flare goes up, bathing the unbelievable whiteness of the snow with ghostly light. The flare hangs in the air, swinging slowly, for a few minutes. In its light our faces look like those of corpses.

'I've knocked off one of the neighbours,' shouts Tiny, above the noise of the storm. It is racing across the tundra in a series of roaring blasts. 'The shit walked straight into my arms carryin' a big bag of Christmas presents with 'im!'

Another flare goes up, and explodes with a hollow thump.

'Wish they'd stop doing that,' scolds the Old Man. 'Up their arses with their flares! Where's the body?' he hisses, pushing Tiny.

'Out there! Dead as a nit!' replies Tiny, pointing to a dark patch on the snow.

'It's a *woman*!' cries Porta, in surprise, when he reaches the body. 'A bloody *woman*! Got a kid with her too! We only need the husband now! Then we've got the whole family!'

In curiosity we bend over the body. She was a pretty, young woman. The child was not hit by Tiny's bullets, but appears to have frozen to death.

'Did you *have* to knock her over straight away?' asks the Old Man, reproachfully, looking at Tiny.

'Dammit man, I thought it was one o' them Soviet chaps comin' after us!' Tiny excuses himself.

'What a dope *you* are!' says Barcelona.

'You can't see no difference 'tween a feller'n a bint this weather,' shouts Tiny, angrily. 'Anyway what's she doin' steppin' around in the snow in the middle of a war with a kid on 'er arm?'

276

'She was a pretty girl,' says the Old Man, quietly, getting to his feet.

'I didn't *mean* to do it,' grumbles Tiny, swinging his Mpi on to his shoulder. 'Always after me you lot are! I'll be off soon, though, an' then you can win your own bleedin' war any way you *like*!'

'Hell, you big dope,' the Old Man explodes, in a thick voice, 'one more trick like that and I'll shoot *you* on the spot! Now you bury those two, and put a cross on the grave. Where'll you get the wood for it? I couldn't care *less*! But a cross she *gets*!'

'Mad,' Tiny defends himself. 'Why should they 'ave a cross? They're Commies ain't they? *They* don't believe *any* of what the parsons preach about!'

'I said they get a cross,' roars the Old Man, furiously, throwing himself down into a hollow in the snow, and pulling his hood up over his head to get a little sleep.

Tiny digs a hole, and pushes the bodies into it. He hammers something into the snow, which might, with plenty of imagination, be taken for a cross.

'The Old Man ought to go shit in 'is 'at,' he confides to Porta. ' 'E's 'ard to get on with ain't'e? Next time I meet one of the neighbours' boys I'll ask him to stand there an' wait while I go back and ask the Old Man if 'e minds me shootin' 'im!'

'Shut your face,' growls the Old Man, from down in his hole.

'Bloody Army,' sighs Tiny, jostling down by the side of Porta. 'Can't even *talk* any more, an' special permission needed to blow the Commie breath out of one of the neighbours' shit-'oles. Life's that sad, it ain't worth livin' it.'

We feel as if it's only been a few minutes when the Old Man starts shouting.

'Come on,' he chases us, impatiently, 'pick up your shit, get your arses moving, before Ivan comes and cuts 'em off!'

'Can't the bloody Army ever give *anybody* any peace?' shouts Porta. 'When, sometime in the future, I become a civilian, I just want to *see* the bloke that'll ever order me out of bed again!'

We've only marched a few miles, when we are stopped by wild shooting from up on a high wall of snow.

At the sound of the first shot I drop down into the snow and sight at a figure on top of the snowbank, but the Mpi sticks. The lock is frozen. I hammer at it, viciously, and the bolt comes loose. I fire off a whole magazine, and the figure disappears from sight.

'Back, back, get *back*!' booms the Old Man's commanding voice.

A rain of bullets falls around us, throwing the snow into the air.

'Covering fire, damn you,' shouts the Old Man, furiously, as the section retreats in disorder. 'You cowardly sods! I didn't give you the order to retreat!'

Heide comes running. He is hopping like a wounded hare. The SMG opens up. We work our way, in short one-man spurts through the deep, powdery snow.

The Russian firing, from the hill-top, grows weaker, and soon stops altogether.

Gasping, groaning and angry, we get up to them. Despite the Arctic cold we are sweating as if we were inside a sauna.

There are only four of them left, and one of these is at the point of death. The two others put up their hands, and do their best to tell us how they have longed for the arrival of the German liberators.

'Where's the rest of 'em?' asks the Old Man, looking around him.

'Taken it on the lam to Moscow,' grins Porta, pointing to the tracks in the snow.

'Seems they don't *all* want to be liberated,' laughs Gregor.

Tiny presses the muzzle of his Mpi against the neck of the nearest prisoner and pretends that he is about to liquidate him.

'*Njet Bolsjevik*,' cries the prisoner, falling to his knees in fear.

'Bloody *tovaritsch* commissars, that's what you are!' shouts Tiny, accusingly, pushing the prisoner roughly so that he falls on his face.

'*Njet* commissar,' they assure him, all talking together. '*Polittruken* is hiding in "The Red Angel". You can find him there.'

With the two converted Nazis guiding them they march into the village. It is literally buried in snow. We move carefully, from house to house, kicking open the doors and sending an Mpi salvo into the dark rooms. If there is a cry we keep firing until there is silence.

A herd of reindeer come galloping, terrified, down the main street. Snow flies about our ears.

Close to one of the houses lies a man wearing an armlet. He is dying. He stares at us wide-eyed and begins to try to crawl away from us. His fur coat is filthy with blood. He mumbles something incomprehensible, and continues to crawl away from us. He is like a man lying on a beach and withdrawing all the time from the tide, which continues to approach him, mercilessly.

'He's mad with fear,' says Gregor, poking him with his Mpi.

'To be expected,' says Barcelona. 'They've probably told him some good stories about us!'

'Let's let the wind out of 'im,' suggests Tiny. 'It's cruelty to animals lettin' 'im lie there sufferin' like that!'

'*Par Allah*, he took the whole burst in his guts,' says the Legionnaire.

'To hell with him,' reckons the Westphalian.

'He's only got himself to thank for it!'

'Put him under cover down by the stables,' says the Old Man. 'We can't do any more for him. Let's move!'

Somebody is waving energetically, with a red curtain, from one of the windows in a long house.

'That's "The Red Angel",' the prisoners tell us. 'That's where the commissar has gone into hiding!'

'They're certainly in a hurry to surrender,' grins Gregor. 'We must *really* have a bad reputation!'

Above the door a wooden sign swings. On it is painted a red angel astride a green elk.

We knock the windows in and send a few shots through them to shake the nerves of the people inside.

'*Vigi vres**,' shouts Heide, in a piercing voice.

They come out one at a time, all of them, both men and women, looking anxious and confused. Last is a big, fat woman with half a shotgun in her hand.

Porta nips the cheeks of her behind in a friendly manner, and runs his hand up under her skirt.

'Where have you been all my life?' he says, lecherously. 'If I'd only known *you* were here I'd've come sooner!'

'Any of these shits still inside?' shouts Heide, importantly, expanding his chest for the benefit of the prisoners.

'Shut it, you sod,' says Porta, looking down his nose at him.

'Which of you is the commissar?' asks Gregor, with a pleasant smile.

* Vigi vres (Russian) = Hands up!

279

'He's been shot,' says the fat woman, 'right through the forehead.' She puts her finger on her own forehead so that there can be no doubt of where the commissar was shot.

'Jesus, but she's *ugly*!' says Tiny, pulling a face.

'She's *lovely*,' says Porta, trying to get his arm around her. 'Just let me get the feel of you,' he smirks, and purses his lips for a kiss.

'You're *pretty*,' she says, pressing him to her huge breasts so closely that his head disappears completely.

'Well, let's you an' me go somewhere and forget the war,' he suggests with a lecherous grin.

'We can go up to my room,' she says, closing her eyes. 'I'm a civil servant and I've got good bed-clothes!'

'Are you a commissar?' asks Porta, and shouts 'Red Front!' quickly three times.

'No,' she said, 'I run "The Red Angel". She throws out her arms like an emperor who has won a great victory.

'Holy Raphael, protector of travellers, what can a busy man ask for better than a lady innkeeper for a girl friend?' grins Porta.

Tiny is getting on well with a tall thin girl with thick pigtails, the colour of new ale, hanging down her back. His entire arm is out of sight under her skirt.

'What do you Soviet people *do* in this 'ole, when you're not killin' Germans that is?' he asks, pushing his hand out through the neck of her dress and waving at himself.

'We discuss the new five year plan,' she says, giving out a little whine and biting his fingers.

'You must be bored to bleedin' death then,' decides Tiny. 'We've only discussed *one* five year plan, an' that took a 'ell of a time. Let's go to your place,' he suggests, 'so I can show you how we roll a girl out on a sheet!'

Suddenly a man rushes out of a doorway, swinging a *Kalashnikov* above his head. He slides down into a potato pit, in a cloud of snow, and begins to shoot to all sides.

'Our commissar,' says Mischa, rolling his eyes towards the heavens.

'I thought he was dead,' says Porta, pinching the fat woman's wobbly cheeks.

'He must've come to life again, then,' she answers, carelessly.

'Looks *like* it,' shouts Gregor, sliding head first into cover.

'If he ain't he's the first corpse I've seen shoot like that!'

'See if you can get him,' says the Old Man to the Legionnaire, who is keeping an eye on things from a window.

'German swine,' shouts the commissar, from the potato trench, 'you'll never get *me* alive. I'll kill the lot of you!' Another burst showers down dust from the ceiling and walls of the bar-room.

Cautiously the Old Man peers from the window, makes a trumpet of his hands, and shouts: 'Drop your shooter, *tovaritsch*, and come over to us. We won't hurt you!'

A new salvo is the only reply. It rattles against the wall.

'The devil take you, you treacherous *schweinhunde*. You're not fooling me!' The *Kalashnikov* roars again.

'Gregorij, Gregorij,' Dimitri tries to entice him. 'Stop all that nonsense and come down and meet the Germans. They're *nice* people!'

'Shut up you *izmeejik**. You don't fool me! *Germanski*, I am an important man and not easily taken prisoner,' Gregorij shouts, from the potato pit.

'*Tovaritsch*,' begs Mikhail. 'Be sensible! Come over and let us celebrate our liberation together. The Germans know you're a big man, and will treat you accordingly!'

'You'll soon realise I'm not a man who can be taken lightly,' comes from the potato pit. Another burst sprays the wall.

'You're nothing but a madman, Gregorij Antenyjew,' cries Fjedor, angrily. 'We've concluded a peace with these Germans, and if you don't come out quickly they'll come and get you, and shoot you on the spot like a mad dog!'

'If we could get *you* over there you could knock his brains out with one blow of your tits!' says Porta to the fat woman.

'I'll strangle the bastard if I ever get my hands on him,' she swears viciously.

'He's a dangerous man,' warns Yorgi. 'He has been to the sniper's school at Moscow and almost always hits what he aims at.'

'Must be out of form today,' says Porta. 'Up to now he's been wasting his powder.'

'He usually has some hand-grenades in his pockets,' says Mikhail, darkly.

'You couldn't throw a hand-grenade in here from over there,'

* izmeejik (Russian) = traitors.

says Barcelona, measuring the distance to the potato trench with a knowledgeable eye.

'He could crawl forward and get into range,' says the Old Man, worriedly.

'*Il est con,*' says the Legionnaire. 'If he leaves the trench we've *got* him! He can't be that crazy – *yet*!'

'What about annoying him so as to make him shoot off all his ammo?' suggests Gregor. 'He can't have a lot with him.'

'Then I'll pick 'im up easy as the devil pickin' up a parson sittin' on the pot on a Easter Sunday,' Tiny laughs, noisily.

'Maybe that's not a bad idea,' says the Old Man, thoughtfully.

A grenade explodes with a sharp bang, some way in front of our position, and throws snow through the windows.

One by one we run from the door and move from one wall of snow to the other to make him waste his ammunition. As soon as one of us is under cover the next man starts running, but the commissar continues firing like mad.

'Let's stop this nonsense,' says Medical Unteroffizier Leth, when we have been moving around between the snow walls for a while. 'I've been a nurse in an asylum and I know how to treat madmen. Got a broom?' he asks, when we are all safely inside the bar-room.

Sofija comes running eagerly with a besom.

'Just the thing,' smiles Leth, with satisfaction. 'We used 'em in the asylum to knock some sense into 'em. I've never met a loony yet who wasn't scared of one of these. Give me one of those Russian hats, and I'll show you how to fix a bloke who's gone off his head.'

Yorgi hands him a green fur cap with a tall, pointed crown.

'Hey, you there,' shouts Leth, when he is outside. 'Drop that gun and come over here! If you don't I'll come up and give you a real beatin' with this broom here! *Na doma.**'

For a moment there is a heavy silence, and it seems as if the mad commissar does not really know what to believe.

Leth walks slowly across the village square and threatens him with the broom.

'Come on down here, you crazy devil,' he yells, his voice echoing back from the snowy walls. 'Or I'll be over and warm your back with this broom!'

* Na doma (Russian) = Come on home.

'Lies and propaganda, you wicked German,' answers Gregorij from the potato pit. 'You are a devil, and neither heaven nor hell will have anything to do with you!'

'Come back,' shouts Gregor, nervously. 'He's mad as a hatter!'

'Don't try to teach your grandmother to suck eggs,' shouts Leth over his shoulder. 'I've been specially trained to deal with German loonies, and I know what I'm doing!'

He approaches the potato trench, step by step, swinging the broom round his head.

Suddenly the machine-pistol rattles out a long snarling burst.

Leth spins round like a top. It looks at first as if he is turning to come back to us, but then he goes down like a sack of potatoes. The snow rises in a cloud around his body.

'*Now* do you understand who it is you're up against?' shouts the commissar, triumphantly. He emits a long peal of crazy laughter, and now none of us can doubt that the man really is insane. 'Men like me are impervious to both fire and water! I'm that tough I could smash a rock to dust just by sitting on it!'

'I'm not standing for this any longer,' roars Barcelona, angrily, emptying his magazine in one long rattling burst.

The mad Gregorij returns his fire immediately. Two hand-grenades fall, not far from the door.

'He must be superhuman,' I cry, in amazement. 'No normal man can throw that far.'

'In the name of all the devils, and by the holy name of Christ's body, I'm coming down there to flay your hides off!'

Again the Mpi chatters. One of the bullets goes through Porta's hat.

'This can't go on,' says the Old Man, with decision. 'Who'll volunteer to take him?'

'Think we've got shit in our heads?' asks Gregor, in angry indignation.

'One bloody madman with a machine-pistol, and he's holdin' up an entire section!' shouts Barcelona, bringing his first down on the table in impotent rage.

The mirror with the angel on it smashes to pieces, and falls from the wall, as another burst crashes through the broken windows.

'That's the limit,' screams Shenja, furiously. 'That mad shit's gonna get to know Shenja from Odessa better! Gimme one o' them Hitler saws!'

Porta hands her a Schmeisser and a bag of magazines. She is so angry that froth rings her mouth and nose. She goes out of the door like a rocket.

'So long, love! Thanks for dropping in!' Porta shouts after her. 'I'll plant three lilies on your grave!'

She zigzags up the hill. The Legionnaire gives her covering fire with the LMG. Tracer makes an umbrella over the potato trench. Suddenly the madman comes into view on the left of the long pit, and sends a burst at Shenja. Her own Mpi goes off like a runaway rattle.

We send a concentrated fire from windows and doors.

The rain of bullets throws him up into the air. He falls backwards, then staggers to his feet again, but before he can fire Shenja is beside him. Now it seems as if *she* has gone mad. She stands over him, like a statue, with straddled legs, and fires down into his body.

'If *she* goes round the bend now,' cites Gregor, worriedly, 'then I'm leaving!'

She stops firing, swings the Mpi on to her shoulder as if she were carrying a spade, and descends the hill with long measured strides.

'That's what the Amazons must have looked like in the old days when they marched back in triumph after a great victory,' laughs the Old Man.

'Anybody say anything about the weaker sex?' asks Porta.

'Call Mum here any time!' says Shenja, proudly, handing Porta back the Schmeisser and thanking him for the loan of it.

Slowly the inn fills up with villagers come to have a look at the Germans. As Shenja's stocks are depleted feelings of friendship grow warmer.

To mark the occasion, the stuffed bear in the chimney corner is wearing a German steel helmet.

Porta takes a balalaika from the wall.

'That was with my father in Siberia,' Shenja tells him.

'Well now,' says Porta, trying the strings.

'Can you play it?' she asks.

'Too true I can,' he answers, pressing it to his side.

The first notes are soft and mellow. Then they become wild as the drumming of Cossack horses crossing the steppe. He wipes his hands on his trousers, and begins to play the clown with the instrument, in Kalmuk style.

Tiny knocks out his mouthorgan. Porta sings in a high voice:

'Einmal aber warden Gläser klingen,
denn zu Ende geht ja jeder Krieg.'*

Soon the inn is shaking to the dancing of the Russians. Mischa springs so high into the air that he splits open his head on a beam. Gregor breaks a finger learning to turn a somersault. Porta gets a crick in the neck when Fjedor persuades him to try jumping over a table with his feet together.

'As soon as this war's over,' Tiny tells Sofija, stroking the insides of her thigh, 'this honourable German uniform of mine goes straight on the muck-pile, and I step proudly into the ranks of the scoundrelly civvies again.'

'Mind you're not disappointed,' laughs Gregor. 'Civilian life's a lot more complicated'n you think it is. You can't go about *there* with your brain shut off an' a set of regulations stuck on your forehead. Life in the Army gets simpler and more straightforward the more stars and braid you've picked up!'

'What does Germany look like?' asks Yorgi, inquisitively.

'Ruins! No matter where you look,' answers Porta, 'and everybody goes round in the same standard clothes, that've been turned God knows how often. A couple of times a year Adolf tells us that he now has victory in his pocket!'

'There's a lot as loses their nuts, too,' explains Tiny, from the far end of the table. 'Them's the ones as don't take the law too seriously, and go on the pinch durin' the blackout!'

'How will it all end?' sighs Dimitri. 'Poltava lies also in ruins.'

'It'll end with one of us losing the war and the winners taking all the loot,' decides Porta, largely.

'If you Germans lose the war you will not be allowed to have an Army any more,' predicts Fjedor, darkly, patting a Schmeisser.

'That'd be bad,' Porta admits, with a false smile. 'The German Army is for us something holy. Like the Church! Prayers on Sunday and drill on Monday. We always close out the week with a parade and start it again with prayers and weapon drill!'

---

* Einmal etc. (German) = (freely)
      But someday glasses will clink again,
      For every war must have an end.

'Hear, hear!' yells Heide, raising his arm. He is too drunk to understand Porta's irony.

'The Army is a gift from God to the German people,' hiccoughs Gregor, saluting the stuffed bear.

'We Prusians are born to the practice of war,' shouts Heide, proudly, raising his arm again. 'God created the uniform and the rifle especially for our use.'

'In the same way as he created the spade and the muck-rake for the Russians,' grins Porta, jovially. 'That German God certainly does know what he's doing!'

'Don't worry about losing the war,' shouts Andrej, lifting his glass to Barcelona. 'If you do, then we Russians will join you and fix our present allies. Together we could beat the rest of the world in no time!'

'Yes, we *do* have a lot in common,' says Porta, thoughtfully, 'particularly holiness and cruelty.'

'Should we get into difficulties,' shouts Gregor, with the voice of a General, 'we will not hesitate to take cruel and unusual methods of warfare into use. We shall mobilize all German and Russian lice, infect them with spotted typhus and throw them at the heads of the Americans. *That* will make them lose the desire to force our peace-loving peoples into making more wars.'

'We could also collect rats from the ruins and from the graveyards of former wars,' suggests Porta, 'and, when he had infected them with all kinds of shit and corruption, send them as gift parcels to our hateful enemies, who are consciencelessly killing our women and children.'

'Yes, we Germans and Russians know how to make other nationalities keep in line all right,' shouts Barcelona, above the noise.

'Helmets off for prayers!' hiccoughs Porta, crawling up on a table. 'We must pray to God to help us finish this World War as soon as possible, so we can get a new one started!'

The village patriach, who is nothing but skin and bones, says he can remember the Crimean War, where some fool of an English general slaughtered his own cavalry, and if he thinks really hard he can remember Napoleon's entry into Moscow.

'It was a brave sight,' he says, quietly. 'What a lot of horses they had with them. Napoleon was riding on a white one!'

'Snow camouflage, I suppose!' says Tiny.

'Do you shoot with cannons in this war?' the ancient asks Porta.

'We do set one off now and then,' admits Porta.

'Do you think, perhaps, one day, a man could see how one of those things works?' asks the old fellow in his thin, reedy voice.

'You can come with us when we leave,' suggests Porta.

'We've got a cannon here,' reveals the aged man, with shining eyes. He smacks his toothless gums together gleefully. 'Somebody forgot it here, shortly after the Revolution, and we've kept it hidden ever since.'

'Why don't you try to fire it then?' asks Tiny. 'No powder, maybe?'

'Yes, yes!' boasts the village patriach. 'A lot of it, of all kinds.'

'Where *is* this shootin' iron you're talkin' about?' asks Tiny, interestedly. He gives Sofija a smack on the backside which sends her flying into the arms of Fjedor.

'In the reindeer stables, hidden in the straw,' chuckles the old peasant.

'Let's go and look it over,' suggests Tiny.

'Yes, let us do that,' the ancient man nods, obviously pleased. 'I have taken part in two or three wars, but I have never seen a cannon fired, and now that I am over a hundred years old I would like to see it before I die.'

'When were you born?' asks Porta.

'More than one hundred years ago,' answers the aged peasant, with a happy smile.

As they force their way through the snow on their way to the reindeer shed, the peasant confides to them that Prince Nicholas had once tipped him five roubles. In those days a whole month's pay.

'The prince was a good and holy man,' he sighs.

'Yes, he had a heart of gold,' smiles Porta, pleasantly. 'His tactical errors in handling the Imperial Army can't have cost more than a few million Russians their lives.'

'Did you know him?' asks the aged man, interestedly, looking with awe at Porta.

'No, I was never lucky enough to,' answers Porta. 'If I had I'd probably have ended in a mass-grave.'

In concert they manage to dig up a 104-mm Austrian field-gun.

'She's an old 'un,' confirms Porta, when they have dragged the gun free of the straw and placed it in position. 'Could blow to bits and take our arses with it, easy!'

Tiny opens the breach with a crash, and examines the interior of the barrel with an experienced air.

'Wouldn't fancy goin' on inspection with this baby,' he grins.

'Where do you keep the powder?' Porta asks the old fellow, who is in transports of joy and expectation.

'Under the straw,' he wheezes. 'It's not dangerous, is it?' he asks as they roll the first shells over to the gun.

'Not when you know what you're about,' boasts Tiny, pushing a shell into the breach chamber.

'We'll take load three,' says Porta, knowledgeably. 'That'll make 'em drop their beers with fright down at the inn!'

Tiny pushes the charge home.

'Hold on to your balls or they might go with it,' says Porta, turning the elevating wheel.

The long, dusty gun-barrel rises, and points towards the clouds.

'Let me have first go at it,' says Tiny, sitting in the gunner's seat.

'Go on then,' grins Porta, pulling the old peasant with him, behind a huge rock. 'Hold on to your hat,' he says, warningly, forcing him down under cover.

'It *is* dangerous then?' he asks, fearfully.

'Dangerous and dangerous,' says Porta. 'There's a certain risk attached to all this war stuff. Now and then people get hit in the head with a cannon, but don't worry, explosions go upwards so if it *does* go wrong all that'll happen is Tiny and the rest of the rubbish'll just fly over the heads of us two.

'There she goes,' shouts Tiny, happily, pulling the lanyard. But nothing happens.

He pulls again and gets the same negative result.

'There's somethin' not workin',' he says, vexed. 'Come and give me a 'and to sort it out.'

'No, I'm only the loader,' Porta refuses, from behind the huge rock. 'It's loaded!'

Tiny screws and hammers, sinks and elevates the barrel, and gives the gun a kick or two for good measure.

'Got it!' he cries, enthusiastically. 'It's the firing-pin that's stuck.'

'Give it one on the napper, then,' suggests Porta, 'That'll get that Austrian shit off its arse, I reckon.'

'Fire!' Tiny orders himself and pulls the lanyard with all his might.

A deafening roar shakes the whole village, and a huge sheet of flame goes up. A new explosion follows, immediately on the heels of the first. A spout of snow rises from up by the potato trench, where the heavy shell has fallen. A rain of potatoes flies through the air. Great quantities of them are blown into the bar-room and smash against ceiling and walls.

Shenja snatches her shotgun from behind the bar.

'Now they're playing with that blasted cannon,' she roars. 'Look at the way those pigs've ruined my good inn! I'm not standing for any more of it. I've had enough of this World War to *last* me!'

She goes out of the door like a rocket and heads for the reindeer shed, where she can see the gun-barrel rocking up and down. But she is only half-way up the hill when she stops and stares in terror out over the snow desert. Eight motorised sledges are coming bouncing over the hills heading for the village.

A machine-gun hammers from the leading sledge. Tracer bullets kick up the snow along the whole length of the street.

'Rotten swine' are Shenja's last words, as she sinks to the snow, shot through and through by the MG salvo.

The sledges come to a halt on the brow of the nearest hill. A voice roars across the Arctic silence, first in Russian then in German:

'Everybody outside! Hands above your heads!'

'What *now*,' sobs Mischa, crawling under a bench, his favourite place of concealment when danger threatens.

'Come death, come . . . ' hums the Legionnaire, readying the SMG.

'Those machine-cannon'll blast us to pieces,' whispers Gregor, fearfully, pulling a pouch of hand-grenades closer to him.

'We've not got much choice,' answers the Old Man, ironically. 'If they take us alive they'll break every bone in our bodies!'

'*On les emmerdent*,' laughs the Legionnaire. 'Let us attack them with hand-grenades.'

'They'll have smashed us before we get near 'em,' says Heide, bleakly.

'Where the devil's Porta and Tiny?' asks the Old Man, angrily.

'In the reindeer shed with the old gun,' answers Gregor. 'It was them smashed the potato pit.'

'For the last time! Come out with your hands above your head,' roars the voice from the loud-hailer.

'Don't you think it'd be wise of you to go outside with your hands up?' says the Old Man to the Russians, who are pressed close to the walls in terror.

'*Nitschewo*** you do not know the NKVD,' answers Fjedor with a tired smile. 'If they do not shoot us down on sight, they will as soon as they realise we have fraternised with you.'

'Then what'll you do when we've gone?' asks the Old Man.

'There will not be any "after",' says Fjedor, fatalistically. 'It is better to die with you than to be slaughtered like cattle.'

'*Je leur pisse au cul*,' snarls the Legionnaire, pressing the butt of the MG into his shoulder.

The sledges rumble slowly down the hillside, and a shower of shells explode out in the snow.

'They're using explosive shells,' shouts Gregor, excitedly, diving behind the bar.

'What'd you think they'd be using?' asks the Old Man, sarcastically. 'Armour-piercing wouldn't be much good against us.'

The three in the reindeer shed are sweating over the antique gun. Tiny is working like a horse. The gun is heavy, and difficult to move, but finally they manage to get it into position.

'Now we'll give it to them bleeders,' Tiny curses, sulphurously, lowering the barrel. He grabs at one of the shiny brass cylinders the old peasant has rolled over to him.

'Hell, the fuse!' Porta demands.

Tiny rummages in some old boxes and finds some fuses.

The ancient goes down on his knees and presses both hands over his ears. The long gun-barrel moves irritatingly slowly, but finally is aimed at the furthest sledge.

'Get a soddin' move on,' whispers Tiny, 'or else let me do it!'

Porta puts his eye to the sighting mechanism, which is of considerably later date than the gun itself.

'Fire!' he shouts.

* Nitschewo (Russian) = Never.

Tiny jerks the lanyard with such force that it is pulled from the eyelet.

There is a terrific muzzle flash and a thunderous crash. Next second the furthest sledge has disappeared.

A leather-clad form is thrown from the open turret, and whirls through the air like a shuttlecock.

Tiny opens the breach and the empty shell casing is ejected. A new shell goes into the chamber.

Metal clangs against metal and with a crash the breach is closed.

'Fire!' shouts Porta.

Tiny rips the lanyard back.

The lead sledge is thrown into the air and falls vertically back into the snow. There is the heavy thud of an explosion and a yellow-red flash shoots out from both sides of it.

A shell goes through the roof of the barn and beams crash down over their heads. A long stream of tracer tracks rushes through the air and bullets smack viciously against the front shield of the gun.

Porta has his eye to the sight again. Slowly the barrel of the gun depresses.

Tiny and the old peasant sweat at the supporting legs. The gun cannot be turned laterally, and they are forced to move the entire carriage.

'Fire!' shouts Porta as he gets the next sledge in his sights.

'Good-bye, you shits!' snarls Tiny, tugging the lanyard.

The heavy gun rocks and jumps. The third sledge is knocked across the snow and hits the sledge in front of it. They go over and slide down the icy slope with caterpillars in the air.

Each time a shot is fired the Old Man roars with laughter and slaps his thighs delightedly.

Porta gets two more hits, before a 50-mm shell comes through the door and explodes inside the barn. Flames lick up from the bales of straw, and in a few minutes the shed is filled with thick, black smoke.

'Shells!' coughs Porta, half-choked.

The breach of the gun closes with a metallic clang. It fires again. A miss this time. The shell whizzes closely past the nearest sledge. Its turret turns and the short-barrelled 20-mm automatic cannon points directly into the barn. Inside, a casing rattles to the ground and the breach of the Austrian gun closes on a new shell.

Porta spins the elevating wheel like a madman, then gives up and sights along the barrel as if it were a rifle.

'Fire, for Christ's sake!' shouts Tiny, who has taken cover under the gun itself.

The gun roars and the motorised sledge, which is coming towards the shed, flies to pieces. The turret whirls through the air and two flaming bodies are thrown from the body of the sledge.

'You got 'im! Dammit all to 'ell, you *got* 'em!' screams Tiny, joyfully. 'Come *on* you shits! We'll show you where Moses bought the beer!'

The ancient peasant jumps up and down with his legs pressed together, laughing away like a hoarse crow.

An armoured sledge glides out from between two houses. Its gun swings around uncertainly as if searching for a particular angle of fire.

'Let's get it *moved*,' shouts Porta, jumping from the gunner's seat to help them turn the carriage.

The gun on the armoured sledge hammers, and shells howl down towards 'The Red Angel'.

'Hell!' cries Porta, 'I thought they were going to have a bang at *us*.'

'They can't see us,' says Tiny. 'The smoke's coverin' us completely!'

'Beat it, old 'un,' says Porta, shoving the old peasant gently. 'This is going to be hotter than the whole of that shithouse war you were in!'

'*Nitschewo*,' answers the ancient man, stubbornly. His eyes are red and swollen from the poisonous smoke, but he is happy, even though he *is* choking. The dream of a lifetime has been fulfilled: He has seen a real cannon fired off.

The heavy armoured sledge pushes slowly forward between the houses and creeps towards the inn. Its guns hammer incessantly and shells send the roof flying away. A huge, canopied bed on which Captain Wasilij Zimsow's body is lying, stands exposed on the remains of the first floor.

'Where the hell's he got to?' Porta strains his eyes to see through the thick smoke.

At the same moment a shell explodes, just outside the barn, and he is thrown from the firing-seat.

The old peasant, who is standing right behind him, is thrown forward and smashes his face into the ground. Tiny rolls towards the empty pig-pens, where a beam lands on him with crushing force.

With blood streaming down his face, the village patriarch climbs up into the firing-seat.

'*Pascholl**,' he crows, pressing his eye to the sight. He turns the nearest wheel, which happens to be the height finder. With fumbling fingers he finds the lanyard and jerks it as he has seen Tiny do.

The gun roars, the muzzle-flash lighting up the whole barn.

The blast throws the ancient from the seat and sends him sliding some way across the packed earth floor. Confusedly he peers out through the wheels of the gun and gives out a cackle of pleased laughter.

Only a couple of hundred yards from the barn a heavy armoured sledge is burning. Coal-black smoke ascends towards the heavens.

'Well I'll be buggered,' cries Tiny, in astonishment. 'There's a good anti-tank man got lost in you!'

'Time we moved. They're blowing the inn to pieces down there,' says Porta, emerging from a heap of bricks.

All hell has broken loose in 'The Red Angel'. A 50-mm shell explodes, in a sea of flame, in the kitchen and blows the stove through the wall.

Yorgi runs about screaming and trying to clutch at his chest with the stump of an arm. A torn-off foot flies across the bar-room and smashes against the wall at the far end.

Under the long table Sofija sits staring in horror at her left leg. Only a little of the knee remains. A growing pool of blood spreads out around her. She opens her mouth and starts to scream.

'*Sacré Nom de Dieu*,' hisses the Legionnaire, and throws a first-aid pack over to her.

Two of the armoured sledges are so close to the inn that we can easily read the numbers and tactical insignia on the turrets.

'NKVD,' comments Heide, drily.

I tie three hand-grenades together and make ready to throw them.

'Wait a minute,' says the Old Man, catching at my arm. 'You can't throw that far!'

But it is too late. I have already pulled the cord, There is no

* Pascholl (Russian) = Forward!

safety on these potato-masher grenades. I tear myself free and take my arm back.

Everything disappears in a hot, blue cloud. I feel a violent blow on my shoulder. The grenades slide across the floor.

'*Milles diables,*' howls the Legionnaire, giving the grenades a kick which sends them flying towards the door.

They explode in the air and tear open Oberschütze Lung's entire chest.

'Jesus, Jesus!' screams Gefreiter Günther. 'My eyes, my eyes!' He staggers to his feet with both hands pressed to the bloody gruel that had been his eyes. Screaming he rushes out of the door and into the snow. He stands still in the square, screaming, with his mouth wildly agape.

An MG rattles and tracer bores into his body. He falls backwards like a log, kicking at the snow so that it whirls up in clouds about him. Sobbing he tries to crawl away. Like a sled he slides down the hillside and disappears in a depression.

A long, thin splinter has gone through my furs and slashed open the flesh along the shoulder. The wound is bleeding freely, but the bone is intact.

The entire village is in flames.

A shell explodes, right in the middle of the bar-room. The floor is a sea of blood. Torn-off limbs and bloody chunks of human flesh are everywhere. A nauseating stench fills the inn, which looks like a slaughterhouse in which the butchers have run amok. Even on the ceiling there are great patches of blood, and the floor is a sticky mass of crushed bone, blood and shredded flesh.

Feldwebel Karlsdorf sits propped up against a wall, staring blankly at the place where his legs had been a short while before. Now there are only a few shards of bone and some long strings of flesh and sinew. He begins to laugh. Quietly at first, as if at a joke. Then his laughter rises to a mad, sobbing howl.

Another shell explodes inside the room with a sharp report. When the blue-green smoke has cleared, a bloody mash marks the place where Karlsdorf sat.

The noise of the shells has sent me completely deaf. I crawl over to the Legionnaire and help him with the LMG.

Up in the burning barn Tiny lies, with his hands folded behind his neck, and stares thoughtfully up at the sea of flame. The fact that the entire barn might fall on him, doesn't seem to worry him.

Porta opens and closes his mouth, as if he were chewing on something evil-tasting.

'The devil,' he groans, hoarsely. 'What sod's been eating cat-shit with my chops!'

'I have seen how a cannon is fired,' whispers the old peasant. He looks down at his mutilated hand, from which all the fingers are missing.

'What a load o' shit,' mumbles Tiny, getting up to help the ancient man. Before he gets to him he is thrown deep into a snowdrift on the far side of Party HQ. Porta is blasted vertically into the air, like a shot from a mortar, and lands behind the remains of the potato trench.

The barn is torn to pieces. All of the shells which were hidden in it have been brought to explosion, and the blast wave which follows sweeps away everything in its path.

'What in the world was that?' pants the Old Man, climbing out of a deep hole into which he has been thrown by the blast.

'Porta and Tiny going up! *C'est le bordel*,' says the Legionnaire, wiping blood from his face.

Has an hour, a day or a year passed? I have no idea. My head is aching as if it had been split open by an axe. Dimly I remember something about a colossal explosion and huge flames. I try to rise to my feet, but a heavy kick sends me down again. A guttural voice brings me completely to my senses. Now I remember clearly what has happened.

They come from the kitchen, a party of small, powerful men with flat Mongolian features and broad NKVD shoulderstraps.

I turn my head cautiously. A little way from me lies Gregor, tied up like a sack. He looks dead. A little further off the Old Man and Barcelona are sitting, tied back to back. The Westphalian is hanging head downwards, tied to a beam like a smoked ham. Round about I can see the rest of the section. All are bound. Porta, the Legionnaire and Tiny are not there. Probably already dead.

An NKVD soldier stands by the smashed door, with a *Kalashnikov* in his hands and a cigarette hanging from his mouth. From a beam over by the staircase swing five hanged bodies. Three men and two women. The civilians have obviously been summarily treated. On the cellar door someone has been crucified. Who it is I cannot see. But he is not dead yet. His body twitches occasionally.

A wiry little officer kicks me hard in the side.

'You saboteur,' he snarls at me in bad German. He bends over me so closely that I can smell the vodka and machorka on his breath.

'Speak Russian?' he asks.

'*Njet*,' I answer.

'Ilgun*', he screams, exposing a row of white teeth. 'You speak Russian! You say *njet*!' He turns to a sergeant for confirmation. Without waiting for a reply, he goes on: 'Was *you* blow up Nova Petrovsk?'

'*Njet*,' I answer.

He spits, and slashes me across the face several times with his *nagajka.*

'Admit,' he roars, wildly. 'We tear tongue from throat! No confess, no use for tongue!'

Again the *nagajka* whistles through the air, tearing the skin from my neck and throat. He waves to two Siberian soldiers and gives them an order in a dialect I do not understand.

The soldiers return with a heavy box, of the kind tinsmiths use to carry their tools in. With a grin the officer takes a pair of long-handled pincers from the box and snaps them at us threateningly. With practised movements the soldiers tear the clothes from Barcelona and the Old Man.

The officers repeats the questions he had put to me.

'Get fucked,' answers Barcelona, staring at the little officer with hate-filled eyes.

'We soften you,' smiles the Russian, wickedly. 'Who lead section?'

'Piss off,' snarls Barcelona, contemptuously.

'I break German balls, if no answer,' promises the Russian, his eyes vicious slits.

A long, wavering scream from the cellar interrupts him. Only a human in terrible pain can scream so.

'Now find one who will talk!' smiles the Russian officer. 'Hang them up!' he orders, brusquely.

A soldier puts a thin rope around my throat. He ties the other end to a beam. I have to stand on my toes to prevent myself from being strangled.

The officer begins to flog the Old Man with his *nagajka.*

'Who is leader?' he asks, after each stroke.

He is a specialist in the use of the terrible Siberian whip.

* Ilgun (Russian) = Liar.

Each stroke opens the skin. Blood streams down the Old Man's body.

In a short while the Old Man's screaming stops. He has collapsed completely, as if he were dead.

I have heard that it is possible to kill a man with three strokes of the *nagajka*, and having seen a *nagajka* in the hands of a Siberian NKVD soldier I do not doubt it.

I look at the Russians around me. They look tired and worn out. Their faces are covered with frost sores, as are ours. One of them is asleep on his feet, with the Mpi hanging loosely against his chest.

'You saboteurs,' decides the little officer, running the *nagajka* caressingly over Barcelona's naked torso.

'No we're *not*, you shit,' roars Barcelona, raging and straining at his bonds.

'What you do here?' asks the Russian, with a dangerous smile. 'You hunt reindeer?'

'We're here to piss on *you!*' shouts Barcelona, viciously.

The *nagajka* whistles, splitting the skin of Barcelona's face.

'I whip you dead,' promises the little officer, the black eyes burning in his flat, Mongolian face. 'You hear, *svinja?*'

'Son of a whore,' shouts Barcelona, hoarsely.

The officer seems to go amok. Blows from the *nagajka* rain on Barcelona. He gives out a long, rattling scream and goes unconscious.

'What about this Finnish pig?' asks a sergeant, coming up from the cellar.

'We'll take him to Murmansk and plaster a cell wall with him,' answers the officer.

The room fills up with Siberian soldiers. They throw themselves to the floor and roll up like dogs. Five minutes later they are snoring loudly.

One of the sentries lets me down from the beam enough to allow me to sit down. Despite the pain from my hands and feet, I fall into a strange, disturbed sleep.

A faint sound wakens me. The trap in the floor opens and the Legionnaire's sinewy body sneaks up from the cellar and crawls like a snake towards the half-asleep sentry.

Faster than thinking, the piano wire is around his throat. Two powerful tugs and the sentry is dead.

Porta creeps from the kitchen and takes the Siberian sergeant, who is sitting by the window. He too is garotted.

Tiny's tough features appear from behind the stuffed bear, his teeth bared in a murderous grin. Like a doll he picks up the sleeping officer from the floor and presses his head against his mighty chest. There is a sound like cardboard being crushed.

Heide comes tip-toeing down the ruined stairs. Half-way down he stumbles over a pack and rolls on into the room with a terrific racket.

Like lightning the three others are over by the wall with machine-pistols at the ready. Nothing happens. A Russian complains in his sleep, demanding quiet.

From out on the square we hear a buzzing of voices. The sentries are changing. They do not bother about the noise, either. We are so far behind the front line that they cannot imagine anything happening.

The guard commander enters the door, yawning, throws his machine-pistol down on a table, stretches his arms towards the ceiling and yawns again, noisily, like a tired horse. His mouth stays open. With a surprised expression he stares down the muzzle of Heide's Mpi.

Heide smiles satanically and salutes with one finger to his cap-brim. Before the guard commander can close his mouth the Legionnaire's wire is round his throat. His tongue sticks out from between his frost-cracked lips, and slowly his face goes dark blue.

A corporal enters the room and immediately catches sight of the dead guard commander, who is lying in a heap on the floor. He stiffens and opens his mouth, but not a sound crosses his lips.

Tiny kills him with one blow across the throat from the edge of his hand. Quickly and quietly as a cloakroom girl accepting a hat from a guest.

'Come death, come . . . ' hums the Legionnaire, softly.

'Rookies,' sneers Heide, contemptuously.

Porta gives the butt of his Mpi a loud slap.

'Up on your feet, you sad sacks,' he roars, in a ringing voice.

Tiny fires a burst at the beams of the ceiling and one of the hanged women falls to the floor with a thud.

Confused and sleepy, the NKVD soldiers scramble to their feet. With looks of utter foolishness on their faces they stare at the four grinning German soldiers lined up by the wall. One of them fumbles for his Nagan. The Legionnaire throws his knife.

It bores into the reckless man's chest right up to the hilt.

'Watch it, *tovaritsches*,' grins Porta. 'Don't even wobble on your feet, or you'll have sat on the pot for the last time!'

'Throw your weapons over here,' orders Heide, in a tough voice, 'don't try anything we might misunderstand or off these go!'

'We're on *your* side,' says a sergeant, his voice shaking.

'Now you tell us,' says Tiny, cheerfully, giving him a blow on the neck which sends him flying across the room and half into the fireplace.

'Kick his balls up in his throat,' suggests Porta, with a broad grin. 'They get me so piss mad, these whining shits who change sides soon as the fat's in the fire.'

In a moment the rest of us are free, but we are hardly on our feet before an Mpi stutters and the whole room is filled with acrid cordite smoke.

Two of the prisoners sink to the floor.

'What the hell did you do that for,' shouts the Old Man, accusingly, at Heide.

'They didn't know the fighting was over,' answers Heide, coldly, bringing down the heel of his boot on the face of the nearest of them.

'Don't stand there starin',' roars Tiny at a sergeant. 'Do somethin' or other so's I can shoot the life out of you!'

'Off with your clothes!' orders the Old Man. 'You can keep your underclothes and socks. Everything else into the fire!'

The fire burns up, and a stench of burnt cloth and singed fur spreads through the room.

'We'll freeze to death,' protests an NKVD soldier, banging his hands together.

'Of course,' Heide laughs sarcastically, 'but comfort yourselves with the thought that death from freezing is quite pleasant. If it had been up to me, you lot of rookies would've been dead by now.'

'We'll meet again,' promises a corporal, sending Porta a look of hate.

'You a prophet or something?' asks Porta.

'I'm telling you, *Germanski*, I'll be *seeing* you,' snarls the corporal, furiously.

'Wooden soldiers are lucky,' grins Porta, patting the corporal on the cheek, 'they can't drown!'

'*Pjors*,'* snarls the corporal, spitting helplessly after Porta.

'Frost in your whiskers, nose all blue,
   Furs all white, and your army socks too,

sings Porta, jeeringly.

'Grab your kit,' orders the Old Man. 'Let's get away from here in a hurry!'

Porta and Tiny go round, solemnly, and shake hands with every one of the prisoners in parting.

'Those wicked *Germanskis* certainly got hold of the arses of the *tovaritsches* this time, didn't they?' grins Porta, delightedly. 'Sit down nicely in the corner, now, and think over carefully what you're going to say to your bosses when they turn up one day to have a chat with you.'

'*Malltschal*,† you devil of a German,' shouts one of the prisoners, viciously, throwing a piece of firewood after Porta.

' 'Ave fun, mates,' chuckles Tiny, and waves as he goes out of the door.

'We should've shot them,' complains Heide. 'If they've got any brains at all they'll soon be after us. If a stupid Eskimo can knock up a pair of skis out of what's lying around, and pinch the clothes off a seal, one of Stalin's NKVD men ought to bloody well be able to! Let me go back and liquidate 'em!'

'You stay here,' answers the Old Man, decidedly. 'We're not murderers!'

'Hell, but it's cold,' complains Porta, knocking his hands together.

'We're up in the Arctic,' grins Gregor, weakly.

Wherever we look the scene is cold and deserted, with nothing living in sight. After a while the high spirits, our escape from the hands of the NKVD soldiers has created, begins to ebb.

We call a halt in a hollow. It is doubtful if the Finnish captain can live through the trip home. His feet have begun to smell like rotting meat.

'Gangrene,' confirms the Old Man, briefly.

'We must amputate,' mumbles the Legionnaire.

'You do it?' asks the Old Man, doubtfully.

'*Par Allah*, if we do not get back within forty-eight hours he

* Pjors (Russian) = Dog.
† Malltschal (Russian) = Shut your mouth.

300

will be dead,' prophesies the Legionnaire, gloomily.

'Let's put a bullet in 'is neck,' suggests Tiny, practically. 'The Finnish Army's got no use for 'im, an' 'e's a burden on *us*. So what else *can* we do with the bleeder?'

'Shut it, you wicked sod!' snarls the Old Man, angrily.

We look towards the captain. He is lying on a wooden sled which we take it in turns to pull. There is fear in his face. More than likely he has heard Tiny's cynical suggestion.

'We'll just have to get him back as quick as possible,' says the Old Man, resolutely. 'Are there any morphine tablets left?'

'Not a one,' answers Sanitätsgefreiter Brandt.

We begin the ascent in the wavering light, but are not even half up before the Old Man has to order a halt. The section is completely worn out.

In a moment we have all fallen into a deep sleep. It is that deadly dangerous sleep which goes directly over into death, and which has struck down so many in the Arctic.

After over twelve hours' sleep the Old Man gets us on our feet again.

'Shut *up*,' groans Porta. 'How I'm longing for a Finnish sauna and some regulation military cunt!'

'My prick's like a little frozen button,' shouts Tiny. 'It'll take at least twenty of the fattest kind of quims in existence to thaw 'im out again!'

'Let's get moving,' wheezes Gregor, jumping up and down on the spot, to try to get some warmth into his body. 'If we stay here much longer we'll all be blocks of ice!'

After several hours of inhuman toil we reach the edge of the cliffs.

The Old Man lies down on his stomach, and examines the steep declivity down which we shall have to go. Listlessly he lowers the binoculars.

Far below us rages the White Sea. Mountains of green, foam-specked water surge and thunder against the fanged rocks.

'Once we reach the beaches,' says the Legionnaire, 'it is not far, at the most one hundred kilometres.'

'That all,' laughs Porta, jeeringly. 'Just a little country walk for a party of heart cases.'

'Go on, laugh,' sighs the Old Man, downheartedly. 'It'll be a rough trip, *I* can tell you!'

'*Par Allah*, we have no choice. We must go over this edge,' says the Legionnaire. 'I have a feeling the Russians are at our heels!'

'Then we've had it,' decides the Old Man, tiredly, lighting his silver-lidded pipe.

'*C'est le bordel*, but I have seen tireder soldiers than this section,' growls the Legionnaire. 'We can still fight!'

The Old Man goes down on his knees and looks round at the section, spread out apathetically in the snow.

'Hear me,' he shouts. 'We're going on a little climbing expedition and we'll have to let ourselves down on ropes. Once we're down there it's not far to home. Now then, spit on your hands, lads, and let's pull together!'

We crawl over to the edge and peer down. The first part of the cliff face looks reasonable and not too difficult to manage, but further down there is a smooth vertical wall which goes straight down towards the sea. Before getting there, however, about half-way, it goes sharply inwards. There we will have to swing ourselves in to obtain a foothold.

'Lord save us,' sighs Barcelona, looking as if he feels like giving up before he has even started.

'We've *got* to do it,' decides the Old Man, heavily, taking the glasses from his coat pocket, where he has put them to keep the lenses from freezing up.

He examines the cliff face all the way along. Then he hands the binoculars to the Legionnaire.

'I think there's a small man-made gap a good way down. If I'm right we can get through there!'

The Legionnaire stares for a brief moment in the indicated direction.

'*Tu as raison*, but what a job it will be to get there, and if we make one mistake we end in the White Sea!'

'If we had suction cups on our hands and feet and an extra one tied on the end of our pricks, we'd never get over that bulge,' says Porta, creeping, shivering, back to safety.

'Oh, arseholes,' rumbles Tiny, crawling back from the edge in his turn. 'Giant bleedin' stones, loads of snow an' ice, an' a 'ell of a lot of cold, green water! More'n enough to drown all the barmy soldiers in this whole World War, who've volunteered to go out an' get theirselves killed!'

'Get ready,' orders the Old Man, harshly. 'It'll be the roughest climb of our lives!'

Gregor makes the ropes ready. He is the only one of us who

has attended the mountaineering school. With a supercilious expression he explains to us how to let ourselves down on the ropes.

Squabbling amongst ourselves we share out the ammunition between us and adjust the balance of our weapons.

The Old Man almost has a fit when Porta suggests our leaving the two light mortars and the heavy boxes of bombs behind.

'If we get home by Christmas,' says Gregor, solemnly, taking cover behind a snowdrift, 'I want a sun-lamp for a present!'

'I'll give you one,' Porta promises him. 'I know a shop that sells 'em, and also how to get into it after closing time!'

Gregor stands on the edge of the storm-battered heights, takes the loop of the rope over his head and makes it fast under his arms. He leans forward against the storm as if it were a solid wall. His chapped lips part in an optimistic grin. With his feet braced against the face of the cliff he begins to slide downwards. At the vertical wall he stops and looks up for a moment. Then he seems to disappear into the abyss. A moment or two later he appears in sight again. He has managed to gain a foothold on the dangerous bulge, from which he will have to swing inwards.

'We could get a job in a circus with this number,' says Porta, shuddering.

'World wars are pure *shit*,' grumbles Tiny. 'Let you in for all kinds of pissed-up jobs! No wonder they've got conscientious objectors in all them free countries!'

'Your turn, Barcelona!' shouts the Old Man.

'I can't go yet,' protests Barcelona, with fear in his voice. 'I want to see if anyone breaks his neck first!'

'If you don't come now I'll see to it you go last!' rages the Old Man. 'And then there'll be nobody left up here to hang on to the rope!'

But before Barcelona can reach the edge, Heide is on his way and after him the Legionnaire goes down.

Barcelona is anxious to go, now. The Old Man's threat of leaving him to the last is enough to give him cold shivers.

We have to lower the Finnish captain down. Several times he is dashed violently against the cliff face, but to our surprise he is still alive when he gets down. One of his legs has been crushed from the foot to above the knee. His chances of survival are not good.

Now it is my turn.

'Take it easy, now,' warns the Old Man, who sees how scared I am.

'Brace hard with your feet all the time. There are enough of us up here to hang on to the rope. As long as you don't lose your nerve, you'll be all right!' He adjusts the hang of the machine-pistol, slung across my chest, so that it will not get entangled with the guide-rope.

'I can't do it,' I protest, in panic fear, staring down into the roaring abyss.

'Off you go,' the Old Man sends me off with a push, and I am over the edge.

Far beneath me the White Sea thunders in all its Arctic fury. I scramble desperately for a foothold, but my boots only scrape on the snow. I hit the first ledge, with a bump which presses the magazine pouch painfully into my ribs.

Porta waves to me and flips the rope.

I hang on for dear life to the narrow ledge. Round me the storm howls and roars like a raging monster trying to smash me.

Three hard tugs on the rope give me the signal to continue. Carefully I crawl over the sharp edge. This is the part of the climb which cannot be seen from above.

I kick the toes of my boots into the snow and obtain a foothold. I inch my way down. Several times the terrible Arctic storm comes close to blowing me over the edge and smashing me against the cliff face. For a moment I consider jettisoning the ammunition pouches, but I know what the others will do to me if I get down without them.

At last I reach the narrow bulge. Only a bit over 300 feet to the bottom. I crawl carefully across the snow. It is slippery as glass. With fear clutching at my throat I slide over the edge and lower myself slowly down. At least the sea is no longer directly below me. To my relief I feel hands clutch at my boots and guide me on to safe ground.

'Well done,' Heide praises me, giving me a playful punch in the stomach.

As if in a dream I see the rope disappear upwards.

Soon the next man is on his way down.

Porta and Tiny come last. They stand right out on the edge and play the fool, Porta throws out one hand.

'After you, sir!' he says to Tiny.

'I'll *shoot* those idiots,' shouts the Old Man, exasperatedly. They come down together, like a couple of Siamese twins, pushing off strongly against the cliff face. The rope shakes above them.

'Bloody jumping-jacks,' shouts the Old Man, fearfully. 'You'll break your necks!'

'It is your duty to report them,' says Heide, solemnly.

'Shut your damn mouth,' roars the Old Man furiously. '*I'll* decide who's to be reported or not reported. Just remember that, will you, once and for all?'

'Got a pain somewhere?' Porta asks the Old Man, when he gets down to him. 'You told us to get a move on, and weren't we down twice as fast as anybody else?'

'I'll get you two a court martial,' shouts the Old Man, angrily. 'This is the *limit*!'

'Blimey, 'ow *mad* can you get?' says Tiny, admiringly. 'Watch out you don't 'ave a stroke, now!'

'I curse the day I ever took over No. 2 Section! You are the biggest shower of shits in the entire blasted German Army!' the Old Man flares up at them.

'If we were to leave you you'd die of grief,' smiles Porta, flatteringly.

'The whole damn world can get to hell far as I'm concerned and No. 2 Section with it! I wish the whole bloody business was all over and done with!' rages the Old Man.

Gregor laughs.

> 'Ja, wenn's aus sein wird
> mit Barras und mit Urlaubschein,
> dann packen wir unsere Sachen ein
> und fahren endlich heim,'*

he sings softly.

Just before we reach the strange-looking ravine a volley of rifle shots splits the icy air.

Unteroffizier Kehr spins round like a top, staggers forward a few steps, and falls to the snow. The bullet has hit him in the stomach. It feels as if a boxer has punched him in the solar plexus.

'What bloody shit hit me?' he asks. With blood dribbling from the corners of his mouth, he goes down like a dog-tired

---

* Je wenn's etc. = A German equivalent of
　　　　When this cruel war is over,
　　　　Oh how happy I will be ...
　　　　etc. etc.

man. The new, powdery snow rises and falls back to cover him like a shroud. 'Hell, the bloody Russians got me,' he mumbles and looks in surprise at his hand which is filled with blood.

Two shots crash, and the snow spurts up in front of me. Frightened, I push myself down into the snow and send a burst of tracer at the ravine. Off to my left an automatic rifle barks noisily. Behind me, in a depression, Heide and Gregor wrestle with the mortar.

'Give 'em a couple of backscratchers,' shouts the Old Man, from over by a big snow drift. Eagerly, Gregor opens the box containing the queer, Japanese grenades, which we call backscratchers. They have a different kind of explosive charge, and are only issued to special service units. We are exhilarated at the thought of what will happen in the gulch when the backscratchers fall there.

'Plop, plop,' goes the mortar.

We follow the curved flight of the vaned bombs with our eyes.

'Forward,' orders the Old Man, giving the hand signal for one man to double forward at a time.

Machine-gun fire hammers viciously at us, throwing up lumps of ice.

'Get opened out,' shouts the Old Man, leading us on in a peculiar sideways run, peering continually behind him. 'Open out,' he repeats. 'Why the hell can't you open out? Get your arses into gear!'

'Cool it, afterbirth!' howls Porta, furiously.

Tiny goes down, throws away his Mpi, and tries to dig himself into the snow with hands and feet to escape from the tracer bullets which buzz around us like a swarm of wasps.

Porta stops at his side, and prods him with the butt of his weapon.

'Come on, you big Hamburg shithouse! Think you can lie there sawing wood all day while we do all the work?'

'I ain't got piss in my nut like you lot,' screams Tiny, hysterically, digging himself deeper into the snow. ' 'Im as kills people with a machine-shooter shall 'imself get a burst in the bonce, Lot's wife says!' He is getting his Bible stories mixed up, as usual.

Heide rushes up in a cloud of snow, and stops in amazement when he discovers Tiny down in the hole.

'Now I've seen it all. Cowardice in the face of the enemy. Cost you your head!'

'Creep back up into the German Nazi cunt you crawled out of,' bawls Tiny, dangerously. He pulls out his P-38 and empties the whole magazine at Heide, who flies off in terror towards the Russians.

'I 'ope they shoot your fascist balls off,' snorts Tiny after him.

'Who's got a Kaspanos?' shouts the Old Man, throwing himself under cover from the violent fire from the gulch.

'I've got two,' I answer, holding them up.

'Off you go, then,' the Old Man orders, brusquely. 'Put 'em both under Ivan's arse!'

'Think I'm mad?' I protest violently.

'It's an order,' roars the Old Man, turning his Mpi on me. 'Get moving, you cowardly shit!'

For a moment there is silence where we lie behind cover. They all look towards me. Then something happens up in front. The Russians are attacking. *'Uhraeh, uhraeh,'* they shout harshly. They come at us at an amazing pace, half sliding, half running down the slope, their automatic weapons rattling incessantly.

'Kaspanos,' shouts the Old Man, crawling further behind cover.

I throw one of them over to him. It is one of the big five kilogram jobs that can tear a Stalin tank to pieces.

Tiny takes the Kaspanos from the Old Man, bites off the pin and slings it forward in a great arc. It explodes with a roar that sounds like the end of the world.

The leading enemy group is literally pulverised.

'Plop, plop,' sounds from behind us, as the mortars spit out their devilish bombs.

They explode in front of us, sending stones and snow into the air. There is a continual roaring and whistling to all sides of us. The sound of the explosions is accentuated enormously in the cold air.

'Allah-el-Akbar!' screams the Legionnaire, fanatically, and gets to his knees. His machine-pistol smashes out death into the deep snow, where the NKVD troops are advancing in a long line.

'Forward,' shouts the Old Man. 'Let's get that gate open!'

We excite ourselves to animal rage and follow the Old Man

uncaringly into the rain of tracer coming at us.

Barcelona falls to his knees, and presses his fur gloves to his face. A stream of blood runs out from between his fingers.

'Dig yourself in, we'll pick you up later,' shouts the Old Man, rushing on.

Barcelona rolls down into a hole and thinks of other head wounds he has seen. Usually they mean instant death, and he comforts himself with the thought that since he is still alive his wound cannot be so bad.

Heide and Gregor come lumbering through the snow with the mortar between them.

'Watch out for the soap,' shouts Porta, warningly, and points to the treacherous packets of TNT which lie, scattered, seemingly casually, in the snow. Tread on one of those small packets and you'll end in the icy sea.

Tiny picks one up and throws it at a giant Russian in a white bearskin coat. The Russian is torn in two and his head goes flying through the air like a football.

Gefreiter Linde, who is running a little in front of me, rises suddenly into the air as if he had been shot from a mortar, and there is a noise like the end of the world. Snow, and blocks of ice, rain down on us. Linde must have set off at least ten soap-tablets by treading on one.

Bullets whistle, ricochet and snarl. Somebody is shouting for help, and calling for stretcher bearers. Our stretcher bearers have been blocks of ice out on the tundra for a long time now.

The shelling and rifle-fire become even more violent. The Old Man is on the verge of desperation. He knows very well that the section has reached the point where it is no longer functioning. The next stage is mindless panic.

He waves the mortar forward, and a little later it begins to sound again.

In front of us the snow is burning, where the bombs have fallen.

Suddenly the Russians are moving, retreating back towards the gulley.

'Plop, plop,' the mortar bombs follow on their heels.

Heide is a genius with a mortar. But a new body of Russians comes rushing out of the ravine and before he has time to correct his sight they have reached cover behind the snow walls.

'Help me with the SMG,' shouts the Legionnaire, struggling with the carriage.

Gregor gets hold of the supporting tripod, but slips and bangs his face down hard on the machine-gun.

'Lift your fuckin' shit yourself,' he rages, kicking out at the carriage.

'*Il est con, comme ma bite est mignonne,*'* roars the Legionnaire, throwing a piece of ice at him.

'Keep that snow wall under fire,' orders the Old Man. 'Don't let them come over it!'

All at once the snow is swarming with Russians.

The 42 spits tracer at the figures in snow-camouflage. I fire like a madman. The barrel steams and the hot cartridge cases hiss and splutter as they sink into the snow.

Porta comes running, and rolls into cover behind a projecting rock.

Behind me the SMG rattles and it almost seems as if the Russian attackers run unharmed straight through the concentration of fire.

I take careful aim at the leading soldier. He has a tall, grey fur cap on his head, with a large, red enamelled star. His head seems to be balanced on the edge of the sight as I fire. Next moment he is gone. The Mpi flies in a great arc from his hand, and seems for a second or two to be suspended in the air.

An explosive bullet sends a rain of stone and ice splinters into my face. Blood runs from hundreds of tiny wounds. Luckily my eyes have not been hit.

I get to one knee and throw the Kaspanos in amongst them. Joyfully, I watch them go up into the air and smash to the ground again.

Automatic weapons rattle. A tapestry of tracer tracks canopies the terrain.

'Uncle Ivan's out to get us, *I* can tell you,' shouts Porta with a broad grin, jumping over the snow barrier with a bundle of grenades in his hand.

Oberschütze Krohn rises part way up. A thick jet of blood spouts from his throat.

Gefreiter Batik comes to his aid but is also hit, and falls, screaming, alongside him.

'The whole world's goin' for a shit,' shouts the Westphalian. 'Let's beat it, before we end up in the garbage can!'

'Shut up and go forward!' shouts the Old Man, from his hole.

* Il est con etc. (French) = He is as stupid as my prick is pretty.

309

'No, we stay here,' shouts Gregor. 'We're throwing our lives away for no reason. Let 'em get inside a hundred yards, *then* we'll take 'em!'

A heavy Maxim MG is placed just in front of us. They've placed it well, and can fire on us with hardly any risk to themselves.

Heide tries to put it out of action with the mortar, but his bombs fall all round the MG-nest without doing it any noticeable damage.

I crawl forward and try to throw grenades into it, but the distance is too great. That damnable SMG has already wounded four of us badly.

Tiny gets up, with a bundle of grenades in his hand.

'Shoot like 'ell,' he shouts, spitting on the snow. 'I'll knock those bleeders' bollocks up for 'em!' He starts off with long strides.

'Mad as a hatter,' says Gregor. 'They'll knock him over before he's got half-way!'

It is a riddle to us how such a huge man can move with such unbelievable speed.

With a long jump he is down behind a fallen Russian. He swings back his arm and throws the grenades.

A fur-clad form appears on the rim of the snow wall, and a hand-grenade whirls through the air towards Tiny. He rolls to one side with the agility of an acrobat. The grenade explodes with a loud crack in front of the body and shatters it.

With a terrific roar Tiny's string of grenades explodes inside the SMG-nest.

'*Vive la mort*,' howls the Legionnaire, jumping up with the Mpi cradled in his arms.

Shouting and screaming, the rest of the section follows him.

The Russians stream in disorder, back towards the gulley.

'Kill 'em,' howls Gregor, murderously. His Mpi chatters.

Suddenly it is all over. We sit down in the snow and try to catch our breath. Porta rolls a cigarette from a bag of machorka he has discovered in a dead Russian's pocket.

The Legionnaire bandages Barcelona, who has received a long, deep slash in the face.

The Old Man fills his silver-lidded pipe, and leans against a powder-blackened snow drift.

'Jeepers in 'ell,' Tiny breaks out. 'We give the neighbours what they asked for there, all right!'

Silently we walk round, examining the bodies. We help ourselves to whatever we have a use for. Some of them are not yet dead. We take their weapons and leave them where they are lying. The cold will soon finish them off. We cannot help them. We cannot even do anything for our own wounded. Curses follow us, but we do not even try to answer back.

The Old Man presses his lips together, and looks uneasily at the flickering Northern Lights.

'Pick up your weapons! Single file! Follow me!' he orders, briefly.

Early in the morning, two weeks later, we are looking for a quiet spot through which we can get back to our own lines.

The Old Man thinks we are on the northern end of the Sala front.

A Russian supplies soldier runs straight into our arms. It was, of course, Porta, who noticed the smell of coffee, long before we heard the supplies soldier. He comes, singing softly, over the hill, with a container of coffee on his back. When he sees us he is quite paralysed with fear, and we shake him violently to get some life back into him.

He begins to weep, and says this war is the wickedest thing he has ever run into.

'Stop your crying, now, you little misery,' Porta comforts the unhappy Russian. 'If the coffee's good we won't hurt you!'

Later he tells us he is from Tiflis, where everybody is in favour of the Germans, and confides to us that he, himself, has always been really fond of Germans.

We go under cover in amongst the fir trees and enjoy his good coffee.

'Think now! The neighbours drink coffee,' says Porta, letting off a thunderous fart. 'I always thought they only slobbered tea with jam in it!'

'Yes, you do learn a lot in these World Wars,' says Tiny, wonderingly, blowing into his mug.

'Keep *quiet*,' hisses the Old Man. 'You chatter loud enough to wake the Seven Sleepers!'

There is a muffled thump from the far side of the trees.

'Cripes,' shouts Tiny, throwing himself flat.

The next minute there is a roaring and creaking in the forest and several trees come sailing through the air like giant javelins.

We change in a moment. Our easy-going attitude has gone. Our faces are tense.

311

They emerge from the trees, over the rolling hills, moving along at ease, quite sure nothing bad can happen to them here.

The Russian artillery roars again, and we hear the long drawn out rushing sound of the shells on their way to the Finnish positions.

'Ready,' whispers the Old Man, excitedly. 'We've got to mow 'em down in one long swing!'

I aim the LMG into the thick of them.

The Old Man lets his arm fall in the signal to open fire. All the automatic weapons roar in one single long salvo, which echoes back from far off amongst the trees.

Some of them manage to reach the long snow ditch, but by far the majority remain lying still on the path.

'The gulley,' shouts Gregor, furiously. 'Shoot the bottom out of it! Those devils are lying there just waiting to get shot!'

The SMG roars, ripping along the whole length of the ditch. We throw hand-grenades into it. There is utter stillness.

During the firing the supplies soldier has disappeared.

'Dammit!' the Old Man swears. 'If he gets back and gives the alarm, we'll have the whole of 238 Infantry Division on our backs.

'We'll knock *them* off too, then,' boasts Tiny, loudly.

'Dope,' snarls the Old Man.

A salvo of shells falls on our side of the front-line. Trees fly towards the skies like giant arrows shot from a bow. Here and there the woods begin to burn.

'Let's get out of here,' says Heide, uneasily, looking nervously about him. 'When that fucking supplies soldier gives the alarm all hell'll break loose! Let's go for a break-through! It's our only chance!'

'*You* break through on your own, then, you fucked up German monkey, you,' shouts Porta, viciously. 'You're so fuckin' stupid you've not even found out yet there's trip wires an' wolf-traps everywhere!'

'Wolf-traps?' mumbles Heide, scared, lifting his feet gingerly, as if he were already standing on top of one of those devilish inventions.

'Yes, wolf-traps,' Porta laughs, sarcastically, 'and if they catch us they'll push us into one of 'em, so they can enjoy the elevating sight of us wriggling ourselves to death on the points of the stakes!'

'An' a puffed-up Nazi Unteroffizier like you,' says Tiny with a sneering grin, 'they'll first cut the prick off of, and send it to the Zoological Museum in Moscow, so everybody can 'ave a good laugh at the Nazi's mini-pricks!'

Heide is too shocked to reply.

A couple of miles further along we run into some Russian MPs lurking about amongst the fir trees. Everything happens so quickly we do not realise what has been going on until the action is over.

Machine-pistols bark, and battle-knives flash in the twilight. We drag the dead policemen away from the path so that they will not be found immediately.

The artillery fire, on both sides, is ebbing out, and a strange, threatening silence falls over the huge forests.

Porta's reindeer has vanished. Despite the Old Man's protests we go back to look for it.

Tiny finds it amongst some trees where it has dragged itself to die. Its throat has been slashed open lengthwise by an explosive bullet.

Porta throws himself down, unhappily, by its side. It looks at him with a glance full of affection, and we are close to tears.

Gregor fishes out a morphine ampoule and gets a needle ready.

'It's the last of them,' he says, 'but why should he suffer because us crazy humans want to knock one another's brains out?'

Soon after, the reindeer dies. We bury it, so that the wolves will not find it straight away.

Suddenly Tiny jumps up and listens, tensely.

'Dogs!' he says. 'Bleedin' dogs!'

'Are you sure?' asks the Old Man, doubtfully.

'Dead sure,' asserts Tiny. 'Can't you 'ear 'em, *really*? It's a 'ole pack of 'em, an' big 'uns too!'

Several minutes pass before the rest of us can hear a deep, continual baying.

'War dogs,' whispers Gregor, nervously. 'They'll tear us to pieces if they get to close quarters!'

'Them stinkin' 'ounds can just 'ave a go at gettin' to close quarters with yours truly,' grins Tiny, diabolically. 'I'll tear their bleedin' tails out their arseholes I will, so they'll forget all about bein' war dogs!'

'Wait'll you see 'em,' says Gregor, with fear in his voice. 'A hungry tiger's like a bloody housecat alongside *them*!'

'What the devil do we do?' asks Barcelona, straightening the heavy bandage which covers the whole of his face.

'Let's go south,' suggests Heide, 'They won't be expecting us and in the forests there's more cover.'

'Not against Siberian war dogs,' says the Old Man, checking the magazine of his Mpi.

'Let's talk Russian to 'em, then,' suggests Tiny, 'then them Communist 'ounddogs'll think we're pals! With the clothes we're wearin' we could just as like be neighbours!'

'You can't fool a war dog,' says the Old Man, with conviction. 'They've tasted the whip so often when they've made a mistake that they just don't *make* mistakes!'

'I'm so homesick, suddenly,' says Porta, beginning to run into the woods towards the west.

'Yes, that way,' shouts the Old Man, grimly, 'forward and straight on through! Spread out, and give one another covering fire, and have your battle-knives ready! Keep the knife pointing upwards when they spring. That way they'll open themselves up when they leap at you!'

With a great deal of noise we force our way through the thick underbrush, run across a frozen stream, and come out into open country.

Behind us we hear a voice bawling gutturally, and a machine-pistol burst throws up the snow around us, but the trees give us good cover. It is difficult to hit a moving target in the forest.

Like a bulldozer, I force my way through the brush.

A shrill scream, which turns into a death rattle, sounds behind me.

'What was that?' I ask, fearfully.

'Feldwebel Pihl,' answers Gregor. 'Looked as if his hair and his helmet went off at the same time!'

In between the trees we fling ourselves into cover. Rapidly we reload our automatic weapons. Silently we lie waiting.

They come at us standing and give one another courage with loud, penetrating shouts.

The Old Man lets them come close, before dropping his arm. At short range the machine-pistol is a terrible weapon. You just have to be careful not to hit any of your own chaps.

The violent automatic fire paralyses them for a moment, and before they have pulled themselves together, they are knocked to the snow.

Raging we run at them, over them, kicking them, smashing their faces with our gun butts.

The Finnish corporal goes down just in front of me. I have no time to find out if he is dead or merely wounded. Now we are so close to our own lines that nobody wants to get killed helping a wounded comrade.

Three huge Siberian wolfdogs come loping out of the forest. The first of them springs at Barcelona but he manages to whirl and finish it off with his Mpi.

The other two seem to work together. They are going straight for the Old Man, who falls over a tree stub and drops his Mpi. Terrified he puts out his hands to protect himself from the murderous animals.

Gregor kills one of the dogs with a pistol shot. Mpis we cannot use, or we'd kill the Old Man too. Mpis spray such a terrible lot.

The last of the dogs falls dead on top of the Old Man with the Legionnaire's Moorish dagger in its back. Even in death it still snaps its teeth at the Old Man's throat.

'Jesus'n Mary,' groans Porta, as a new baying is heard in the forest, and half a score of fierce, bloodthirsty hounds come rushing over the cleared ground.

The Westphalian goes down, screaming and kicking, with two slavering hounds on top of him. In a few seconds there is nothing but a heap of bloody rags left of him. An Mpi salvo kills the two animals, as they look up, with blood-dripping jaws, from the heap of bones and bloody flesh which a moment before had been a living human being.

A great, grey hound, like a ghost, comes straight at me. I duck instinctively and the monster soars over my head and rolls in the snow.

Heide catches one of them in the air on his battle-knife and rips up its belly so that its entrails fall to the ground.

The dog which has attacked me is making ready for a new spring. For a moment I stare, hypnotised, at its great, yellow incisors, bared in a demoniacal snarl.

Desperately I empty the whole magazine into it. The burst throws it backwards and literally rips its coat to ribbons.

Tiny catches one of the great dogs in mid-air, tears off its head and throws it at the next attacker. He catches the next one by the tail and swings it furiously round above his head. Whether it is the dog which makes the most noise, or Tiny, is hard to say, but the dog flies back the way it came, without a tail. Tiny has *that* in his hand.

Now there are only two dogs left. They stop in the middle of their attack, turn off a few yards from Tiny, and fly, whining, towards the forest, with Tiny after them, shouting at the top of his voice.

Just before they get to the forest Tiny catches the rearmost dog by the neck and picks it up as if it were a puppy and not a vicious Siberian wolfdog, trained to kill. He comes back on the run with the dog trailing behind him like a sack.

'Shoot that vicious cur,' screams Heide, furiously, lifting his Mpi and aiming at the dog.

'You shoot *'im*,' snarls Tiny, 'an' I'll tear your Nazi 'ead off of your lousy shoulders! 'E's goin' 'ome with me an' I'm gonna teach 'im to clean them Kripo sods out of David's Station!' He pats the growling dog, which is sitting undecidedly in the snow showing its teeth. 'You're goin' with me to 'Amburg, you are, *an'* you're goin' to bite the arse off of *Otto* (bleedin') *Nass*!* *Panjemajo, tscharny trohort?*†

'I won't have you take that devil of a dog back with you,' decides the Old Man, briefly, his Mpi held ready, and pointed at the snarling dog.

'Shit on that,' shouts Tiny, stubbornly, pulling the dog close to him. 'Frankenstein, that's 'is name, is from now on a member of the Greater German Army! 'E'll take the oath, soon as we get back!'

'Let him go,' orders the Old Man. 'Let him run off home!'

' 'E's *stayin'*,' shouts Tiny, stubbornly.

'Cross of Jesus, but he's a wicked-looking bastard,' says Porta. 'Watch out he doesn't bite your face off!'

'You may pat 'im,' offers Tiny. 'Won't touch any friend of mine, 'e won't. Do you like 'im?'

'Ye-e-es, when I look at him properly. I *do* like him,' says Porta, hesitantly, 'but he's not what I'd call a lapdog!'

'You're mad, mad, *mad*,' the Old Man gives in. 'Always animals in tow. But this Siberian war dog is the *limit*, understand! That devil's only waiting his chance to eat the lot of us!'

The silence is shattered by long bursts of firing behind us. It is the dog soldiers who have caught up with us, and are

* Danish text: Kriminalkommissar *Otto Nass* = Superintendant Otto Nass (why 'bleedin'?).

† Panjemajo etc. (Russian) = understand, you black devil.

furious at the sight of the dead animals lying in the snow. Completely disregarding our defensive fire, they rush forward, shouting, intent on avenging their dogs. Only a few of them live through the attack.

From the German-Finnish lines flares go up in all colours. They have obviously been disturbed by the violent firing from the Russian side.

The Old Man breaks open the flare pistol, and inserts a shell. With a thump the flare flies towards the heavens, and opens out into a five-pointed star, which slowly descends, and goes out over the forest.

'We're back!' mumbles the Old Man, exhaustedly.

We stumble and fumble our way across the rough ground, with our weapons at the ready and every sense alert. The last, short distance is often the most dangerous.

I fall head over heels into a communications trench and knock my shoulder out of joint by the fall. Despite the pain I snatch at my Mpi. It's happened before that people have jumped down, happily, into the wrong trench.

The section mixes with the trench company, Finnish *Jäger*. The OC, a lanky, young first lieutenant, with the Mannerheim Cross around his neck, greets us, and hands round cigarettes from his private stock. A dirty, bearded lieutenant, who looks fifty, but is probably not yet twenty, brings out vodka and beer.

We have no more than sat down, when a whistling and roaring is heard in the air, and the whole position rocks as if struck by a violent earthquake.

'The Avengers,' smiles the Mannerheim knight, passing the vodka bottle to the Old Man. 'They never miss. They throw everything at us, but the kitchen sink, every time a band of partisans gets through.'

We are asleep before we reach our quarters in the rear area. Somebody says something about the sauna being ready for us, but we couldn't care less. We have only one wish. To be allowed to sleep.

It is far into the next day when we finally get up on to our wornout legs again. We have slept so deeply that we did not even hear an air attack that left half the village in ruins.

Porta cooks up mashed potatoes with small cubes of pork. There is melted butter too. It isn't *real* butter, and the margarine is rancid, but we couldn't care less. We eat like men preparing for a seven-year famine.

The sound of the guns is a faint rumble in the distance.

'This is how I enjoy being *me*,' says Porta, stretching luxuriously. His stomach bulges, as if he were nine months on the way, and he is annoyed at the fact that he cannot get another spoonful of food down. For once he is filled up. Right up to his uvula.

'Coffee, anybody?' asks Porta, rising to his feet.

Just as the coffee is ready, and we are relaxing in the light of the Hindenburg candles, Hauptfeldwebel Hofmann pushes open the door and enters in a whirl of snow.

'Hell, but it's cold,' he says, blowing into his hands. 'Got a cuppa coffee for me?' He takes a couple of sips, and swears when he burns his tongue. He looks round at us for a moment. Takes another sip. Then he pulls a sheet of paper from his cuff and hands it to the Old Man.

'You're off in two hours' time! You get artillery cover when you go over!'

All conversation has ceased. It is as if the angel of death had passed through the low-ceilinged room. We cannot believe what we have just heard.

Hofmann narrows his eyes and watches us. He pushes his pistol holster in front of him, as if accidentally.

'By hell!' shouts Porta, flushing red. 'We've got a right to eight days rest after a six-week trip!'

'You've got no rights,' answers Hofmann. 'The order came from the top. Oberst Hinka complained! He didn't *stop* complaining until they threatened him with a court martial!'

'What about the section? We're short of men!' asks the Old Man. 'I can't bloody well go over on the other side with nine men! And my 2 i/c, Barcelona Blom, is in hospital with a smashed-up face!'

'Don't worry about that,' says Hofmann, drily. 'The Army looks after all that sort of thing. Your replacements are here already. You're gonna be the most mixed section that ever existed. There's Russians, Lapps and Finns amongst 'em. The lorries'll be here in two hours' time, and so's not to tire you they'll stop right outside the door. *Hals und Beinbruch!*' he says, and goes out of the door.

'This is the kind of thing that can make a man pray to get a leg shot off,' shouts Porta, trembling with rage. '*Then* you'd know, once and for all, you'd never have to go farting about in never-never land with the guerrillas no more.'

'A leg! Are you nuts?' shouts Tiny. ' 'Ow'd you be able to run away when the David's Station bleeders come after you, with their truncheons an' their blue, bleedin' lights? No, sonny! An *arm*! *That's* all right! You can't use a machine-popper with only one arm! *See?*'

'An arm's worse,' says Gregor. 'What'd a moving-man do with only one arm?'

'Get a pension for the rest of his life,' says the Old Man, 'if he's left it out here!'

'You won't get a sausage if we lose this war,' considers Porta, 'even if you throw *both* arms away.'

We begin to get our equipment together, and have hardly finished the task when the lorries are at the door.

It is snowing so heavily that we can hardly see anything, but that is to our advantage when we have to cross the front line. A night like this makes the job of the observers a difficult one.

Tiny is having trouble with his war dog. It doesn't want to go. It growls and bares its teeth. We have to lift it into the lorry.

'I can well understand him protesting,' says Porta, patting the dog. 'Once they've got out of the Soviet Union who'd *want* to go back?'

Chief Mechanic Wolf is standing, leaning against a tree, and watching us with a broad grin.

'Last night I dreamt I saw you shot so you fell apart in in two halves,' he shouts to Porta, as the lorries swing from the unit lines.

We can hear him laughing a long time after he has disappeared from sight.

The lorries swing on to the Sala road. We know where we are off to. The Arctic front!

We fall asleep before we reach the front, and fall up against one another when the lorry brakes.

Some soldiers, from the Finnish Sissi battalion, take us on from there. Silently they watch us as we crawl over the parapet of the trench and through the barbed-wire.

A machine-gun barks, viciously, at an angle to us. A flare whirls up into the sky and falls slowly to earth.

We wait, quiet as mice, until it blinks out!

THE END

A SELECTED LIST OF WAR BOOKS
PUBLISHED BY CORGI

WHILE EVERY EFFORT IS MADE TO KEEP PRICES LOW, IT IS SOMETIMES NECESSARY TO INCREASE PRICES AT SHORT NOTICE. CORGI BOOKS RESERVE THE RIGHT TO SHOW NEW RETAIL PRICES ON COVERS WHICH MAY DIFFER FROM THOSE PREVIOUSLY ADVERTISED IN THE TEXT OR ELSEWHERE.

THE PRICES SHOWN BELOW WERE CORRECT AT THE TIME OF GOING TO PRESS (JANUARY '84).

☐	12007 3	HIT!	Chris Dempster	£1.50
☐	10807 3	FIREPOWER	Chris Dempster & Dave Tomkins	£2.50
☐	10869 3	THE WILD GEESE	Daniel Carney	£1.75
☐	11976 8	O.G.P.U. PRISON	Sven Hassel	£1.95
☐	10400 0	THE BLOODY ROAD TO DEATH	Sven Hassel	£1.95
☐	09761 6	BLITZFREEZE	Sven Hassel	£1.95
☐	09178 2	REIGN OF HELL	Sven Hassel	£1.75
☐	08874 9	SS GENERAL	Sven Hassel	£1.95
☐	08779 3	ASSIGNMENT GESTAPO	Sven Hassel	£1.75
☐	11414 6	LIQUIDATE PARIS	Sven Hassel	£1.75
☐	08528 6	MARCH BATTALION	Sven Hassel	£1.75
☐	08168 X	MONTE CASSINO	Sven Hassel	£1.75
☐	07871 9	COMRADES OF WAR	Sven Hassel	£1.75
☐	11259 3	WHEELS OF TERROR	Sven Hassel	£1.75
☐	11417 0	THE LEGION OF THE DAMNED	Sven Hassel	£1.75
☐	11987 3	MOSQUITO SQUADRON	Robert Jackson	£1.25
☐	12226 2	THE LAST BATTLE	Robert Jackson	£1.50
☐	12148 7	TEMPEST SQUADRON	Robert Jackson	£1.25
☐	12105 3	OPERATION DIVER	Robert Jackson	£1.50
☐	12285 8	SS STUKA SQUADRON 2: HAWKS OF DEATH	Leo Kessler	£1.50
☐	12277 7	TALE OF A GUINEA PIG	Geoffrey Page	£1.75
☐	11355 7	CONVOY	Dudley Pope	£1.25
☐	12046 4	633 SQUADRON: OPERATION TITAN	Frederick E. Smith	£1.50
☐	11824 9	633 SQUADRON: OPERATION COBRA	Frederick E. Smith	£1.35
☐	11075 2	633 SQUADRON: OPERATION VALKYRIE	Frederick E. Smith	£1.50
☐	10155 9	633 SQUADRON: OPERATION RHINE MAIDEN	Frederick E. Smith	£1.95
☐	08169 8	633 SQUADRON	Frederick E. Smith	£1.25
☐	12026 X	JOHNNY KINSMAN	John Watson	£1.75

All these books are available at your book shop or newsagent, or can be ordered direct from the publisher. Just tick the titles you want and fill in the form below.

CORGI BOOKS, Cash Sales Department, P.O. Box 11, Falmouth, Cornwall.

Please send cheque or postal order, no currency.

Please allow cost of book(s) plus the following for postage and packing:

U.K. Customers—Allow 45p for the first book, 20p for the second book and 14p for each additional book ordered, to a maximum charge of £1.63.

B.F.P.O. and Eire—Allow 45p for the first book, 20p for the second book plus 14p per copy for the next seven books, thereafter 8p per book.

Overseas Customers—Allow 75p for the first book and 21p per copy for each additional book.

NAME (Block Letters) ....

ADDRESS ....

....